Praise for
Always the Bridesmaid

"A charming, rollicking commentary on weddings in the twenty-first century. I loved the Jane Austen-ish heroine."

—Jeanne Ray, author of
Julie and Romeo and *Eat Cake*

"The ultimate bridesmaid gift."   —*Publishers Weekly*

"Full of comedy, style, wit, and romance."   —FictionAddiction.net

"Quite entertaining . . . [an] amusing charmer."
—*Midwest Book Review*

"Written in savvy style . . . displays clever wit and crafts a handful of priceless scenes."   —FictionFactor.com

"Phenomenally entertaining. The pace of the story is perfect."
—TheRomanceReadersConnection.com

"Engrossing, amusing and surprisingly heartfelt."   —myshelf.com

"Talented newcomer Lyles has written a compulsively readable novel. Her descriptive gifts transport readers to the single girl's San Diego, with its beaches, bars, and bistros."   —*Romantic Times*

Roommates

Whitney Lyles

BERKLEY BOOKS, NEW YORK

THE BERKLEY PUBLISHING GROUP
Published by the Penguin Group
Penguin Group (USA) Inc.
375 Hudson Street, New York, New York 10014, USA
Penguin Group (Canada), 90 Eglinton Avenue East, Suite 700, Toronto, Ontario M4P 2Y3, Canada
(a division of Pearson Penguin Canada Inc.)
Penguin Books Ltd., 80 Strand, London WC2R 0RL, England
Penguin Group Ireland, 25 St. Stephen's Green, Dublin 2, Ireland (a division of Penguin Books Ltd.)
Penguin Group (Australia), 250 Camberwell Road, Camberwell, Victoria 3124, Australia
(a division of Pearson Australia Group Pty. Ltd.)
Penguin Books India Pvt. Ltd., 11 Community Centre, Panchsheel Park, New Delhi—110 017, India
Penguin Group (NZ), Cnr. Airborne and Rosedale Roads, Albany, Auckland 1310, New Zealand
(a division of Pearson New Zealand Ltd.)
Penguin Books (South Africa) (Pty.) Ltd., 24 Sturdee Avenue, Rosebank, Johannesburg 2196,
South Africa

Penguin Books Ltd., Registered Offices: 80 Strand, London WC2R 0RL, England

This is a work of fiction. Names, characters, places, and incidents either are the product of the author's imagination or are used fictitiously, and any resemblance to actual persons, living or dead, business establishments, events, or locales is entirely coincidental.

Copyright © 2005 by Whitney Lyles
Book design by Kristin del Rosario

PRINTING HISTORY
Berkley trade paperback edition / November 2005

Library of Congress Cataloging-in-Publication Data

Lyles, Whitney.
　　Roommates / by Whitney Lyles.
　　　　p.　cm.
　　ISBN 0-425-20253-4
　　1. Roommates—Fiction.　2. Female friendship—Fiction.　3. San Diego (Calif.)—Fiction.
4. Triangles (Interpersonal relations)—Fiction.　I. Title.

　　PS3612.Y45R66　2005
　　813'.6—dc22

　　　　　　　　　　　　　　　　　　　　　　　　　　　　　　　　　　2005048063

PRINTED IN THE UNITED STATES OF AMERICA

10　9　8　7　6　5　4　3　2　1

For my husband, Rob Dodds

Acknowledgments

I owe many thanks to the two godmothers of this book, my editor, Leona Nevler, for her priceless expertise and invaluable feedback, and my agent, Sandy Dijkstra, for always being such a wonderful guide and source of motivation.

I would also like to thank the SDLA team for all their hard work, especially Elise Capron for her insight during early drafts of this book.

Much appreciation to Mike Sirota for all his feedback, and for continuing to be the fresh set of eyes that sees all the bad stuff.

Many thanks to my sister, Jennifer, whose opinion always shapes a better novel.

Again, I am forever grateful for my parents for all their support. Thanks to my dad who taught me this past year that you can overcome anything. He is truly a hero, and I am so thankful he is always here to talk writing with me. And to my mom who is probably responsible for selling more of my books than any media source in the country. Endless thanks for all her enthusiasm!

Finally, I can't thank my husband, Rob Dodds, enough for his never-ending encouragement and whose smiles and laughter during last-minute readings made it all worth it.

Roommates

Cribs with Justine and Jimmy

1. The Runaway Mustard Mobile

The first time Elise had ever lived with a complete stranger had been nine years ago when she'd packed up her parents' station wagon and relocated from the suburbs of San Diego to the freshman dorms at the University of Arizona. Talk about anxiety. She'd seen *Single White Female* that summer, and to this day blamed the movie for scaring roommate hunters all over the world.

She watched while her friends from high school had called their future roommates ahead of time to "get to know each other." Rather than imagining their roommates as psychotic versions of Jennifer Jason Leigh, they knew what kind of music they listened to, which sororities they planned to rush, and what their favorite movies were.

Elise had been assigned to live with a Russian exchange student named Anya Gordeeva. Icebreakers had been out of the question.

"Russia? You want to call Russia?" Her father responded to her request to "briefly" become acquainted with Anya Gordeeva. "A two-minute phone call to Russia costs more than your tuition!"

For the duration of her last summer in San Diego, she wondered whether or not Anya Gordeeva would copy her haircut, and if she might share her affinity for Alfred Hitchcock movies. As it would turn out, Anya Gordeeva copied the hairstyles of the female cast of *Baywatch*. When asked if she liked Alfred Hitchcock movies, Anya wanted to know if he had been on Howard Stern. She was consumed with the idea of ending up on a *College Girls Gone Wild* video, which of course would ultimately land her a guest appearance on Howard Stern, who would launch her career as a "model" and introduce her to Vince Neil of Mötley Crüe. *American Dreams*.

Instead of dating Vince Neil she found her American beau at the Tucson miniature golf course where he worked and frequently parked his tricked-out Honda Accord. He looked like Eminem on crystal, and they had sex on the squeaky bunk above Elise's at least four nights a week.

When Elise had summoned up the nerve to ask if they could please have sex at his place, Anya Gordeeva threw her head back and laughed as wickedly as Cruella De Vil. Then in a very thick Russian accent said, "You very jealous because you don't get any."

Living with Anya Gordeeva for her first year of college had been like belly flopping the first time she'd dived as a child. Having the wind knocked out of her on her first diving attempt had left her forever wary of diving boards. And having a total weirdo for her first roommate had made her forever cautious of living with strangers. She wouldn't have minded living with an interesting weirdo. If Anya had been, say, a stripper who was considerate and friendly, Elise probably would've found it intriguing. She would've asked her fifty million questions about her profession and overlooked that she was saving up for implants so she could qualify for *Penthouse*.

Throughout undergrad and graduate school Elise had lived with friends—people she knew. Girls with solid references. For the most part, they'd been pretty decent roommates, occasionally annoying her when they did little things like leaving *one* chip in a huge bag. A cruel way of fooling her into believing there was actually something to snack on until she pulled a bag as light as a Kleenex from the cupboard.

By the time she received her master's in criminal psychology, her roommates had either left Tucson or found a husband. Elise decided it was time for her to move on as well.

The dating scene in Tucson was about as dry as its climate, and if Anya Gordeeva could see her now, she just might have a point. At twenty-seven she was heading back to her southern California roots and living with a stranger for the second time.

At times she wondered if she had been crazy when she'd made the decision to leave. Socially, she'd be starting all over again in San Diego. Though most of her Arizona friends were married, she still had lots of friends. Economically, Tucson was great. She could probably afford to buy her own home within a year or two if she stayed there. California was much more expensive, and she'd have to rely on roommates to cover her rent. Furthermore, her only real friends in San Diego were her family and her best friend, Carly. She was leaving a lot behind. But she needed change. After a string of terrible dates she really wanted to see what else was out there. It was an adventure.

Her skinny arms vibrated like a pair of dentist's drills as she steered a beastly U-Move truck across the Arizona desert highway. Ever since they'd left Tucson she'd been peppering the trip with silent prayers that the bike lane would be empty until she reached her new home in San Diego.

Driving this rig called for a lot more than just paying attention to the road and pressing on the gas. It required strength. At five foot three and one hundred pounds, she felt as if the truck had more control than she did.

When she'd gone to U-Move Rentals for a vehicle, she'd asked for something small. Just like the ones she'd seen in their spiffy ads. A newer model, a sporty van with eagle's wings painted on each side and the gold U-Move logo dangling from a raptor's beak across the hood. However, U-Move had been out of those and had provided her a with a vehicle the shade of Grey Poupon and comparable in size to a mattress delivery truck. It smelled like mustard and looked like

mustard. Her brother had dubbed the truck The Mustard Mobile before they'd even driven it off the lot, and she felt like an insect trapped
inside a hot-dog stand.

Furthermore, a rattling noise from somewhere in The Mustard
Mobile had been irritating her since they had left, and the radio was
broken. Without realizing it, she hummed the Buzz Burger commercial jingle. "Buzzz Buhurrrrger," she sang to herself in a voice that
had potential to break the windshield.

"Where the burrrrger makes a buzz!" Stan sang before he sat up.
He'd been dozing in the passenger seat next to her. "I gotta take a
leak."

Her Boston terrier, Bella, woke, too, and released a yawn so large
that her pink tongue curled into a leafy loop.

"Can you wait until we get to Centro Mesa?" Personally, she
could. Centro Mesa was the capital of Buzz Burger, and she'd been
thinking about the number-two combo since they'd started their road
trip three hours earlier.

Stan propped his feet on the dashboard. "No. I can't wait. And
quit driving like an old lady."

She ignored the last comment. Carly was following them in Elise's
red vintage convertible Volkswagen bug. Sixty was the maximum
limit for the bug, and even that was pushing it. Besides, if he thought
she was driving like a grandma, he had only himself to blame.

The original plan had been for Stan to drive the U-Move and
Carly to serve as copilot. Two people needed to man The Mustard
Mobile for backing up and changing lanes. Being a tour guide for the
Wild Animal Park, her brother was the best candidate to drive. His
tram at the park toted over thirty passengers. Elise had planned to follow in her convertible behind them. However, Stan had gotten
smashed at Elise's going-away party, passed out an hour before they
had planned to leave, and was still drunk while they packed the truck.

As she turned into the rest stop she got the same creepy feeling
she associated with watching *Unsolved Mysteries*. It seemed as if

most of the missing in America were "last seen" at a rest stop off some desolate highway. Fragrant with urine and decorated with carvings that said things like, "Kenny 'n' Amber 4-Ever," they were places where her mother had always advised her not to touch anything or talk to anyone.

Pulling into a parking space was a task reserved only for seasoned truckers. There were a million opportunities to nail someone's bumper or take out a car door with a single swipe. She ended up parking in a dirt field that made the restrooms appear to be tiny cream-colored bumps on the desert horizon. They needed to stretch their legs, she reasoned.

Smothering heat covered her as she climbed from The Mustard Mobile. She pulled Bella's leash from her purse and clicked it onto her little red collar.

"I like what the weather does for my hair," Carly said, touching the bottom of her blonde bob as if she'd just gotten a haircut. "My straightening iron has never been able to make it this flat."

"Having straight hair is definitely God's way of making up for destroying your CD cases and favorite lipsticks." Ever since Elise had moved to Arizona, her wavy brown hair hadn't experienced a single day of frizz. However, she'd stopped buying expensive lipstick after several melted tubes and a couple of destroyed purses.

Carly squeezed her arm. "Are you excited?" she asked. "We're getting closer."

"Yeah. I'm kind of nervous. I feel like a freshman in college again, heading into the unknown. Remember how horrible that turned out."

"You really did get a shitty roommate. Has Stan told you anything else about Justine?" Carly asked as they neared the restrooms, the scent of urine hovering like a nuclear cloud.

"I wish. Stan has been asleep ever since we left Tucson."

"I'm sure she's cool. Stan wouldn't be friends with her if she was a total weirdo."

Elise picked up Bella before they entered the ladies' room, and in doing so caught a whiff of her hands. They smelled like Dijon, and the dog smelled like mustard, too.

After she scoured her hands with powdered soap, which felt like sand and made her fingers smell like a hospital, she returned to the lovely Mustard Mobile.

"I'm feeling much better," Stan said. "I can drive the rest of the way." He pulled the keys from her hand.

"Are you sure? I'm actually getting used to it."

Ignoring her, he quickly climbed into the driver's seat. "I can't wait to drive this thing," he said, like a child playing Nintendo for the first time.

"Really? I don't mind driving."

The engine roared to life. "I'm fine! Hop in!"

She could feel the bridge of her nose turning slick and sweaty where her cat's-eye sunglasses rested, and she wanted out of the sun. "All right."

The Mustard Mobile was pleasantly freezing when she climbed in, and the rattling noise was as loud as ever.

"So, tell me more about Justine," she said once they were on the highway.

"Well, what do you want to know? You probably know just as much as I do. You've talked to her on the phone."

Elise had spoken to her a few times but knew only the basics. Her soon-to-be roomie worked at her uncle's coffee shop, was twenty-six, originally from Nebraska, and had a boyfriend named Jimmy who played in a local band called Potter. Stan was a huge fan and a good friend of Jimmy's.

Justine was nice on the phone, and Elise had imagined them becoming close friends, hanging out at the coffee shop where she worked, sharing their favorite books and recipes. Maybe they would double date—if she ever found a date.

"What does she look like?" She kicked off her flip-flops and stretched her feet on the floor in front of her. Elise always liked to have a visual of everything. For example, if Carly was telling her a story about a coworker, Elise would have to know what she looked like, or more specifically, what kind of shoes she was wearing.

"I don't know." Stan said. "A girl."

"How can you not know? You're the one who set this up."

"She's got red hair and she's skinny."

She'd forgotten how horrible Stan was with details. He turned on the radio but found only static and switched it off. "Oh, there is one thing I forgot to tell you about her."

Something about his tone made her muscles stiffen. "What?"

"Oh, well. It's probably nothing. I should really just let *her* tell you."

She sat up. "No. You have to tell me."

"It's none of my business. Besides, it's really something she should tell you."

"You can't do this to me. You're the one who set this up, and you're going to tell me whatever it is. Now." It suddenly seemed much hotter in The Mustard Mobile.

"All right. Fine." He took a deep breath. "Well." He paused to look in his rearview mirror.

"Speak, Stan."

"Okay. Some people think she has a gift. I guess she's kind of psychic, and she occasionally holds séances in the house."

"What?"

"Yeah. I've actually been to one. It was weird."

"You're kidding?"

"No. She called in this spirit who went by Père. She said that meant *father* in French, so we were all trying to figure out if it was someone's grandfather. He was killed in some war. I can't remember which one."

She wanted to believe he was kidding, but this description was far too detailed for Stan's imagination. He didn't know French. "You never told me this. I thought you said you had never been to her house."

"Well, I forgot. Sorry." He scratched the bridge of his nose and began to hum the Buzz Burger song.

"How can you forget something like this?"

"I don't think she does it anymore. Jimmy mentioned something about it getting a little out of hand."

Her visions of double dating and drinking caramel lattes together turned to scenes from *The Exorcist*. What if Justine was possessed by the devil, and Elise had to contact a priest?

"This is not something you just *forget* to mention."

"Sorry."

She looked at him: his baseball cap turned backward, his big blue eyes gazing at the highway as if it were no big deal that he had arranged for her to live with someone who called in the dead.

She remembered the time in middle school when he'd convinced her that their parents were adopting an African child named Diana Momsabu. According to Stan, she was eight years old, was good in math, and hoped to become a doctor one day. Her parents were waiting to surprise Elise with her new sister at Christmas. He had even provided a picture of a young African girl with a shy smile and a beaded necklace. The real story, which she'd gotten from her older sister Melissa, had been that her parents had attended a benefit dinner for children in Africa and had simply signed up to sponsor Diana Momsabu's education.

She looked at him again. "You are *such* a liar."

"I'm not lying." He sighed. "I shouldn't have even told you."

"Yes. You should've told me. You should've told me when you gave me her phone number and told me what fun it would be to live with her." It was going to be hard enough to start her life over in San Diego, and now she had this to worry about?

They passed a sign for Centro Mesa, and Stan broke into one of the loudest and most profound versions of the Buzz Burger song that for a moment she actually thought he should sing in their ads.

Despite her anger, seeing the red and yellow sign sent a little bolt

of excitement through her veins. Not only was Buzz Burger her favorite fast-food restaurant, but it was also a sign that they had
crossed the Arizona border. Buzz Burgers were only in California,
and there was absolutely nothing like their secret sauce in Tucson.
However, her excitement was fleeting. She was moving in with the
type of person who inspired the spine-tingling tales that were told at
sixth-grade camp.

She would've found it absolutely fascinating if Stan were the one
moving in with a person like this, and might even consult with the
roommate for a psychic reading every once in a while. However, she
didn't want to be the one whose living situation became an urban leg-
end, and Elise wondered if ten, maybe twenty years from now her
name would still be accurately included in the tales. Or would she become Lisa, maybe Ella—the girl who was murdered by Père.

"What are you going to have?" he asked as they pulled up to the
microphone at the drive-through.

"What I'd really like is a screwdriver."

"Huh?"

"Yes, a screwdriver. So I can screw your head on straight," she
said. "What the hell were you thinking, Stan? How could you do this
to me?"

"Oh c'mon. It could be worse. Now tell me what you want."

"I'll have a number two combo with a Seven-Up," she answered
coldly.

"That's the cheeseburger combo, right? I'm going to get the same
thing." He smiled as he pulled up to the menu board. "Two number
two combos. One with a Seven-Up and one with a Coke."

Elise reached for her wallet on the floor. When she sat up, there
were still two more cars ahead of them. But what she saw made her
freeze.

"Stan, I don't think we can fit through there," she said as she
studied the overhang that created a small passage from the ordering
board to the pickup window. A tin roof supported by long, metal

poles created shady coverage for the passage. Perhaps it was provided to keep passengers cool while they waited for their food. From the top of the roof hung a sign that read **11' Clearance.** "Seriously. Stop the car. We're not going to fit through there."

"Hmmm," he mumbled. "That is pretty tight."

"Let's just park and go in."

"There is no way this thing is taller than eleven feet."

"Stan, even from where I'm sitting it looks like we could scrape the roof. Let's just park and go in."

She put the strap of her camel-colored purse over her shoulder. He stuck his head out the window and looked to the rear. "How are we going to get out of here?" he wanted to know. "There's like three cars behind us."

Elise looked as well, and waved to Carly in the process. Not only were they trapped in a one-way ordering lane with curbs and landscape islands on either side of them, but another car had pulled in and there were now four cars behind them. She could hear the voice coming through the drive-through microphone. "Welcome to Buzz Burger. Would you like to try a strawberry shake today?"

"I don't know how we can get out," she said. "But I know we can't make it through there."

"Sure we can."

He began to inch forward.

"No we can't. You're crazy."

She caught a whiff of hamburgers and greasy fries. There was only one car ahead of them, and as soon as it pulled out of the drive-through it would be their turn to pass through the Buzz Burger tunnel. "Look. As soon as the car ahead of us leaves, I'll walk up to the window and explain that we can't . . ." Her voice trailed off when she realized they were moving. "Stan? What are you doing?" Instead of listening to her, he stepped on the gas pedal and proceeded to move forward. "You're even crazier than I thought. We can't fit though—"

To her surprise they barely slid under the clearance sign. In fact, it was so close that the truck stirred a slight breeze, causing the sign to blow back and forth on its squeaky hinges.

"Thank God," she sighed, as they waited for the car ahead of them to leave.

"See? I knew we'd fit." He smiled triumphantly before continuing. So, he'd been right about this, but if he thought he was off the hook for setting her up to live with a medium, he couldn't be more wrong.

As Stan inched forward she thought of ways she could torture him. Perhaps she'd run ads in every San Diego newspaper for a thousand-dollar yacht with his phone number: *Bankrupt. Must sell this luxury yacht for the bargain price of $1,000. Call Stan.* She was imagining the incessant irritating calls he'd be plagued with morning, noon, and night when a jarring bang startled her. At first she thought there had been a car wreck in the parking lot. But one glance out her window indicated *they* were the wreck.

What followed next sounded like an explosion. Metal screeched as the truck scraped through the sides of the drive-through. They were so focused on the height of The Mustard Mobile that they'd completely overlooked the width. It sounded as if the world's most powerful espresso maker was mixing up the truck. She looked out her window and watched as the passenger-side rearview mirror was ripped from its mount. She feared the doors would be gone if they ever made it out. In a state of excitement, Bella propped her paws on the window and yelped.

Rather than stopping at the pickup window for their food and explaining the accident to the cashier, her brother gunned the gas pedal and peeled out of the Buzz Burger drive-through, taking what sounded like half the establishment with them. They bounced over the curb so hard that Elise thought she felt a lung in her throat.

"Stan! You're not stopping? We *have* to stop!"

"No we don't. No one saw us."

"You just took out half the Buzz Burger! And what about Carly? She's back there in the wreckage!"

She stuck her head out the window and caught a glimpse of her rearview mirror bouncing like a soccer ball over the pavement behind them. Carly tailed them in the bug. Thank God she was okay. From her angle, she could still make out the Buzz Burger. The steel poles that once supported the tunnel were as bent and crooked as elbows. Half the drive-through roof hung awkwardly, and the metal roof flapped over the poles like a gigantic steel flag. She didn't get many other details because Stan fled from Centro Mesa wearing the same scary expression she'd seen on Robert De Niro during a car chase in *Heat*.

"Stan. Stop. The. Freaking. Car. The U-Move is in my name. I will be liable for a hit-and-run."

He glanced at his sister. "Hit and run? Please. We didn't hurt anyone. Buzz Burger won't give a shit. They make millions of dollars every day. They won't mind some broken metal roof. They can go to Home Depot today and replace that thing in an hour."

Where he got this logic from she had no idea. She was about to further explain the damage they caused and the potential lawsuits when her cell phone rang.

"What the hell happened back there?" her best friend asked.

"Stan decided to tear through the eleven-foot drive-through roof. I told him the U-Move couldn't fit, but he insisted on taking matters into his own hands. He won't go back."

"If it makes you feel any better," Carly said, "I could still fit through the drive-through to follow you guys, so the wreckage can't be that bad. They can probably still run the drive-through for the rest of the day. As long as somebody isn't driving a big car they can squeeze through there."

She imagined the bad karma they were racking up as the franchise lost business because trucks weren't going to be able to order food. She clung to Bella as Stan sped onto the highway, dust and debris forming clouds outside their windows.

"Also," Carly added. "You guys took off so fast. There is no way anyone could've taken your license number." She began to laugh.

"That was the funniest thing I have ever seen in my life. The rearview mirror bounced right off the side of The Mustard Mobile."

Ha-ha.

She was stunned that her best friend was finding this as thrilling as her brother. Carly. She only wore two kinds of clothes. DKNY and Ann Taylor, and she'd been dressing this way since high school. While Elise had been experimenting with torn jeans and combat boots, Carly had always stuck to sensible loafers and sweater sets. She'd worn the same perfume, Chanel No. 5, since the seventh grade, and owned a clean and matching set of makeup brushes. She was a practical person, and here she was, willing to be an accessory to crime.

"I think it's okay," Carly said. "I don't think they're going to come after you. I'm starving, though. Can we stop in the next town for food?"

Elise imagined their descriptions being wired through the Middle of Nowhere police dispatch as they were speaking. Young male. Late twenties. Medium build. Blue eyes and brown hair. Female companion, mid-twenties. Petite build. Hazel eyes. Brown shoulder-length hair.

"No. We can't stop until we get at least a hundred miles away. Then I'm driving. Stan isn't allowed to drive anymore."

She said good-bye to Carly and leaned back in her seat. She was starting her new life in San Diego as a fugitive.

2. A New Hood

The only good thing that had come out of the accident was that the rattling noise had gone away. Whatever Stan had done had apparently knocked something back into its place, and she had never appreciated silence more.

They'd stopped briefly in the dry, remote town of El Centro to assess the damage. "By the way," Stan said as they pulled into the Carl's Jr. parking lot. "I was just kidding about Justine. She's not really psychic."

"What?"

He lowered his eyes. "She's not psychic. I made that up."

"What the hell is wrong with you?"

He shook his head. "Why are you flipping out? I thought you'd appreciate the truth."

"Thanks, Stan. Thanks for being a total asshole and completely traumatizing me for the past one hundred miles."

"I'm sorry. I thought it would be funny."

If he thought confessing was going to put her in a better mood, he was wrong. She knew what he was up to. She'd done the same thing. For example, in high school she told her parents she got an A in math right before revealing that she'd also received her first speeding ticket. He was trying to make her feel so relieved that she wouldn't care about the damage he'd done.

After parking, they both circled around the truck.

"See! I told you!" he yelled, joining her at the tailgate. "You can't even tell!"

It was *partly* true. The Mustard Mobile had been in crappy shape to begin with, and it was hard to tell which scratches were new. However, it was missing a mirror on the passenger's side, and the mirror on the driver's side dangled by a thick black cord. One hubcap was gone, and the right corner of the front bumper showcased a dent the size of a small banana.

Guilt nipped at her conscience as she wondered how the poor Buzz Burger was faring. In the Carl's Jr. parking lot she promised God if she ever made it big as a mystery writer, she'd send them an anonymous cash donation.

They didn't spend a ton of time surveying the damage. She'd been nervous that if they stopped for too long someone might recognize them, and she was anxious to get to her new neighborhood in North Park. This time, she took over the wheel.

Her last month in Arizona had been filled with daydreams of packing a beach bag and walking to the coast to edit her novel and soak up sun. She'd bodysurf and throw crumbs to the seagulls while getting a tan that would attract a brilliant and sun-kissed surfing boyfriend. These fantasies, however, came to a screeching halt when she realized that the rent near the ocean was not designed for struggling writers.

When Stan gave her Justine Viccar's phone number in North Park, she investigated her options inland. North Park was one of the oldest areas of San Diego, and centrally located. She recalled charming little Craftsman-style houses, swanky coffee shops, and hip record stores that specialized in selling hard-to-find music. It was a haven for starving artists and one of the only places in San Diego that still had affordable rent. So her fantasy had switched to hanging out at coffee shops and meeting a hot vegetarian poet.

As she exited the freeway her palms became as damp as a moist kitchen sponge, and she kind of hoped Justine wasn't home to shake her hand. She followed Stan's directions and turned the U-Move down a one-way street, careful not to sideswipe any cars parked next to the curb. She began to feel nervous when she trucked past houses with bars soldered to windows and barbed wire framing yards. Where were all the little vegan restaurants? The meditation centers and indie record stores? Pit bulls were chained to trees.

Furthermore, it suddenly occurred to her that they weren't in North Park. Wasn't North Park west of the freeway? They were heading east into City Heights, North Park's closest neighbor and a regular feature on the eleven o'clock news for its drive-by shootings and liquor store stickups. Billboards in City Heights encouraged saying no to drugs and provided specific locations for free HIV testing. In City Heights, the neighbors held gang initiations instead of welcome-to-the-neighborhood parties.

"Are you sure I didn't make a wrong turn? We're in City Heights, Stan."

"City Heights. North Park. We're right on the fringes of both. What difference does it make? It's all the same."

"What difference does it make? In case you didn't notice the hooker with gold teeth who just waved to you, this is not North Park."

"Go right here," he said, oblivious. "By the way, Arnold Schwarzenegger visited the area recently to talk about reforming education. Right here at the city hall in this neighborhood. Right in City Heights."

What was his point?

"Stan, this is not North Park."

"Well it's so close. I'm telling you. This whole area is on the rise. You just don't know because you've been out of the loop for so long. It's a cool place to live."

Cool if you owned a bulletproof vest. She was going to have to take karate lessons.

Stan directed her to pull into a sagging apartment complex. Orange paint peeled from the walls like shredded cheddar cheese. Bars covered most of the windows, and a mildewed couch that was missing every single cushion sat on the neighbor's dead lawn. A rusty staircase wrapped around the front of the three-story building, and a couple of limp palm trees lined the entrance. A sign reading "Casa de Paradiso" was posted in front of the building. The "a" in Casa hung upside down by an old nail. Elise had taken French in high school, but she knew enough Spanish to understand that *Casa de Paradiso* meant "House of Paradise." She wondered if whoever had named the building couldn't figure out the Spanish word for *squalor*.

"This is it?"

Stan looked at the directions. "Yup."

She wished Stan would tell her this was all one big joke, like the séance thing. He was just screwing with her, and her real house was across town in the cute Spanish-style complex that she had been dreaming about. But he wasn't kidding. Casa de Paradiso was going to be her new home.

"Aren't you going to park?" he asked.

She was still debating. Part of her wanted to open Stan's door, shove him out of the truck, and speed back to Tucson.

This will only be temporary, she told herself. She was renting month to month. She could leave *as soon* as she found a new place.

Justine had mentioned that they each had their own parking space, but fitting The Mustard Mobile into her space only invited the opportunity for more disaster, so she parked next to the curb.

"This isn't North Park," Carly said as she joined them.

"I know. Tell Stan. He seems to think it is."

"Why don't you just stay with me for the time being?" Carly offered.

"In your studio? With Bella? I think it would be a little too cramped, but thanks."

Carly sighed. "I wish I wasn't locked into my lease for another year. Otherwise, it would be you, me, and Bella in our own little beach bungalow. I'm going to start looking for a new place for you tonight. You can't stay here."

Carly was perhaps the most reliable and efficient person she knew. She was the type of friend that Elise could call at three a.m. on a Tuesday night from a Mexican jail and ask for ten thousand dollars' bail and a ride home. Not only would Carly cross the border, but she would probably show up with Gloria Allred and a tube of antibacterial hand lotion to kill all the germs from the jail. Not that Elise had ever been arrested. She just knew her best friend well, and was glad to be moving closer to her.

She found the key stashed under the mat. It was in a little white envelope with a note attached. This would be the last time they would ever stash keys under the mats again. For crying out loud, people don't leave keys under mats in City Heights.

Hi Elise!

Sorry I couldn't be here to help you get settled. I wish I didn't have to work, but I can't wait to meet you later. Help yourself to anything.

Justine

God only knew what lay inside. At this point anything was possible. The blinds were drawn when she entered. Even though it was three o'clock in the afternoon, it appeared to be past dark. As she searched for a light switch, she inhaled the scent of stale cigarette smoke—the kind of smoke that seeps into the curtains and makes the wallpaper turn the same shade of yellow featured in "before" pictures for teeth whitening ads. She'd never lived with a smoker and hadn't even thought to ask if Justine smoked when they'd spoken on the phone.

In the dark, she fumbled for a light switch. "It reeks in here."

"I know," Carly said. "But I'm sure you can set some regulations. She has to understand. Being a smoker myself, I know that we smokers have to be the accommodating ones."

She really began to consider staying with Carly until she flicked on a light switch. Illuminating the apartment cast a new light on Elise's disappointment. Not only was the furniture nice, but the entire inside of their apartment looked renovated. Faux marble countertops in the kitchen. New beige carpet. Crown molding. Bella's nose was practically glued to the carpet as she immediately began to sniff out her new surroundings.

"I told you," Stan said. "This place is on the rise. People are fixing up these little condos and turning them over."

She noticed two pairs of shoes by the front door, both very fashionable. A pointy pair of black heels, and a funky pair of retro-looking sneakers, brown with tan stripes on the sides.

"I think we're supposed to take our shoes off," Elise said, slipping off her flip-flops.

Carly slipped off her loafers. "Well, that's a good sign. Obviously she's clean."

That was an understatement. The Spanish tiled floors in the kitchen shined like brand-new copper pennies. There wasn't a speck of dust or clutter to be found. Elise never knew what to do with old phone bills or scrap pieces of paper and ended up leaving them in little stacks next to her desk. She'd never thought it was possible to live a clutter-free life.

She felt like a miner who had just stumbled upon the mother lode when she noticed pictures on the wall. "Look," she whispered. "Pictures. We can see what she looks like!"

Carly rubbed her hands together as she approached. "I've been curious."

Except for one tiny photo of her family, all of the pictures on the wall were what appeared to be Justine with her boyfriend. She was much prettier than Elise had imagined. Long auburn hair hung past her shoulders, and her pale skin looked as if it had never met with sunburn. Her green eyes were framed beneath two well-sculpted and dramatically arched eyebrows.

"She's pretty," Carly whispered. "And apparently she really likes her boyfriend."

"I know. How many pictures of them do you think there are?" Elise's voice was practically inaudible. Why they were whispering neither one knew.

A couple of photos featured Jimmy alone. In one, he was playing his guitar in front of a stage full of people, his Rod Stewart haircut hanging over his ears and resting on his neck. There was another picture of him standing next to a Thanksgiving turkey looking as if he didn't belong in the tie he was wearing. After assessing all the photos, the girls continued to inspect every room.

A small bar separated the kitchen and living room, which meant that she could watch TV while cooking a meal. There was no flaky goop or crust gathered around the dispenser on the hand soap pump. Sure, Elise was clean. But her soap dispensers tended to resemble a runny nose.

Furthermore, Justine had seemed welcome to sharing her place with Elise's dog. But Elise knew how often Bella shed coarse little black and white dog hair. In fact, Elise had dozens covering the tank top and shorts she was wearing. What if Justine hated Bella?

Her worries were squashed when she noticed the tiny laundry room attached to the kitchen. This was the most exciting aspect of moving in with Justine. No more hoarding quarters and digging in the trenches of couch cushions in search of spare change. Her days of hauling heavy laundry baskets and a good book to the Laundromat were over. Having a washer and dryer made her temporarily forget that her new neighbors probably sold drugs out of their condo.

Small signs of Justine were revealed in the laundry room. A wool sweater laid flat on the dryer, size small. A pair of hoop earrings apparently fished out of a pocket and set on top of the washer. Her attention was distracted when she noticed Stan rummaging through the fridge.

"Get out of there," she said.

He closed the refrigerator door. "I'm starving. We haven't eaten since El Centro."

"I'm hungry, too. But Mom and Dad are going to be here in a little while, and we're all going out to dinner." It was time to give Stan something to do. "Why don't we start unloading?"

Outside, the scent of orange blossoms wafted through the path that led back to the truck, and she hadn't realized how much she missed that fragrance. The sweet scent of the blossoming white flowers was California's perfume in spring and early summer.

Somewhere in the moving process Carly had vanished. Elise figured she was either still looking around or had gone outside to smoke.

"Where do you want this?" Stan asked, holding her TV.

"Just set it on top of the dresser. I wonder if I get cable in here."

Stan placed the TV on her dresser before screwing the cable cord into the wall. Once plugged in, he hit the Power button. "I think you only get local stations." He scanned the channels, stopping occasionally to watch something.

They peeked inside her closet and discovered that two of the shelves had come loose and looked as if they might fall from the wall if she placed anything on top of them. "I can fix those," Stan said, running his hands over the wood.

"You can?"

"Of course." He patted her on the back. "I brought some of my tools with me, so I'll tighten those. Then you'll have much more space in there for your stuff."

"Thanks."

Despite his jackass tendencies, he really could be nice when someone needed a favor. She knew he would fix them, even it meant staying until midnight. She remembered the time she had driven to San Diego two Christmases ago, and her car had broken down near Gila Bend. She was going to call for a tow truck and stay the night in a run-down motel in the truck stop town until someone could pick her up the next morning. However, Stan wouldn't hear of it. He ditched the Coldplay concert he had tickets to and drove five hours to pick her up so she didn't have to stay overnight in the middle of nowhere by herself.

She decided to leave several boxes unpacked, and instead stacked them in her closet. She was getting ready to put her sheets on her mattress when she heard Carly's voice.

"Hey, check this out," she called from somewhere in the apartment.

Stan had begun setting up her desk, and she brushed past him as she followed Carly's voice.

She found her in Justine's room. "You've gotta see this!"

"What?" Elise was back to whispering. "We shouldn't be in here."

"You know you were planning on peeking in here, too."

She had already *peeked* inside. She'd stolen a quick glance before an eerie feeling that Justine could enter at any moment sent her racing back to her half of the apartment. She knew what they were doing was wrong. Her conscience told her they were trespassing. However, she was also dying to see what Carly had found. Whatever it was would reveal something about the *real* Justine. Of course, her imagination immediately assumed it was something sexual or raunchy. She took a step forward, Bella at her heels.

She looked around and noticed that the two bedrooms were exactly alike, spacious, and each with its own bathroom. Elise was amazed that someone had actually figured out a way to prevent that bumpy layer of sedimentation that forms at the end of the toothpaste tube. Maybe if Elise squeezed her paste the same way it wouldn't look like a science project.

It suddenly occurred to her what kind of pressure it was going to be living with Justine Viccars. Elise was going to have to be as clean as a Windex commercial if she didn't want to be branded the slob. With her old roommates she was considered pretty clean, but with Justine she could be coined a disaster. No more leaving the occasional coffee mug in the sink or brushing crumbs onto the floor instead of sponging them off the counter. She was going to have to start making her bed every day.

"Okay, come look at this." Carly pulled her deeper into Justine's world.

"All right. Show me. Quick."

Carly pointed to a wall next to Justine's bed. Elise looked at an eight-by-ten photo of Justine and Jimmy. Her arms were thrown over his neck, and he was holding her piggyback style. They were both laughing, and the wind blew Justine's long hair away from her face. They looked like they were posing for a breath mint ad. For a moment Elise wondered why Carly had dragged her into Justine's bedroom to show her this. They already knew Justine had a lot of pictures of her boyfriend. She had even spotted a few more in the kitchen. Then she looked at the picture hanging beneath it. The photos were exactly the same.

"She has two of the same exact pictures hanging next to each other. Can someone please say obsessed?" Carly said.

It was strange, but she had to pee, and visions of Justine popping up behind them while they discussed her bizarre choice in wall décor made her nervous. "Maybe she just really likes the picture." She could hear Stan using his electric screwdriver in her bedroom. "I don't know. Let's get out of here."

"It's so weird," Carly said, not budging.

The fine hair on the back of her neck sprang to life when she heard what sounded like the rough turn of a door handle. She listened to a swoosh of air enter the apartment as the front door opened. Holy shit, she was home, and they were in her room. She yanked Carly by the elbow back into the living room. "We were just trying to figure out whose room is whose," Elise said.

"That's nice, honey," her mother said, holding a large pot of flowers. "I thought your new roommate might like these."

Elise sighed. "Mom and Dad." Stan must've given them directions.

"Come give me a hug, Slugger," her dad said. Still tingling from surprise, she fell into her father's bearlike embrace. She could smell his spicy aftershave as he planted a kiss on her forehead.

"Slugger! Slugger! Slugger!" He shouted so loud that she wondered if the neighbors might complain on the first day. And she really didn't want everyone to know the nickname her father had given her when she gave Stan a black eye after he ripped her Ken doll's head off when she was eight. She was twenty-seven years old now.

Her father was wearing khaki shorts with a golf shirt tucked in. An outfit her mother undoubtedly picked out. If it were up to him, he'd be sporting penny loafers with no socks and the University of Arizona sweatsuit Elise had given him her freshman year of college. His fashion sense was as savvy as a two-year-old.

The shorts and shirt her mother had selected did a good job covering his basketball-sized tummy. Her mother, however, had failed to find him a decent pair of shoes. Hal Sawyer had the kind of toes that made little kids run from swimming pools when he got in. They were an unnatural shade of yellow and as gnarled and exotic looking as something from *Lord of the Rings*.

He moved his smothering hug to Carly. "It's great to see my girls again!"

"Did you see the Padres game last night, Mr. Sawyer?" Carly asked.

"You bet. Wouldn't have missed it for the world. And you're too damn old to be calling us Mr. and Mrs. Sawyer. We're Hal and Marge now."

"Your roommate smokes?" her mother asked, opening windows. "That's going to get old fast."

Her father shook his head. "It's awful in here!" Again, the neighbors.

Marge looked around the apartment the same way she had looked around Elise's bedroom in seventh grade after she had plastered her walls with posters of Billy Idol. "Stan set this up?" her mother asked.

Elise nodded.

"What is wrong with him?" Marge wanted to know. Elise had actually been questioning her own judgment. She should've never trusted his suggestion. The atmosphere in his own apartment was similar to a camping trip. However, Stan had tons of friends, most of whom were fun-loving, good people. So she was still counting on Justine to be cool.

A mixture of skepticism and disgust covered her mother's face. "Well, at least it's clean in here." She released a cough, which to an untrained ear may have sounded real, but Elise knew better. "I don't know how you're going to be able to handle it."

"I'm sure if I ask her to smoke outside she will. It's going to be fine."

"You know, Elise, when your father and I were driving into this area, we were very concerned. Just remember this isn't like Del Mar or Tucson. Just a couple of blocks over we saw a homeless man pushing a shopping cart and digging through someone's trash. Didn't we, Hal?"

Her father nodded. "Do you still have that pepper spray I gave you? And what about that flashlight? Do you keep that in your glove box?"

Elise had no clue where the pepper spray was. He'd given it to her years ago, and to tell the truth, she'd been scared of the canister, afraid if she held it the wrong way, or if she placed it in an awkward angle in her purse, it was going to accidentally dislodge and go off in her face. "I don't know where the spray is. But I think that flashlight is still in my glove box." The batteries were probably dead by now, but she kept that to herself. "I'm not staying here long. Believe me, it's just temporary."

"I have a great idea," her father said as if he'd just found the master solution to all her problems. "Why don't you move home?"

While her mother's face lit with joy, Elise wanted to ask, *Why not just become a confirmed spinster?* She didn't want to discuss the issue any further. "Let me show you my room. It's huge, and Justine had the carpets cleaned for me."

Her mother looked around the room. "Well, at least you'll have your own private space. Maybe you can just keep to your room and block out that smoke." She looked at Stan, who was still bent over the desk, his brows furrowed in concentration. "Hello, Stan. How was the ride over in the U-Move?"

"Fine." He reached for his screwdriver.

"Stan crashed into the overhang at the Buzz Burger in Centro Mesa," Carly said.

"Oh please," he said. "Did you have to bring that up?"

"What?" Marge screeched. "Good grief. Is there damage?"

"Not much to the U-Move, but who knows about the Buzz Burger. He took off too fast to tell."

Her mother threw her hand over her chest. "Oh my word. Did you hear that, Hal? Your son crashed into a Buzz Burger in Centro Mesa."

"Uh, that's too bad." Her father had returned to the living room, seized the remote control, and was in a world of his own as he watched a Padres game. He wouldn't have cared if Stan had driven the U-Move through a police station. "Dammit!" he shouted as someone struck out.

She turned back to Elise. "Will they sue?"

"No," Stan answered. "They're not going to sue."

"Well, who is going to pay for all that damage?"

"Stan is," Elise said. Since he had recklessly decided to take his chances and rip through the drive-through like a raving maniac, he was going to be responsible for returning the U-Move and explaining the damage. Money owed was coming out of his pocket.

They spent another hour organizing Elise's room while her father watched a baseball game from the edge of the couch, shouting obscenities at the pitcher. Chances were Trevor Hoffman, star pitcher for the Padres, couldn't hear Hal Sawyer, but all the neighboring streets in City Heights could.

When they were finished unloading, Elise looked around. Compared to Justine's nicely organized pale greens and creams, Elise's room looked like an explosion of color from Thrift City. She'd always liked warm, bright colors, and her red sheets and comforter were mismatched and covered with patches of gold and pink. She hung a few pictures, just to make herself comfortable. A large oil print of a dramatically green cactus with huge yellow cactus flowers that she'd purchased in Arizona. Her ex-boyfriend, whom she'd dated all through college, was an artist and had painted her a watercolor of Bella lying on her plaid dog bed.

She'd hung the framed cover of the only mystery book she'd published, *Double Deceit*. The book was about twin sisters who each blamed the other for a string of murders in their neighborhood.

Elise wondered if Justine would think she was a cold loner for having so few photographs on her wall. She had one of Carly and her in Italy the summer after they graduated from college. Her other framed photo was of her nephew, Jeffrey. The picture had been taken a year earlier as he sat with a birthday crown perched on his blond head waiting to blow out his first candle. Jeffrey was her older sister's son. Thank God Melissa had stepped up to the plate and produced a child by the time she was thirty. It took some of the pressure off Elise to get married and have grandkids. No one expected anything from Stan.

"I need to eat," Stan said. "I'm ordering a pizza."

"That's a good idea," Marge said. "Why don't we just eat pizza here while Elise gets settled?" She reached for her purse. "Here's my credit card. Go ahead and order."

Elise was hungry, too, but she didn't want her family commandeering her apartment before she had even met Justine. "Maybe we should go out. I'd kind of like to explore the area." She looked at Stan. "I thought you said there was a good Mexican food restaurant around here."

Ignoring her, he pressed the phone against his ear. "One pepperoni pizza. And another with half green peppers and olives. And a large cheese. And can you bring a six-pack of Coke with that?"

A half an hour later a weathered-looking pizza man arrived holding several boxes and a six-pack of soda. Marge immediately began pulling Justine's plates from the cupboard. "Everyone come grab a piece," she called.

"What kind would you like?" Stan asked Carly.

"Just plain cheese for me," she said. Stan slapped a piece of plain cheese on a plate for her, then served his father. Quite the little helper.

"I think we should ask her if we should use those plates," Elise said, ripping off paper towels to use instead.

"It's fine," her mother said. "Aren't you guys going to share?"

"Yes. But we can't take over before I've even met her."

"Oh, relax."

Elise put her piece of pizza on a paper towel. She took a bite and hoped that everyone ate quickly.

"So, don't forget to mark your calendar for Melissa's shower," her mother said.

"Oh, don't worry," Elise said. "I already have."

"Good. Why don't you see if there is anything you can do to help? I'll give you Crystal's phone number. She might need something."

Knowing Crystal Klingsburg, she probably had everything planned before Melissa was even pregnant, or married, for that matter. She was Melissa's best friend in the whole world and had been responsible for every shower, bachelorette party, and celebration in her adult life. It was a good thing she was so gung ho about event planning, because if it had been left to Elise, her sister's bridal shower probably would've consisted of a six-foot sub and a case of Two Buck Chuck. Elise had never been a big planner and frankly thought showers and other such events were kind of boring. At least her sister was having a female child. Girl baby clothes were absolutely precious, and watching her open her gifts would be cute.

"Come look at this," her mother said, pulling her digital camera from her purse. She carried the thing with her everywhere, and no matter who you were, if you started a conversation with Marge Sawyer, you'd end up being exposed to the most recent pictures of Jeffrey. "These were taken last weekend," she said as she began scrolling through several pictures of Jeffrey standing next to a goat. "We went to the petting zoo. And you should've seen him. He wasn't afraid of any of the animals. There were all these kids crying, and he just ran right up to the goats and fed them, just like he'd had goats his whole life!"

"Great."

She was looking at the fiftieth picture of Jeffrey with a goat when she heard the familiar sound of the door handle turning.

"She's here!" her mother whispered excitedly. Open pizza boxes and piles of crumbs covered the countertops. She quickly brushed her hands over the crumbs, letting them scatter over the tiles where they were less noticeable.

"Hi," Justine said to no one in particular, her eyes wandering over the room.

Elise was about to introduce herself when Stan stood up.

"Hey!" he said, before giving her a hug. "It's good to see you again!"

She looked like the pictures, but much smaller. Elise was small, too, but she felt large next to Justine. Her new roommate had a tiny boyish figure with square shoulders and a washboard stomach. She wore khaki cargo Capri pants and a black tank top with rhinestones on it. As she turned toward Elise and Carly, she flicked a tongue ring in her mouth.

"Hi. I'm your roommate. I'm Elise. It's so nice to finally meet you," she said as they shook hands.

"You, too. I'm glad you made it." She glanced at Stan. "You guys look nothing alike." It was true. Except for their big blue eyes, they looked different. Both of Elise's siblings took after their father. However, Elise resembled Marjorie's side of the family, the Bradford square nose and heart-shaped lips.

"This must be Bella," Justine said. She reached down and rubbed Bella underneath her chin. "I'm so excited that you have a dog. I've wanted a pet ever since I moved to San Diego. I miss my parents' golden retriever in Nebraska."

As Elise introduced her to the rest of her guests, she noticed that no one in her family had taken off their shoes and had been wandering all over the apartment.

"Would you like some pizza?" Marge asked.

She put a small hand over her flat stomach. "Oh, no. No thanks. I'm really not hungry."

"How long have you lived here?" Curious Marge asked.

"Two years now. It's great. Downtown is five minutes away. The beaches are fifteen."

"And we see you have a boyfriend? A musician?" Her mother beamed. It was really time for them to go. Elise could feel a CIA inquisition coming on.

Justine's head cocked to the right, and her cheeks became the color of pink tulips. "Yes. He's away in Los Angeles, recording his album."

"Well, that's neat. What kind of music is it? Rock music?"

"Yes. It's kind of like The Beatles but more modern, a little more edgy."

"The Beatles?" her mother said. "I love The Beatles. Maybe we could all go to a concert sometime."

This type of questioning continued until her mother knew which hospital Justine was born in, that her father was a contractor, and which brand of cleaning supplies she liked best. She even busted out the digital camera. The whole time Elise stood at the sink, scrubbing their dirty plates.

Carly had long since yawned, called it a night, and headed home. Eventually her parents said their good-byes, too. Stan was the last to leave. He stayed a little longer, helping carry her empty boxes to the Dumpster behind the apartment complex. She suspected he might actually be worried about her walking to the Dumpster alone. However, he would never admit this, being that he was the one who had arranged for her to live here.

"I'm so sorry," Elise said after she had closed the door behind him. "I'm sure you weren't expecting an onslaught of questions from my parents when I moved in."

"Oh, that's okay. My parents are the same exact way, only my mother would be stuffing you full of food the whole time she interrogated you." She flicked her tongue ring. "So, do you need help with anything? Let's see your room."

They stood in her doorway, surveying Elise's setup.

"That's so cool that you're a famous writer," she said, pointing to the cover of *Double Deceit*. "I'm living with a celebrity."

Elise tossed her head back and laughed, but really inside she just felt irritated. Being called a celebrity only made her remember just how broke she was. If she were indeed famous, there was no way in hell she'd be sharing an apartment in City Heights for five hundred dollars a month. Instead, she'd be dividing time between her beach-front property in Kauai and a five-bedroom house in La Jolla. "I wouldn't really say I'm famous."

Justine stared blankly. "Why?"

"Well, it's not that easy. I'm pretty much scraping by to survive, and everything is so uncertain with my career."

"I wish I could make money doing something like that, working out of the house. Jimmy has a great job, too. He can sleep in and work whenever he wants."

"Creating your own schedule is definitely nice."

Justine thought for a moment. Depending on the angle in which she arched her eyebrows, she could either look playful or evil. She looked a little of both. "So is your book scary?"

"I guess. Somewhat. I think it's probably more suspenseful than scary."

"What are you working on now?"

"Another mystery. This one is about a woman who gets framed for murdering the elderly woman she takes care of. It's called *Cold as Ice*, and I write about the same detective as my first one. Her name is Ashley Trent."

Both her eyebrows shot up. "Woooow. That sounds good."

"Thanks." Elise suddenly realized how gross she looked and felt. Her new roommate probably thought she was wearing L'Eau de Mustard.

"Do you want a glass of wine?" Justine asked. "I have a bottle of red."

"That sounds great. Lemme just rinse off and change into sweats."

Elise quickly showered, then changed into her favorite pair of sweats and a tank top. When she returned to the living room, Justine was waiting on the couch. Her acrylic nails looked long on her little hands as she lit a cigarette. Even though she didn't plan on staying long, she wondered how on earth she was going to endure the smoking.

She sat on the love seat and reached for the glass of wine that Justine had poured for her. The television was on, but neither one paid attention as they chatted. Justine explained that she worked at a small coffee shop in North Park that her uncle owned. "It gets really boring in there during the day when it's slow, and I have to work a lot of doubles so I can afford rent." She petted Bella while she spoke. "It sucks, because I don't get to spend as much time with Jimmy as I'd like on the weekends. But sometimes he'll just come sit with me at the coffee shop all day."

Soon, Elise found that the conversation had turned to her love life, or lack thereof. "I had a boyfriend all through college," she explained. "Everything was great between Tim and me. The only problem was that he had a serious case of altar phobia."

Justine raised an eyebrow. "Altar phobia?"

"He was afraid of meeting me at the altar. I dated him for four years, and he kept saying he wasn't sure about marriage. Breaking up with him was like losing my best friend, but I had to do it. I couldn't put in another four years waiting for him to grow up. I'm not getting any younger."

She took a sip of her wine. "Jimmy has tons of friends. We'll find you a boyfriend."

Elise was about to ask more about Jimmy's friends when she remembered that she'd left some boxes of stationery and photo albums in the bug. If it were any other neighborhood, she'd leave them in there until morning. However, she lived in the ghetto now. "I need to get some boxes out of my car."

"I'll help you. By the way, I meant to tell you that we have a storage area above our parking places. I'll give you the key, and you can put whatever you want inside."

The air outside was cold and the scent of orange blossoms still heavy.

"Yo. Justine!" A boy of about seventeen came running toward them. He wore a wife beater tank top, blue pants that hung so low they would've exposed his butt cheeks if it hadn't been for his white boxers. A heavy gold chain hung from his neck. Skinny as a rail, he was only a few inches taller than she. He was out of breath when he reached them. "Is this your new roommate?"

"Yes. I told you about her."

"Yeah, yeah. That's right. She from Tucson." His voice sounded like Jay-Z, but his skin was as white as Vanilla Ice.

"Elise, this is Glorious D. He's our next-door neighbor on my side of the building."

Elise extended her hand. "It's nice to meet you."

"Yeah, hey check this out. I been rhymin' about you guys." He began to move his head back and forth. "That's right y'all. Glorious D's in the house," he said as if a huge audience awaited his performance. "Now let me holla about our hood. I gotcha back cuz we all good. Bustin' around wit yo boxes. Lookin real fine, cuz you two's foxes. Trickin' out yo pad. It might get loud around here. So dontcha get mad." He stopped. "Uh, that's all I got right now."

Applause came from several open windows on the second level of the building, and Glorious D's arms shot up like two little antennas. "Thanks y'all. I see you around," he said before slapping Justine's hand with a high five and heading back to his pad.

"He makes up raps all the time," Justine said. She seemed irritated, but Elise loved it. Having Glorious D as a neighbor would provide loads of entertainment, and as far as being interesting, he kicked ass over the yuppie couple and two small children she'd lived next door to in Tucson.

They each carried a box back to the house. Without removing her shoes, Justine went straight for the answering machine. She pressed the button and stared at the machine as if she were waiting for something critical. They'd only been outside for about ten minutes.

"No new messages," the electronic lady indicated.

The arch in her eyebrows suggested trouble.

"Is something wrong?" Elise asked.

"No. I just thought that Jimmy would've called by now."

Justine punched in numbers on the phone while Elise carried the boxes to her room. When she returned, Justine still hovered over the answering machine. Once again, the electronic lady told them in so many words that they were total loners for the evening.

"I'll check my cell phone," Justine said.

Elise decided to get ready for bed. While she was brushing her teeth, she was certain she heard the electronic lady saying there were no new messages for the third time that night.

3. Hunting

A loud, thunderous heartbeat pulsed above her, making the walls vibrate. In her semiconscious state she wondered if she had moved to a neighborhood near Camp Pendleton. But when she opened her eyes she realized that she was in City Heights. There was a helicopter circling above. This meant that there was something going on, and she might be on the news. When she threw her covers back, Bella jumped from the mattress and ran to the bedroom door.

Entering their living room was similar to setting foot in the smoking section of a cave dwelling. At nine o'clock in the morning their apartment was as dark as a grave and as smoky as an Alcoholics Anonymous meeting. It had been two days since her arrival, and she couldn't help but wonder what her new roommate had against natural lighting and fresh air. Rarely did she open a single blind or window during the day. More intriguing, her reasons for keeping everything sealed during the day didn't seem to involve measures of safety. At night she left everything open, inviting creeps and Peeping Toms to spy from all over City Heights. It was so bizarre.

Elise opened the blinds and several windows before she stepped outside to let Bella go to the bathroom and to see what all the excitement was about. She could actually see the pilots inside the chopper and was tempted to say good morning.

Her neighbor's door flew open, and a squat Mexican woman with more facial hair than Stan and an apron tied around her waist emerged. She shook her head and mumbled something in Spanish as she surveyed the view above. Elise had never seen this particular woman. However, she'd noticed dozens of other tenants coming in and out of her apartment. She'd lost count after about twelve and was beginning to wonder how many people actually lived there. Her bedroom shared a wall with their place. For the past two days Elise had been exposed to the kind of Spanish music that featured a lot of accordions and gave her an urge to slide a flower between her teeth and kick up her heels.

She was about to introduce herself and ask if she knew what was going on when an authoritive male voice descended over them. "Lock all doors. And windows," the voice barked from a loudspeaker above. "Stay. Inside. Do. Not. Open the door. For anyone. We are looking for a white male. Medium height. Wearing a red and black plaid flannel shirt. He is armed. And dangerous. I repeat. Stay inside the building."

Elise shot the Mexican women a thrilled look, but her neighbor was already running for safety. Elise grabbed Bella and thought about what a great story this would be. Nothing like this ever happened to her. When a convenience store across from Stan's apartment complex caught fire and he was forced to evacuate, she felt a slight pang of envy. Or when Carly's next-door neighbor turned out to be a white-collar criminal and was arrested right in front of her building, Elise hung on her every word, wishing she might be interviewed by a newscaster while holding grocery bags.

She closed the door, dead-bolted it, and began sliding all the windows shut. Though exciting, she didn't want the fugitive to choose their apartment for his hideout.

"Good morning," Justine said as she reached for her cigarettes on the kitchen counter.

"There is a fugitive on the loose, wearing red plaid. And a helicopter hovering over our roof."

"Oh. That. I thought I heard something."

"We have to keep all the doors and windows locked, and we can't leave the building."

She looked freshly showered and outfitted in her low-rise jeans. Her French-manicured fingertips squeezed the end of a cigarette. "They'll catch the guy in a few minutes. They always do." She inhaled and blew a huge cloud of smoke into the kitchen.

"This happens frequently?"

She shrugged. "Yeah. I guess." She walked to the kitchen and lifted a package from the counter. "Look what I got for Jimmy." Elise watched as she opened a brown cardboard box. She imagined that Justine had bought Jimmy a vinyl record collection of his favorite bands. Or perhaps a cool vintage jacket for his next concert. Instead, Justine pulled out a series of small lighthouses, one by one. "After he gets back from L.A. I'm going to give him one of these almost every day until he leaves for his tour," she said. "There are thirty-five lighthouses here. And they're all hand-painted."

"Oh. Does he like lighthouses?"

"I don't know. I just saw them in this catalogue and thought it would be a nice collection for him to have from me." She began to thumb through a catalogue. They looked like a product of the Thomas Kinkade Gallery. Something her grandmother would relish. "Look at this." She pointed to another lighthouse, much larger and fancier than the little ones that sat on the counter. "I'm going to order this lighthouse and give it to him the day he leaves for his tour." She further explained that the top of this revolving lighthouse lit up and played "You Light Up My Life" when plugged into the wall. "It will be the final gift for the collection. I'm going to attach a note that says, 'Jimmy, *you* light up my life.'"

"That's very sweet of you." For some reason she had a hunch that guitar-wielding Jimmy probably wouldn't have come up with the idea to collect hand-painted lighthouses on his own. But maybe he had a soft, sentimental, gay streak.

"I'm going to hide them in the storage space above our parking places," Justine said. "I hope he doesn't find them. When you meet him, *don't* tell him where they are."

Elise thought it odd that they were discussing a collection of hand-painted lighthouses while a helicopter combed the area for an armed fugitive.

"He's coming back in a couple of weeks. I miss him so much." She headed for the kitchen cabinets. Elise had added some of her dishes to the cupboards and caught a glimpse of them when Justine pulled opened a door. Over the years Elise had acquired a mishmash of stemware and kitchen accessories from garage sales, thrift stores, and her mother's hand-me-downs. She'd never owned a set of matching dishes and felt slightly self-conscious when she noticed her World's Greatest Mom! mug next to Justine's even rows of matching white mugs.

Justine looked over her shoulder as she poured coffee. "So, what are you up to today?"

"Working on my book."

Elise was heading to the kitchen for a bowl of cereal when a startling knock at the front door nearly sent her sprinting for cover in the utility closet. "Who do you think it is?" she whispered, fully envisioning the knocker in red plaid.

Stealthily, her roommate tiptoed to the front window. Elise watched as she moved, as quiet as a bunny on grass, toward a slit in the blinds. She spent a few seconds squinting through a narrow slit before she whipped her head back to Elise. Judging from the panicked expression that contorted her face, Elise knew it wasn't the Girl Scouts. "Quick! Hide!"

Elise darted toward the utility closet, taking the cordless phone with her.

"No! Not you," she huffed. "The *lighthouses!*" Her harsh whispers came out between gritted teeth as she raced to the counter.

The lighthouses? Elise's concerns actually centered on whether or not they should call 911. "Who's out there? Are they wearing red plaid?"

"No. It's a friend of Jimmy's. I don't want him to see these." Frantically, she stuffed each figurine back into the box.

"Maybe you should let him in."

"I will in a second." She rearranged a row of cleaning supplies before sliding the box beneath the sink. "Coming," she called as she stood up, running her hands over the front of her jeans.

She offered a wide-open space in the doorway and signaled for him to enter.

"Hi, Max," Justine said. "This is my new roommate, Elise. She's Stan Sawyer's sister."

"Hey, Elise." He set down a guitar case to shake her hand. A small black tattoo of a star covered the space between his thumb and index finger.

"Nice to meet you," she said.

"Max fixes Jimmy's guitars."

"Jimmy said that I could just drop this off here, and you'd get it to him."

"Of course."

He pointed an index finger upward. "Welcome to the neighborhood, Elise. Nothing like a helicopter hovering over your apartment to make you feel at home."

"It's definitely not Tucson."

"No. It's uh . . . interesting. I used to live over here. You guys should really get a better dead bolt for your door." He glanced at the simple security device above their door handle. "And for just a few bucks you can install little alarms on all the windows."

"I don't know how to put any of that stuff in." Justine seemed bothered.

"I'll show you. It's easy. You just go to Home Depot, get the parts, and I'll help you install them."

"I think that's a great idea," Elise added.

He had the type of haircut that suggested he had just rolled out of bed but was also very stylish. Thick yet nicely trimmed eyebrows framed his dark, round eyes, and he had a nose that would only look good on a male. A rugged strip of facial hair grew just below his bottom lip, tracing its way to his chin. He was gorgeous, and she was open to a security system.

He turned back to Elise, and she suddenly felt very silly in her pink flannel pajamas. A Christmas gift from her aunt Caroline in Vermont, the pj's were cut from a lively cloth that featured dogs holding balloons. "So you're Stan's sister?"

She nodded.

"Cool. Your brother's a good guy."

She wasn't surprised he'd said this. As irresponsible as he was, Stan had tons of friends, and they all loved him. He was a blast to hang out with, always the life of the party.

"How long have you lived here?" he asked.

"Just a couple days." She made a mental note to wash her face and apply a moderate amount of makeup before even setting a toe outside her bedroom door every morning. "What about you? Do you live in this area?"

"North Park," he said. "In a loft above my shop." They chatted a bit about the neighborhood and helicopters, and she noticed the inky outline of a couple other tattoos peeking from beneath the sleeves of his T-shirt. A closer glance revealed a sultry high-heeled female foot dangling from a sensuous fishnet-clad leg. So he definitely wasn't someone she'd take home to meet the parents. But he could be fling material, and boy did she ever need it. While her parents watched *The O'Reilly Factor*, they'd never have a clue.

"So, what do you do?" he asked.

"I'm a novelist. I write mysteries."

"That's great. I've never met a published writer." He rubbed the little crumb duster beneath his chin. "Mysteries, too. That's really impressive. Anyone can sit down and write a story about everyday life, but to incorporate plot twists and turns, you've got to be pretty genius. I'll have to pick up a copy of your book."

The phone rang, and Justine's eyes darted to the caller ID as if she were hungry. Judging from the glow that came over her face, Elise knew it was Jimmy. In fact, even if Justine hadn't been radiating bliss, it would be safe to assume it was Jimmy. Yesterday he'd called about ten times. By midafternoon Elise was starting to wonder if he called just to tell her he had pooped.

Her voice became low and singsong. "Hello, Chee Chee Cheechers."

Max and Elise exchanged glances.

"How's my Chee Chee Cheechers this morning?" she continued.

The way she said *Chee Chee* sounded like she was speaking to a monkey. "Max is here. Do you want to talk to him?" the zookeeper asked. "Okay. Hold on."

Smiling, she handed the phone to Max.

"What do you call him?" Elise asked in a pleasantly curious tone.

A wistful smile turned the corners of her eyelids. "Chee Chee Cheechers."

And he lets you?

"That was the name I used to call my teddy bear who slept next to me every night. But now Jimmy sleeps next to me. So he's Chee Chee Cheechers. We've kind of made a little game out of it. He calls me Meechee Meechers. They're our little names."

"Cute."

Justine took a heavy swig of coffee and then dumped the remaining contents into the sink. She pulled out her rubber gloves, turned the faucet to scalding hot, and proceeded to scrub the mug for a solid minute with a bristled sponge. Steam wafted around her face as her lips tightened with determination. After finishing, she dried the cup, examined it for water spots, and returned it to its exact spot in the cupboard, perfectly aligned with all of her other matching dishes. These were the standards Elise had to live up to.

Max clicked off the phone and set it on the counter. "All right, girls. I've gotta go. It was nice meeting you, Elise."

"Do you want to take a knife or something with you to the car?" she asked as if she were suggesting he might need to borrow an umbrella for the rain.

He threw his head back with laughter. What was really funny was that she was only half kidding.

"Thanks for the offer," he said. "But I doubt I'll get carjacked on my motorcycle. Let me know when you guys want to go to Home Depot. And tell your brother I said hi."

She locked the front door behind him.

"So, he seemed nice," Elise said, subtly providing an opportunity for Justine to elaborate on Max's personal life.

"Max. Yeah, Jimmy loves him. He is nice." She reached beneath the sink and pulled her box of trinkets from their hiding place. A little vein bulged from her forehead as she returned the box back to the counter. "I hope I didn't break any of these."

"So he owns a guitar shop?"

"Yes."

"And drives a motorcycle?"

"Uh-huh," she mumbled, totally engrossed in her lighthouses. She was worse than Stan when it came to providing details. Being a writer, Elise naturally had a nosy side. People fascinated her, and gathering details about their lives often gave her better insight into creating well-rounded characters. She wanted to know if he was married. Divorced? A single parent? Was he a womanizer? Okay, she was interested in him. And she was bored. Her love life was as exciting as watching golf. She needed someone to at least daydream about, even if her parents would probably peg him a Hell's Angel. Anyone with tattoos was trouble, as far as they were concerned. Different generations.

Instead of providing details about Max, Justine grabbed the box of figurines and headed for the front door.

"Do you think it's safe to go out there?" Elise asked.

She shrugged. "I don't know. I have to go to work though. Have fun today!" With that, she and her lighthouses were off.

Elise ate breakfast on the fluffy cream-colored couch that Justine's parents had purchased for her on their last visit. While munching on raisin bran she watched the news, hoping to find out what the man in red plaid had done. After thirty minutes of traffic, weather, and sports, she realized that there wasn't going to be a broadcast about the events in her neighborhood. Chasing armed renegades in City Heights was too mundane to make the headlines.

The sound of the blaring helicopter had been replaced with a very honest rap song. *"So I grabbed the bitch's neck and I told her hold my fo-tay. You better do me good cuz I'm feelin really ho-nay."*

The song was stuck in her head, and she mindlessly sang under her breath as she called her sister. "You better do me good . . ." Ring. Ring. "Cuz I'm feeling really horny . . ."

"Elise?"

Good grief, she hadn't realized she'd been singing aloud until she heard Melissa's voice.

"What are you singing?"

"Sorry, this rap song was stuck in my head."

"That's so weird," she said. "I was just thinking about calling you! I want to hear all about your new place and your new roommate."

Elise was about to give her all the details when Melissa spoke instead.

"Jeffrey, it's Aunt Elise. Do you want to say hi to her?"

"No." A small voice squeaked. Elise had sent him a Wiggles video for Easter, and this was how he thanked her?

"Here. Say hello to Aunt Elise. Tell her you love her."

"Me no want to."

She listened to the muffled sound of the phone being passed to a new hand, and then the sound of shallow breathing. "Say, hi, Aunt Elise," her sister's voice sang from the background. There was more breathing, and what sounded like the sucking of candy. "Jeffrey. Say. Hi. Aunt Elise."

"Hey, Jeffrey," Elise said. "How are you? I can't wait to see you!"

More sucking.

"All right. You're welcome for the Wiggles video. Why don't you give the phone back to your mom now?"

Then he spoke. "Aunt Lise."

"Now say, I love you, Aunt Lise," her sister said quietly.

"Love you, Aunt Lise."

She loved being Aunt Lise. Stan got to be Uncle Tan.

"Isn't that the cutest thing ever?" Melissa said as soon as she took the phone back. "You're Aunt Lise. I love it!"

"He is cute. When do I get to see him? I miss you guys."

"Well, I had an idea. I know you're scraping by and Mom told me about your new place and how you can't afford to live without a roommate. I was thinking you could do a little baby-sitting for me while I run errands tomorrow. I'll pay you well."

She hadn't baby-sat since high school when she'd looked after kids who were eight and ten. She'd taught the kids how to play a couple of card games before letting them stay up past their bedtime to watch *Jaws* and pig out on snacks and sodas that were usually off-limits. The kids had apparently never mentioned what kind of baby-sitter she was, because the parents called her over and over again. She'd never been left with a toddler. However, quality time with her little nephew would be fun, and it was true. She could use the money, and if she ever wanted to get out of City Heights, she was going to have to start earning more. "All right. I'd love to watch Jeffrey."

"Great. So, how is everything going?"

She began to tell her about the helicopter until she was interrupted very early in the story.

"Jeffrey, don't touch that. Here. Give it to me. Sorry, go on."

"So, as I was saying. I was jolted from my sleep, and when I walked outside—"

"Okay, sweetie, let me make you a peanut butter and honey sandwich."

She had forgotten what it was like to talk on the phone with people who had small children. Ever since her sister had given birth, Elise's side of the conversation had been interrupted with some form of cooing, soothing, or whining. She understood though. Jeffrey was just a small child, and his needs were much more important than any of her stories. They could catch up later. "Listen, Melissa. I'll let you go. What time do you want me to be there tomorrow?"

They agreed on a time and said good-bye.

She was excited to baby-sit her nephew. Spending more time with her family had definitely influenced her decision to move back to San Diego. She missed them and especially felt as if she were missing out on a lot of stuff with Jeffrey. After Elise hung up with Melissa, she realized it was nearly noon and she'd accomplished nothing in the way of writing.

A half hour into her work, the phone rang. Carly Truesdale popped onto the caller ID. "You must be on your lunch break," Elise said.

"Sure am."

Elise could hear her chewing. "What are you eating? It sounds good."

"A Chinese chicken salad." She swallowed then took a loud slurp from a straw. "How is everything going over at the new place?"

"Well, let's see. My apartment is smokier than a drug rehab center. There was a manhunt for an armed criminal in our neighborhood this morning. And some hot guy with tattoos of naked women and a star on his hand came to our apartment to drop off a guitar. At least there is never a dull moment!"

"Whoa, whoa, whoa. One thing at a time. You met a hot guy?"

Never mind the helicopter story. "Yes, but I don't know if he is my type. I mean, he is. He'd be good fling material, but just not take-home-to-meet-Mom-and-Dad material."

Carly paused to finish chewing. "Well, I have another love prospect for you, and he *is* take-home-to-meet-the-parents material. Marcus wants us to go on a double date with you and his friend Toby. He wants to set you up with him."

Marcus. Elise had practically forgotten he'd existed, mostly because he gave Carly the same amount of attention a crack-addict prostitute would provide to her crack-addicted child. "Have you met Toby?" Elise asked.

"No. But Marcus said he's a Realtor and doing really well. Please say yes," Carly said. "You have to come."

"I've never been on a double date before, but it could be fun." She paused. "All right. What the hell? What do I have to lose?"

"Yeah! It'll be so fun," she announced before lowering her tone. "I think I'm in love with Marcus," she whispered. "But at the same time I think I'm cursed."

"Cursed?"

"No one has ever called me their girlfriend, including him. I have never been able to make it out of the gray phase."

"What's the gray phase?"

"It's the phase where nothing is black or white. You don't know if you're just having fun or if you are committed. The white phase is when you are just having fun, seeing where things go, and everyone knows it's too early for a commitment. The black phase is when you are fully committed to someone, like how you and Tim were in college. I am perpetually stuck in the gray phase. I'm in the phase where we spend enough time together that we're past the white phase, but we don't check in with each other or take each other home to meet our parents. Everything is gray and foggy, and that's pretty much always where I am."

It was true. Carly had never had a real boyfriend. She was smart, cute, and fun. But no one had ever been willing to commit to her.

Elise had reasoned it was because of the lack of quality men in the world. For every ten great girls there was one okay guy.

"I really like him, Elise."

"Maybe you should tell him. It's been four months. Ask him where the relationship is going. Maybe you're always in the gray phase because you've never discussed anything with anyone." She thought for a moment. "At least you're *in* a phase. I'm in the phase of fantasizing that I might hopefully meet *someone* who could *potentially* lead to something in my uneventful love life. What phase is that?"

"I don't know. But I have to run. My break is over."

4. A New Arrival at the Zoo

"Yo! Elise!"

Glorious D. Every time she left the building she passed him. From what she could tell, he hung out in the driveway all day. Sometimes it was just him. Sometimes he was with his mom's Chihuahua. His raps were pretty good and were probably the only thing she liked about Casa de Paradiso.

"Hey, Glorious D! How are you?"

He sported a blue and gold oversized Chargers blazer and a matching baseball cap perched sideways on his head. His gold necklace glimmered in the sun. "Cool. Whatch you been up to?"

She almost blurted out that she had been searching for a new place to live all morning but then remembered that he might include this detail in his next rap to Justine. "Just working on the novel. Now I'm off to baby-sit."

The smile dropped from his face like an ice cube when she said the part about baby-sitting. "*Man*, that sucks. I baby-sat my cousin once, and it was boring as shit. Then the kid bit me."

"Oh." *Well, my nephew is not like that,* she wanted to say. *He is the cutest child on the planet.*

"But hey. Check this out. I made up a new rap. About you."

So far, he hadn't rapped about anything but her.

He began to nod his head. "She's a killa writin' a thrilla. Typin' so fast. She gotta make it last. Right to the end. She makes a new trend. Nice girl hangin.' Hangin' in da hood. Takin' her pimp ride does her some good." He always became animated, throwing both arms to the side as he rhymed, moving his body with each beat. "That's all I got right now. But I'll get more for ya later."

Her bug was far from pimp, and a lot closer to clunker, but nevertheless she loved his rap. "Thanks, Glorious D. That was the best I've heard yet."

"Really?"

"Yeah. That was really great. I loved it."

A boyish smile spread across his face. "Cool."

As she drove to her sister's place in Poway she sang Glorious D's little tune. No one had ever made up songs or raps or even poems about her, and she really enjoyed it.

Her sister lived in a nice neighborhood in Poway, consisting primarily of families with friendly Labrador retrievers and swing sets in the backyard. Elise felt slightly nostalgic as she passed her high school and turned down her sister's street.

When she pulled up to their home, she noticed Jeffrey riding his tricycle in circles in the driveway. He wore a helmet, and his chubby hands held on tight to the handlebars. Perhaps she was biased, but she really thought he was the cutest child she had ever seen. Blond ringlets and large blue eyes. His cheeks were a bit chubby, but it only added to his adorable features.

"Hi, Jeffrey," she called as she closed her car door. Instead of jumping from his trike, calling out, "Aunt Lise," and running to her open arms, he slammed on his brakes and turned his helmeted head in her direction. Lips pursed, he gave her one long stare before turning his back and pedaling away.

"I brought you something," she cheerfully called after him. He sped up and pedaled toward his mother, who waved from the garage.

"He's just being shy," Melissa yelled. She held one hand over her stomach. Though she had just entered the second trimester of her pregnancy, she was already starting to show. Melissa was tiny like Elise. Her little legs looked like she was holding a large egg above them. She was dressed in light pink cropped pants and a matching maternity top with a collar and buttons down the front. Shortly after giving birth to Jeffrey, Melissa had hacked her long, layered hair and shaped it into something maternal. It was the kind of hairdo that screamed, *I drive a minivan and fold laundry in front of Dr. Phil.* Frankly, Elise thought she looked older, and she had always secretly wondered why having children made women feel like they needed to look as if they were constantly equipped with a Ziploc of Pepperidge Farm Goldfish and a packet of wipes. Did bringing a life into the world mean that you could no longer be cool? When she had kids, she was keeping her hair long and wearing faded Levi's. She'd be the cool, hip mom, like Madonna or Kate Hudson.

Jeffrey stood with his hands on his hips, eyeing her as she approached. He was wearing orange and black velour shorts that looked about ten sizes too small for him, cowboy boots, and a T-shirt with the state of Colorado on the front. "Cool outfit," Elise said.

"He's really into dressing himself these days. There's nothing I can do. And besides, I want him to make his own decisions."

She gave Melissa what was supposed to be a hug but turned out to be a clasping of forearms because of her protruding belly. Then she knelt down in front of Jeffrey and handed him the coloring books and crayons she'd purchased for him.

"Hey, bud," Elise said. "I brought you something."

"Ohhh, wooow," Melissa said in a baby voice. "Look at those. You're going to have fun with Auntie Lise today, aren't you?"

He looked up at his mother. "I wanna go with you."

Melissa laughed. "No, sweetie, you're going to stay here. With Aunt Lise." Elise hadn't expected him to love her right off the bat. They'd only met a handful of times in his short life. But she did want to click with him. She imagined by the end of the day he'd be begging his parents to have her back. They'd have so much fun together, he'd be asking about Aunt Lise nonstop for weeks to come.

"So, let me show you where everything is." Melissa picked the child up, and Elise followed them inside. "Things should be easy," she explained. "I'll show you where all the diapers are, and what toys he likes to play with. We have movies, and he'll probably take a two-hour nap around one." Elise immediately heard the sound of a vacuum roaring when they entered the house. "Oh, and Lupe is here today cleaning. I'll introduce you to her."

She was sort of annoyed to learn that Lupe was there. She wanted the house to herself, the freedom to see what kind of food they had in their kitchen cabinets without Lupe watching her.

Every time Elise visited her sister she longed to have her own spacious home with new Pergo floors and throw pillows that matched. Her sister's house felt like a home, a place where people felt secure in their lives and didn't worry where the hell they would be five months from now. It was a place where you could curl up with a blanket in front of the fireplace during the winter or suck on a Popsicle while resting your feet on an ottoman in the summer. She hated to torment herself with daydreams, but she couldn't resist wondering if she would ever have a place like this. At this point, she'd take the house without the husband and kid. She just wanted some sense of stability.

"All right. Well, I'm going to head to South Coast Plaza for the afternoon, so I'll see you in about seven hours."

"Seven hours?" Elise said, startled. "I mean, seven hours. That's fine. I just didn't realize you were driving so far." South Coast Plaza was over an hour away.

"Well, I need to do some shopping, and you know . . . it is the best mall around." They followed her to her minivan. "We'll have to catch up on everything when I get back. I still haven't heard about your new place."

They waved to Melissa until she was out of the driveway.

"Well," Elise said as soon as the garage door had closed behind them. "Would you like to color? Or maybe you could show me some toys that you like? Why don't we take your helmet off?"

He released a whiny grunt when Elise reached for his helmet. "Leave on!" he screamed before kicking her in the shin and running inside.

"Okay, fine."

She followed him to his bedroom and found the cleaning lady in there, vacuuming. Her shoulder-length curly hair and high bangs were crunchy with gel. The bottom half of her body appeared long and skinny in her stretchy jeans, but she was clearly an apple in terms of shape. Her tummy stuck out like a pouch, and she had huge boobs and soft, round cheeks. Gold rings decorated every single finger except her thumb, and she wore a gold chain with a charm reading "Ramon" hanging from it. She stepped on a pedal sticking from the vaccum cleaner with her L.A. Gear high-tops, and the room became silent. *"Hola,"* she said in a heavy Spanish accent. "What your name?"

"Elise. And you?"

"Eleeze. I'm Lupe. You speak Spanish?"

"No. I actually took French in high school."

She laughed. "Why you take French when Mexico so close?"

"I don't know. It was a stupid mistake. I guess I wanted to be sophisticated and thought that speaking French was going to do that for me."

She threw her head back and laughed as she fluffed a pillow. She noticed Jeffrey standing with his arms folded over his chest and an evil stare fixed in his eyes. Why he had taken such an instant animosity to Aunt Lise she had no idea.

"*Qué pasa, Heffrey?* Why you stand in the corner for Mrs. Eleeze?"

Elise took a step toward her nephew and smiled. "Heff—I mean Jeffrey. Why don't you show me your favorite toy?"

With that suggestion, he began to scamper away. For a moment Elise thought she had sparked something fun. He was running for his toy, and they would play and be great pals before Melissa returned from shopping. However, he didn't stop at his closet or toy chest but rather sped toward the bedroom door. Elise chased after him, but he was too fast and slammed the door behind him, barely missing her fingers. Though his actions were very abrupt, it seemed like slow motion as Elise listened to the sound of a dead bolt sliding in the doorframe and clicking shut. He had locked them in. She turned the door handle, hoping for a miracle, and it didn't budge. "Jeffrey," she said gaily, as if nothing were wrong. "Open the door, you silly goose."

"No," he squeaked. "You locked."

"Please, Jeffrey. I want to show you a magic trick." She didn't know any magic, but he wouldn't find that out until after he opened the door.

Lupe moved toward the door. "Heffrey! Why you do this to Mrs. Eleeze, Heffrey? Open the door, Heffrey. Now, you Heffrey. Open that door."

Elise listened to the little pitter-patter of tiny feet trailing down the hall until his footsteps became so distant she could no longer hear him. Naturally, visions of her nephew playing with matches while holding a steak knife between his teeth popped into her head. However, there was no time to panic. She needed to get out of there. She was actually more irritated with Melissa and Brice. One, they had let him turn out this way. And two, who in the hell put locks on their toddler's bedroom door?

"This eese bad," Lupe muttered.

"No shit. Do you have a cell phone?" No sooner had Elise asked the question did she hear the sound of the "Mexican Hat Dance" from behind the closed door. Lupe did have a cell phone. One with a very lively ring, actually. And it was in the other room. Elise could see her own cell phone sitting on the dashboard of her car, useless in a time of need.

"Eye yi yi," Lupe breathed. "We have to break window. They have pool in backyard. What if he jump in pool?"

This was only getting worse. "Let's see if we can pop the screen." It was the only alternative, and luckily they were on the first floor of the house. She just prayed there was a way back into the house from the outside. She watched as Lupe pried the screen off with her long acrylic nails that were painted fuchsia with tiny little blue flowers airbrushed on the tips. After popping the screen, Elise looked down. Even though they were on the first floor, the window wasn't exactly close to the ground. It was going to be a jump. She slid through the open frame and felt her knees jolt as she landed on her feet. She ran to the front door. Relief washed through her veins when the handle turned.

"Jeffrey," she called. "Where are you?" She heard something and stopped to listen so she could pinpoint exactly where it was coming from. She listened to a succession of quick scratching sounds and suddenly imagined Jeffrey jumping on the bed while sharpening a steak knife. She followed the noise upstairs and found her nephew. The crayons that she had brought over were scattered around his cowboy boots. He didn't bother to look up at her as he scribbled all over his parents' bedroom door with a brown crayon. "Jeffrey, holy—" She stopped herself. "What are you doing?"

As she pried the crayon from his sticky hand, she wondered why he had picked brown. There was lavender and red in there. She was wondering how she was going to explain this to her sister when the "Mexican Hat Dance" came to life again.

"All right. Come here," she said as she stuffed him under her arm like a pillow and shuffled downstairs to free Lupe. "Want to go to zoo!" he yelled.

She held on to him while she unlocked the bedroom door and released Lupe. *"Heffrey, qué pasa?* You be bad boy today."

Instead of admitting his faults, he ignored Lupe, turned to Elise, and began to whine "peener" over and over again.

"I'm sorry I don't know what peener is," she said, starting to feel helpless. "Do you have to go to the bathroom?"

"No! Peener! Peener. Peener now!" He slammed a cowboy boot against the tile.

She looked at Lupe. "No ask me." Lupe shook her head before reaching for some furniture polish.

"Can you point to what peener is?" Elise asked him. "Why don't you show me?"

"Peeeeeeener!"

"Is it a toy?" She picked up a stuffed dinosaur and held it out.

He pushed the toy away before stomping his left boot. "Peeeeeenerrrrr!"

She started to feel like a terrible aunt who was not privy to the language of Jeffrey. "Is it food?"

"Want peener!"

"All right. I'm calling your mother." Melissa didn't answer the phone, and Elise wondered if she had secretly packed a suitcase before leaving.

She tried her own mother. Grandma knew the meaning and origin of every word in the language of Jeffrey. Grandma wasn't home either, so she tried Stan. He'd spent more time with him than Elise had.

"Yeah," he answered after the first ring.

"What is peener?"

"Huh?"

"I'm baby-sitting Jeffrey, and he's stomping his feet and demanding peener. Help me."

"Oh. Peener. It's a peanut butter and jelly sandwich. Where have you been?"

"Sorry, I had no idea."

"Here. Put him on. I want to say hi."

"Jeffrey," she said sweetly. "Guess what? I figured out what peener is, and Uncle Stan wants to talk to you." She expected him to kick the phone from her hand, but instead his eyes lit up as he greedily snatched the receiver. A pang of jealousy nipped her when Jeffrey giggled into the receiver and even said "I love you" to Uncle Tan. When he was finished talking, he kicked Elise in the shin before dropping the cordless on the floor and demanding "pru." What the hell was pru? She wondered while touching her throbbing leg. At least she'd figured out peener. Maybe that would distract him. She quickly made peener, cut it into four cute squares, and delivered it to him on a plastic plate with Pinocchio on it.

She expected delight from him and was surprised when he shoved the plate away and began to cry. "Jeffrey," she said quietly. "Please stop crying." She tried to pick him up, but he only screamed louder and began to flail his arms and legs.

What the hell had she done? She would've paid money to know. "Jeffrey, please tell me what's wrong."

"Go away!" he screamed through his tears.

When the phone rang she prayed it was her mother, offering to come baby-sit, or Melissa telling her that she'd changed her mind and was headed home. It was for Lupe.

"Lupe, the phone is for you."

She explained that her cell phone was getting bad reception before speaking in rapid Spanish to the caller.

Jeffrey was still wailing when the sound of cleated feet came in from the foyer. Who could be wearing cleats through her sister's house? Did Lupe invite a friend over? No. It was Melissa's husband, Brice. "Hey," he said in his golf shoes. "I just came home to get my golf clubs out of the garage, and I heard Jeffrey crying. What's wrong with him?" He picked up his son and looked to Elise for an explanation.

"I have no idea what is wrong. He asked for peener. I gave him a peanut butter and jelly sandwich, and now he's upset. I don't know."

Jeffrey's face looked like a prune with teeth, and by the way he was crying you would've thought that Elise had run his hand over with a tractor. Brice glanced at the sandwich. "Oh," he said, as if the problem were so simple that only an idiot wouldn't have figured it out by now. "He likes his sandwiches cut in triangles. That's usually how Melissa does it."

"Oh," she said, wondering what other minor details were important to this young dictator.

"You can just throw that one out," Brice said. "Start over."

She started over, thinking optimistically about how nap time was just a half hour away. After Brice left for his golf game, Jeffrey pooped in his diaper, then refused to have it changed. He hid under the pool table for twenty minutes and then tried to persuade Elise to open one of Melissa's gifts that had arrived early in the mail for her shower. Elise couldn't help but wonder what had possessed them to bring another child into the world, and then felt bad. They were her family, and she had heard about the terrible twos. Perhaps her nephew was just going through a phase.

He finally fell asleep in front of *Finding Nemo*. She spent thirty minutes scrubbing the brown crayon off the bedroom door with one of Lupe's sponges. Then she decided to go make her own sandwich. She found Lupe in the kitchen, scooping mint chocolate-chip ice cream into a bowl.

"So, you have boyfriend?"

"No."

"Why not? You *muy bonita*. You need boyfriend."

Elise looked at her necklace. "Is Ramon your boyfriend?"

"Husband. Where you live?"

"City Heights."

"*Díos mio*. Why you live there?"

Even the cleaning lady lived in a better neighborhood. "It's a long story. But I'm leaving soon."

"Where you wanna live? I bet you wanna live in a neighborhood like these? Huh?" She smiled. "Me, too. I also want to drive four runner. Silver one." Elise spent the next two hours listening to Lupe gossip about all the neighbors she worked for, including a very well-known newscaster who lived two doors down from Melissa and Brice. "She cheap. I ask for five dollar raise because she so picky, and you know what she tell me? No. She say I can't have five dollar more, and you know what she want? She want me to scrub all her vases with a toothbrush. Don't say nothing though," she said as she helped herself to a beer.

Toward the end of the afternoon Elise was debating becoming the mysterious aunt who sent birthday cards stuffed with a twenty but never made too many appearances. The kid was a terror in miniature cowboy boots, and having quality time with him wasn't worth getting kicked in the teeth.

With only an hour left of baby-sitting, he managed to hide the cordless phone. While she was scouring the kitchen for it, he came up to her and tapped her on the leg.

She looked down at his dimples and marveled at how cute yet bad he was. The thought of what he held behind his back terrified her. His little arms were locked behind his waist, and she immediately realized that he could be armed with a snail or a giant-sized booger that he was waiting to assault her with.

"What do you have there?" She took two steps back.

His grin became even bigger. She debated calling in Lupe for backup. "Jeffrey, what is behind your back?"

Slowly, he revealed his hands. He held a tiny gold frame that he had clearly taken from some mantel in the house when she had been searching for the phone. She looked closely at the picture and thought she might actually have to fight back a tear. Inside the frame was a little photo of Elise holding an infant Jeffrey at his first Christmas. "I love you, Aunt Lise," he said as he lifted his arms toward her. She wanted to melt.

As she picked him up, the phone rang. She followed the sound to the freezer, then found the phone hidden inside a package of waffles. It was Melissa, calling to say she'd be home in an hour.

"How is everything going?"

Jeffrey rested his head on her shoulder.

"Fine. Everything is fine."

As she drove to her apartment she could hear the leftover pizza in her fridge calling her name. She'd ordered it the night before, and there were three slices of mushroom and pepperoni left, and she planned on eating each one. After eating, she'd take a long, hot bath, curl up on the couch, and watch *Trading Spaces*.

Glorious D wasn't around, and she wondered if perhaps he had gotten a record deal. Light glared from their windows, and she felt a flicker of irritation as she approached the front door. She knew she wasn't perfect, but the house was lit up like the president of the electricity company's wet dream, and no one was home.

What she faced when she opened the front door was so surprising that a little wasted energy instantly became the least of her concerns. Behind a cloud of cigarette smoke sat a man. Frozen, she stood in the doorframe. Had she entered the wrong apartment? Quickly, her eyes darted over the room. Those were her shoes sitting next to the front door. She felt a physical urge to run screaming for her life. Who was this lanky stranger sprawled out on their couch, feet resting on the coffee table? His toenails were long. Good God, he had Bella.

"Hey. How's it goin'?" Suddenly, it occurred to her. It was Chee Chee Cheechers. She'd been passing dozens of pictures of him for three weeks and wondered how his face had managed to escape her subconscious. His mug shot should've been permanently etched in her memory by now. However, he was much skinnier than the photos, and his hair was longer. He still styled the early seventies 'do, but it was less Rod Stewart and a little more Carol Brady. He looked as if he hadn't shaved in days.

"You must be Elise!" He stood, and she was surprised by how tall he was. "I'm Justine's boyfriend, Jimmy!" He grabbed her hand, gripped it hard, and shook it like a drumstick. The rumors really were true. Musicians, no matter how weird or unattractive they were, could get gorgeous girls. This wasn't how she had pictured the love of Justine's life.

"Uh, yeah. Yes. I just didn't recognize you from the pictures. But now I do. Uh-huh." She tried not to sound flustered. But she never expected to find this pale rock-star version of Ichabod Crane sitting on their couch.

"You look different from your pictures, too." This was disturbing for two reasons. One, after seven hours of baby-sitting Rosemary's Baby, she looked like hell. Two, the only pictures of Elise were in her room, which meant that he must've ventured in there.

"I've heard so much about you," he said. "Justine loves you. I gotta tell ya, her last roommate was a *real* bitch."

"I've heard so much about you, too," she said, wondering how he had gotten in. "I thought you were in L.A., recording your album."

"Oh yeah, man. I was. Thank *God* it's over now." He shook his head and released a chuckle. "We finished up early. It was getting old, and we were getting sick of each other, so we decided to cram and just power it. I decided to surprise Justine." He ran his fingers through his hair. "Man, I couldn't wait to get out of there." He motioned to the couch. "Hey, have a seat. Grab a beer."

"Thanks. But I'm actually really hungry. I think I'm going to grab something to eat." Still flustered, she headed to the kitchen. "Where's Justine?" she asked over her shoulder.

"At work. She'll be home around midnight. She has to close, and there is an acoustic guitar show at the coffee shop tonight. She wants me to go, but I'm just too tired."

Her eyes darted over the shelves in the fridge as she searched for her pizza. She moved a milk carton and peeked behind a loaf of bread, but her search for the pizza turned up nothing.

She found her empty pizza box sitting on the countertop next to the trash can. A greasy paper towel rested nearby with a shriveled piece of half-eaten crust on top. Justine and her guests were welcome to Elise's food. She wasn't Scrooge. However, she did mind if they ate the last piece of her pizza.

She was imagining what Jimmy would look like with an empty cardboard pizza box smashed over his head when she heard the sound of a beer cracking open.

"Sure you don't want a beer?" he called.

At this point, she could really use one. "Yeah, okay. Thanks."

He reached into the twelve-pack, which rested by his feet. "Here. Catch." As fluid as an Olympic disc thrower, he tossed the beer in her direction. Instead of landing in her hands, the silver bullet soared past her and into a framed photo of Justine and Jimmy. The picture shot off the wall like a Frisbee, nearly swiping Elise's cheek. The beer whizzed into the wall like a cannonball, ripping through the plaster and creating a hole as ugly and large as a rotten cantaloupe.

"Shit!" Jimmy yelled as the frame crashed next to Elise's feet, spraying bits of glass over the carpet. He leapt over the back of the couch. "Are you okay?"

"Yes, I'm fine. It didn't hit me," she said, touching her face. She glanced at the wall. "Good God," she breathed. "How are we going to fix that?"

Drywall and plaster drifted from the hollow like snowflakes. She peeked inside the cavity and could see the Coors Light can resting in a little grave between a pink cushion of insulation and chapped drywall on the floor. A layer of cold moisture glistened off its rim.

"Look at the size of that hole!" Jimmy exclaimed. "Justine is gonna *wig*."

Their landlord's reaction had actually been the one she feared most. Common sense told her that having a hole in the wall was one of the worst things imaginable in the world of deposit refunds. In fact, it was probably a close second to spilling red nail polish on the carpet. "I have no idea how to fix something like that."

"Oh. It's just drywall. It can't be that hard. Maybe we can just put the frame back over it for now, and no one will notice."

"I don't think we should do that," Elise said. "The weight from the frame could create an even larger hole."

They both glanced at the frame on the floor. It was in a million pieces, and their sappy smiles were forever embossed with a ring from where the beer can had struck. "Damn. That was a cool picture," Jimmy said, surveying their now alienlike facial expressions.

She felt like mentioning that Justine probably had several other copies of the same print stashed away somewhere, but kept that to herself.

She looked at his bare feet next to the glass. "Let me grab the vacuum." As she headed to the laundry room, she prayed he knew a good handyman. She could only imagine how much their landlord would deduct from the deposit.

"Dammit," he muttered. "I thought my aim was perfect. I can't believe the size of that hole." He shook his head. "I'm sorry, man."

"Let me see that," he said, taking the vacuum from her hands. "I'll clean it up."

That was good, because she was still starving. She needed to eat something so she could rationally figure out how they were going to repair the giant trench that now occupied their wall.

When she opened the refrigerator, she couldn't remember what she was looking for. Oh yes, food. Her mind was still reeling with shock from the way her day was turning out. First Jeffrey. Now Jimmy. In addition to having horrible aim, he wasn't supposed to be here. How had he gotten in? Justine must've been here when he arrived.

There were all kinds of pastas—macaroni, rigatoni, penne—but no sauce. She found cucumbers, broccoli, and carrots. However, her search turned up no lettuce. What was a salad without lettuce? Peanut butter with no bread. Tuna with no mayo. Her quest for food was worse than searching for a new roommate, and eventually she decided to invent some kind of pasta-vegetable concoction with a butter-garlic sauce. It took her a an hour to make, and she ended up overdoing it with the garlic. She ate her mediocre meal at the counter while Jimmy watched *Jackass* on MTV.

She wondered how long he planned to watch television. She wasn't in the mood to watch a group of deranged skaters crash golf carts and sample delicacies like goldfish all night.

The phone rang, and she snatched it up. Carly. "Hey. I just wanted to call for your advice. I'm going out with Marcus tonight. Should I wear my black sweater with the bell sleeves, or the red angora V-neck?"

"Have you talked to him yet?"

"No. I can't get the nerve. But maybe tonight."

Elise had kept up with her end of the deal. "You said you were going to talk to him before our double date tomorrow."

"I am, but you know how it is. I haven't found the right opportunity. It's not like I can just bring it up at the copy machine in the office. So which sweater?"

"The red angora."

Jimmy tossed his head back and howled with laughter at something he'd seen on television.

"Who's there?" Carly asked. "I hear a man in the background. Is it the guy with the tattoos? Is *he* there?!"

She slipped into her room and closed the door behind her. "No. It's Jimmy. Justine's boyfriend." She explained how she had come home to find him on their couch.

"Where the hell is Justine?"

"Work. She won't be home until midnight."

"She just left him there for you to find?"

"Apparently."

"That is so wrong." Carly's voice burned. "You don't just leave your boyfriend with your roommate and let him do whatever the hell he wants in the apartment. You need to get out of that place. But listen, Marcus is going to be here in two minutes. I gotta run. I can't wait till tomorrow night! We'll talk more about it tomorrow."

After she said good-bye to Carly, she took the phone back in the kitchen.

"Oh hey," Jimmy said. "I almost forgot. Your mom called. And uh . . ." He thought for a moment. "Carol called, too."

Carol? Who the hell was Carol? She racked her brain, trying to remember *anyone* named Carol. Then it occurred to her. "You mean Cheryl? Cheryl Adams?"

"Oh yeah. Cheryl Adams. That's right."

He'd talked to Cheryl? Cheryl Adams was her agent. She was business, and one of the main people responsible for making sure she had food on her table. She was about to ask if there was a message from her when the phone rang again. This time it was her mother.

"What's going on over there?" she asked, worried. "Who answered the phone when I called?"

She returned to her room. "It's Justine's boyfriend."

"He answers your phone?"

"I guess so." Elise gave her mother the same information she'd relayed to Carly.

"Is he on drugs?"

"Not that I know of."

"How long is he staying there?"

An excellent question. "I don't know. I think he has a place of his own *somewhere* in San Diego. I'm sure he's just visiting."

"Well, listen. Your father is bringing you a new can of pepper spray this weekend. Okay?"

After saying good-bye, she flopped face-forward onto her bed. What next? She wondered. A *Tyrannosaurus rex* could come tearing through her front window, and she wouldn't be surprised at this point. She allowed herself five minutes to wallow in a miserable yet totally inviting pit of frustration and self-pity over her move to San Diego. For a moment she lounged in a place where she felt completely sorry for herself and wondered why she ever left Tucson. When her five minutes had expired, she told herself the following:

You can move.

At least Justine is clean.

Best of all, there is a double date to look forward to.

And there is Max.

There is hope.

She scanned the local stations in her room, and she found nothing of interest on TV. She decided to take a bath, knowing she was probably missing a good episode of *Trading Spaces*, but not having the nerve to ask Jimmy to change the channel. While she soaked, she could hear Jimmy's laughter burning through her bedroom walls.

5. Adventures in Blind Dating

A drumroll jolted Elise from her dream. Oddly, she was very relieved. For a moment she'd thought it was gunshots. She rolled out of bed, Bella at her heels, and washed her face in the bathroom sink. Music blasted from the living room—music with lots of guitar and the kind of beat that made people speed on the freeway.

"Morning," Jimmy yelled when she entered the living room. He stood in front of Elise's stereo wearing only boxers and playing the air drums. A small hand-painted lighthouse sat on the coffee table nearby.

Instead of apologizing and asking if they had woken her, Justine announced that they were listening to Jimmy's new album. She wore the shirt Jimmy had sported the night before, which barely covered her G-string–clad butt. It really was too early to see this. "What do you think of the album?"

Oh, I'll tell you what I think, she wanted to say. *It's too early to be listening to this, and Justine, please cover your privates when you're in the living room.* "It's great!" Elise said before opening the front door to let Bella out. When she closed the door behind her, she could still hear the blasting music and was confident the entire complex was listening to Jimmy's album for the first time as well.

It was a beautiful morning, perhaps the most beautiful Elise had witnessed since she had returned to San Diego. Warm breezes tickled her cheeks, and the sky was a shade of blue that insisted everyone must go to the beach. She was mentally picking out a bathing suit when she remembered that she had to call Melissa's best friend, Crystal, to find out if there was anything she could do to help with the baby shower. Her mom had been on her case all week.

When she returned to the apartment, Jimmy was standing at the kitchen counter drinking a beer at the fresh hour of nine a.m. and making toast with her bread.

"Hey," Jimmy said. "Do you want some toast? I'm making it for me and Justine. We're going to eat as soon as she gets out of the shower."

"Thanks. But I think I'm going to have cereal."

He'd only been there for one night, but Elise couldn't help but wonder how much of her food he was going to eat by the time he left.

Needing a break from the hood, she decided to spend the afternoon at Mission Bay with Stan. She packed a beach bag, and when she left she could hear Justine and Jimmy giggling behind Justine's bedroom door.

Saturdays at the Bay were always packed, especially during the summer. Parking spaces were sacred, and it was nearly impossible to avoid kicking up sand on someone's picnic basket and towels. But she loved it, and for the first time since she'd returned to San Diego she felt at home. She loved the crowds, the lazy way suntanned bodies lounged on colorful beach blankets and cheap chairs.

She walked through a maze of scantily clad beach bums, inhaling the delicious scent of hot dogs roasting over coals and the occasional blast of coconut suntan lotion. This was where she wanted to live, walking distance from the beach. She found Stan toward the end of the sand strip on the west side of the bay. Already sunburned, he was playing Over the Line with several of his friends.

She was happy to see that there were a couple of girls lounging at their camp. So far, the only other potential female friends she'd met since she'd moved back to San Diego had been Justine. Considering that Justine's entire existence centered on Jimmy, Elise assumed she wouldn't be hitting the singles scene with her anytime soon. She'd been longing for more girlfriends. She missed her group of friends in Tucson, the way they had gotten ready for fun nights together and swapped stories about all the cute guys they had met the following morning over mimosas. She had Carly, but Carly was also trapped in a world of infatuation with Marcus.

A lurking fear of spending many Friday nights alone with a video rental and cheap wine had been creeping up on Elise lately. Even worse, she'd been haunted by visions of transforming into the weird chick sitting at the end of the bar alone if she didn't find some other comrades quickly.

She introduced herself to the girls.

"We just moved here, too," Brooke said. "I'm from Pittsburgh, and Tracey is from North Carolina." Judging from their tans, they had been here a lot longer than Elise, and she was afraid she might permanently scar their vision when she removed her T-shirt and shorts.

"Please, help yourself to some snacks." Tracey held up a bag of Ruffles with one hand and pointed to some onion dip sitting atop a cooler. "They're for everyone. We've got plenty."

"Thanks." Something about potato chips and onion dip made her feel right at home. It was classic beach food, and the sight of salty ridged chips and a sour cream carton with sand glittered around its edges gave her a strange sense of nostalgia and pleasure.

Tracey and Brooke were sweet girls who unfortunately had roommates but promised to keep on the lookout for Elise. Tracey was an accountant, and Brooke attended law school at USD while waiting tables at a Japanese restaurant in La Jolla. They spent the day lazing in the sun, sharing stories about their recent moves over the buzz of Jet Skis.

She couldn't help but listen with envy and admiration when they both told her they had walked to the bay from their apartments and described living situations that didn't include helicopters and loser boyfriends who ate their food and ruled the television set.

"I wish my move had been as easy as yours," she said to them.

"Well, you know why you're having trouble," Brooke offered. "Because you have a dog. It's impossible to find places anywhere around here that will take dogs. I had to send my dog back to my parents' house in Pittsburgh. It was better than giving him away to some stranger. You could always give her to your parents for a while."

Not an option. Elise would never part with Bella. Even if it meant living in the ghetto until she was able to buy her own place. At the rate her career was going, she might never be able to own a home. She had a bond with that dog as if Bella were Elise's own child, and frankly, she liked the dog more than most kids.

She'd saved Bella from her weird neighbors, the Fosters, in Tucson. From the outside, Cathy and Mark Foster appeared to be a charming young yuppie couple. She drove a Volvo, toting around their well-groomed young children to flute lessons and karate. He drove a Mercedes sedan and belonged to one of the nicest gyms in the area. When they got a puppy, Elise thought it was cute that they had completed their family. Nice parents, two cute children, and now the pup. They had asked Elise to feed Bella when they went to visit family in Scottsdale. Bella was a good puppy, not the type that jumped all over you and ripped at your shoelaces with razor-sharp teeth. Rather, she was affectionate and seemed to crave cuddling as if she were starved for attention. After just a couple days of pet-sitting Elise let Bella stay at her place for the rest of the Fosters' vacation. She'd fall asleep with the dog's warm body curled next to her and wake up looking at her big pointed ears and puggish face.

Seven months after the Fosters had taken Bella into their home Elise learned that they "were getting rid of her."

"Know anyone who wants a dog?" Mark Foster had asked casually one morning as he grabbed the newspaper. "We just can't keep *that dog* anymore."

"Why?"

Mrs. Foster shrugged. "Oh, I don't know. We don't have time for a dog, and I just don't think we're pet people. I've never really liked animals. We just thought she might be good for the kids." She chuckled. "And Mark told me I could get a new coffee table if we gave her away."

Weren't animals supposed to be a lifelong commitment? You don't go buy a pet and then trade it in for furniture several months later.

"She's kind of funny looking, too," Mark added. "She gives me the creeps. Maybe someday we'll get a nice golden retriever for the kids."

"A golden retriever will probably look better on the Christmas cards," Elise said. She couldn't help it. Though she was being sarcastic, they actually nodded. And this was why they were weird. One, they were shallow. Two, as far as Elise was concerned, anyone who wasn't "pet people" was suspect. People who didn't like animals couldn't be trusted. Who didn't like the warm feeling of a puppy licking her face, or the sound of a cat purring? She didn't have any friends who jumped in circles and leapt for joy when she walked through the front door.

"I'm running an ad," Cathy said. "So far no one has called, but if I don't get rid of her by next week, I'm going to take her to the shelter."

The shelter? She'd said it as if it were no big deal, like Bella would be going to some kind of doggie summer camp. Elise had always had pets growing up. Dogs and cats. Since she'd been in college she'd missed having a pet. She thought about it overnight and the next morning went to retrieve the dog. A week later she saw a Bekins truck delivering a brand-new oak coffee table. It was so ugly.

Not long after adopting Bella she had realized that not only were the Fosters shallow assholes, but their kids were complete fuckers, too. It became obvious that Bella had suffered much torment at the hands of the Foster children. Every time a child came near her, she would whimper before hiding beneath the nearest piece of furniture. What those kids had done, Elise would never know.

They'd been together for two years now, and Bella was the most loyal and steady companion Elise had ever had, especially since she wrote alone all day. Bella was like a coworker and a companion. Giving up her dog would never happen.

Stan raced over and grabbed a beer from his cooler. His team had won, and he was in an exceptionally good mood. She noticed that Tracey and Brooke both seemed to laugh more freely after Stan sat down. They ran their fingers through their hair and sucked in their stomachs, too. She wondered if one of them had hooked up with her brother, or if they were hoping to. Surprisingly, Stan never had a hard time getting women. He'd always been active, doing things outdoors—surfing and bike riding daily. As a result, he was tanned and chiseled, and his big blue eyes often reminded Elise a little of Jared Leto's. She had often wondered if he would ever find the right girl and settle down. He tossed a cold beer on Elise's towel. "So who is this guy you're going out with tonight?" he asked.

"I don't know. It's a blind date."

Tracey and Brooke raised their eyebrows and released surprised gasps. For some reason the words *blind date* elicited the same response she'd get if she told them she was going bungee jumping over the Bermuda Triangle. "God! That's scary. Do you know how brave you are?" Brooke said. "I did that *once*. And I'll never do it again. Oh no. Never again." She shook her head.

"Do you know what he looks like?" Tracey asked.

"No idea."

"Aren't you dying of curiosity?"

"Well, I've made a promise to myself not to expect anything. Not one thing. It's been hard, but I've tried to avoid fantasies where he's drop-dead gorgeous, has a heart of gold, and loves dogs. If I don't think about it too much, I won't be disappointed."

"That's a really good attitude," Tracey said.

Her brother laughed.

"What?" Elise asked.

"Oh nothing."

"What?"

"I just had this image of a complete nerd picking you up."

"Thanks."

He laughed harder, then stopped suddenly as if something had come to mind. "Seriously, if the guy is a creep, call me, and I'll come get you."

"Oh, that is so sweet," Brooke cooed. "What a good brother you are. My brother is the same way, so protective."

"I'm sure it'll be fine," Elise said. "Carly is going to be with me." She flipped onto her stomach and let the sun soak into her back. "What happened on your date?" she asked Brooke.

"Ugh. It was awful. I felt like his therapist. He talked about his ex-girlfriend who cheated on him all throughout dinner. He kept comparing her to everything I did. I wanted to get up and leave."

"My roommate went on a blind date once, and the guy had a gold tooth. She found out later the guy was technically still married, too," Tracey chimed in.

Talking to them had done the opposite of what she'd been trying to avoid. She was starting to have fantasies of Toby, her real estate agent blind date. The rest of her afternoon at the beach was spent warding off visions of him with teeth that would be stylish on a pimp, and a whole load of baggage.

Getting ready for her date made her realize just how badly she needed to go to the nearest shopping mall. It had been a long time since she'd been on a real date. If they were doing something casual, then she would knock Toby's socks off with an adorable Urban Out-fitter's tank top and fantastic jeans with just the right amount of wear and tear. However, Carly said they were going downtown, which meant jeans weren't allowed. If she attempted to set foot in any down-town establishment wearing jeans, she'd be greeted with the kind of stares that made her feel like she had a gigantic booger hanging from her nose.

It took her twice as long to get ready because she couldn't decide on anything to wear. She hadn't worn black pants since the days when the fashion industry had just begun to introduce boot cut. All her black pants were tapered and made her look like she needed a formal introduction to the millennium. She finally settled for a skirt that she'd forgotten she even owned and that surprisingly seemed to fit in with the current trends. It was short, light pink, and had several layers of ruffles toward the bottom. She put on a white blouse and jean jacket and thought she looked pretty hot with her new tan.

She spent another ten minutes digging like a gopher through the mountain of shoes on her closet floor for the strappy heels she'd worn to her graduation. After several minutes of frantic digging, she finally found the heels. The right one was smooshed and looked malformed from being smothered beneath the pile. When she put the shoes on, she noticed that her foot looked deformed.

She needed a second opinion.

Justine's bedroom door was open, and she popped her head in. She found her alone in her bedroom and on the phone. This time she wasn't murmuring monkey talk, and she looked startled when she noticed Elise in the doorway.

"I'm sorry," Elise said, unsure of what she was apologizing for. She quickly turned from the room.

"No. It's okay. Come in!" she called.

"Sorry. I thought I scared you."

"No. I'm just checking Jimmy's messages. I figured out his code for the voice mail on his cell phone."

"Where is he?" Elise asked.

"He just went to the liquor store. We're having some of his friends over and then going to The Whistle Stop with them. He went to get beer for before we go to the bar. Do you want to come out with us?"

"I actually have a blind date tonight."

Instead of lifting her eyebrows and telling her how risky blind dates could be, she ignored her and pressed something on the phone. "Listen to this," she said as if she were Nancy Drew. A female voice came crackling to life on the speakerphone. "Hey Jimbo," she said. "It's Bettina. I hear the whole band is in L.A., and I want to meet up with you guys. I haven't seen you in forever, and I heard everything is going great with your little lady from Nebraska." To that, Justine rolled her eyes. "Well, call me. I'm in L.A. for business, and I want to buy you a drink." She clicked off the speakerphone. "I can't stand that chick."

"Who is she?"

"Some freaking groupie who used to date Adrian Potter, the lead singer. She has never gotten over him. So she *stalks* the other band members and tries to be their friend. I mean, why can't she just leave my boyfriend alone and get a life?" She said the last part while she was standing in her dark bedroom on her day off, busting into her boyfriend's voice mail message account.

"Anyway, what's up?"

"What do you think of the shoes?"

"Ummm. They're all right." She thought for a moment. "Come here."

Justine opened her closet door. What lay inside was the most organized shoe rack in America. Really. Elise thought someone should
write Oprah about this. The world needed to see. Not only were all
of Justine's shoes neatly lined and organized, but each shelf was
arranged in rows according to color and style. Beneath each pair was
an index card listing the outfits that went best with the shoes.

She reached a thin arm into her closet, pulled a pair of pink
pumps from a rack of heels. She presented them to Elise as if she were
handling the Hope diamond.

"Those are so cute."

"Thanks," Justine said. "Try 'em on. I just bought them the
other day."

The black soles were as sleek and unmarked as an untouched
chalkboard. "You just bought these." Elise shook her head. "I can't
wear them."

"Why not?"

"You haven't even worn them yet."

"So. Try 'em on. I bet they're perfect with your outfit."

Elise slipped on the shoes. Both girls studied her feet in the mirror. Her claves looked long and sexy above them, and the shoes were
the same shade of pink as her skirt.

"They're perfect," Justine said.

"I can't wear these. You've never even worn them. You just bought
them, and I can't trounce around town all night in them."

"You're wearing those shoes, and I don't want to hear another
word about it."

"But—"

"Go get ready. You can let me borrow something of yours when I
need to."

Elise was applying the finishing touches of her makeup when the
doorbell rang. They were here, and five minutes early. She took a

deep breath and squashed a last-minute hope that her date looked like Brad Pitt.

Every time she became nervous her mind seemed to go on vacation. Clear, sharp thinking departed, and a slow and spacey substitute with delayed reactions and a lack of quick wit moved in. Sometimes if she took a few deep breaths she could bring her mind back. She inhaled deeply and could hear the muffled voices of Justine and Jimmy as they answered the door. She grabbed her purse from her desk and headed to the living room.

"Oh, hi," she said.

"Hey, Elise," Max greeted her, looking even cuter than the last time she had seen him. "What are you up to this evening?"

She was about to tell him she was just going out with some friends when Justine beat her and announced that she had a blind date.

He nodded. "Right on." He set his helmet on the couch. "I meant to ask you, what's the name of your book?"

"*Double Deceit.*"

"Cool. I was in Borders the other day and wanted to grab a copy."

"Really? Thanks."

"Yeah, I was looking for a good book to read. I ended up getting some other mystery book that was okay, but not that engaging."

She wondered how this calm, cool, seemingly intelligent person was friends with Jimmy. "If you ever need recommendations, I can give you all kinds of books to read. I read all the time."

They talked about good books, and for a moment she wished Carly wasn't bringing Toby and Marcus here. For some reason, she didn't want Max to see her going on a date.

The doorbell rang again, and it was several more of Justine and Jimmy's friends. She wanted to visit with Max more, but a tall blonde smelling of patchouli and wearing Birkenstocks cornered him. Justine introduced her to some of the new arrivals, and Elise felt a little overdressed around their casual bar attire. She also felt an urge to ditch her skirt and heels, throw on jeans, and head to The Whistle Stop with them.

When Carly entered with Marcus and Toby, the entire room fell silent. Elise was too overwhelmed by the fact that every single person was staring at them to realize that Toby was pretty darn cute. She just wanted to get out of there as quickly as possible.

This wasn't an episode of *The Bachelorette*. She didn't need an audience while she met her date for the first time.

"Well, good-bye, everyone. It was fantastic meeting you," she said as she quickly herded her group to the front door.

Outside, music blasted. "I said sucka watch yo ass. Cuz you gonna get tagged. Bleedin till ya die. You gonna say good-bye . . ."

"Nice neighborhood," Marcus said sarcastically.

She'd only had the opportunity to meet Marcus a couple of other times, and each time she was exposed to his company, she liked him less. She had forgotten how much better Carly could do. Going bald, he had bug eyes that popped from his little skull and looked as if they might produce beams and zap you if he stared too long. Worst of all, he was one of those people who always pointed out the obvious.

"I've gotten used to the rap," Elise said. "Just like I expect to hear cheesy love songs in the grocery store, I expect to hear rappers singing about gang warfare and blow jobs in my neighborhood."

Toby laughed. "This is actually going to be a really great neighborhood someday. Investment-wise, City Heights is moving up. Just like North Park."

"When?" Elise asked. "Tomorrow?"

He laughed, and she thought he was cute, someone her mother would love. He and Marcus both wore freshly ironed button-down polo shirts with black pants. Toby's hair was cut short, and though it was getting a little thin, he made the best of what he had and managed to comb it stylishly. He smelled like a good, clean masculine deodorant, but not in an overwhelming way, and he had a friendly smile.

"Why don't we go in separate cars to Dakota's?" Marcus said.

"That way, Elise and Toby can chat. They should get to know each other." Nothing like being put on the spot.

She climbed into the passenger seat of Toby's Camry and was pleased to know the rims hadn't been stolen during the brief time he'd been in her apartment. She felt a little pang of first-date awkwardness. She was nervous and conscious of the way her hair fell around her face and the way she crossed her legs. Even though her thighs were pretty muscular, if she crossed them at the wrong angle she could accidentally flash Toby a grisly shot of cellulite. She'd never struggled with her weight, but she had areas on her thighs that tended to appear problematic if in the wrong light. As of right now, she wanted to go out with him again.

"The owner of your place is going to make a killing when he sells your place," he said as they pulled out of her street.

"The inside of my apartment is nice. But let's face it. I live in the ghetto."

"I'm actually thinking about buying property in this area. Rental property. It's a great place to invest. I tell all my first-time buyers to look here."

They talked about real estate, and though she thought Toby was very nice and polite, she felt a growing sense of frustration.

As he explained the benefits of buying a house and how much money she would make if she turned a property over in two years, it just reminded her even more of how broke she was and how much she craved a place of her own.

Listening to him made her feel even worse about living with Justine. Toby was only a year older than she was, and he already owned three condos, two of which he rented out. Elise was getting too old to roommate hunt. Even Stan talked about buying a place.

When they arrived in the Gaslamp Quarter, Toby pulled right up to Dakota's valet. This was perfectly fine with her, because she was wearing Justine's shoes and didn't want to scuff them up. They found Carly and Marcus waiting for them at a table inside.

When the waiter came to their table for drink orders, Elise's disappointment over her living situation faded, and she suddenly felt excited about being out with a new guy and doing something fun. "I'll take a gin martini with two olives," she said, the melody of optimism ringing in her voice.

Carly's eyes lit up. "That sounds great. I'll have the same."

Marcus eyed them both before ordering a Bud Light.

"Just iced tea for me. I'm not really a drinker," Toby said as his eyes wandered over the menu.

She witnessed her moment of optimism suddenly plunge off a cliff and explode in flames. The evening was destined for a safe and boring path of polite talk about real estate investments. On the other hand, so what if he didn't drink? He was driving, and maybe he had a spontaneous and fun sober side. She just hoped he didn't mind if she ordered a few drinks.

Toby seemed like an insightful person. He came from a large Catholic family in Michigan and loved baseball.

"Sometimes I get box seats from my office," he said. "You and I should go to a game sometime."

"Yeah. That would be fun," she said, and she meant it.

When the conversation moved to Elise's career, both Marcus and Toby were more interested in the publishing industry and how profits were made as opposed to the plot of her novel. But that was okay. They were businessmen and naturally curious about the financial side of everything.

When it came time to order, Toby ordered a broiled chicken breast and steamed vegetables. This selection was not listed on the menu, but rather was Toby's own heart-friendly creation. He also requested no butter or oil.

No drinking and a healthy diet. His lifestyle seemed boring, but perhaps he could be a good influence on Elise if they started dating. She'd ordered a personal pizza and had asked for extra cheese.

"I'm training for a marathon," he explained after the waiter left.

"Toby runs ten miles a day," Marcus added.

"It shows," Elise said, polishing off the last of her martini. "I mean, I didn't mean to be so bold, but you look like you're in good shape."

"I love working out. I'm really into fitness."

Okay, so he would be a very good influence on her. Life changing, actually. Elise had never played sports, and her idea of a good workout had been parking far away from her classes at grad school.

After dinner they went to The Bitter End. Carly and Elise both ordered martinis. After finishing their drinks, they had a chance to escape to the ladies' room together.

"Are you having fun?" Carly asked.

"Yeah, he's nice and cute."

"Good! Marcus is getting tired. I think he wants to leave soon."

After another drink, the couples said their good-byes. Elise could feel the effects of her martinis. As soon as they slid into Toby's car, he kissed her, a soft slow kiss with lots of lips. *Pretty bold, for being sober*, she thought in her buzzed state. Kissing him felt good, and she realized that she'd never gone so long without being kissed. How long had it been? Five? Six months? As they headed back to her place, he kissed her at each stoplight. When they pulled up to her building, he reached for her over the center console. She clicked the button on her seat belt and slid closer to him. Slowly, he traced his fingertips up her inner thighs, and then his hands made their way up her skirt. She hadn't planned on any of this, but the alcohol made her feel brazen, and it felt good to be touched.

Gently, she reached for him, pulling him closer. He pulled her panties aside, and she thought she would explode with need. This was a lot for a first-date good-bye kiss, and she wondered through a haze of lust if they should stop.

Part of her ached for him to touch her more. And part of her was afraid they were going to get carjacked. She was about to suggest he walk her to the door when he stopped kissing her.

"Go down on me," he breathed.

"What?"

"Give me head," he moaned. "Please."

He was *asking*. She hadn't been asked for "head" since the eighth grade. And even then, she'd had the sense to know it was bad manners. Who the hell did he think she was? Because he was about to find out that she definitely wasn't the type of girl who gives blow jobs in the front seat of cars on a first date. Just because she'd had a few drinks didn't mean she wanted to live out the lyrics of a rap song for Mr. Fitness.

"I really should go," she said, instantly losing her sexual desire. "Thanks for dinner."

"Wait." He grabbed her arm. "Can't you just touch it some more? Please?" She looked at the tip of his penis sticking out from his zipper.

"Let go of me."

He released his grip, and she instantly reached for her purse.

"Wait just a second," he said as he began to climb out of the car, too.

She tried to get away from him quickly but missed a step and almost tripped over the curb. He pulled her elbow. "Aren't you going to kiss me good-bye? I kind of wanted a tour of your apartment."

He pulled on her elbow, and the way his fingers latched around her arm made her a little afraid. "Another time, okay? My roommate is sleeping right now. And her boyfriend is in there. He threatened the last guy who woke him up. He's really mean."

He wouldn't let go, and she was completely relieved when Glorious D joined them. "Hey Elise," he said. "This your boyfriend?"

"No. It's not. In fact, I was just saying good-bye to him."

Toby wore a guilty expression on his face and looked at Glorious D with a mixture of fear and respect, as if Glorious D were her father. "Well, I should get going. I'll call you sometime."

"I'm moving," she called after him. "Don't bother."

Glorious D walked her back to the apartment. After explaining what a horrible evening she had to Glorious D and listening to him rhyme about blind dates, she said good night.

Cigarette smoke assaulted her when she opened the front door, and she went to open a window.

What a disappointment Toby had been, she thought to herself. She'd been looking forward to Padres games with him, and he'd seemed so normal. It was just as well, though. She hated working out and was actually thinking how irritating it would be to date a guy who ate less than she did.

The blinds were wide open, and a streetlamp cast a glow over a motorcycle in their parking lot. She wondered if it was Max's. She felt tempted to take a cab to The Whistle Stop, salvage her night. Max would be there with Justine and Jimmy, and she could still have fun. But then she heard a faint groan behind Justine's bedroom door. They were back from The Whistle Stop, which meant that wasn't Max's motorcycle, and he was probably at home, too.

A few seconds later she heard the kind of grunting that made her cheeks turn red. She quickly returned to her room, feeling as if she had invaded their private moment.

As she walked to her bedroom alone, she also felt a pang of yearning. She didn't bother to turn on the lights as she slipped out of her clothes. After she slid into bed, she wondered if Max was alone, too.

6. The Unspoken Roommate

Jimmy didn't leave. He became as much a part of their apartment as their furniture. A smoking, beer-drinking armchair that hogged the remote control and was terrible at taking phone messages.

Furthermore, the grunting only became louder and more obnoxious. Justine's moans and gasps could be heard even with water running at full blast. Nearly every morning since his arrival, Justine would stroll out of the bedroom, wearing one of his T-shirts and the smile of a satisfied cat. First she'd giggle. Then she'd turn to Elise. "I hope you didn't hear us last night. We weren't too loud, were we?"

Something told her that Justine wanted her to say yes, to tell her their frantic sex had kept her awake. "No. Didn't hear a thing."

A flash of surprise would cross over her eyes before she would say, "Oh good. But definitely let us know if we're ever too loud."

Not only had their living room become a fogbank of cigarette smoke, but Jimmy hogged the remote control, watching episodes of MTV *Cribs* religiously. She had a strong hunch he was probably fantasizing about the day he'd be a guest on *Cribs*— if that day ever came. And that was a big *if*. Seeing how Jimmy didn't even have a crib of his own, it would be a long time before his episode aired.

At night, Elise sought refuge in the private quarters of her bedroom. Occasionally, she would leave her room for food and water. During these quests she usually found Justine and Jimmy curled up on the couch, a look of pure contentment in Justine's eyes and a look of childlike yearning in his while Blink-182 showed off waterfalls in their hot tubs and Tommy Lee took a ride in his elevator. Every time she entered, he always offered her a beer.

"Yeah, come hang out with us," Justine would add as an afterthought.

Once or twice she had accepted but couldn't visit for long. The smoke had made her eyes water and then she'd remember that chilling commercial from the American Lung Association of the middle-aged woman with a voice raspier than Satan smoking a cigarette from a hole in her throat while attached to an oxygen tank. Then she'd return to her room. She often thought about asking them to smoke outside, but she also thought about moving at the first possible opportunity. Since she was secretly planning on bolting from the apartment the first chance she had, she felt bad setting smoking rules.

She'd gotten so used to Jimmy that when she wrote all day she knew he was behind Justine's closed bedroom door. She could feel his presence even if he wasn't in the same room as her.

He usually popped out of Justine's half of the condo around two, made himself a late breakfast before skateboarding to the liquor store for a twelve-pack of whatever beer was on special that day.

Once she had caught him taking apart their couch cushions. "Did you lose one of your lighthouses?" she asked.

"No. I'm just looking for spare change. I'm starving, and I only have two bucks on me."

She took pity on him. "Just help yourself to *some* of my food."

"You sure?"

"It's fine. You can eat some of my stuff today."

"I'll pay you back next week. I'm getting a check from the label, and I'm going to hook you and Justine up. I swear." He headed for the kitchen. "Then I'll make some money when I'm on the road, so I'll be in good shape after that. I'll be able to contribute more."

Thank God his back had been turned and he hadn't seen the shock that registered on her face. Elise knew he was going on tour in a month. He was supposed to be gone for several weeks, wreaking havoc all over the country doing Lord only knows what, but she didn't know he planned to return to *their* apartment. Furthermore, his current status was supposed to be as a guest until his bandmates found another place. Justine had been acting as if he was moving in with his friends. Elise had never planned on a third roommate, especially an unemployed alcoholic rock star who left the couch only to grab another cold one from the fridge.

There was, however, one bonus of living with Jimmy. He was sort of a slob. If he made a sandwich, he left crumbs on the counter. He built pyramids with his beer cans on their coffee table, and he occasionally left empty dishes in the sink. His memory was horrible, too. His sister's name had shown up on their caller ID once, and he didn't even know who she was because he'd forgotten that she'd changed her name when she'd gotten married five years ago.

His bad memory combined with carelessness took a lot of pressure off Elise to be so immaculate. If she got sidetracked and left a mug in the sink, she could be certain that Justine would never be sure who had left the mess.

She had hoped he would invite Max over again, but no such luck. Jimmy seemed perfectly content by himself.

Several days after his arrival Elise fell into a writing groove, plugging out twenty pages. She had a feeling about this book. It was much better than her other one, and she prayed to sell foreign rights, perhaps even movie rights.

She was feeling pleased with her progress when a loud bang on their front door interrupted her. Time had flown, and she was stunned to see that it was three o'clock in the afternoon. She hadn't heard any bling-blinging on *Cribs*, and it suddenly occurred to her that Jimmy hadn't come out from his den yet.

"Coming," she called. Rarely did someone come to the front door. For this reason she never made an effort to improve her appearance. She wore red and black plaid pajama bottoms and a University of Arizona T-shirt. Her reading glasses were perched on her nose, and her hair was tied in a bun on top of her head, thin pieces sticking up like overgrown weeds.

A little man wearing gray slacks with a button-down short-sleeved shirt and a clip-on tie greeted her. For a moment she thought he might be selling encyclopedias. However, he looked really familiar. She thought she recognized him as one of the tenants from upstairs. He was bald in the front and wore thick glasses.

"Hi," Elise said, waiting for him to explain his visit.

"Hi. I'm Walt Carter, head of the homeowners' association. I realize you guys are renting this place. But most of the tenants here are owners, and we've had some complaints about the truck parked in front of the building."

Truck? Homeowners' association? They have a homeowners' association? In City Heights?

"In fact, we've had several complaints," he continued. "For one, it's leaking oil, and two, well frankly, it's an eyesore."

"Um, sir. I'm sorry, but I don't drive a truck. I drive a Volkswagen, and my roommate drives a Hyundai Accent."

"Well, apparently it belongs to a guest that's been staying here. Several tenants have reported seeing a young man leaving this apartment to retrieve things from the vehicle."

Jimmy. Elise knew he had a jalopy parked *somewhere*. She just didn't know it was parked in front of their building. She'd occasionally noticed the truck when she had walked to her car. It was a small model from the early eighties, covered with rust spots and painted a shade of green that should only be reserved for the military. On the tailgate it read, "Yo." Some clever little soul had decided to rip off the other four letters in Toyota.

"I'm serving you a notice and a fine of sorts. It's a demand that you must move the truck within forty-eight hours, or it will be towed at your expense and you will also be fined an additional seventy-five dollars for failing to comply with the homeowners' association. Also, every time you are served a complaint by the homeowners' association it is accompanied by a seventy-five-dollar fine."

He talked so fast, throwing information at her like a child armed with sand at a playground. "So there is a seventy-five-dollar fine today?"

"That's right."

"What about the couch that's been sitting in front of the building for two months now?" she asked. "Why haven't those people been fined?"

"That couch actually belongs to the neighboring complex, and it's not in our jurisdiction. There is nothing *our* homeowners' association can do about that. If you have a complaint you can take it up with the neighboring building or perhaps the City of San Diego."

"What happens if we fail to pay the fine?"

"Well, then it's handed over to your landlord. He can choose to do as he wishes. But typically the landlords will deduct it from your deposit when you move out. Or he might raise your rent."

He handed her a stack of papers, nodded his head, and was off. Elise looked over the papers. Sure enough, they had been cited with a fine and a notice to remove the vehicle from the premises. As soon as Walt was gone, Glorious D cruised up, a blue bandana tied over his head.

"What up, Elise?"

"Do you know that man who was just here?"

"Yeah man. That dude's a prick." He began to move from side to side, shifting his weight to opposite feet with each beat. "Walt. Walt. It ain't his fault. He got no life. Takin' a knife to yo door. Wreckin yo day cuz he can't play." He popped out of rapping mode. "Man, screw that asshole. What'd he do now?"

Elise told him about the fine.

"You want me to tag his car?"

"No! It's okay. Don't do anything to Walt."

After she said good-bye to Glorious D she debated waking Jimmy. After all, most people had put in a full day of labor, and he hadn't even crawled out of bed yet. Furthermore, he needed to make arrangements to move his truck within the next forty-eight hours. Who knew when the clock had started ticking with those forty-eight hours? This Walt Homeowners' Association guy could've started the forty-eight hours whenever he wrote the citation, which could've been last night. She was heading toward Justine's bedroom when the front door burst open.

She spun around, expecting to see smoke blowing from Walt's nose, horns growing from his head, and a stack of complaints up to his waist.

Instead, a large brown upright piano greeted her. Behind the instrument she could see Jimmy's shag haircut. A cigarette dangled from between his lips. "Lemme try to push it through, man." He had company. She felt a flicker of hope that he'd brought Max with him. Then she realized that she was in her pajamas and wearing her reading glasses. She hadn't even wiped the crust from her eyes from when she woke up six hours ago.

"You sure you don't want me to get on the other side and lift it?" A male voice called. It wasn't Max's voice, and she felt a strange combination of relief and disappointment.

"No. I think I can slide it."

Elise watched as Jimmy pressed his skinny body against the piano, his bony shoulders shoving the wooden frame. The little wheels beneath the instrument jolted over the doorframe.

"Hey, what's up?" he said when he noticed her.

"We have a piano?"

"Yeah." He continued wheeling it toward the empty half of the living room. "And a drum set."

His friend followed, carrying large drum pieces in each hand.

"Just set those over there, dude." He turned back to Elise. "We just got kicked out of our studio, and we don't have anywhere to store this stuff." He motioned toward his friend. "Elise, this is my buddy Elliott Potter. He's the drummer for our band."

She recognized him from the flyer. He was stocky and had a head full of curly dark hair and long sideburns that extended to his chin. He wore jeans and a T-shirt that read, "Say No to Drugs." They shook hands before he headed to the couch and proceeded to roll a joint on their coffee table, right next to five lighthouses.

Last week she was making herself dinner when Justine had presented him with one of the lighthouses. Elise had slyly eyed them from the kitchen while he opened the gift.

"Another lighthouse," he'd said with a polite twinge of fake happiness in his voice. "Cool."

Beaming, Justine had kissed him on the cheek before they'd proceeded to make out right there on the couch. The lighthouses never moved.

"I really need to get high before we unload the rest of that stuff," Elliott said. *The rest of that stuff? What else did they have?*

Elise remembered an episode of *Oprah* she'd seen the previous week. It had been one of those Let's Take Cameras Inside the Homes of the Rich and Famous So the Rest of the Country Can Feel Totally Poor and Unstylish for an Hour episodes. They had toured makeup guru Bobbi Brown's house and discussed heated towels and the television set in her bathroom before they were off to the grand designer of Pottery Barn's home where she showed off her kitchen island and chic little chalkboards in every room. Watching this episode had unleashed a craving for heated towels and chalkboards that she couldn't explain.

As she stood in her living room while they passed a joint across her coffee table, she wondered what it would be like if Oprah had an episode about them—those who can't afford their home let alone heated towels, but rather roll joints next to a row of trinkets.

She wanted out. She wanted her own place with a matching set of dishes and fluffy white couches. She was too old for this. Five years ago she probably would've thought it was a blast to have a couple of musicians turning their living room into a studio and offering her pot. For a moment she considered a career change. Real estate? Pharmaceutical sales? But she was doing what she loved. Unfortunately, it was a career that involved a lot of sacrifices in the beginning—and had a very long beginning, for that matter.

She was about to tell Jimmy about his fine and the notice, but he left to gather more instruments. He returned with a giant electric keyboard. Their parade of instruments continued until four guitars, two trumpets, and several amplifiers occupied the empty space in their dining room. Within minutes, their apartment had become the Grand Ole Opry. Elliott sat down in front of the drums and banged out a drumroll loud enough for people in Mexico to appreciate. His curls shook over his forehead, and his mouth turned to a contorted line as he threw his heart and soul into the set. The whole time she couldn't help but imagine the next visit from Walt.

"That's awesome!" Instantly, Jimmy slid onto the bench in front of the piano and began to play music to accompany the drum set. She had to admit, they sounded great. She found herself caught in the moment, tapping her feet. She was about to ask the name of the song when she remembered the fine and notice in her hand.

"Uh, Jimmy. I hate to interrupt, but um . . ."

He continued to play while Elise spoke.

"You need to move your truck. A man came by here a little while ago with a fine and a notice saying that you had forty-eight hours in which you needed to move your truck."

"Shit. Really?" He still tapped away on the keys. "How much is the fine?"

"Seventy-five dollars."

"Man, that sucks. My truck doesn't start."

"Listen, I have to hop in the shower. It's my brother's birthday, and I'm going out to dinner with my family tonight. But I'll set the stuff right here on top of the piano." As she headed back to her room, she prayed he wouldn't forget.

She had just stepped out of the shower when the doorbell rang for the second time that day.

"Coming," she yelled. She threw on her robe and wrapped a towel around her head. She glanced at the clock just to make sure she wasn't running late. Her parents weren't due for another half hour.

When she opened the door a three-hundred-pound grizzly faced man with stubble and pants that were too small for him invaded her view. His hairy stomach bore a striking resemblance to a mohair sweater she had recently turned over to the Salvation Army, and his belly button was as deep and dark as the drain in her bathroom sink. She tried to remember if the helicopter that had been combing the area that morning had been looking for him. No. The fugitive du jour had been a young Mexican male, mid twenties, on a red bike.

"Somebody call Triple A?" he asked.

"Oh yeah. That would be my roommate's boyfriend. He should be here any minute."

His face remained blank, but something about the way he sighed made her believe that he didn't want to wait.

"I'm towing the Toyota in the front, right?"

"Yes. That's the one."

She heard the sound of wheels rolling over concrete as Jimmy swiftly glided toward the driver on a skateboard. His bangs were blown back, and he held a paper bag in his hand.

"Hey man. Sorry. I had to go get a brew. You want one?"

"No. I don't drink on the job."

Elise left them to sort out Jimmy's truck issues. Minutes later, she heard the door open again. Only this time it was Justine. "I got here just in time," she said, out of breath. "The guy almost wouldn't tow Jimmy's car without my Triple A card. I had to leave work."

She set her purse on the counter. "I got the cable bill and electricity bills today." She reached for them inside her purse. "I just split them in half. You can look them over if you want. But I've written down how much we each owe on the top of both bills."

"Oh, okay. I'll write you a check." She was heading for her checkbook when it occurred to her that Jimmy had practically moved in. He watched television more than anyone, which used both cable and electricity. Furthermore, it didn't seem as if he planned to leave until he went on tour next month. They should divide the bills three ways. And for that matter, they should be dividing the rent three ways as well. She suddenly felt as if she were being taken advantage of. The idea of confronting Justine seemed terrifying. However, if she wrote a check for half the bills, she'd feel like a spineless doormat, and that was worse than facing her roommate.

"Justine, um, do you think it would be possible for Jimmy to contribute? I mean, he watches television more than anyone and he, well . . . it seems like he, um, lives here."

Justine stared at Elise, her eyebrows twisting into a sinister shape that Elise had not yet become familiar with. Maybe she shouldn't have mentioned it. After all, he was leaving for his tour. Perhaps he was just a guest who had free rein of their television and refrigerator. She didn't want to be The Evil Stingy Roommate that charged Justine's guests rent.

"Well, if he doesn't have the money now, I understand. He can contribute another time."

"Fine," Justine said. Her long nails curled over the bills, and her voice was as chilly as a polar bear's breath. "I'll tell him you mentioned that he should contribute."

Elise wrote a check for her half of the bills, feeling as if she had just pulled a sweater from the sales rack at Nordstrom only to find when she'd paid at the cash register it had been full price.

"I have to go back to work," Justine said. "So I'll just mail the bills on my way."

Her parents arrived sharply at six o'clock. Her father wore a sport coat with crisply ironed gray slacks. Her mother had on one of her signature monochromatic matching pant and sweater sets. She had a million of these outfits. This one was various shades of pink. The sweater, made of fine silk, was a light rose, while her pants were a deeper mauve hue and didn't reveal a single crease or wrinkle. A baby pink shawl was draped over her shoulders, and she wore expensive Ferragamo sandals. She was the utter image of sophistication combined with comfort.

Elise was dressed more appropriately for the Mexican restaurant Stan had selected in Ocean Beach. She wore jeans with flip-flops and an off-white peasant blouse.

Her mother's round eyes immediately darted over the living room as if she were searching for some kind of evidence. "Where is he?" she whispered. "The boyfriend?"

No sooner than she had asked did Jimmy come strolling from Justine's bedroom, bare chested and beer in hand. Unaware that Elise had company, he belched loud enough to raise the dead while scratching his crotch. "Oh, hey!" he said. "These must be your parents." He set down his beer and wiped his hand on his pants before offering it to her mother.

"Yes. I'm Marjorie Sawyer," she said, holding out a delicate hand. "Elise has told us quite a bit about you."

He lifted his brows before shaking hands with her father. "Really. Well, I gotta say, it's been great staying here. Elise is the coolest roommate Justine has ever had."

"You've got quite the collection of instruments there," her father said, surveying the new studio at their apartment. "Is that a trombone?"

"Yeah. We got kicked out of our studio today. Luckily, we can store our stuff here for the time being."

"Used to play the trombone in my high school marching band," her father said. This was something Elise had never known about her dad. "Do you practice here?"

"We might." This was when Elise would no longer become the "coolest roommate ever." They couldn't have band practice here. She had to write, and he didn't even pay rent!

"That's an interesting collection of lighthouses," Marge said. "Are those yours?"

"Uh, yeah," he said before discussing trombones with her father. They visited with Jimmy for a few minutes before Elise shuffled her parents out the door.

She slid into the backseat of her father's Mercedes sedan. As soon as he started the engine, the voice of a talk radio host joined them, as if he were riding along with the Sawyers to Rancho's.

Her parents listened to talk radio so often that Elise imagined what it would be like to ride with them in the car without the sound of an aggravated and excited radio host. Furthermore, she often wondered why they listened to it. From what she could tell, it mostly just put them in a bad mood. If they heard something they didn't agree with on a program, they'd spend the remainder of the ride fuming and ranting about the idiocy of the views expressed. Talk radio was so much a part of their lives that they spoke of the hosts as if they knew them, like they were personal friends they'd had lunch with that afternoon.

"Well, Dr. Christine mentioned that the problem with America's youth today is all these working mothers," her mother would say. "I always knew I was doing the right thing by staying home with you kids. Although sometimes I wonder about Stan. Maybe it was because I let him watch MTV. Dr. Christine says that's a no-no, too."

The other result of talk radio was that it unleashed a hostility inside her parents that most people outside the Sawyer family never caught a glimpse of. No one at their country club would ever suspect that smooth and polished Marge Sawyer with her monochromatic Neiman Marcus outfits and manicured hands had just been shouting some of the worst obscenities in the English language at a car radio only minutes before arriving at a tennis match.

"I hope you're still planning on looking for a new roommate," her mother shouted over the radio. "I don't know how you can stand living there."

"I will soon. I've just been busy finishing up my book and haven't had time."

"What?"

"I said I'm going to start looking for a roommate soon."

"I can't hear you."

"Could you turn off the radio? Please," Elise said.

"Hal, turn down the radio. I can't hear Elise."

"I just want to hear this one last comment," he said before driving straight through a red light. Her mother's scream made Elise's ears ring. Elise covered her eyes and couldn't hold back her scream, either.

"Good grief!" her father yelled as they miraculously avoided being broadsided by a Ford Ranger and made it through the intersection in one piece.

"Hal!" her mother yelled. "What were you thinking? How could you not have seen that light?"

This was the other thing about talk radio. Elise had some serious concerns that talk radio might hold the fate of her parents in its agenda. She'd lost track of how many times they'd both escaped fatal accidents by a mere millimeter. She'd witnessed dozens of separate occasions when each one of them had become so wrapped up in a program that they just switched lanes without even looking. Elise had begun to theorize that most accidents could probably be attributed to Dr. Chrstine and that conservative host Roger Tremwhatever.

Whenever Elise passed some poor soul on the side of the highway holding an ice pack to his forehead and miserably surveying the bumper he'd rammed into, she thought of one thing: talk radio.

"Please. Would you just turn off the radio?" Elise said, her heart still racing at the near-death experience she'd just been involved in. "You guys are going to really hurt someone one of these days. I'm serious. I'm really worried about you guys."

Thankfully, they turned the radio down. "So, are you excited for the shower tomorrow?" Marge asked.

"Yes. And I'm bringing the cake."

"Fantastic. I'm so glad you can be a part of this shower since you missed the last one when Melissa was pregnant with Jeffrey."

"What? What's going on?" her father asked.

"I was just saying that I'm glad Elise is back."

"I am, too, but I don't know why you don't just move home," her father said as he parallel parked in front of Rancho's. "Rent is such a *waste* of money. You may as well just take your five hundred dollars and throw it out the window every month. You're just paying for someone else's investment."

"Why don't you and Stan go in on a place together?" her mother said. "Right now is a great time to buy property. When I was at the club the other day I played tennis with Vicky Landon. She's one of the top Realtors in San Diego, and she said if you went in on a place with Stan, the two of you could probably afford a nice condo."

"I love hanging out with Stan. But if we lived together we'd kill each other." Elise was far from Justine on the neat scale, but Stan was in completely different realm of the solar system when it came to cleanliness. She changed the subject. "So Melissa isn't coming to dinner?"

"No. They're just coming for dessert. Jeffrey skinned his knee today."

Perhaps this was the only benefit of having a child. It got you out of everything, whenever you wanted. All Melissa had to say was Jeffrey wasn't feeling up to it, and there were no questions asked. Not that she wanted to miss having dinner with her parents, but there were other things in life she wouldn't mind having a hall pass for.

They found her brother standing outside Rancho's. He was also in jeans and looked as if he'd just woken up.

"Happy birthday," Elise said, handing him the card and scented candle she'd gotten him. She thought a nice fragrance might add some appeal to his apartment.

Her parents gave him a hundred-dollar gift certificate to Jake's. It was one of the best restaurants in San Diego, and her mother figured if Stan ever did go on a date he should pay. "Take someone out with this," she said. "There has to be a nice girl you could take to dinner."

The best part of Rancho's was the menu. Of course it featured all the regular delicious Mexican entrees, carne asada and chicken enchiladas. But it also included vegetarian selections. Though she wasn't even a vegetarian, Elise always ordered the shiitake burrito. The burrito was so good that she had actually debated abandoning meat for a healthier lifestyle. If things like this were so available, why not? Her father even ordered vegetarian, too, the shiitake chimichanga.

"So, how was that date you went on the other night?" Stan asked, reaching for a chip.

"Oh yes!" her mother said. "With the Realtor, right? Are you going out again?"

Elise really didn't feel like going into it and quickly tried to think of something to divert their attention. "The date was not great, but I am kind of interested in someone else." The moment the words left her lips, she regretted it. Her relationship with Max was little more than a crush, and furthermore, even if it did transpire into anything she'd have to gradually tell her parents about him.

"Really? And who is this?" Marge wanted to know.

"What does he do?" her father asked.

"Um . . . well I don't really know him that well, actually. He's just someone I'm sort of interested in."

She remembered her high school boyfriend, Greg. He had an earring and had taken it out as if he were concealing a weapon every time he came to her parents' house. He and Elise had both feared the discovery of that earring, as if they were serial killers worrying about the bodies in their freezer being found. Their worst nightmare came true when by pure chance they'd run into her mother at the mall. After noticing the earring, her parents were so disappointed in Elise's choice in boyfriends that there had actually been talk of sending her to a psychiatrist.

Then she remembered Stan. He had a small tattoo of a clover on his back. For five years he'd successfully kept it a secret. One Thanksgiving he'd spilled red wine on his shirt. Maybe it was the wine that made him momentarily forget the clover, but he made the grave mistake of removing his shirt in front of everyone. Her mother had reacted to the tattoo as if they'd discovered that Stan was secretly leading a double life as a gay porn star. The whole holiday was ruined. So ruined, in fact, Marge couldn't continue cooking the turkey. She locked herself in her bedroom, letting only Hal in for consolation. Melissa had lucked out and was with her in-laws. But Elise and Stan went hungry while watching a lousy football game.

Every Thanksgiving since, there had been tears and devastation while Marge stuffed the turkey and sadly remembered the horrible Thanksgiving when they found out about Stan's awful secret. Elise had spent the last three Thanksgivings in the kitchen saving the holiday and distracting her mother from dwelling too much on Stan's tattoo, reminding her that it was only a clover, not a naked lady.

What would they think if she brought Max home? If they rode up to her parents' house on the back of his motorcycle, his tattoos peeking out from all edges of his T-shirt? Every holiday for the rest of Elise's life would be ruined.

"Who is it?" Stan asked.

"No one. Just somebody I met through Justine."

Her mother raised an eyebrow. "Are you sure you trust her choice in friends? Look at *her* boyfriend."

Why had she ever brought this up? Why? But then something occurred to her. Stan knew Max. She could find out more about him. Her thoughts were interrupted by the sound of boots running toward their table. She looked over her shoulder and saw Jeffrey weaving through tables as he ran toward Stan with a gift in his hand. He wore his cowboy boots. This time with khaki shorts and a child-sized blazer with gold buttons.

"Oh!" her mother gasped happily. "Isn't it great that Melissa is letting him think for himself?"

"Hand Uncle Tan his gift," Melissa said.

He shoved Uncle Tan's gift toward him and then said, "Me open."

Melissa and Marge thought it was the cutest thing ever, and Stan handed the gift back. "Okay," he said.

They all watched as Jeffrey ripped the gift wrap from what was shaped as a book. It was a cookbook called *Gourmet Cooking* and featured a small piece of steak atop a pastry shell shaped like a basket.

"Thanks," Stan said as he took the book. Whether he would ever use it would remain to be seen.

"Let's see," Marge said. "Why don't you pass it around?"

"Condy," Jeffrey whined to his mother. "Want condy."

He sounded British when he said *candy*. Melissa frantically searched through her purse. "Condy," he said again.

She listened to her nephew ask for "condy" at least twenty more times while waiting for the cookbook to make its rounds to her. Her father passed it to her without looking inside. She was actually kind of curious to flip through the pages. She could use a few cooking tips. She opened the first page and noticed that Melissa and Brice had actually written something to Stan inside the book. *What a sweet gesture*, she thought. This made it so much more meaningful. Being nosy, she had to read.

Melissa and Brice,

*   You two are a fabulous couple. Hope this comes in handy in your married life.*

*   Love, Diane and Rick*

Who the hell were Diane and Rick? Clearly, her sister had done a horrible job of regifting.

After Rancho's, Elise decided to head with Stan to Winston's in Ocean Beach. She called Carly, who was sitting around waiting for Marcus to call, as usual. After several minutes of persuasion, she finally convinced her to meet them for a drink.

"Those girls you met the other day at the bay are going to be there," Stan said as they walked to the bar. "Brooke and Tracey. Remember?"

The ocean air was crisp, and she pulled her sweater tight around her shoulders. "They seem cool, and they're cute. Why don't you date one of them?"

He shrugged. "They are pretty. And they're nice. But I don't know. They're both just missing something."

"What do you mean?"

"They're just kind of . . . I don't know. Not what I'm looking for."

She never knew he was looking for anything more than some fun.

"What are you looking for?" Having conversations about women with her brother was always interesting. His insight was a valuable and rare glimpse into the male species, and she was curious as to what made him stable.

"Brooke slept with two of my friends when she first moved here. Tracey gets drunk and tries to hook up with me, but something about her just turns me off. I don't know. She's kind of an airhead. I want someone who wants to have fun but also has her head screwed on straight."

Elise was proud of him. She knew he had gotten plenty of action throughout bachelorhood. He could've easily taken advantage of his good looks, hooked up with both of them by now, and used them a million times for booty call. However, he was maturing into a good guy, looking for more substance than an easy fling. She hoped he found a great girl, someone that she could be friends with, too.

Winston's was crowded when they arrived. A band Elise had never heard of was playing, and the lead singer reminded her a little of Pete Yorn. She was dying to ask Stan about Max but realized it was going to be difficult with all of his friends there.

Tracey had brought a date, and Brooke was dressed as if she were out on the prowl in her hip-hugger jeans and hot pink halter top. Brooke was one of those girls who had a way of making Elise feel like a Smurf—small and unshapely. Unlike Elise's thin little body, Brooke had voluptuous J.Lo curves, and the kind of boobs people paid a lot of money for. She caught up with them for a few minutes before they said they wanted to hit the dance floor. Elise would've joined them but was waiting for Carly to meet her at the bar. She was standing by herself, sipping a Long Island when she felt a presence next to her.

"What are you drinking?" a male voice asked.

She was afraid to face the person. If he was beastly and offering to buy her a drink, she'd be stuck making polite conversation. She always felt bad refusing drinks from a guy. She turned around and felt adrenaline rush through her veins when she looked at Max leaning against the bar beside her. "Hi," she said, trying desperately to mentally murder the giddy little monster that threatened to reveal herself at any moment. "I had no idea you were here."

He nodded. "I'm a guitar tech for this band. I'm helping them with sound tonight."

"Oh. Cool. Do you do sound for a lot of bands?"

"Yeah. I might go on the road with these guys next month." *No!* She wanted to shout. *Then I'll really never be able to see you.* "What would you like to drink?" he asked.

She looked at her glass, which now consisted mostly of ice. "A Long Island."

"I read your book," he said.

"You did?"

"Yeah, I liked it. I told my mom to read it, too. She loves mysteries."

"Thanks." She couldn't help the enormous grin that consumed her face.

"I think you have an awesome career." He was really gorgeous, and she had to admit his tattoos turned her on. They weren't loud and obnoxious like he was trying to be Mr. Tough and Trashy Tattoo like that motorcycle guy with the dreads on the Discovery channel. Rather, his tattoos were a little more chill, like Johnny Depp. He looked at the bartender. "A Long Island and another Budweiser."

"You got it." The bartender popped the cap off the beer and made Elise's Long Island in a bigger glass. "No charge for these," he said as he knocked on the counter.

"Thanks man. This is for you." He set a five next to a stack of napkins.

"Thank you," Elise said as Max handed her the drink.

She looked at the way his fingers curled around his glass. They were long and callused and he wore a couple of large silver rings.

"So why don't you play anymore?"

The corners of his lips turned up, as if he wasn't prepared for the question. "It got old."

"What did?" The Long Islands had claimed her shame.

"The touring, mostly. I made a lot of mistakes. It was just time to quit."

She wanted to know exactly what the mistakes involved, but even she had her limits with prying. "Do you miss it?"

"Do you miss grad school?"

She thought for a moment. "Sometimes. But I'm happy to be here, moving forward."

"Me, too. Sometimes I think about riding in the bus with the guys, sharing stories from the night before. It makes me laugh. I love the memories, but I am where I am now, and it's better this way. I'm thirty-two now."

She'd thought he was a little older than she was, and was actually happy to hear that he had a few years ahead of her. She thought of Toby who was twenty-seven. She remembered how immature he was.

They discussed Elise's latest book until she felt a presence next to her and noticed Max's eyes wander to her left. "Hi! I'm Brooke."

Max offered his hand. "Max. It's nice to meet you."

She watched as they shook hands, Max's rough hands pulling in her tanned manicured hands. "Great to meet you, too," Brooke said, giving him a huge smile and a flash of cleavage. "Are you a friend of Elise's?"

"Yeah. I'm friends with Elise's roommate, Jimmy." Funny, Jimmy wasn't her roommate.

"Cool. Are you in the band?"

"No."

Max nodded to someone near the stage. "Well, hey, it was nice meeting you, Brooke. I hate to rush off, but I have to go help set up."

"Great meeting you, too." She beamed.

"I'll see you, Elise." He squeezed Elise's shoulder as he walked past.

"Who was that?" Brooke asked as soon as he was out of earshot. "He is the hottest thing I have seen since I moved here. I'd love to let that guy see what color my sheets are tonight."

"Yeah, he is cute," she said. She was feeling slightly irritated until something wonderful occurred to her and washed away any irritating Brooke thoughts. He had asked if she missed grad school. She'd never told him that she'd gone to grad school. This could only mean one thing. He'd been asking about her. Who? Stan? Jimmy?

Carly arrived and bought everyone a round of shots in honor of Stan's birthday.

"Max is here," Elise whispered in her ear after they drank their first shot.

"Who?"

"Max. The guy I told you about, you know the hot one with the tattoos."

"Ohhhhh. Where?"

Elise looked around the bar. "He's over there, talking to Stan."

"Are you kidding me? Your parents would shit a pineapple." She looked a little longer. "He is hot as hell though."

"And he's nice."

"And he knows your brother. Why don't you ask Stan what his story is?"

"I thought about it. He'd probably just end up embarrassing me."

"True. Looks like your little friend has her eyes on him, too." They watched as Stan walked away and Brooke moved in, perching herself on a barstool next to Max. She was the only person in the bar who hadn't been affected by the heat. There wasn't a peck of sweat on her body, and Elise could tell by the way her eyes danced over his face that she was using all her charm on him.

"Well, if fake boobs are what he wants, then I'm definitely not the girl for him."

"Good attitude, sweetie."

They hit the dance floor, and Elise realized she was starting to feel pleasantly potted herself. She danced shamelessly with a bunch of Stan's friends. When she left to fill up on another Long Island, she looked around for Max. He was near the stage, turning knobs on what looked like a gigantic speaker.

"Hey listen," Carly said. "I'm really tired. I'm going to take a cab home."

"Are you all right?"

"Yeah, I'm just tired, and I have that convention tomorrow, so I want to get a good rest. But I'll call you afterwards, okay?" She gave her a hug. "Have fun at the shower."

"I wish you were going to be there to commiserate with me."

After Carly left, Elise scanned the bar for the rest of the group. Her brother was nowhere to be found. She felt drunk and decided she should probably hop in a cab as well. She wanted to say good-bye to Max but didn't want to disturb him while he was working, and he had left the stage anyway. She was turning for the door when she practically walked into his chest.

"Are you leaving?" he asked.

"Yeah. I was going to grab a cab," she said, trying to sound as sober as possible.

"It was good seeing you."

"It was nice seeing you, too."

For a moment he stared at her as if waiting to say something. He swallowed before speaking. "Well listen, I want to get . . ."

"There you are!" Brooke interrupted. "We've been looking everywhere for you, Elise. And Max, I wanted to say bye to you. Lemme give you my number. I'd love to stop by your shop sometime."

She watched as Brooke whipped out a pen and scrawled her name, number, and e-mail address on a napkin. If Elise wasn't mistaken, she thought she saw Brooke draw a heart next to her name.

Politely, Max took the napkin. "Well, you girls have a good night," he said, nodding. Elise looked over her shoulder as she walked away, and he was still watching them. She felt as if she'd just turned on a fantastic suspense movie, and five minutes before the ending the electricity had gone out. If she wasn't mistaken, Max was about to ask her something before Brooke interrupted. The title of her new book? Her phone number? She'd never know.

7. The Baby Storm

The first thing Elise felt when she woke up was the dry, chalky texture of her mouth. Water. She needed it badly, but also felt as if she would barf if she swallowed anything. She was hung over in the worst way. If she had a higher tolerance she wouldn't have gotten so drunk to begin with and probably could've avoided a hangover altogether. She glanced at the clock and thanked God that she still had several more hours of sleep before her sister's baby shower. It took all her strength to crawl from bed and drag her feet to the kitchen. If she had to drink straight from the Sparklett's water tap, she would.

She turned on the light and for a moment wondered if she were still dreaming. Standing at the refrigerator, naked as Michelangelo's *David*, was Jimmy. His legs looked like two long, hairy pencils, the pink eraser standing out brightly as his privates. "Holy shit!" she spat when she realized this was no dream.

"Oh shit, man. Sorry. I thought you were asleep." He cupped his hands over his genitals.

She threw a hand over her eyes before quickly shuffling back to her bedroom.

"Sorry!" he called.

She closed the door behind her. Not only did she drink straight from her bathroom sink but also slapped a wave of cold water over her face, trying to wash away the memory of Jimmy's penis hanging between his skinny legs like a limp celery stalk. She swallowed two Aleve before pulling the covers over her head and praying she wasn't plagued with bizarre dreams for the rest of the night.

She woke three hours later, feeling somewhat refreshed but also slightly afraid to set foot outside her bedroom door. How awkward would it be now? She had seen him. Nude. It was bad enough that she was privy to all the sexual noises they made, but now she felt as if a line had been crossed. However, knowing him, he wouldn't even care. He'd probably think it was funny rather than embarrassing.

She rolled over and nearly screamed aloud when she looked at the time. Her alarm never went off. She had to pick up the cake and drive to Crystal's house in Carlsbad, which would take an hour. The shower started in forty-five minutes. She spent about ten minutes getting ready and cursed herself for not being more like Carly when it came to wardrobe planning. Carly always knew what she was wearing to every event at least a week prior. Elise had no idea what to wear. Furthermore, having access to a washer and dryer still didn't make her do her laundry on a regular basis. She had no clean clothes and ended up in a wool turtleneck sweater in the middle of summer and a denim miniskirt.

She entered the living room wearing sunglasses. This way she wouldn't have to make eye contact. However, neither one of the Cheecherses were around, and she cruised out of the house, avoiding any embarrassing encounters.

Being late usually didn't stress her out. For example, going to the movies. She rarely saw the previews but rather cruised into the theater just in the nick of time. No big deal. She kind of liked sitting in the front row. However, there were occasions when being late really alarmed Elise, like midterms or missing a flight. Melissa's shower was one of these occasions, and she honestly felt as if it was worse than walking in late to a wedding. She might get in trouble or be reprimanded at this shower.

Just as she sped onto the freeway, her cell phone rang. For a split second she debated answering. She didn't recognize the number, and whenever she didn't recognize the number, she never bothered answering. Why run the risk of facing an undesirable ex-boyfriend? Or someone who wanted a favor. However, after the second ring, she realized it might be part of Melissa's shower committee with last-minute instructions. She picked up.

"Hello," she said.

Instead of being greeted by her mother or Crystal, she was greeted by an electronic voice, which informed her she had a collect call, before the familiar and disturbing voice of Jimmy was spliced in to identify himself. "To accept these charges press pound," the robot said.

For a moment she was thrilled. Maybe he was in jail! Then he couldn't live with them anymore. In fact, she would never have to see him again. Of course, she would accept. If anything, it would be a great story to share at the shower.

"Uh, hello," Elise said after pressing pound.

"Elise?"

"Yes."

"Thank God," he sighed. Elise waited for him to explain that he'd been arrested for driving under the influence that morning, but instead he went on to explain that he'd been driving Justine's car to pick up a drum set, and it had broken down in Sorrento Valley. He was stranded and needed a ride. If Elise remembered correctly, Sorrento Valley was an industrial town with little to no shops or restaurants. He really was stuck in the middle of nowhere.

"How did you get this number?" she immediately wanted to know.

"Well, Justine gave it to me. She would pick me up, but obviously she doesn't have a car, and I don't have a Triple A card. I'm stuck."

"Well, I'd love to help you, but I'm actually on my way to a baby shower right now, so I can't get you. I just don't have time."

"Really? Because you're the last person I tried. No one is home."

"I'm sorry, Jimmy. But there is no way I can pick you up and take you back to City Heights at this point."

"Well, I can wait in the car while you're at your shower."

He wanted to wait in the car? Why couldn't he be in jail? "All right," she said. "I'll pick you up. Where are you?"

She found him sitting curbside with his elbows propped on his knees.

"Thanks man! You are the greatest, and boy does it ever feel great in here!" He slid into the air-conditioned car, and obviously felt no embarrassment or discomfort for their encounter in the kitchen earlier that morning.

Just as they were pulling away, her phone rang again. A feeling that she was in serious trouble washed over her, but then she realized that she had the perfect excuse. She had to save a stranded motorist. Anyone would've done the same thing if they were in her shoes. "Hello!" she said with confidence before immediately launching into her story about how she had come to Jimmy's rescue. "He's going to wait in the car though," she said.

"Oh, don't be ridiculous," Melissa said.

"I knew you would understand. It's not my fault that I'm late."

"No, I mean don't make him sit in the car. Bring him in."

"Uh . . . well. Um, actually he'll probably do better in—"

"Do you know how hot it is today? Besides, who says showers are only for women? Bring him in. And I want to meet him, after all the stories I've heard about him from you and Mom."

Oh good grief. What had she gotten herself into? Maybe she should drop him off at a strip mall in Carlsbad and let him roam the aisles of the grocery store. It was cool in there. She didn't want him coming to the shower. He'd probably get drunk and start singing at inappropriate times.

"Well, maybe I'll drop him off—"

"Oh hey, gotta run. Aunt Sherry just got here. Can't wait to see you guys." The line went dead.

When they arrived at the bakery to pick up the cake, he said he would wait in the car and asked if he could use her cell phone. When she returned, he was speaking to someone. "Yeah, Max will be there," he said. "We can ask him to do it." Her ears perked so high, she imagined she must've looked like an Australian shepherd. It really was a blast having a crush on someone, even if she'd only been around that person three times in her life. Where was he going to be? She wanted to be there. Jimmy said good-bye to whoever he was talking to, and she debated asking him about Max. However, like Stan, he'd probably just do something to embarrass her. She wondered if Max would call Brooke, or if she would stop by his shop. She was gorgeous, so who could blame him if he did?

She thought it was actually nice to have Jimmy along, because he held the cake the whole way to Carlsbad.

After parking outside Crystal's town house complex they followed a trail of pink ribbons. Jimmy held the cake and immediately began skipping. What in the hell was he doing, and with the cake in his hands? "Follow, follow, follow, follow the piiihhhnk ribbons," he sang in munchkin voice as they headed down the path leading to the shower.

"Ha-ha!" Elise laughed. "I do feel like we're following the yellow brick road." And right now it wouldn't surprise her if the shower turned out to be like Oz. She hummed *The Wizard of Oz* tune as she traced her way through a maze of condominiums. Her stomach ached when she knocked on the front door, and for a moment she wondered why she was suddenly stricken with nervous anxiety. There would be food and games and hopefully alcohol for those who weren't expecting. And she could just ignore Jimmy. But there was a fear that crept up on her, the same kind of nervous fear she had come to associate with giving speeches.

Then she remembered. It was Crystal. Elise normally liked her, and she had been best friends with Melissa for as long as Elise could remember. She was like Melissa's Carly.

She really had nothing against Crystal. She was a fantastic person with a heart of true gold. But for some goddamn reason that Elise would never understand, she loved doing sentimental, speechy things at every single event that involved Melissa. Elise still woke up in cold sweats, fighting off nightmares about Melissa's bridal shower and bachelorette party when each guest was forced to go around the room saying their name, how they had met Melissa, and their favorite Melissa story. She had even upped the ante at the bachelorette party and made them all share a story and say what they liked best about the bride. It had been painful to say the least. And why?

Elise had always been one of those people who loathed the first day of school for the simple reason that the teacher might make everyone go around the room sharing their name, favorite color, and what they did for the summer. She had even asked for the hall pass on a few of these occasions and had camped in the bathroom until the icebreakers were over. If she had wanted to be a public speaker she would've become a priest. She was a writer, and writers felt comfortable behind things like their computers.

As she waited for someone to answer the front door, she tried to be optimistic. Perhaps Crystal would show mercy at this event. After all, what could she possibly do for an icebreaker at a baby shower?

It's not like they could tell stories about the baby. She wasn't even born yet.

"Hello," Crystal cooed from the door. The past few times Elise had seen Crystal she reminded her of a newscaster. Pretty, thirty-something face. Flawless makeup and perfectly cut and styled shoulder-length hair that looked like it could withstand a hurricane. "It's Elise! Come in, and here, let me take that," she said pulling the gifts from her hands. "And you must be Jimmy." She extended a manicured hand. After the introductions she set Elise's gift on top of a mountain of presents all decked in pink wrapping paper and extravagant ribbons. She clapped her hands together after setting Elise's stuff in the pile. "Now, what can I get you guys to drink? We have—"

"A beer would be great," Jimmy interrupted.

Crystal was silent for a moment. "Um, well okay. I think we have some beer in the fridge. My husband occasionally drinks it, so let me see."

They followed her into the kitchen. "And Elise, the same for you?"

"Uh, no." She saw some champagne chilling on a table. "I'll just have champagne."

"Great."

She handed Jimmy a beer. "Now, go introduce yourself to everyone, but before you do that, please visit Madison and Kayley over at the game station. We have a little icebreaker planned."

Shit. Here it was. They'd probably have to write letters to the infant and then share them with the rest of the group while gathered around Melissa. Instead of joining Madison and Kayley at the icebreaker station, Elise felt like yanking a long ribbon from the gift pile, binding Crystal, and hiding her in the closet. Maybe it was unethical, but she'd really be doing the whole shower a service.

Elise looked at her young cousins standing behind a small card table, drinking Sprites and grinning devilishly as if they had a mischievous secret. Perhaps they, too, had plans to hide Crystal.

"Game station?" Jimmy said as they approached card table. "We're playing a game? That's what goes on at these things? Like are we going to play poker or—I don't know—quarters?"

"No, Jimmy. It's an icebreaker to get people to mingle and chat amongst themselves."

"Hmmm," he mumbled before taking a swig of his beer.

Kayley leaned over and whispered something in Madison's ear before they both burst into laughter. However, the girls quickly became very composed when Elise and Jimmy arrived. "Hi, Elise," they said.

"Hi, guys." She hadn't seen her two young cousins in a while and thought they were blossoming into pretty young girls. Madison actually reminded Elise a little of herself at thirteen, experimenting in a realm of fashion that few dared to go. "This is Jimmy Chee—" Shit, she had almost called him Jimmy Cheecher. What was his last name, anyway? She had no idea. She chuckled, and began to cover up the mistake. "Brain fart! I started to call you Jimmy Cheekonimos. I knew a guy named Jimmy Cheekonimos in high school, and every time I think of the name Jimmy, I just think of Cheekonimos."

It was a blatant lie, but it seemed to work, because he said he knew someone named Steve Freebin in high school, and he always called every Steve he knew 'Freebee' out of habit.

"This is the game table, and here is what you do," Kayley said. "We stick a name of a celebrity to your back, and then you go around asking people yes and no questions only."

"Like for instance," Madison chimed in, "you can ask, 'Am I married?' or 'Is my hair brown?' but you can't say, 'Who am I married to?'"

"Then everyone is going to reveal who they think they are, and we'll see if they're right." Kayley finished with a smirk on her face.

"Fun," Jimmy said. "Hook me up with someone cool. Like Mick Jagger."

"They're all women," Madison said.

"Well, even better," he said. "Give me someone hot then."

Elise caught a glimpse of the girls exchanging smiles before they began applying sticky name tags on their backs. She wondered if Jimmy was getting Gwyneth Paltrow or Julia Roberts. Maybe she should ask for someone hot, too. She realized she ran the chance of getting pinned with someone really undesirable. She had played this game at a good friend's bridal shower a couple years back and had been Courtney Cox, which was a winner.

She thought this icebreaker was a great idea for a couple reasons. One, it would force Jimmy to mingle, and she wouldn't have to be responsible for him. Two, it sure beat writing letters to the unborn.

As soon as they left the game station, they looked at one another. "Let me see your back," Elise said, turning him around. She expected to see J.Lo or someone like that. Instead, written in childish handwriting was Mary Kay Letourneau.

"What the . . . ?"

"What?" Jimmy twisted his neck around. "Is it bad?"

"Um . . . I'm just surprised," Elise said, wondering if she was Martha Stewart. When had shower games taken on such a twist?

"Well, let me see yours," he said, excited as he spun her around. Elise waited for him to say something. Chuckle, or even nod. However, he just stood there. "I don't know who this is," he said, his brows knit.

"You have no idea?"

He shook his head. "No. Do you know who I am?"

"Oh yes." She knew all about the thirty-four-year-old delusional schoolteacher who had seduced her twelve-year-old student and then mothered two of his children, one from behind bars.

"Well, am I single?"

"Um, no."

"Do I have dark hair?"

"No."

"Have I been in any movies lately?"

"No."

"Am I an actress?"

"No."

"Am I a singer?"

"No."

This line of questioning continued until she was certain he would never, in a million years, figure out who he was. He thought he was the kind of celebrity that was known for her talent or good deeds. He'd even guessed Oprah at one point.

"Let's mingle," she said. If she was going to figure out who she was, she needed to talk to people who watched the news. As they headed toward the rest of the party, she looked at the other guests' backs. She caught a glimpse of Crystal, who was arranging hors d'oeuvres and was totally oblivious to the fact that she was Heidi Fleiss. Utterly brilliant.

She glanced at Tanya Harding and Lorena Bobbitt and wondered how Madison and Kayley had gotten away with it. Crystal never would've allowed this.

Then she realized that the girls had managed to infiltrate some celebrities that weren't criminals. Their eighty-three-year-old frail grandmother with dementia was Lil' Kim. Elise noticed Courtney Love and Pamela Anderson in the mix, too. On a lighter note, there was also Gwyneth Paltrow, Nicole Kidman, and Kelly Ripa.

Melissa noticed Elise and came toward her, arms outstretched. Except for her belly, she still was a complete twig, and Elise hoped that she looked as thin and spritelike when *she* was pregnant. She was also glad that her sister would be able to meet Jimmy. She would now have a visual to refer to when she listened to all of Elise's roommate tales. "You must be Jimmy," she said.

And who are you? Elise wanted to ask. Amy Fisher? God, what if

Elise *was* Amy Fisher? She was so naïve, getting involved with that Buttafuoco man. She'd rather be Belle Starr, "Petticoat Terror of the Plains," from the historical Wild West.

She looked at Melissa's back and read in the same childish writing: Melissa Holden. This might be perhaps the best hoax of all. Melissa was herself. "I can't figure out who I am," Melissa said. "I honest to God have no idea." If only she knew how ironic that sounded. "Let's see yours?"

Elise turned around. "That's odd," Melissa muttered. "I wonder why Madison and Kayley picked such strange people. Mom is Lizzie Borden."

Then she looked at Jimmy's back. "This just gets even weirder."

Elise's Aunty Sherry walked up and immediately gave her a huge hug. "So introduce me to your boyfriend."

She had to keep from choking on her champagne. "Actually, this is my *roommate's* boyfriend, Jimmy. His car broke down, and I just brought him along. It's a long story."

"Let's see your back," he said to Aunt Sherry.

"I can't figure out who I am for the life of me," she said as she turned around. "I was thinking maybe Maria Shriver?"

Tammy Faye Baker. "I don't know who any of these people are," Jimmy said. "Are all these people in all those old Alfred Hitchcock movies you like to watch?" He pointed to one of Melissa's friends across the room. "There is one I recognize. Pamela Anderson."

Elise asked her aunt several questions and surmised that she had blonde hair and was in jail for some time. It wasn't for murder, robbery, or extortion of any kind. Her crime was sexual and involved a minor. She was about to ask if she was Mary Kay Letourneau, too, when she noticed Crystal, name tag removed, frantically removing labels from each guest's back, ripping them off as if she were preventing them all from realizing the game hadn't gone according to plan. Her mother looked startled when she was interrupted from conversation and had her name tag peeled off her back like a Band-Aid. "Is the game over?" she asked, slightly disappointed. "I never figured out who I was."

"No. The game has been canceled. There was a mistake, and we're going to do another kind of icebreaker."

Elise scanned the room for her cousins, who were nowhere to be found, and wondered what kind of game they would all be playing now. She saved Crystal the task and had Jimmy remove her name tag. She was indeed Mary Kay Letourneau. Those little devils had given them the same one. Jimmy went to the fridge to help himself to another beer. Apparently he was feeling right at home here. She found her cousins hovering over a cheese platter.

"Looks like your game got called off," she said.

Madison shrugged. "Crystal flipped out when she found out that she was Heidi Fleiss."

"Whatever," Kayley said. "She never said what kind of celebrities she wanted us to use. She just said celebrities." She giggled. "Then we gave you and your boyfriend the same one to see if you guys would ever figure it out."

"He's not my boyfriend."

"He's not?"

"No!"

"I didn't think your parents would be happy if you had a boyfriend like that," Madison said. "He just looks like he would play in a band."

She thought of Max and his tattoos. Even her preteen cousins knew how conservative her parents were.

"All right, everyone!" Crystal clapped her hands together. "If I could get your attention, please!" The room became hushed as all eyes focused on the camp director. "We're going to move into the living room to do an icebreaker, so please grab your drinks and make yourself comfortable."

Jimmy strolled up with a new beer and followed Elise to the living room. She felt her stomach become twisted and painful and knew they were in store for a solid dose of public speaking. She slid into a folding chair in the farthest corner of the room. Jimmy sat down next to her, and she hoped they would somehow be skipped.

"All right," Crystal said once everyone had taken their seats. She looked at the group as if she were Barbara Mandrel, getting ready to serenade them. "Since most of us don't know each other, we're going to go around the room and say our names, how we know Melissa." She spoke slowly and enthusiastically. "And a wish or hope for the baby."

Elise could've sworn she heard a few muffled groans and sensed she wasn't alone in her opinion. At any rate, her mind immediately began to think of a wish or a hope for her unborn niece.

The first person to go was a woman Elise didn't recognize.

"My name is—"

"Stand up," Crystal interrupted. "Just so we can all hear you."

She stood, and Elise noticed that her cheeks looked a little flushed. "My name is Gina Young, and I'm Melissa's husband's assistant." Her eyes nervously darted over the room. Why were they doing this? Couldn't Crystal see that the woman was suffering? Behind her Fox News smile, Elise thought the woman must have a sadistic side. "Um, well, I guess I just wish the baby a lot of happiness and laughter."

Everyone clapped. "Very nice," Crystal said.

Moving on, there were all the obvious wishes like good health, success, good relationship with parents. Someone wished that she had lots of great girlfriends and an *ahh* fell over the room. Once all the easy wishes were used up, Elise wondered what in the world she was going to say.

She felt an elbow in her ribs. She expected to see terror in Jimmy's eyes when she looked at him. However, he hadn't even meant to elbow her and had actually been clapping enthusiastically for the person who had just gone.

She thought of all the things she valued in life, what she was most thankful for. Most of them had been mentioned already. She could say that she wished the child success by twenty-eight so that she didn't have to live with roommates anymore and could decorate her own place. Suddenly she thought of the perfect wish. For as poor as she was, she wouldn't trade her career for anything. That's what she would say. She wished her niece the ambition and creativity to pursue her dreams. She wanted her to be happy in her career. It was golden. She felt relieved that she had come up with something, but her palms were still sweating when it was Jimmy's turn. She was next. Clearly comfortable in the spotlight, he stood without hesitation and smiled at the whole group. "Well, you're probably all wondering what I'm doing here. I mean, how many guys do you see at baby showers?"

He paused to absorb all the amused chuckles that came from the audience. Elise looked around the room. It was like an audience for *Oprah*. They all watched with delight. He had the crowd eating out of his hands. "Anyway, I actually met Melissa today. I'm Elise's roommate's boyfriend, and it's a long story how I got here, but I'm thankful that Elise invited me, and I'm glad to be here with all you ladies." There was a long *ahhhhh* before he continued. "Anyway, I'm a musician, and it's taken a lot of sacrifices to be in this career and do what I love doing. But it's been worth it." Was he using hers? "I'd like to wish the baby courage and creativity and the ambition to pursue her dreams. I hope she does what she loves doing." He practically got a standing ovation. And while the group roared with applause, Elise sat, shell-shocked, wondering how he had read her mind. The bastard. She sat there for a moment, confused, wondering what in God's name she was going to say. Then she felt a tap on her shoulder. It was Jimmy. "It's your turn." The whole room waited.

This part she had rehearsed in her mind a million times for the past twenty minutes. "Well, most of you know who I am. But for those of you who don't know, I'm Elise, Melissa's younger sister." She caught a glimpse of her mother smiling and then locked eyes with

Crystal, who was beaming like Kathy Lee Gifford. Her eyes wandered over the rest of the room before her settling on a large bowl of bean dip. "Anyway, um, I wish that . . . the baby, um, has a real flair for cooking." Dead silence followed. "Because you know, um . . . food is important."

"Well, all right. Thanks Elise," Crystal said. "Moving along."

She slid into her chair and waited for the day to end.

8. Jimmy's Invitation

Elise spent the following day at her computer, editing her book and eating from a box of Wheat Thins that she kept hidden in her bottom desk drawer. She also had licorice and potato chips stashed in there, too. She left her bedroom late afternoon to replenish her water supply and was surprised to find Jimmy away from the TV. He stood in front of his pile of instruments. The phone was tucked in between his chin and ear, and he held one of his guitars in his hands.

He looked agitated, and she wondered what sort of crisis he faced in his couch-potato life. She filled a glass of water and returned to her room. A few minutes later a light tap on her bedroom door interrupted her work. For a moment she thought she had imagined the noise. It had been so soft, and Jimmy never knocked on her door.

"Yes?" she said.

"Elise. It's me, Jimmy."

"Yes, Jimmy. I know it's you. You can open the door."

He poked his head inside like a young child peering into a

strange place for the first time. "Um. Are you busy right now? I need a favor."

She could afford to take a break from her writing but was afraid of what he wanted. A loan. Groceries for the next two weeks. A gift certificate to Ray's Liquor. "What do you need?" she asked.

"I really need a ride to Max's store. It's just right around the corner in North Park. But I've gotta get my guitar fixed. I have a show coming up, and Max said he'd fix it for me for free." Of course it was free.

She grabbed her keys. "Sure. Let's go."

"Thanks, man. You're the coolest."

She stole a few minutes to apply a light coat of lipstick and brush her hair. She also slipped into her favorite pair of jeans. The light wash down the front of them gave the illusion that she had thighs like Sarah Jessica Parker.

"You have the best car in the world," Jimmy said as he made himself comfortable in her convertible. The top wasn't down, but he immediately rolled down his window and perched his elbow in the open frame.

"Are You Gonna Go My Way?" by Lenny Kravitz played on the radio, and he moved his head to the beat of the music. "Did I ever tell you that we opened for this guy?"

"You did?!" Elise couldn't contain her surprise. She'd been a Lenny Kravitz fan since the seventh grade, and a good portion of her youth had been spent imagining herself attending the Grammys with him.

"Yeah. He's a short little guy. I mean tiny. He's probably not much taller than you."

"Really? I'm pretty small."

"I'm serious."

"Was he nice?"

"Yeah, he was a cool cat. I only met him briefly—like maybe a minute. But he seemed nice."

She had a million questions, but Jimmy directed her to park in front of a small store with glass windows. Dozens of guitars lined the windows. It was tucked in between a dry cleaner's and a thrift shop. The sign above the store read, "Max's Axes."

Bells sounded when Jimmy pushed the door open, and a Johnny Cash CD played from the speakers. Max stood behind the counter and didn't glance up when they approached. He messed with some kind of metal device with tiny wires. He looked up only when they stood right in front of the counter.

"This pedal is driving me nuts," he said calmly. He didn't seem to be going nuts. In fact, he seemed quite the opposite. "Kenny from Big Sugar brought it in yesterday, and I just can't figure out what's wrong with it." He set down the pedal and shook Jimmy's hand. "It's good to see you."

Then he turned to Elise, and a smile lifted the corners of his cheeks. "It's great to see you, too. How's the book coming?"

"Great. I still have quite a bit of editing, but it's getting there."

"I look forward to reading it."

"Oh yeah." Jimmy nodded. "That's right. Your book. You're a writer. I think I'll read something of yours while I'm on the road."

Hell would freeze over before Jimmy read anything.

Elise heard a yawn from behind the counter, before a black dog stood up. The dog gazed up at Max before shaking her thick coat. One of her ears stood straight up, while the other lay folded and floppy. Max scratched behind both her ears.

"This is Maggie," he said.

Elise let the dog sniff her hand before scratching her under the chin. The guys began to discuss Jimmy's guitar problems, so Elise took the opportunity to browse around the shop. Maggie followed her, and Elise petted her on top of the head as she looked around.

The walls of Max's store were covered in layers of overlapping flyers and posters of musicians. There were signed posters from bands that she recognized like Blink-182. They were from San Diego. Posters of bands with purple Mohawks and body piercings covered corners of the store. There was a poster of a chick band named Bitch Rocket. The girls wore torn jeans with biker boots and T-shirts with the sleeves ripped off. A couple of the girls had sleeves of tattoos covering their arms, and one had a shaved head. Buried in a far corner of the store she noticed an old flyer, frayed and yellow around the edges. Once black and white, the picture had faded to gray. Her eyes almost wandered right over the flyer until she spotted Max. Much younger, his hair hung to his chin, and he had a full goatee instead of the little soul patch that rested beneath his lip. Though his features looked softer with youth, aging had made him more attractive.

"You guys hungry?" Max asked.

"I could eat," Jimmy said.

She hadn't eaten since lunch and was actually starving. "Yeah, why don't we grab dinner?"

"How 'bout Paesano?" It was Max's suggestion.

They walked from Max's store to the restaurant. It was a warm evening, and Elise removed her hooded sweatshirt.

Aside from their waiter and the cook tossing a pizza crust behind the counter, they were the only customers at Paesano. It wasn't the kind of Italian restaurant where you needed to get dressed up and make a reservation. Rather, it was a place where you could wear jeans and order a pitcher of beer, which was exactly what Jimmy did as soon as they were seated.

"I don't know about you guys, but I want the white pizza," Jimmy said.

"It's all I ever get," Max added.

Elise scanned the menu for this white pizza and found it under the appetizers section. The sauceless pizza actually sounded a little bland with only olive oil, cheese, and garlic. But she trusted their opinions. Jimmy could qualify as a pizza connoisseur, he ate so much of it.

"That sounds good," Elise said, closing her menu.

Max took a swig of his beer, then looked at Elise. "So what's it like living with this idiot?" He smiled. "You ready for him to go on tour?"

She burst into laughter.

"She loves me," Jimmy said. "Don't you?"

Love was a strong word. *Tolerated* was more accurate. However, she felt like being polite and nodded.

"I bet Elise was thrilled when you returned from L.A. Nothing like a deadbeat rocker crashing at your house."

Max had it all figured out, but Elise didn't want to step on any toes. "Jimmy's great. He . . . he always makes me laugh."

Jimmy nodded as he squeezed her knee. "Thanks. Thanks, man. I went to my first baby shower yesterday," he said. "And I gotta say, it was pretty fun. There were games and—"

He was interrupted by the sound of his cell phone. It was Justine. She proceeded to call three times before their food had even arrived. Each time, Jimmy explained to her that he was eating at Paesano and that he would see her after she got off work. It seemed like a clear-cut conversation. However, there was something Justine failed to get, and she continued to call. The fourth time Jimmy's cell phone rang, they all exchanged glances.

"Justine," they said in unison. Sure enough, it was her.

"I already told you!" he barked into the phone. "I'm having dinner with Max and Elise." It was the first time Elise had ever seen him angry. "Fine! I'll eat *again* with you later. You told me you weren't getting home until eight!" He snapped the phone shut and set it on the table. "I'm putting it on vibrate," he mumbled. "This is starting to fuckin' irritate me."

Minutes later their conversation was interrupted by his phone vibrating on the table. He ignored it. But it vibrated again. And again. It wouldn't stop. Elise was tempted to answer for him. *Go away, you freak! He's eating!*

He finally jumped from the table and answered the phone. This time, he took the call outside.

"Now *there* is a woman with a purpose," Max said. "She's really got a leash on him."

Elise had plenty of insight she could add to this conversation, but she didn't know how close Max and Jimmy were. What if Max repeated everything she said? But Max wasn't the gossiping type. *What the hell?* she thought. *Go ahead and share your thoughts.* "Yes. She treats him like her pet."

He shrugged. "Women and bands. I don't know what it is with musicians, but women turn crazy around them."

"You were in a band. Did you make anyone crazy?"

He chuckled. "Probably. And I probably shouldn't have."

"Where are you from originally?"

"Here. I grew up in Carlsbad. Went to Berkeley for a couple of years. Dropped out to play music."

"What were you studying?"

"Political science. What about you? What did you study?"

She told him about her graduate degree in criminal psychology, and how she'd been fascinated with what motivated people to commit crime. "It's why I love writing mysteries so much. I like to use my imagination. However, I don't like living on a mystery set. I feel like I'm going to end up in a real live novel plot if I stay in City Heights for much longer."

"What about living with your brother in Ocean Beach?"

"No. We'd kill each other."

"I have two sisters. I don't think I could live with either one of them. We're all so different."

The pizza arrived around the same time Jimmy returned.

After one bite she decided that white pizza might be her new favorite food. Covered in soft little chunks of garlic, she knew it was a guarantee for terrible breath, but the mozzarella and soft crust melted in her mouth. For as long as she lived in the area, she'd be eating at

Paesano on a regular basis. "This is delicious," she said in between bites. "Why don't all Italian restaurants have this?"

"It's a specialty here at Paesano," Jimmy said. "It's the best."

Between the three of them, they managed to polish off most of the pizza. Stuffed, she still continued to nibble at her third piece. It tasted so delicious, she couldn't help herself.

"Does anyone mind if I take this last piece back for Justine?" Jimmy asked.

"No," Elise groaned, her stomach nearly popping buttons off her jeans. "Take it away."

"It's all yours," Max said.

Jimmy went to the counter for a take-out box.

"I think that may have been the best pizza I've ever had in my life," she said. She folded her hands over her stomach.

He nodded. "Any time you want to stop by the shop, I'm always up for white pizza. I'll go with you. And hey, you guys never called me to put new locks on your doors."

"Well, I'm sure you're busy and have better things to do. I don't want to bother you."

"And they've got me!" Jimmy chimed in. "I won't let anything happen."

That made her feel much better. Jimmy and his huge muscles. He'd probably offer a burglar a beer.

The check arrived, and they all reached for their wallets.

Elise pulled a ten from her purse, enough to cover her share of beer, pizza, and tip.

"Damn," Jimmy muttered. "I only have three bucks. Do you guys think you can cover me? I'll pay you back."

Of course he only had three dollars. If he'd contributed his share, Elise probably would've had a heart attack right there in Paesano. She took pity on him and reached for another ten.

"I got it," Max said. He placed thirty bucks on the little tray, then pushed her ten back toward her.

"Take my ten," she said, shoving it back.

"Oh. And here is my three," Jimmy said weakly as he held on to his money.

"Don't worry about it," Max said "I got it." He began to slide from the booth.

Elise followed him with her cash, but he wouldn't take it. "You buy next time," he said.

As they walked back to his shop, she thought of his offer for her to stop by the shop. Though she'd be dying to see him again soon, she had always been stricken with a shyness around anyone she was romantically interested in. She'd probably spend days entertaining the idea of a luncheon getaway to Paesano with Max. But she knew that day would likely never come. She just hoped Jimmy's tour came soon. They needed new locks.

Justine was watching an interview with Dr. Phil when they returned. He was on *Larry King* taking phone calls from viewers, and for a moment Elise thought it might be beneficial for Justine to call in with a question. *Um, yeah. Hi, Dr. Phil. I'm not a frequent watcher of your show, but my roommate says I should be. I hang pictures of my boyfriend on every free inch of wall space in my apartment. I call him twenty times a day and make him get permission from me before he does anything. I also secretly listen to his voice mail. Is this okay?* His response would be glorious.

It was so smoky in their apartment that Elise thought she should stop, drop, and roll back to her bedroom. Justine's feet were propped on the coffee table, and her arms were crossed over her chest. "Carly called," she said without looking at them.

"I gotta take a shit," Jimmy mumbled beneath his breath before heading to the bathroom. "And it freakin' reeks in here. How can you sit in here like that? At least I crack a window!"

Very interesting, Elise thought. This comment about the air quality coming from Jimmy was slightly hypocritical. Perhaps he and Justine were getting sick of each other.

"So, how was dinner?" Justine asked as soon as he was gone.

"It was great. Jimmy brought you some pizza." She pointed to the box on the counter. "How was work?"

"Boring as ever."

"I told you that you can borrow any of my books to take with you. For when it's slow."

She shrugged. "I don't really like reading." She set the remote control on the couch next to her and reached for a lighthouse from the coffee table.

"So, Max seems really cool. Does his girlfriend ever hang out with you guys?" she asked as nonchalantly as possible.

"Girlfriend? No," she said, examining the latest addition to Jimmy's collection. "As far as I know, he's single."

Luckily, Justine was too busy studying the lighthouse to notice the smile that had crept over Elise's face.

9. The Sound of Music

The only thing Elise heard when she answered the phone were the muffled whimpers. She knew these whimpers well.

"Carly? What's going on?" She pushed her chair away from her desk. "Carly? What's happened?"

"Marcus dumped me," she cried.

"At work?"

"Yes. The coward sent me an e-mail. He said it was just too complicated to be dating a coworker. Then Tracey in human resources told me she heard he went out with the vice president's daughter who works in marketing for drinks over the weekend!" She burst into loud, wailing sobs.

"Oh, C! What an asshole. I'm so sorry. Where are you now?" She could hear the light buzz of traffic whizzing past.

"I took the afternoon off. I told them my cat died and I was still upset about it."

"Your cat died two years ago."

"I know," she sniffed. "So it's not really a lie."

"You can't go home and sit by yourself. Why don't you come over here? Justine has to work until midnight, and Jimmy will be in the studio, so we won't have to deal with either one of them. I'll make—"

She was interrupted by a blaring horn. "MotherFUCKERRRR!" Carly screamed. "Take that, ya fuckin' bastard!!" *Beep! Beeeeep!*

"Carly? Are you there?"

Her voice collapsed again. "Sorry I just had a little road rage. Somebody cut me off, and I gave him the finger."

"Well, anyway. I was saying, why don't you come over and we'll have a girls' night?"

"Can we watch *The Sound of Music*?"

"Of course." It had been their favorite movie to watch together since they were small children. In fact, they'd been so inspired by the movie that they had each sported Julie Andrews bowl-cut hairdos in the third and fourth grade. "Come over whenever you want. I'll get us wine and food, and we'll watch the movie and make a dartboard of Marcus's face. Asshole."

After they said good-bye, Elise decided to take the day off as well. Her best friend didn't get dumped every day. This was an emergency, and she needed supplies for her Heartbreak First-Aid Kit: Junk food. Alcohol. Maybe matches and scissors, depending upon how angry Carly felt, and if she had any pictures or other Marcus memorabilia on her. After showering, she headed to Vons with Bella.

There, she purchased an economy-sized bottle of Chianti, a frozen pizza, a chocolate cream pie, microwave popcorn, and something healthy—a box of low-carb chocolate chip cookies.

She was humming "Climb Every Mountain" as she carried her grocery bags back to the apartment. She owned *The Sound of Music* DVD but rarely watched it without Carly. Once, when she'd had the flu and had been confined to her bed for two solid days, she watched it by herself. But it hadn't been the same without Carly. There was no one to talk to about what a bitch the baroness was and how cool it would've been to have a baby-sitter like Maria von Trapp. And that idiot Rolf, turning them all in, trying to send the von Trapps to a fate worse than death with the Nazis. Hating him with Carly was much more fun than feeling angry alone.

Carly arrived wearing a tear-stained face, a velour sweatsuit, and her white fluffy bedroom slippers. She began to weep again as Elise pulled her into her arms.

Elise forever wondered how Carly always managed to smell good, even on the worst days of her life. If Carly were in a plane crash and stranded in the Amazon for three months, she'd still come out of the jungle smelling like Chanel No. 5.

"I'm so humiliated," she cried.

"Breaking up is the worst. There is just no easy way around it."

"I'm going to be in the gray area for the rest of my life. I'm probably the only twenty-seven-year-old who has never had a real boyfriend."

"You just haven't found the right guy. Would you want to be in the black area with the wrong guy?"

She thought about this. "Yes."

"No you wouldn't." Elise headed for the kitchen. "Here. Have a glass of wine. I got us a chocolate cream pie, too."

Her face lit up. "You did?"

She nodded as she poured the Chianti into two glasses.

Carly sat on the couch holding Bella, stroking the dog while she sniffed back tears. "I love this dog," she whimpered.

"I know. She's the best little therapist. Always there when you're feeling down. She never says anything to make you feel worse, and she doesn't care if you gain a few pounds or are having a bad hair day."

"I miss my cat." She began to cry even more.

They sat on the couch, Bella curled between them, as they drank wine and ate pie straight from the tin with two forks. Carly cried over Marcus, and Elise told her that he would end up overweight, alone, and dining on TV dinners loaded with ingredients that caused heart attacks. This seemed to lift her spirits.

They were ten minutes into the movie when Jimmy came cruising through the front door.

"Hey, ladies," he said. "Adrian had a date tonight, so we got out of practice early."

She imagined thrusting his twelve-pack from his fingers, knocking him unconscious with it, then dragging him to Justine's closet where she'd bind him in guitar strings and gag him with a lighthouse. Irritation surged through her veins as he plopped onto the couch right next to Carly. This was the one time she truly did not want him around. Carly needed a girls' night, dammit. Not an evening of smelling his belches and watching him laugh out loud while Johnny Knoxville and the rest of those lunatics on *Jackass* hosed themselves with poop. There was going to be no *Jackass* tonight. Or *Cribs*, for that matter.

He slid his twelve-pack in between his Converse high-tops and pulled out a cold one. "Holy shit!"

"What?" Elise immediately looked for some kind of broken object resting at his feet.

"*The Sound of Music*! I love this movie!"

"You do?" Carly said.

"Yeah. This is one of the greatest movies ever made."

A true shocker.

"Did you rent this?"

"No. I own it."

"This is a *good* one to own."

Elise waited for him to say he was kidding and ask how much longer the movie was going to be, and when could they watch MTV. Instead, he sat back, propped his feet on the coffee table, and asked if anyone wanted a beer. "Have they gotten to the part where she makes their clothes from the drapes?" he asked before chugging several gulps of Keystone and crushing the empty can like a grape.

"That's coming right up," Carly told him. "I love that part."

"Me, too. It just makes me feel so happy." He was dead serious.

They watched the movie until the von Trapp children raced into Maria's room, petrified of thunder and wearing hideous pajamas. Off the top of her head Maria made up a clever and consoling song, chasing away their fears as she bellowed about kittens and apple strudel in her nightgown.

"Hey, let me show you guys something," Jimmy said as soon as the scene ended.

He got up from the couch and pulled a guitar from his stash of instruments. "This is gonna be good," he said. Upon returning to the couch, he began to strum away. "You guys recognize it?"

"It's a faster version of 'My Favorite Things'!" Elise shouted.

He stopped playing and pointed to her. "You got it. Wait till you hear the rest."

The girls gathered closer to Jimmy, just like the von Trapps inching closer to Maria as she made up lyrics and chords from scratch.

"That is so cool," Carly said.

Jimmy began to sing. "When the dog bites . . ." His voice was much punchier than the movie. Way more rock. But it was cool.

Before long they had emptied a bottle of Chianti, abandoned the movie, and moved to the piano.

"You are sixteen going on seventeen," Elise sang. She had the part of Rolf.

"Innocent and naive . . ." Carly followed.

They went through just about every song from the movie. If Jimmy couldn't remember the notes, they would just find it on the DVD and he'd play it by ear.

The more wine they drank, the louder their voices became. They all sang "How Do You Solve a Problem Like Maria?" in unison at the top of their lungs, Jimmy working up a sweat when he threw all his strength into the climax on the piano.

Eventually they moved from show tunes to pop hits. He was quite the piano man, playing their every request. He could even play "Careless Whispers" by George Michael. This had been Carly's suggestion.

She had a real hang-up with Wham and offered to sing solo. He moved to his electric keyboard for this song.

"It's more eighties this way," he explained. Sure enough, he synthesized a rather impressive version of the song. "You've got a great voice," he said to Carly. "Really." He thought for a moment as he hovered over the keyboard. "I have an idea. Let's sing a duet!"

Carly gasped, "That is such a good idea!"

"How 'bout 'Don't Go Breakin' My Heart' by Elton John? It's one of my favorites to play on the piano." He paused to open another beer. "Elise, you'll play percussion. It'll be wonderful."

She made herself comfortable on the little stool in front of the drum set. "I don't have a clue how to play the drums."

"Well, you're not going to play the drums the entire song. Just when I point to you." He had a whole plan. "God! This is going to be great!" he exclaimed as he rubbed his hands together. Next, he produced sheet music, which he handed to Carly. "Here. You look over the lyrics while I give Elise a quick lesson on the drums over here."

He knelt down next to her and pulled the drumsticks from her hands. "First of all, you're gripping them like they're going to run away. Relax a little."

He wrapped his fingers over her hands and held on to them as he demonstrated precisely how to tap the cymbals to produce a shimmery sound.

"How do you know how to play all these instruments?" Carly asked. "I mean, why don't you play the drums for your band? Why do you play bass?"

"Because. We have an awesome drummer." He shrugged. "And let's face it. I'm the most bitchin' bass player around." He tossed his head back and chugged enough beer to make Keith Richards drunk. What followed was a belch loud enough to send Bella scurrying into Elise's room. "I guess long hours in the studio have forced me to learn how to play all kinds of instruments. I'm not a drummer. I just know enough to get by."

He left his empty beer can on the piano before continuing to teach Elise a little beat. In the simplest form, he showed her exactly where to strike the drumsticks. "Now. You have to count if you're going to be a drummer."

This was the most confusing part. Anything involving numbers had always been difficult for her. She was a writer. She'd never made it past algebra in high school. She never thought she'd get the hang of it. But when she produced something that sounded like a decent drumroll, she felt adrenaline surge through her veins. Now she understood why so many people aspired to be musicians. There was a rush involved with jamming, even if it was just a tiny string of beats. It was like when she read her work and loved the way it had turned out, only drumming was more physical.

While Elise tapped away, Jimmy reached for his cigarettes. Slightly buzzed and feeling confident, she figured this might be a good time to ask him not to smoke there. "Uh, Jimmy? Would you mind smoking outside?" She was about to provide a good reason, but he spoke instead.

"Of course, man! Why didn't you say something sooner?" He went to the front door with a cigarette dangling between his lips. Carly flashed a thumbs-up to Elise while he was on his way out.

"I can't believe how cool he's being," Elise whispered. "I should've asked him to smoke outside ages ago."

"I know. He's so nice!"

When Jimmy returned, he sat down behind the piano. "Okay, let's all practice together. Now Elise, remember you just tap the cymbals until I point to you. All right?"

She nodded, holding the drumsticks. Maybe if she got really good, she could learn to twirl them like Tommy Lee.

When Carly sang Kiki Dee's part, it was almost frightening to listen to the similarity.

They practiced the song several times. In the process they decided Elise would also sing background vocals. He handed her a tambourine. "All right. You're going to shake this when you're not play-ing the drums," he said before sliding back onto his piano bench. "Okay. Let's do it for real this time," Jimmy said, as if they were recording the piece for an album. "One. Two. Three." He nodded his head and then pointed to Elise. She produced one of her best drum-rolls yet. "Yes!" Jimmy yelled, as he continued to play the piano. "Don't go breakin' my heaaaart!" He sounded a lot like Elton John. He nodded in Carly's direction.

"I couldn't if I triiiied."

She grabbed his empty beer can from the top of the piano and pulled it up to her mouth like a microphone. "Baby you're not that kind . . ."

"Elise," he called, and she produced another drumroll. Maybe she was drunk, but she thought they sounded fantastic. She grabbed the tambourine and couldn't help but dance behind the drum set, put-ting as much passion as she could muster into shaking her instrument. "Ewwwheewww!" She sang in the background.

She raised both hands as Carly and Jimmy sang to each other. Wait. They were really singing to each other. Carly leaned into Jimmy, singing to him as if he were the only person in the room. "I won't go breaking your heaarrrrt!"

He moved closer to her, their eyes locking, noses practically touching. "And when I was doooown!"

She shimmied in front of him. And he shimmied back. "Ohhhhh," Carly sang. They had succumbed to their own little duet world, a place that involved teasing facial expressions and adoring gazes. They were better than Sonny and Cher, or Elton and Kiki, for that matter.

Elise was so consumed with filling in the background and watch-ing their performance that she didn't hear the front door open.

When the song ended, Jimmy jumped from the piano, raised his arms in triumph, then grabbed Carly and spun her around. He stopped midspin. A startled look seized his eyes as he slowly returned Carly to the floor.

Elise had no idea how long Justine had been standing there. She was wearing Jimmy's leather jacket, and she hadn't removed her shoes yet. "I could hear you guys from the street."

Elise searched for words to fill the silence. Their apartment had never been this quiet. However, the cold stare in Justine's eyes seemed to speak volumes. "Jimmy was just teaching me how to play the drums because we were all watching *The Sound of Music*. Um, Carly was sad and . . ." Where the hell was she going with this? "She came over so I could cheer her up, and Jimmy ended up making us all happy when he taught us how to do a duet. Wasn't that nice of him?"

She pulled her purse from her shoulder and set it on the coffee table. "Very sweet." Then she headed to her bedroom. "Jimmy, I need to talk to you."

Without making eye contact with them, he followed her, stopping only to grab his twelve-pack from the fridge.

As soon as the bedroom door shut behind him, Carly turned to Elise. "I feel bad," she whispered. "Did we get him in trouble? We were just having *fun*."

Elise was about to respond when they heard Justine yell. Her words weren't decipherable, and Jimmy's voice was too low for the girls to make out his response. "I don't care if she's pissed," Elise whispered. "She needs to get a grip. It's not like we were having a threesome. We were making a duet."

"I feel bad, though. It probably looked so much worse than it really was."

"Whatever. She'll get over it. She's not his keeper." But then Elise remembered the way she spoke to him like an animal and practically led him around on a leash. "Well, actually, she *is* his keeper. The zookeeper."

Disappointed that the singing was over, the girls heated the frozen pizza. To avoid any further disturbances from the zoo, they ate their midnight snack on Elise's bed. They giggled and chatted about the time they had karaoked at a twenty-four-hour karaoke bar in Tucson when Carly had come to visit Elise during grad school. While Carly munched on a piece of pizza, Elise heard her humming "A Few of My Favorite Things." She hadn't mentioned Marcus in hours, as if she'd forgotten the state of misery she'd been in when she arrived. For the first time, Elise was thankful for Jimmy.

10. Lights Out

A cold chill hung in their apartment for several days following the duet. There was no more Cheechersing. Justine now only referred to Jimmy as "him." There were other changes, too. Jimmy was quiet and indifferent when he found out there was a *Cribs* marathon on MTV or a special on Newcastle at Ray's Liquor. Furthermore, a ruthless sense of humor had been released from Justine. Elise was all for dark humor but found it odd when Justine laughed with enthusiasm after Glorious D tripped in front of their doorstep and ripped a hole in his pants. Instead of offering a Band-Aid, she stood over him, pointing and shrieking with delight at how badly he'd "biffed."

She also burst into laughter when an old man hobbled across their parking lot, holding a three-legged dog, and found it especially humorous when a contestant tripped in the Miss USA pageant on television. However, her biggest outburst occurred one day when Elise returned from having lunch with Carly. Justine had begun laughing the moment Elise had said hello.

"What?" Elise asked with a large smile and a hint of curiosity. She wanted to be let in on the joke.

Justine clutched her stomach and laughed even harder. Her laughter was contagious, and Elise giggled, too. "What? What is it?"

"You have lettuce stuck in your teeth!"

Jimmy zoomed in to see.

Wasn't she aware of the universal hand gesture of subtly scratching your tooth? That was usually enough to inform someone.

After the lettuce incident Elise kept her distance. Luckily, Stan had stopped by a couple times to hang out with her, so she wasn't left entirely by herself with them.

She decided to call her brother to see if he wanted to meet for lunch, and was disappointed when she reached his voice mail. She remembered that he was strapped for cash after paying off the damage to the U-Move and had been taking on extra shifts at the Wild Animal Park. Elise could hear the rough and raunchy voice of a female rapper. "Lick me . . . lick it good . . . lick it like you care." It was, after all, lunchtime. She grabbed her keys from her desk.

Jimmy wasn't around when Elise entered the living room. It was Justine's day off, so perhaps they'd actually peeled themselves from the couch. Just as she started to think by some miracle she had the apartment to herself, Justine emerged from her bedroom, holding a box of Marlboro Reds and a lighter.

"Hey," she said as she prepared to light a smoke. Apparently, her little talk with Jimmy about smoking outside had only applied to him. It had also only seemed to apply to him on that particular evening, because she suspected that he was still smoking in the house as well.

She was tired of going to lunch with Carly or running errands and catching nauseating whiffs of cigarettes, thinking how gross it was and then realizing moments later that the smell was actually coming from her. Every article of her wardrobe had taken an ashy scent, and Bella smelled as if she were one of the Cheechers's ashtrays. Confronting Justine about the smoking would be like ripping off a Band-Aid. Though painful, she needed to do it. Quickly.

Should she say something now? It might be the perfect opportunity, while she was smoking. She could just casually bring it up. She took a deep breath and braced herself. "Um, Justine." Her voice was low and weak when she spoke. "Would you mind, um . . . Would you mind smoking outside? It's just that, well . . ." For a moment Elise thought that Justine might light her instead of the cigarette. ". . . And it makes my eyes water, and I just think it might be better . . . maybe it would be better if you smoked outside or just in your room with the door closed and your window open on days when there is a manhunt." She still held the lighter midair, frozen. "Well, and Bella is allergic to it, too." Where this had come from, she had no idea.

She shoved the lighter in her jeans pocket. "Bella is allergic to it? Why didn't you say something?" She touched Elise's arm. "No wonder she's been hiding under the couch lately. I'm sorry, sweetie. Of course I'll smoke outside. From now on." She turned and headed for the front door, her auburn mane swishing across her back.

A small sense of relief came from this triumph. Now, if she could just avoid getting mugged, this might not be such a bad place to live. While grabbing her keys and wallet, she considered Max's offer to join him at Paesano. He'd said to stop by the shop anytime. But what if she stopped by and he was going to lunch with another girl? Only her imagination could explain how awkward that would be. Or what if he had only told her to stop by, just to be nice? What if she interrupted his work?

Elise could hear Glorious D outside. "Cuz she's smokin'. Smokin' outside. Take it outside."

She had the courage to confront Justine about the smoking, but yet she couldn't find the guts to spontaneously drop by Max's shop. She'd always been a wimp when it came to the male species. This was probably why she could count on just a few fingers the number of men she had slept with. Carly was much more brazen than Elise and probably would've stopped by Max's store only a couple of days after he'd made the offer. They probably would've had lunch and sex by now. However, the mere idea of walking in his store unannounced made her palms sticky.

Glorious D was still singing to Justine when Elise left for lunch.

"The smell. It's like hell, she say. No it ain't okay. Take it outside." Elise wished he didn't have to rub it in so much. Also, she felt a nip of guilt for making Justine smoke outside.

"Do you guys want to go to Mama's with me?" Elise asked.

Justine shook her head. "No, thanks. I have a lot to do today." She grinned. "I need to get one of Jimmy's little gifts ready for him. I still have fifteen lighthouses left to give him before I get to the final one."

"I just ate," Glorious D said. "Or else I'd go wit you."

"All right. I'll see you later."

On the way to the restaurant she thought about Max again. She could always use Stan as a resource. He could set something up for them to all hang out. However, being her older brother, he'd been known to turn weird and protective and had never let her become involved with any of his friends when they were growing up. This was mostly due to the fact that he knew what they were all capable of. However, he seemed to like Max and think highly of him. But there was also the risk that Stan might do something to embarrass her. She decided it was probably best to leave him out of the plan.

As she neared Max's street, her heart began to race. Should she drop in? Yes? No? Yes? At the last second she slammed on the brakes and screeched down his street. As she approached his shop, she debated speeding past and forgetting the whole thing. Eventually she'd see him again, and they could make official plans to go to Paesano then. But who knew when she would see him again? She was tired of waiting for Jimmy to ask her for a ride to his shop or eavesdropping on all his conversations to see if he mentioned Max. It was time she took matters into her own hands.

She pulled up to the curb. There was no turning back now. He'd probably seen her from the window. As she turned off the ignition, she went over what she would say in her mind. *Hi, Max. I was just taking a break from the book. Thinking of heading to Paesano by myself, and then I remembered that you said to stop by if I was ever going. So I thought you might want to come along.* No. Too much explaining. He'd definitely know she had rehearsed. *Hey, Max. Just heading to Paesano for white pizza. Want to come?* That was cooler and more casual, but it would be calmly getting those words out that would be hard. She'd sweat and probably stumble over a syllable or two, and end up saying something completely different.

As she exited the car, she realized there was no turning back now. Her eyes wandered over his shop window and came to a screeching halt on his front door. Closed? His shop was closed—lights off, doors locked, and a sign that said he'd be back later. Her nerves stumbled over a tumultuous path of relief and disappointment. She had mentally prepared herself for this moment. And now she'd go to lunch alone before heading home to a life of daydreaming and wondering when Jimmy would need his guitar fixed again. Who knew when and if that would ever happen? Possibly never. Perhaps she should leave him a note, casually offering a rain check. It was totally against that rules book and very forward, but she couldn't sit around for the rest of her life, wondering. She found a Nordstrom receipt in her purse and wrote on the back of it.

Hey Max,

Stopped by to see if you were up for white pizza. Guess we'll have to take a rain check. See you soon.

Elise

For a moment she held the pen midair, wondering if she should write her phone number on there. Too desperate, she decided. If he wanted to find her, he knew where she lived. She stuffed the note under the door and drove to Mama's for lunch alone.

The Lebanese restaurant was crowded when she arrived. Mama's was truly a hole in the wall. There was no indoor seating or friendly waitresses that told you to take a seat wherever you wanted. Instead, there was a walk-up window for placing orders and a tiny patio that offered a few beat-up picnic tables. Mama's was a diamond in the rough—a wonderful discovery—that attracted its regular patrons through word of mouth. People didn't drive past Mama's and stop because of its appealing décor. In fact, it was a place most people drove past daily and had no idea what they were missing. She ordered her falafel in saj bread to go and took the same path home.

While driving, she pulled out her lunch. As she stuffed her face she didn't think much of the two police cars parked in front of her apartment complex. After all, seeing the black-and-white vehicles, their lights spraying fruit-juice-colored beams over their neighborhood, was just another part of the scenery in City Heights. She pulled into her parking place, then brushed a few crumbs of falafel from her jeans. When she looked up, adrenaline shot through her veins. Her front door was wide open. Two police officers stood in her foyer.

She jumped from the car and ran up the path that led to their apartment. Something had happened to Justine. And it was Elise's fault for making her smoke outside. Her eyes scanned the lot for Glorious D. She wanted to see a familiar face, someone to tell her what happened before the police did. She needed to be prepared.

Out of breath, she darted toward the front door. She should've just endured the smoke. Bought an air humidifier. She could've found a new apartment or roommate.

Two officers and Justine stood near the couch. They stopped speaking when Elise entered and eyed her as if she had just interrupted something very important. Justine's thin arms were folded over her chest, and her cheeks were tear-streaked. She clutched a snotty-looking Kleenex.

"Oh my God. What's happened?" Elise said, throwing her arms around her roommate.

In between sobs, Justine managed to choke out a few muffled words. "It's . . . ahuuuh ahuuuuhhhh ahuuh. Awwful."

"Just take your time." Elise rubbed her shoulders. "Were you hurt?"

"No," she squeaked. Taking a deep breath, she blotted her eyes. "Oh, it's the worst thing ever. Just awful."

"Is it Jimmy?" The suspense was killing her.

"It's the lighthouses," she said before bursting into a full-blown crying frenzy, choking on hiccupping cries. "They're all gone! They've been stolen!"

Elise stopped rubbing her shoulders for a moment. Did she just say the lighthouses had been stolen? Elise understood disappointment. In college, her entire collection of eighty CDs had been ripped off from her bug. She'd been so angry that she wanted to hunt down the thief himself and rub honey all over his body before rolling him over a bed of bee-infested ice plant. But getting the police involved had never crossed her mind. Didn't they have murderers to track down?

"Okay," Elise said, still rubbing her shoulders. She suddenly felt conscious of the police watching them and wondered what they must think. Were they relieved that they didn't have to deal with regular City Heights crime—domestic violence, gang warfare? Or did they think Justine was insane? Elise hoped the police weren't forming the same opinion about her. She didn't own any lighthouses, not a single one. She looked at the coffee table and was confused when she noticed several ceramic lighthouses still decorating their living room.

Then she remembered Justine had a whole other box of them in their storage space outside.

"When were they stolen?" Elise asked.

"Sometime last night," she said in between sobs. "Someone cut the lock on our storage space and took the whole box of lighthouses. There was even an old VCR and some jumper cables in there, and they didn't touch those. Just the lighthouses."

Elise could've sworn she saw one of the officers holding back laughter from the corner of her eye. When she looked at him, the smirk fell from beneath his mustache and his features immediately turned stoic. "They were probably after something they could sell to get money for drugs," he said. "Maybe someone walked up on them and they grabbed the box and ran. Or maybe it was all they could carry, and they thought there was something more valuable in there."

"They are valuable," Justine hissed. "Sen-ti-ment-al value."

"I understand," the officer said. The officers asked a couple of more questions and filled out some stuff on their clipboards before saying they had another call to respond to.

"Aren't you going to take fingerprints?" Justine asked, following them to the door.

"That would require calling in our forensic team, which is usually only done if there has been grand theft or a homicide."

"But this *is* grand theft."

"Well, you estimated the worth to be about . . ." He flipped through a small notebook. "One hundred and twenty dollars. Grand theft is typically thousands of dollars."

"So, you're not going to do *anything*?"

"We took a report. And if it happens again, call us. In the meantime, get a better lock for your storage space."

Elise imagined a crusty drug addict who, for some reason, had the same physique and hairdo as Jimmy. She imagined the pleasure this person must've felt after busting into the storage space and finding a box filled with what they assumed to be the kind of valuables their crack dealer would gladly swap for drugs. This smelly individual had probably run for blocks, believing he held a treasure large enough to keep him satisfied for weeks. She could only imagine the disappointment the crackhead must've endured after he opened the box and found a bunch of trinkets worth less than a bag of chips on the black market.

"Jimmy will never even get to see the final one. The one that played 'You Light Up My Life.' This is so horrible."

Elise put her arm around Justine's shoulders and told her about the time all her CDs were stolen. "I can totally understand your feelings of disappointment. All of my favorite CDs were gone. Fleetwood Mac, Lenny Kravitz. All my Ramones CDs. Over a thousand dollars' worth of music."

Justine cried even harder. "It's not the same," she said. "CDs don't have the same kind of sentimental value. You can replace those. This was a gift with *special* meaning." Justine blotted her eyes and looked up at Elise. "So, does Carly have a boyfriend?"

What did this have to do with anything? "No. She just broke it off with someone. She's single."

"Hmmm. So, she's on the rebound then?"

If she thought for a minute that Carly was interested in Jimmy, she was even more insane than Elise had thought. One, Carly would never go for Jimmy. An unemployed couch potato, aspiring rock star. Not a chance. Not only were they night and day, but Jimmy wasn't even close to her type.

"No. She's not on the rebound, Justine. She doesn't need to have a man in her life every minute. She's fine by herself." *Unlike you.*

11. Special Mail

Several days later Elise tortured herself with images of Max opening the front door of his shop, her Nordstrom receipt getting blown by a gust of air and carried to a hidden location behind a guitar, lost until the next time he cleaned the store. Ten years from now he'd rearrange his guitars and find a shriveled receipt covered with two inches of dust and enough dog hair to stuff a small pillow. He'd read her faded writing while one of his children played with a vintage Les Paul behind him, and he'd rack his mind wondering who the hell Elise was.

She checked her e-mail and was pleased to see one from her agent's assistant. Perhaps something was brewing on the book front.

Hi Elise,

I've tried to call you twice this week. Maybe you're out of town? I left a message with your roommate. Anyway, maybe he forgot.

Well, exciting news here. Jennifer Bloom has signed on

to represent the film rights for your book. She absolutely loves it, and she is one of the top film agents in Los Angeles, so you're in great hands. I'll keep you posted when we know more. Hope all is well!

Best,
Carissa

She popped from her chair. "Oh my God," she breathed. This was news. She called her parents first but made them promise not to tell a soul. "Everything is so iffy in this industry. Just because I got signed on with a film agent doesn't mean anything yet. It just means that a very well-connected person is going to try to sell the movie rights. So just try to keep it hush-hush, okay?"

"Of course," her mother said.

"Our lips are sealed," Hal chimed in from the speakerphone.

"I mean, you can tell Melissa and Brice, but just don't go spreading the word everywhere. I don't want to jinx anything."

"We won't say anything."

She called Stan next, but he didn't answer his cell phone. Unable to contain her excitement, she left the news on his voice mail, emphasizing that it was top secret. She dialed Carly next.

"Oh my God! What if Julia Roberts is in it? Can I come to the premiere?" She yelped. "This is great!"

She repeated the same secrecy lecture she had given her parents. "Nothing is ever certain in this business, and besides, I don't want to have to explain to fifty million people that nothing ever happened with it if the movie rights aren't sold. I'd rather just keep it between my close friends."

"I know. Have I ever repeated anything you've told me?"

"No. You haven't."

"But we can at least discuss the cast? Does that jinx it?"

"Probably. But it's just too hard to resist. So, I'm thinking Julia or Sandra Bullock."

"Yes!"

Carly threw out a few more ideas before her boss neared her cubicle, and she had to go.

After she hung up, she went to the kitchen for a cup of green tea and found Justine curled beneath a blanket on the couch, watching *Cribs* by herself. Elise decided not to tell her roommates about the latest twist in her career but wondered if they would notice the perma grin that had now taken control of her face. She was about to ask where Jimmy was when he came bursting through the front door with a huge smile on his face. "Guess what? I got a job!"

"You did?" Justine sat up.

"What about your tour?" Elise asked.

"It's just a temporary job. Just a couple of days." He went straight for the fridge, pulled a cold one out, and popped the cap off. It was one o'clock in the afternoon. "I met this guy today at Max's store." Now he had her attention. "This dude has a face-painting business. We're going to paint faces at the Del Mar Fair. It's the last week of the fair, so they're expecting a huge turnout."

Justine released a condescending laugh. "You? Paint faces?"

"Yeah." He smiled. "Me."

"That's great, Jimmy," Elise said. *But back to the part about Max's store.* "So how did you say you met this guy again?"

"Oh. He is a friend of Max's. Hanging out at the—"

"How much do you get paid?" Justine rudely interrupted.

"He charges between five and ten dollars per face, and I make half of whatever we make for the whole day. He said I could probably make about two hundred dollars."

"I didn't know you were such an artist." Justine smirked.

"Well, the guy, Leonard, that's his name, has stencils, and all I do is airbrush inside the stencils. Some people might want a rainbow.

Others might want their favorite football team. He said they do a lot of butterflies. Stuff like that."

"Maybe somebody will want Potter painted on their face. The band logo." Justine laughed. "Or maybe they'll want an autograph of the big famous San Diego bass player on their cheek." Her wicked tone was masked with a condescending playfulness.

Elise wondered why she was being so mean. He was finally doing *something*. Contributing.

Jimmy released a little chuckle. "Maybe. Well, I gotta go get ready for the fair."

He went into Justine's bedroom, and as soon as he was gone, she turned to Elise. "What an asshole."

"Uh . . . why?"

Justine stormed to the counter and grabbed her cigarettes. "Come outside with me while I smoke. I need to talk to you."

As soon as the front door was closed, Justine began to fume, literally. Elise watched as she took several furious drags of her cigarette. "He's leaving soon for his tour," she exclaimed. "He is going to be gone for over a month! We aren't going to see each other for over *thirty-five* days. See?" She pulled a folded piece of paper from her back pocket.

It was a handmade calendar of Jimmy's tour. Not only had she taken the time to write each date, city, and venue in calligraphy on a perfectly aligned grid, but she'd also gone the extra mile and glued a different picture of his face to every single day. "I made one for him, too. Only it has my face on every day. We're keeping them in our back pockets at all times."

It was one of those odd occasions in Elise's life when she was truly at a loss for words.

"Anyway, I can't believe that asshole got a job."

She looked at Elise as if she were waiting for her to tell her what a prick Jimmy was for getting off the couch and earning a living.

"That means that three out of his five remaining nights that he is here we won't be spending together."

"Well, don't you get tired of paying his way all the time?"

"No," she snapped. "Why would I? I love him, and when he hits it big, he can pay me back."

"Okay."

She looked at Elise, terrified. "What's the Del Mar Fair like?" she whispered. "I've never been."

"Well, there are a lot of animals. And rides. Giant cheese sticks and cinnamon rolls. Haven't you ever been to a fair?"

"No. Are there girls there?"

"No. Fairs are only for men. Of course there are girls. Justine, there are girls everywhere."

"I know. But he'll be touching their faces. And you know how girls are. Once they find out who he is, they'll want more than a face-painting."

Reality check. Even if they did, by some far-fetched chance, find out he was in Potter, weren't they going to wonder what he was doing painting faces? It's not like he played bass for Aerosmith. He was painting faces for a living!

"Justine, he loves you. You guys have your Cheechers names."

"He can cheech off."

"What are you going to do when he goes on tour? There are going to be girls around him all the time."

"Well, I already told him he has to call me at least four times a day."

That should be a blast for him.

Glorious D strolled up. "Howz the ladies doin' today?"

"Fine," Justine said. Then she lowered her voice. "Jimmy just got a job painting faces. At The Del Mar Fair."

"No shit?"

"What's the fair like, Glorious D?"

"You know. There's rides and a pettin' zoo. And, damn. I don't know. It's a fair. Hey, you guys want a knockoff bag? My friend jus' got a whole truckload. They look real good. Prada. Gucci. Kim Spade."

Justine threw her head back and howled laughter. "It's *Kate* Spade, you moron."

"Kim Spade, Kate Spade. What difference does it make? It's a nice price." He turned his gaze to Elise. "And you could use a new bag. That one you carry looks real fake."

As far as she knew, her bag wasn't a knockoff of anything. She'd bought it for fifteen dollars at a mall kiosk in Tucson. "Thanks, Glorious D. I'll keep those bags in mind."

Jimmy was whistling when he came outside. His hair was wet, and he had gotten dressed up for the job, changing into a new T-shirt. He held a white envelope in his hand. "All right. I'm on my way. Oh, I almost forgot." He lifted the envelope and started to hand it to Elise. Her heart lurched. Had Max sent a note for her with Jimmy? It was sort of juvenile, yet also sort of romantic. The thought of him being romantic made him sexier.

"This was taped to the door," he said.

"Really?" Had Max stopped by and not bothered to knock?

"It was addressed to you and Justine."

"What is it?" Justine asked before throwing her lit cigarette butt into a dry hedge next to their apartment.

Elise felt her heart sink. The note wasn't from Max, and was likely some neighbor complaining about the sound of Jimmy's piano.

He shrugged. "I don't know who it's from. I was going to open it, but it wasn't addressed to me. But, hey, I gotta run. Have fun tonight."

As soon as he was gone, Elise opened the envelope. She pulled out a pink slip, and before she even had a chance to read it, Glorious D spoke up.

"Holy shit, man. You guys been evicted."

12. The Hunt Begins

They had thirty days to pack up and get out. In college, the word *eviction* had been associated with raging parties and excessive complaints from lame neighbors. Back then, eviction had signified the end of an era. The end of keg stands and live music.

However, their landlord wasn't kicking them out because he'd reached the end of his rope. The owner wanted to sell, cash in, and profit from the soaring California real estate. For the first time in Elise's life she actually felt warm when hearing the word *eviction*. It would force her to leave City Heights.

The afternoon after they learned of their eviction, Elise found Justine and Jimmy in the kitchen, making scrambled eggs that were brown. Elise tried to ignore the turquoise and purple guitar airbrushed on his cheek.

"So," he said. "I picked up the paper this morning at Ray's, and I think we better get looking soon. There are a lot of good ads in there for the City Heights, North Park area."

As he slid the classifieds toward Elise, she felt a pang of guilt. They expected her to move with them, to continue as their roommate? She figured they would ask what her plans were and she could politely bow out, using the excuse that she really wanted to live by the beach. They, of course, wouldn't be able to afford to relocate with her and would wish her well. "Oh," Elise said. "Um, well . . . I don't know if I want to stay in this area."

They both stopped and looked at her as if she had just told them they had bad hair.

"Oh," Jimmy said.

"You're not going to live with us?" Justine asked.

She suddenly felt an overwhelming sense of guilt. Maybe she should stay with them. Even though they made her want to kick the piano with annoyance on a regular basis, they weren't mean people.

On the other hand, what was she thinking? They drove her nuts, and Jimmy didn't even pay rent! They probably only wanted her around to cover the other half of the apartment for them.

"It's just that I've always wanted to live by the beach, and Carly's lease might be ending soon. We might look for a place together."

They nodded in unison. The excuse about Carly was a lie, but this seemed to make them feel better. "Well, you'll have fun living with Carly," Justine said. "But I'm sooo sad you're not going to be my roomie anymore."

"Man, this eviction sucks," Jimmy said as he picked up Bella and kissed her on the top of her head.

It didn't take them long to find a place. That afternoon, Justine signed a lease for a studio in City Heights. Elise could've also found a studio in City Heights, but she'd been telling the truth about living at the beach.

She spent her afternoon scouring every kind of classified ad for roommates. After dozens of phone calls she'd heard the same things over and over again.

"Sorry. Our landlord doesn't accept pets."

"Oh, you're a little late. I just found a new roommate."

"Rent is fourteen hundred a piece."

The final call was to a two-bedroom house in North Park. The girl on the answering machine identified herself as Jules. She spoke with an upbeat southern accent and promised to call back as soon as she got the message.

She had just hung up the phone when it rang. She glanced at the caller ID and was surprised to see Carly. Elise had called her last night to tell her about the eviction, and she hadn't answered. She had been hard to find lately, and Elise was surprised that she had called back so soon.

"Okay, so who's the guy, and why haven't you told me about him?" Elise asked.

Carly laughed. "What? There is no guy."

"You've been missing in action lately, and I can tell by the lilt in your voice that someone is making you happy."

"No, seriously. I just got assigned a great project at work. If I can impress my boss enough, I might just get the raise I've been waiting for."

"Oh, that's great! Why didn't you say something before? I've been wondering what's been going on."

"Well, you know. I guess I just didn't want to jinx anything. So anyway, what's going on with you?"

"I've been evicted. Max gave me the cold shoulder, and I can't find a new roommate," Elise said happily.

"Okay, start with the eviction."

Elise told her about her new shot at freedom.

"I wish I hadn't signed that stupid lease. You and I could be looking for a place right now," Carly said. "But I'll spread the word around the office that you're looking for a roommate. Now tell me about Max."

"It's no big deal, really. I just dropped by his store the other day, and he wasn't around, so I left him a note, which I know I probably shouldn't have done. It's so, I don't know . . . And now he hasn't made any effort to contact me, and I'm feeling really lame about the whole thing."

"Oh get over it. This isn't nineteen fifty-two anymore. Women can make the first move, and furthermore, stop worrying about your image. Everyone knows you're cute and talented and not desperate. Forget your ego already. Did you leave your number?"

"No."

"Well, what do you expect?"

"He knows where I live. He can make a little effort, too. And I didn't want to seem too forward like Brooke who offered everything but her social security number that night in Ocean Beach. I just thought that was kind of obnoxious."

"She *was* obnoxious. But it's about time you made a move with him. You can't sit around wondering forever, and I'm proud of you for leaving a note. But next time please leave a way to get in touch if you ever want to make it out of the gray phase."

Carly was making her feel better. However, Carly was the type to leave notes and pursue someone. She had sex way before Elise had in high school, actually at the young age of fourteen. Elise had saved herself until college with her first serious boyfriend, Tim. Carly had also never had a serious boyfriend; rather a series of sex partners who never made it to the point of meeting Mom and Dad.

Elise hated the gray phase, the hunt. There was such a fine line between making an ass out of yourself and making the first move.

"Well, do you want to meet for drinks tonight or something?" Elise asked.

Carly paused. "Um, well, I should probably work on this project, but sometime soon."

After they said good-bye, Elise wished for roommates who were single and wanted to have fun. Without Carly, she really had no single girlfriends. She decided to grab lunch and a copy of the *Reader* so she could scour the classifieds. She drove to Mama's, grabbed her falafel, then stopped for the *Reader* at a liquor store on the way back.

"Did anyone call?" she asked Jimmy. If she didn't ask, she'd never find out.

"Uh . . . let me think. Yes! I wrote it down. Jules called."

He handed her a piece of paper with "Jewels" scrawled across it and a phone number. "She told me to spell her name that way, just like the diamonds or emeralds."

"She did?"

"Yeah."

Elise quickly ate her falafel before calling the little gem back.

A bright southern accent greeted her. "Hi there!"

"Hi, Jewels. This is Elise Sawyer. I'm calling about the ad."

"Yes, sweetheart. Of course! Tell me a little about yourself."

They exchanged information about one another as if they were going on a blind date. Jewels worked in sales and was looking for a clean, quiet roommate. Her house was "darlin'," and she honored privacy and personal space. She struck Elise as a younger version of Dolly Parton. But Dolly Parton was kind of cool and probably a real blast to hang out with.

"Well, listen, honey, why don't you get your sweet little self over here this afternoon."

"Sounds great."

A few hours later she left the barriers of the ghetto and headed into North Park. When she turned down the final street listed on the directions, she felt the same kind of excitement involved with stumbling upon a blowout sale at her favorite bookstore. Lined with adorable Craftsman-style houses and pert little picket fences, the whole block looked like the type of neighborhood where Girl Scouts could safely sell Thin Mints and neighbors exchanged gardening tips. She could already picture herself slipping on a pair of dainty gloves and tending a rosebush.

Unlike City Heights, this neighborhood didn't look as if it had been hosed in paint thinner. She slowed down in front of a cozy white cottage with a spray of colorful roses bordering its emerald lawn. She studied the street address, just to make sure she was in the right place. After she was positive this wasn't some cruel joke played by Mapquest to mislead her, she pulled up the parking brake.

The sweet scent of orange blossoms followed her all the way to the front door. She took a deep breath and silently asked God to make Jewels as cool as the house. If all went well, Elise would soon fall asleep to the lullaby of sprinklers softly raining over the landscape instead of sporadic gunshots and bloodcurdling screams. *God, let Jewels be cool.*

"Coming!" A voice called from inside.

A perky brunette with a smile as big as Alabama and purple eye shadow opened the front door. She had a pert little nose and was one of the few people who matched Elise in size.

"Hi! You must be Elise!" she said in her southern drawl.

"It's a pleasure to meet you." Elise extended her hand.

She took Elise's hand into both of hers and held it for a little longer than Elise liked to shake. "It's a lovely pleasure to meet you, Elise." Her lips were so glossy that Elise imagined them serving as glue traps for small flying insects. "You come right on inside here, and I'll getcha a drink and give you a tour of the place. It'll be just wonderful. Are you hungry? I know it's getting close to suppertime."

"Oh no. I'm fine. Thanks." Her southern hospitality was charming, and Elise found herself sort of wishing for a southern accent so she could sound as interesting and warm. She'd be the life of the party.

They stepped into a pink, lacy, rosy, country, baskety land. The house was a small palace of wicker furniture and paintings that featured barns and quilty things drying from clotheslines. She half expected Jewels to pull an apple pie from the oven and offer her a tall glass of lemonade, which would've actually been nice. In fact, she could get used to living here, even if Jewels seemed a little high strung and wore more makeup than a dancer at Cheetah's.

"Now. What would you like to drink, missy?" She put her hands on her hips.

"Oh, nothing. Really, I'm fine."

"You sure?"

"Yeah. I'm fine. I don't want to trouble you."

"Oh c'mon. Have something. It's a hot day. You must want *something*. A Coke? Water? I make great lemonade."

"It's okay." Elise was really anxious to see the place.

"All right. Suit yourself."

"So, you're a writer?" she said as she led her down a hallway adorned with a gallery of picket fence and patchwork paintings.

"Yes. And you never told me what field of sales you were in when we spoke on the phone."

"Well, I work out of the house, too! I actually sell a wonderful line of makeup called 'Glow.' Have you ever heard of it?"

She hadn't but didn't want to hurt Jewels's feelings. "I think so."

"Well, it's *the best* there is. And I mean *the best*. The only other place you can get it besides a Glow Girl, like me, is on QVC. And let me tell you, you don't want to get it there. The prices are marked up, and they won't give you a free consultation. I can get you a deal you won't be able to believe on a whole entire line of products. I can match your skin tones and tell you what season you are. It'll be great." She pushed open a door. "Now. Here is where you would be living." Elise looked at a tiny bedroom with a window peering into the front yard. It was minuscule but had hardwood floors and a cute bookshelf built into the wall.

When she turned around, Jewels was watching her with a vacant look in her eyes. But in a split second, a smile snapped onto her face and she clapped her hands together. "Let's show ya the rest!"

They looked at a tiny bathroom and Jewels's bedroom, both covered with fluffy pink things. While walking back to the yard, the phone rang.

"Let me grab that! You show yourself to the back, and I'll meet you out there."

Elise let herself out a sliding door and into a small yard with a cobblestone path and a small, perfectly trimmed square of green lawn. Perfect for Bella.

"Well, whatdaya think?"

The place was the Ritz-Carlton compared to her current living situation. But there was something odd about Jewels. However, Jewels had a strange way of looking at her, as if she were trying to figure her out. "The place is really cute."

"Well, c'mon inside. We can sit down and talk a little bit more about the place."

After Elise sat down on the couch she noticed it. A square, patent, pink case with shiny little snaps and the *Glow* logo written across the side of it. A small tag dangled from the case, which read, "Jewels Anderson, four-star consultant and master of makeup artistry."

That's when she knew she should get up and run for her life. Clutch her purse to her chest and claim she had a contagious form of diarrhea. If she didn't come up with an excuse to get out of there quick, she was going to be sucked into the clutches of relentlessly high-pressured makeup sales from Jewels. Then she remembered that she'd already mentioned she was free for the rest of the afternoon. What the hell had she been thinking?

"So, do you think you'd be interested in moving in?" Jewels asked.

"Umm . . . well, I actually have another place to look at on my list." It was a bold-faced lie, but she really didn't know if she wanted to move in. She needed to think about it, get to know Jewels a little more. "A friend of a friend. I promised I'd stop by. So, I'll have to wait to give you an answer."

"That's fine. I know this isn't a decision that you can rush into." Jewels told her a little more about the technicalities of the lease, and that utilities were included in the rent. Elise had foolishly begun to think she'd make it out of there without having to look at a single Glow product when Jewels stealthily crept in, as smooth and skilled as any assault at a department store makeup counter. "When I was on the phone just a minute ago I was just thinking about your lovely hazel eyes, and this new line of eye shadow we just got in. I haven't tested it on anyone yet, and I thought well . . . since you're here, it would really help me to get an idea of what this would look like on a pretty face. You have such lovely skin tones. I can only imagine it would look perfect. Do you have just a second for me to test it out? I'll give you a free sample of the shadow?"

Come up with an excuse. Now.

"Um . . . er . . ." She listened to little snaps unclasp, like a nurse peeling the protective wrap off a fresh syringe.

"The color is called Lava Green. Don't you just love that?"

"Well, I never really wear eye shadow, actually. I'm not big on makeup. Just a light amount of lipstick, and mascara."

"That's it?" She began to pick through her box, pulling out tubes and vials. "Gosh, well this is going to be a real blast for you then. I'm gonna make you look great." She paused and looked at Elise, her eyes wide, her face stern as if she were a neurosurgeon. "This is going to be a life-changing experience, Elise."

Elise prayed for another phone call, for Jewels to be distracted by the doorbell, or even a fire. However, she decided to make the best of the situation and find out more about Jewels. This was not a difficult task. Jewels was more than willing to discuss her life. In fact, Elise probably said five words during her entire makeover.

Born and raised in Alabama, her parents divorced when she was five. Her mother then took the kids to Baton Rouge where she married a Baptist minister who was later arrested for fraud. She had five brothers, two sisters, and a passel of stepsiblings, two of whom worked in the adult entertainment industry. She dropped their sparkly pseudonyms, as if Elise were supposed to jump from her seat and beg Jewels to hook her up with autographed headshots. She'd followed her boyfriend, a sailor in the United States Navy, to San Diego.

Elise found it all very interesting and was so absorbed in Jewels's

stories that she sort of didn't mind her drawing all over her face. The
most exciting thing that ever happened in her family was Stan's tattoo.

An hour later Jewels had applied three different face creams, two
different eye shadows, tear-proof mascara, blush with sunblock in it,
flavored lipstick, and a waterproof, food-proof, and kiss-proof lip
liner.

"Are you ready?" she said.

Ready to leave? Yes. Her stomach was growling, and her mind
searching for ways to make it out of there without purchasing a single
Glow product.

Jewels held up a hand mirror in front of Elise. It took all her
strength to swallow the shriek that nearly exploded from her lips.
Worse, this was one of those grueling moments when laughter struggled to cut itself loose from her throat like an out-of-control puppy
slipping from its leash. There were certain times laughter was totally
inappropriate, and this was one of them. It would hurt Jewels's feelings, but she feared that if she opened her mouth to say one single
word, her ability to maintain composure would go down like a ship
on fire. She used all her strength to control the muscles in her face, to
keep from revealing the hysteria she felt inside.

She looked like a cheap and colorful piece of artwork sold on the
side of intersections on Sunday afternoons. Her eyes were a green
sunrise, her lashes as dark and looming as spiders' legs. Her cheeks
popped out like two red traffic lights, and her lips looked like the
same kind of pink glue traps that Jewels sported. She realized that if
she didn't leave soon, Jewels could start spraying her with self-
tanning cream. She'd seen a few bottles in there.

"Well . . . what do you think?"

She swallowed. "Well, it's uh . . . different . . . than what I normally wear."

"I knew you'd love it!"

"Um . . ."

"You are not going to believe the kind of deal I can get you, sweetheart. This whole entire set will cost you eight hundred dollars on the QVC. Eight hundred dollars. And guess how much I'm gonna charge you?"

"No idea."

"C'mon guess."

"Ummm . . . I don't know. Four hundred dollars?"

She slapped Elise's knee hard. "Do you think I would charge you, my future roommate, that kind of money? No sir. I can get you the whole set for two hundred and fifty dollars. This cream alone would cost two hundred on the Home Shopping Network. She held up a small tub of cream, then unscrewed the lid. "Here. Smell it again." Elise inhaled something similar to the tea rose perfume her grandmother had worn for over twenty years. "And let me tell you something. All the celebrities are using this. Jennifer Aniston just bought a case of it."

Who did she think she was fooling? "I really can't afford it. As you know, I'm in the middle of moving, and I'm trying to save."

"I can work out a little special for you. I usually don't do this, but I'd be willing to take off fifty dollars. Off the whole set. It's a real bargain."

Even if Jewels took off two hundred and forty-nine dollars and ninety-nine cents, Elise wouldn't fork over the penny. "That's still way too much. I really can't afford to be splurging on makeup right now."

"Well, which products do you like? I can work out a little package for you."

"Actually, I didn't even bring my wallet. I didn't think I'd need it. I always thought roommate hunting was one activity that was supposed to be free. Ha!" She chuckled, but the stoic expression on Jewels's face suggested that she couldn't take a joke. For once, she looked defeated.

"Well, all right. I'll send you home with some pamphlets and brochures, and you can look them over. Just get back to me when you make up your mind." But judging from her dry tone, they both knew Elise would never be ordering a single thing from Glow.

"I also have this, if you're interested. I don't tell everyone about this, but you seem . . . like you would be open to it." She reached for another case. Elise felt like kicking the box like a soccer ball from her hands and running to the car. "I also host Passion Parties. They are the latest rage and a real blast. You might know some girlfriends that are interested in having one."

She didn't know anyone who would want to host a party for a makeup line called Passion, or any makeup line for that matter.

But when she opened the box, Elise immediately realized she wasn't talking about makeup. What lay inside was X-rated. Dildos, vibrators, creams, and sex toys galore rested inside the little chest. "Now, I know you said you didn't have a boyfriend. But you might need a little helper."

Maybe she did need a vibrator, but she had come here looking for a roommate. She grabbed her purse, popped from the couch, and blurted out, "I just remembered something. I have to pick someone up at the airport."

"Oh?"

Elise was already heading for the front door. "Yes. They're flying in from . . . Singapore. Thanks for doing my makeup. Gotta run."

She was practically sprinting down the driveway when Jewels called her. "Wait. You forgot these!"

Elise turned around and found her waving a stack of Glow pamphlets and brochures. She was afraid if she took one step toward Jewels she might pull out some other briefcase, this time filled with cocaine and opium. "I'm in a hurry. Just mail them to me."

She sped from North Park without looking back.

When she pulled into Casa de Paradiso, Justine was standing outside their apartment smoking and watching Glorious D. His head bobbed up and down beneath funnels of cigarette smoke as she eyed him. She was edging into her parking space when she noticed their door ajar. Inside stood Max, holding a guitar and chatting with Jimmy. Her lava green eyes nearly exploded from her face. Even from her distant and slightly obscured view he looked hot. She could see his muscular forearm, the way veins ran down the muscle. She looked at his hair hanging loosely around his neck. Justine and Glorious D waved, and she noticed that her arm was a little unsteady from surprise when she waved back.

Remain calm. Calm, she told herself. Inhale. Exhale. She'd saunter inside, after making a few witty and insightful comments to Glorious D and Justine, which Max would overhear and think how sharp she was. Then she'd calmly say hello to him as if they were old friends. Hopefully, he'd tell her how happy he was to run into her because he'd gotten her note and had been meaning to take her up on the offer for white pizza.

She glanced in her rearview mirror just to make sure she didn't have anything in her teeth. A startled moment passed as she actually thought that a local prostitute had snuck into the backseat of her car and was now waiting for the right opportunity to carjack her. "Damn," she mumbled. She had forgotten about how bad she looked. There was no way in hell she was going in there looking like she'd just come from a meeting with Elvira's makeup artist. She looked for something, anything, to wipe away the remnants of Jewels's project. A week ago the Volkswagen had been littered with napkins and receipts, and now she wondered what in the world had possessed her to clean her car.

When she glanced back at the door, she noticed something even more alarming than her extreme makeover. Max was backing out of their doorway, saying good-bye to Jimmy. She had only one choice. She threw the car into reverse and screeched from her parking space. Glorious D turned to look, and Justine held out a hand, her brows furrowed. Elise had no idea if Max turned around, too, because she sped from the lot.

Driving from the parking lot like a madman was repairable, but facing Max looking like a stripper could cause irreparable damage.

13. By the Beach

"What the hell happened to you?" Justine asked after she got home.

"Yeah," Jimmy said. "You drove off like the cops were after you."

"Oh, that." She'd stopped at Jack in the Box, had wiped off her lipstick, and was now sucking on a vanilla shake. "My sister went into false labor."

"Oh," they said.

"Is she okay?"

"Oh yeah. Fine."

"You look different," Jimmy said. "Did you cut your hair or something?"

"No," Justine said. "It's her makeup. Did you get new makeup?"

She shook her head and told them about Jewels. "So what have you guys been up to all afternoon?" She asked, hoping to get some information on Max.

The only information she managed to pull from the Cheech-erses about Max's visit was that he had stopped by to drop off a guitar for Jimmy, who was getting ready to leave for his tour. If he had any interest in going to Paesano with her, he certainly wasn't showing it. She might as well accept that she'd been blown off.

She spent the following week searching for a roommate and working on her novel. Late Friday afternoon, Carly called. Elise was in the mood to hit up a good happy hour and had actually been thinking about calling her to see if she wanted to join.

"What's up? I was just thinking about calling you actually."

"Really? I'm just getting ready to leave the office. But I wanted to call you quickly and tell you that I have good news," she said.

"You got the raise!"

"Raise? Oh, um, no. I didn't get that yet. That's not what this is about." Her voice sounded a tad discouraged, and Elise sort of wished she hadn't asked. "Actually, I have good news for *you*," Carly said. "I think I found you a place."

"You did?"

"Yes. It's just temporary, though. Three months. Our intern, Nicole, is going to Germany to study abroad for a semester, and she needs to find someone to cover her spot in the apartment. She wants to sublet to you. I know it's not ideal to move for just three months, but at least it's something. And while you're staying there you can look for a new place. It's close to me and by the beach, and the rent is unbelievable."

Relocating for only three months didn't sound ideal, but nevertheless she was curious. "Do they take pets?"

"Yes, they do. They actually have a cat. They said it was fine if you have a dog, just not a big dog. And I told them your dog was small."

"Where do they live?"

"Mission Beach."

"Are they still in college?" Mission Beach was a cross between college town and tourist land. It wasn't her first choice for a beach town, but it was definitely a step up from City Heights.

"Yes, they are in college. But Nicole seems very responsible and mature, and I'm sure she wouldn't live with people who partied the way we did in college. Ha!" She began to laugh. "But listen, I've gotta run."

"Do you want to meet up for happy hour?"

"Um . . . That sounds good, but I really should try to get some work done tonight."

Elise was a little disappointed. It was Friday, and she didn't want to sit home with the Cheecherses all night. She wanted to go out, and it was times like these when she really thought a boyfriend would come in handy.

"Nicole said to just go ahead and call them. Their names are Iris and Megan, and they're sisters. They'll be expecting you." She gave Elise the number before saying good-bye.

She wasted no time and called them. Living with college students wasn't her dream come true, but it was better than living in a cardboard box with her dog. And lately she'd been wondering if she would end up in a cardboard box or living with her parents.

An hour later she had a meeting.

It was around four o'clock in the afternoon when Elise arrived in Mission Beach. The ocean was as sparkly as a gold Christmas tree ornament as the late afternoon sun crept closer to the horizon. She figured many people had decided to leave work early, because the waves were dotted with surfers.

South Mission Beach was one large cul-de-sac of run-down beachfront apartment complexes and bars where not only did customers without a shirt and shoes get service, but they were welcome. There was sand on the floors of almost every establishment, and the whole city seemed to be filled with the faint odor of surf wax and beer. If one was shopping for "I Love San Diego" shot glasses or postcards of frighteningly tanned women lying topless on beach towels and sporting fluorescent G-strings, South Mission was the place. It was a mecca of cheesy tourist souvenirs, which strangely bore no actual representation of the area. Elise had always imagined people from all parts of the world receiving postcards of women who looked like they belonged in a Whitesnake video. People in say, Canada, must believe that these half-naked creatures of eighties rock ran rampant along the southern California coast, when in reality there might be the occasional woman with a Coppertone tan, bleached hair, and fluorescent G-string, and she was usually visiting from somewhere else.

The first thing people saw when driving into Mission Beach was the gigantic wooden roller coaster. Painted white and colossal in size, the coaster never seemed to stop running, and every time Elise thought of Mission Beach she could hear its wheels rolling on the tracks and the faint sound of excited screams.

She passed the coaster and searched for the address Megan had given her over the phone. Her first impression of the complex didn't knock her socks off, but she reminded herself that it was walking distance from the beach and the boardwalk. She'd been living in a part of town where armed fugitives were hunted daily. Though a little crusty, the duplex was just fine. Parking was also a real problem in the area. It always was at any beach in San Diego, and she drove around for a solid ten minutes before finding a tiny spot that left a good two inches of her back tires in the red zone.

She walked for several blocks feeling bad that she was late but also feeling very happy that she could smell salt water.

Moments after ringing the bell, a gorgeous blonde answered the door. She was so pretty that Elise just had to assume that God really did put extra time into making some people. She looked as if her infant skin had never experienced a single zit, and her long, skinny thighs had never suffered from even a millimeter of cellulite. She had long, straight hair that looked as if it belonged in a J. Crew catalogue.

"You must be Elise!" she said before shooting her hand toward her.

Elise shook her hand. "And you're . . . Iris or Megan?"

"Megan! For God's sake. Iris is my sister."

"Oh, sorry."

They walked up a long flight of steps to what Megan referred to as the first floor of their apartment. The décor was pretty much typical college décor. Sheets hung over the windows instead of curtains. The couches were definitely from a thrift store or a hand-me-down from some relative. The television stand looked as if it were older than Megan. Van Gogh's *Starry Night* and a couple of Monet prints were pinned to the walls with thumbtacks.

A girl rose from the couch wearing flannel pajama bottoms and a Ramones T-shirt. Pockmarks dotted her chubby cheeks, and dark smudges of mascara decorated the circles beneath her eyes. She had sideburns, and her short frizzy hair looked as if she'd tried to dye it a rebellious color but had ended up with a brassy shade of copper.

"Hi. I'm Iris."

Elise extended her hand. "You guys are sisters?" She couldn't help it. The words had just come out. They looked nothing alike. Where Megan was long, Iris was squat. Where Megan was smooth, Iris was rough. Shaped like a bulldog, Iris had rubbery, squat arms and legs. Her jagged fingernails were proof that she was a nail biter, and she had a black tribal tattoo around her pale ankle.

"We are sisters," Iris said. "I just look like my dad. She looks like well . . . no one."

"That's not true," Megan said. "Everyone says I look like Great-grandma Sylvia."

"She's our step-great-grandmother, you idiot. She's not even related to us."

"You are such a dumb ass," Megan said. "She had Grandpa's brother. We are too related."

"That still doesn't make us related."

"Yes it does. I know we're related to her somehow. Ask Mom how."

Before Iris could retaliate, Elise interjected, "Wow, look at that stack of magazines you guys have." Elise was just trying to think of something to say to end their bickering. It worked, because they both took their heated gazes away from one another and looked at Elise.

"Oh yeah," Megan said. "We have prescriptions to both *Us* and *People*."

"It's subscription, you idiot. Not prescription."

"Whatever. Subscription. Prescription. It's the same thing. We just got the one that tells everything about J. Lo's latest wedding. You're welcome to take any of them with you to the beach if you move in."

This was music to Elise's ears. She rarely bought magazines, but if she were going to the dentist or the doctor, she always hoped they had several good issues of the juicy tabloids. There was nothing worse than waiting for an appointment and being sorely disappointed when she found that their magazine racks only held piles of *Highlights* and *Good Housekeeping*. Now these magazines would be at her fingertips.

They showed Elise the room she'd be staying in if she chose to move in. Nicole's belongings were still in the room, but Iris and Megan told her she'd be putting them all in storage before her big trip to Germany.

"She's also letting me drive her new car while she's gone," Megan said.

"No. She's letting *us* drive it," Iris corrected.

Megan turned to Elise. "We've been sharing a car since high school. It's total hell."

"You can move in next weekend if you want," Iris said, "Nicole is packing up her stuff next week, and after that there's only ten days left of the month. We won't charge you rent for those days." This was great! The sooner she bailed City Heights the better.

"Let's show you the rest of the place," Iris said.

When they opened Iris's door, the faint odor of cat urine wafted through the air. Her room was cluttered with stacks of essays and textbooks. A Bob Marley poster hung on one wall, and her bed-spread looked a little stained and weathered. Her sliding closet door was closed, and Elise noticed some clothes sticking out from beneath it. A skinny black cat with a rough coat came out from underneath the bed and immediately began to rub against Elise's legs.

"This is Scrubbles," Iris said. "I got him last year from some homeless guy on the boardwalk who was giving kittens away."

Elise reached down and petted the cat. He purred loud and rubbed his face against her hands. "Does he like dogs?"

"I think so," Megan said. "One of our friends had their dog here once, and they seemed to get along. And there are dogs all over the place around here."

"Well, good. I hope he gets along with Bella."

"Does this mean you're moving in?" Megan asked.

"I think so. Yes."

"Good. We've never lived with a famous writer before."

For a moment she was tempted to throw her head back with laughter and elbow them. Famous writer. Sure, she had fans. But maybe she should explain that she wasn't Mary Higgins Clark yet. But then she thought, *What the hell?* If they wanted to think she was a celebrity, it was fine by her.

She left Mission Beach with a smile on her face and a feeling of excitement she hadn't felt in some time. She'd found roommates. Even if they seemed like they hated each other and their apartment was a little cluttered, it was a decent situation. She could walk to the beach whenever she wanted. She could smell the ocean air, and she'd be able to leave her window open at night.

Instead of driving back to City Heights she decided to drop by her brother's place in Ocean Beach. As far as she knew, he had Fridays off from driving the tour tram at the Wild Animal Park, and she wanted to see what he was up to for the evening. They might still be able to make a happy hour if they hurried.

She lucked out and managed to find a parking place in front of his building. While walking to the front entrance she noticed his beat-up Honda Accord in front of the building. The car was so filthy she could probably write a short story with her fingertip in the layer of dust on the hood. His surfboard was wedged tightly in the car, and she was certain he had to be home.

His doorbell had been broken for years, and she didn't even bother ringing. She knocked and waited. There was no response, and she was starting to wonder where he could be without his surfboard or car. She was about to knock again when she heard the familiar sound of his laughter inside. "Stan!" she called. She waited and listened to him laugh again. She knocked again and waited a couple of minutes before she decided to let herself in.

She expected to see him sitting in front of the television, his feet propped on the coffee table while he ate from a bag of chips. However, the only thing on his couch was an abandoned carne asada burrito, which he clearly had no sense to clean up. Spanish rice was falling in between the couch cushions.

The candle she had bought him for his birthday burned, and she thought it smelled rather nice. Where the hell was he? His bedroom door was closed. Maybe he was getting ready to head out for happy hour. Perfect timing. She was about to call for him again when it hit her. He had a girl over. She knew her brother hooked up, but it was something she'd always chosen not to think about.

She felt her heart lurch when she heard the sounds of panting peppered with grunts. She gripped the handle of her purse before sprinting full speed back to her car. One thing that people should never have to endure in their life is listening to a family member have sex. For that matter, they should never listen to anything involving sex about a family member. No stories. No details. She liked to believe that the only three times her parents had done it had been to produce Melissa, Stan, and herself. And her brother, well, he just kissed girls. And even thinking of that was enough to make her stomach turn.

After speeding from the front of Stan's complex, she instantly dialed Carly. She needed to tell someone about the shock she'd been through. Her phone rang several times before voice mail picked up.

"Hello. You have reached the voice mailbox of Carly Trusedale . . ." Elise had heard her businesslike greeting a zillion times and knew the whole thing by heart. "Please leave a message with your name and the best number to reach you, and I will get back to you as soon as possible. Thank you and have a great day."

"Oh my God! You will never believe what just happened to me. I drove into Ocean Beach after my meeting with Iris and Megan, which went great by the way. Thank you. And anyway I thought I would stop in to see Stan and, oh my God, I almost walked in on him having sex with someone. Anyway, I heard enough to run for my life. I mean you don't have any siblings, but Stan is practically like your brother, so I'm sure you can imagine the grossness I've just been exposed to. Call me back at once."

After partially recovering from the initial shock of Stan's affairs, she began to wonder who this person was that he was involved with. Was it just a casual fling? Someone he had met at a bar or on the beach? She knew he didn't tell her about every fling he had. If he really liked the girl, he'd mention her, so this must be casual sex.

Elise had met a few of Stan's chums, and the poor girls always tried to befriend Elise, flattering her and trying desperately to find things they had in common. Though she could see right through them, she never blamed them. She would probably do the same thing if she were trying to win someone's brother.

Marge called just as she was heading into City Heights. For a split second she actually debated asking her mother if she had any idea who Stan was dating, but then she realized how completely absurd she was being. There was no way in hell her mother would have a clue, and mentioning anything about Stan having a close female friend would just give her mom false hope that she would someday be able to plan a rehearsal dinner. Instead she told her about her new roommates. "Are you sure you want to live in Mission Beach?" she asked. "It's just so touristy down there. And the riffraff that walks around that boardwalk."

"Riffraff? It's all college students and some tourists."

"Last time your father and I were down there, I don't think I saw one person without a tattoo."

"Mom. It's fine."

"So anyway, your father and I are having some people over on Sunday afternoon for an early dinner, and I wanted to make sure you're coming."

"Um, yeah. Okay. This is the first I've heard of it, but, uh, yeah, count me in."

"All right. Good."

"Is Stan coming?"

"I haven't called him yet. I'm going to try him as soon as we get off the phone." Elise wanted to tell her not to bother. "Who is coming?"

"Melissa and Brice and the Yackrells."

"The Yackrells? Who are the Yackrells?"

"June Yackrell is in my San Diego League of Women Voters, and I've invited her family over. Just a minute. Listen, your father needs me, so I'll see you Sunday around four."

When she returned to her apartment she heard giggles from behind Justine's bedroom door. Jimmy was leaving for his tour the following day, and apparently they were making the best of each other's company before he left, because she'd also heard them going at it that morning. All around her was sex. Everywhere she turned. She escaped to her bedroom, closed the door behind her, and decided to start packing.

14. Call Me

Jimmy's departure was similar to a movie where the hero is called to duty, perhaps a war or the hunting down of an outlaw, and the heroine weeps hopelessly into a handkerchief, gripping her chest and pleading for a safe return. Only Jimmy wasn't going off to war. He was touring the country with his rock band. He'd most likely be doing tequila shots with breakfast and getting into the sort of mischief that would be kept between him and God.

Minutes before his departure he feigned bravery and offered assurance for his emotionally frail woman, stroking the side of her cheek and whispering tender words into her ear. However, when his tour van pulled up in front of the complex, Elise noticed his eyes light up like a child discovering candy on an egg hunt. He grabbed his duffel bag from the couch, plopped one last kiss on Justine's forehead, and practically skipped toward his future of binge drinking and party-filled nights.

Justine, on the other hand, clutched a snotty piece of toilet paper and wept just as delicately as Kate Beckinsale in *Pearl Harbor*.

He stopped outside the front door to pet Bella. "Hey, Elise, good luck with . . . everything. Hope to see you when I get back."

He began to walk away, and though he was a complete nuisance, she sort of envied him. Not a care in the world, he'd be partying while most people were fighting traffic in their Monday morning commute. She wanted to be a rock star. Then she heard a sonic-sounding fart followed by a chorus of laughter come from the open door of the van, and she decided maybe not.

Jimmy turned back toward Elise, his bangs whipping over his eyebrows. "Oh, hey. I almost forgot. Max was asking about you last night."

"He was?" She asked a little too quickly.

"Yeah. He asked me if you had a boyfriend."

"He did? What did you say?"

"I said I didn't know."

"You said you didn't know? Don't you know that I don't have a boyfriend?"

"Well, you went on that date that one time."

She couldn't believe that they lived together, and he knew so little about her. "Are you talking about that blind date I went on? That was three months ago. And that was a terrible date. I'm not dating that guy."

He shrugged. "Sorry, I didn't know."

"Max is a cool guy," Jimmy said. "One of the best I know. I didn't want to give him your number because . . ." He shrugged. "I mean, I don't know. I didn't want you to get mad."

"No. I mean, yes. I don't mind if you give him my number." Her heart was racing.

"All right then. I will. Next time I talk to him."

For a moment she envisioned Jimmy drunk and sandwiched between two groupies. Partying one day in Portland, signing autographs in Denver the next. The likelihood of him remembering was as great as him quitting the band and entering the seminary. In between bong hits and encores he'd never find the time.

"Well, don't for—"

"Jimmy!" Justine's voice burst from a window and shattered like glass over their conversation. "I need to talk to you. Now, please."

He gave Bella one last stroke before heading back inside. "I'll, uh, give him your number," he said.

"You will?" Elise followed him, trying not to sound too pushy. He couldn't remember conversations he'd held in the same day.

"You almost forgot this," Justine said, handing him his advent calendar.

Elise recognized the same look on Jimmy that Stan had featured the year Marge had given Stan a tie for his birthday. He shoved the calendar in his pocket and headed back to the van.

The girls watched from the doorway as Potter's van peeled out of Casa de Paradiso parking lot with music blasting and something that looked like a jacket sleeve dangling out the sliding door. As soon as they stepped inside, Justine threw herself on the couch and wept.

"He'll be back soon," Elise said. "It's only a month. Think of how fast that will go by. Think of it on the bright side," she said. "Soldiers' wives don't even get to talk to their husbands for months. At least you'll be able to talk to him. Four times a day," she added.

She replied with hiccupping cries. "You don't know what it's like."

"Justine, I want you to feel better," Elise said, feeling slightly guilty that she didn't feel very much sympathy for her roommate. She was really thinking of Max and wondering if Jimmy would remember to give him her number. "Almost everyone has experienced missing someone. He'll be back. Soon."

Instead of drying her eyes and agreeing that Jimmy would be back soon and five weeks really seemed like nothing in the grand scheme of things, she cried even harder. "Please. Just stop," she wailed.

Then it occurred to Elise. Perhaps she had seen the happiness in Jimmy's eyes when the van pulled up. Maybe she'd noticed that he'd seemed eager to break out of there.

She looked at the hole Jimmy had created on their wall the first time she had met him. A small spider was crawling from the edge, and it reminded her that they needed to fix it before they moved. Elise needed her deposit back, and she had a feeling that if they didn't fix the hole before her departure this weekend, she'd end up paying for part of it.

However, now was not the best time to discuss this. She spent several more minutes consoling Justine until realizing it was useless. She wanted to be miserable. If she wasn't pining over Jimmy, she'd have nothing to do. She looked at the clock and realized it was time for her to leave for Poway. "Do you want to come to my parents' house for dinner?" she asked. "They're having some friends over, and my brother might be there. Why don't you come? It might cheer you up."

"No." She shook her head. "I don't feel up to it."

"Oh, c'mon. You can see what a complete terror my nephew is."

"Really, I just want to figure out his password for his new e-mail account."

"All right. Well, see you later."

A gold Jaguar and a silver Bentley were parked next to Stan's Honda Accord in her parents' driveway. Who drove a Bentley? And what did the Yackrells do for a living? Elise had been under the impression that her mother had invited a couple of people, but there were two cars. She sort of wished she'd gotten a better background of who exactly these people were, but her mother hadn't been available for comment.

She was glad to see Stan's car. She hadn't been able to get a hold of him all weekend, and he still had no idea that she had dropped in unexpectedly. She was kind of curious to see his reaction.

She let herself in and immediately felt underdressed. Her father was wearing a sport coat and slacks. Her mother, a gold monochramatic outfit, and even Melissa had a dressy maternity frock on. Elise thought her mother had said it was a BBQ, and she'd imagined them in the backyard, her father flipping burgers while her mother arranged condiments while wearing a pair of shorts and a nice summer blouse. Elise was dressed in jeans and a white wife beater.

"Elise, darling," her mother said. Darling? Something was up. She never called anyone "darling." "Let me introduce you to June and Bud Yackrell, and their son Thomas." Silence fell over the room when Thomas stepped forward to shake Elise's hand. Something told her this was a moment they had all been waiting for.

The whole point of this event had been to introduce Elise to Thomas Yackrell, who looked as if he were going yachting. A sly move on her mother's part. Elise politely extended a hand. *Be a good sport,* she silently told herself. *Be polite. He's probably a nice person.* "I've heard so much about you," he said through pale lips.

Great. I've never heard of you. As she gazed up at his lanky frame she resisted the urge to ask if he had the same hairdresser as Sam Donaldson. "So, you're the author?" Mrs. Yackrell said from behind.

"Yes, I am."

"That is just wonderful. Romance novels?"

"Actually mysteries."

"Mysteries!" she exclaimed. "That's amazing. I love mysteries. Do you ever read anything by Mary Higgins Clark? Or what about James Patterson? They are both so successful."

"Yes, I have read their work."

"So does your character carry a magnifying glass and wear a plaid cape?" Thomas asked in a low, chortling tone. Elise sensed he was trying to be funny, and while they all laughed she sincerely wondered if his glasses were as thick as a car windshield. She had never seen anything like them, and for a moment she imagined a small piece of asphalt flying into his lenses, or a fly splatting across his frames.

"Elise just got signed with *the* biggest film agency in Los Angeles, and they're marketing her book to all the huge production companies and several big-name actors. Aren't they, Elise?" her father said.

She was glad her parents were proud of her, but she felt as if a terrible jinx were being cast over her career. When she'd told them about the latest development with her book, she'd forgotten that her parents had no idea what the meaning of *secret* was. Two years earlier when her agent had begun submitting the book to publishers, her mother had told everyone, even though Elise had asked her not to. When she came home for Thanksgiving, even the bag boy and checker at Vons knew. And what's worse? Her mother had exaggerated, telling them all the book was going to be published before she ever even had a deal. Thank goodness the book was published, because if it hadn't been, she probably would've had to go into seclusion and change her identity after the shame she'd endure.

"Her book is going to be a movie!" her mother added.

"Wow!" The Yackrells said at once. "Who is going to star in it? Maybe Britney Spears?" The odd thing was that Mr. Yackrell was sincere when he said this.

"Oh! She would be good," June Yackrell chimed in, nodding.

At this point she couldn't be picky about who played Ashley Trent. She just wanted her book to be on the big screen. But Britney Spears? They might as well cast Paris Hilton in the movie as well.

"Well, we'd be happy with Sandra Bullock. Maybe Ashley Judd, wouldn't we?" Her father's elbow felt like a spear in her ribs.

"Well, I just got *signed* with an *agent*." She felt a desperate need to clear things up for them—to really downplay the situation, banish the jinx they had just set upon her career. "I haven't gotten the deal yet, and the way the film industry is, who knows what will happen? It's very difficult, so I don't want to get my hopes up, and I try not to even think about it that much. I mean, the odds are so slim. It's really like winning the lotto." She could feel her armpits sweating, and she wished someone would change the subject.

Thankfully Stan emerged from the kitchen. He obviously wasn't aware of the dress code either, with his backward baseball cap and flip-flops. Brice trailed behind wearing a tie. Jeffrey squirmed in his arms, and the red and blue stains that covered the entire perimeter of his mouth were signs of "condy."

"Look who is here," Melissa said to Jeffrey. "It's Aunt Lise. Do you remember Aunt Lise?"

"No," he said promptly without so much as glancing at Elise.

"You had so much fun with her that day when she stayed with you."

"No. I did not."

Marge and Melissa hooted with laughter. "Isn't he such a little character?"

Marge said. "He's just so honest and you have to love that about him."

"Just sharp as a whip," Grandpa added.

"Elise, why don't you show Thomas your book? I left a copy on the coffee table in the living room," her mother said.

What she really wanted to do was raid the liquor cabinet before scheduling an appointment to have her tubes tied. But she had to be polite. It wasn't Thomas's fault that her parents were exaggerating schemers.

She found her book on the coffee table and felt lamer than she had in ages as she stood there showing it to this stranger.

"So does the detective have a cap and smoke a pipe?"

Would you please get off the Sherlock Holmes thing, you jackass?
"My detective is actually a woman."

He raised an eyebrow, and she sensed another ridiculous attempt at humor coming on. "So does she live in Cabot Cove?"

"No. Ha. She is not Angela Lansbury on *Murder She Wrote*."

"Then does she speak with—"

"No."

"Oh." He seemed a little stung by her abrupt response and took a sip of his Coke. "You're famous, then?"

"So what do you do, Thomas?" Changing the subject seemed like the best way to handle him.

"I run a financial software company that deals with international relations."

"Oh." She nodded. "Neat."

"Yeah, most of our clients are in international trade and marketing, so we focus primarily on . . ."

She found her thoughts drifting to the cheese platter that sat on the coffee table behind her while Thomas described things that could lull a crack addict to sleep. She could see a hunk of Havarti just waiting for her. This was one of the best things about coming to her parents' house. There were always good appetizers and snacks and a refrigerator stocked with gourmet food. Her mother really did know how to put out a good spread, and Elise hoped that she'd be able to host events the way she did one day. She watched with envy as Stan dipped a buttery cracker in a warm block of brie with cranberry sauce spilling over the edges.

"So do you use a Mac or a PC when you write your book?"

She snapped out of it, realizing he was addressing her. "Oh. Um. I don't know." This was probably an easy question, and she knew that at some point she might have known the answer, but she really didn't care about these things. She knew how to check her e-mail and work on her book. Anything beyond that was meaningless.

"Well, is your computer upright?"

"Yeah. It looks like that."

"Interesting. What kind of program do you use?"

She felt like a total idiot. Was this something she should know? "Uh, Windows? Or no. Maybe it's Word?"

"Word. Yes. Do you know what year?"

Look dude, she wanted to say. *I don't know! It works. I type. It prints. That's all I know.* She endured another twenty minutes of this kind of conversation. Then she listened to Thomas talk about some kind of something he was developing for his company. What was really interesting was watching Jeffrey in the background as he fed her parents' fourteen-year-old cocker spaniel, Maxine, pastel-colored pillow mints from a bowl on an end table.

Thomas finally excused himself to use the bathroom, and Elise immediately went to her brother. "I've been trying to call you all weekend."

"Oh yeah? My battery is dead on my cell phone."

"I figured it was something like that. I also stopped by on Friday afternoon, around four." She thought the words would land on him like a bomb, but he didn't seem fazed in the least.

He shrugged. "Really? I must've been surfing or something."

"Hmmmm. I thought for sure you were home. I saw your car and your surfboard in front of the building."

"I don't know. Maybe I was in the shower." He gave no indication that he was nervous or hiding anything. She decided to ask him, point-blank.

"So, have you been seeing anyone lately?"

"No." He shook his head.

Obviously, he'd been having a fleeting sexual affair that he didn't feel was worth mentioning, and on that note she decided to drop it. She didn't want to know.

"Thanks for saving me over there with ol' T. Yackrell," she mumbled. "You could've come over."

"And interrupt the start of something beautiful?" He grinned.

"Did you know that Mom was trying to set me up?"

"No idea. But they mentioned they have a daughter that was supposed to come but backed out at the last minute. I don't think you were intended to be the only victim. I'm going to say I'm coming down with something, and I don't want to get Jeffrey or Melissa sick while she's pregnant. Excuse me."

"You can't leave," she called after him. "Please."

"See ya."

She'd never felt more envious and wished she had come up with a brilliant excuse, too. They couldn't both be sick. She watched as Melissa grabbed Jeffrey and moved quickly to another room as if her brother were oozing germs. The Yackrells all stepped away as well. "You definitely should not be around Melissa and Jeffrey if you're sick," her mother said. "Now hurry and go."

Dinner was just as droll. Elise scooted into a corner chair at the table next to Jeffrey's high chair and pretended to play with him while everyone else took their seats. If her plan worked, she'd end up at the end of the table and nowhere near Thomas. But when Jeffrey took a dinner roll and rammed it into her forehead, her plan fell apart. "I, uh, better sit there, Elise," Brice said.

"Oh, yes," Marge nodded. "Elise, let Brice and Melissa sit with Jeffrey, and you can sit here." She patted the back of a chair. "Right next to Thomas."

She dusted the crumbs from her forehead and slowly moved to her seat.

Dinner was like attending a really boring lecture in college. It moved slowly, and she couldn't wait for it to be over with. Fortunately, most of the conversation centered on Thomas's company, and Elise didn't have to endure any more jokes about her book.

However, when the conversation turned to real estate, Elise knew she hadn't escaped yet. "Thomas just bought a house in Rancho Santa Fe," June said. "It's great for him because he just loves tennis so much, and it has two tennis courts."

"It must be beautiful," Marge said. "Elise plays tennis, too."

The last time she had picked up a racket had been in seventh grade PE.

"Oh, wonderful," Thomas said. "Do you have tennis courts in the area where you live?"

"No." She thought of Casa de Paradiso, Glorious D rapping in the parking lot while pedaling stolen knockoff bags. "There are no tennis courts there."

"And where do you live?" he asked.

She thought she saw a small amount of shame pass her mother's eyes, and for some reason this made her feel better about answering. "City Heights. Right in the heart."

"Oh!" June laughed until she realized Elise was serious. They all stared at her, and she felt like telling them that she wished she could afford her own place in Rancho Santa Fe and that she was tired of renting and having roommates. And if they thought she lived there because she loved the area, they were all dead wrong. No, she didn't drive a Jaguar, but she worked hard and she was determined to buy her own place someday, and could someone please pass the wine? "It's just temporary though. I'm moving to Mission Beach soon."

"Oh yes. That's an interesting area," Bud said.

Sorry they don't play polo there, but it was the best I can do right now, she felt like shouting.

"Shall we move to the living room for dessert?" her mother said, making the best move she had made all night.

While her mother served up tiramisu, Elise thought of excuses to leave. She was considering using Justine. Her roommate needed consoling, as her boyfriend had just left on a long business trip, and Elise was worried about her.

Her parents' cocker spaniel jumped up onto the couch next to June Yackrell.

"Get down from there!" her father yelled at the dog.

"Oh, she's fine." June said. "I love dogs."

She was just starting to tell them about a Lhasa apso they once had when Maxine barfed a gigantic pastel blob on June Yackrell's lap. Thank God for Jeffrey. The party moved quickly after that, and Elise found herself moving for the front door just as quickly as the Yackrells did.

"Well, your parents told me you do quite a bit of public speaking," Thomas said in the foyer.

Whose parents was he talking about?

"They mentioned you do quite a bit of speaking at your book signings." Who did they think she was? Anne Rice? She had done two book signings, and both had produced a turnout of five. She had spoken to her small crowd briefly about the book and had read a few pages from the first chapter.

"I've done a couple of book signings, and I'd hardly say—"

"Well, the reason I ask is because I belong to a public speaking group, and I was wondering if you'd like to attend a meeting with me. It's great fun, and a wonderful way to network. Then we could go to dinner afterward."

She couldn't think of anything she wanted to do less, except hurt his feelings. She decided to give a vague noncommittal answer "Um. Let me know the details, and if I'm available, it might work out."

"Well, why don't I take your phone number?"

Maybe she should say her hand was broken and she was incapable of writing, or even getting a pen for him to use. However, Marge overheard their exchange and immediately shouted, "Oh! I'll grab a pen." She'd never seen her mother run so fast.

Then she had a thought. She could always write down her number in City Heights. She'd be leaving there, and he'd never be able to track her down. It was genius. "Elise, make sure you write down your cell phone number. You're moving," Marge reminded as she handed her a pen.

She wrote down her number in very poor handwriting.

The Real World:
Iris and Megan

15. Orientation

On the eve of Elise's big move she dreamt she would be residing with two friendly werewolves who were running against each other for a seat in Congress and who listened to Elton John. It was a bizarre yet vivid dream, the kind that stays with a person all day. She was humming "Daniel" when Carly arrived to help her load up the car.

Seeing Carly made her realize how long they had gone without spending time with one another. She looked as if she had lost a few pounds and gotten a tan.

"Hey!" she said, arms agape, when Elise greeted her at the door. "I brought you a caramel latte."

Elise hugged her and felt a strand of Carly's hair cross her cheek.

"Stan flaked," Elise said. "He called this morning and said he wasn't feeling well."

"Translated: he's hungover."

"You would think. But I tried to call him three times this week, and he didn't answer. I really think he might be seeing someone."

"Really?" She looked at the pile of boxes stacked in Elise's room.

"Well, I told you what happened the other night. He was obviously with someone."

"I know. Did you ever ask him about it?"

"I tried to, but he said he was in the shower or something like that."

She shrugged before setting down her coffee. "Speaking of love lives, how is yours? Did Max ever call you?"

"No." Elise picked up a box of shoes. Bella followed her to the door and waited with anticipation while she turned the handle. She'd been following Elise back and forth all day, sniffing every single box and wagging her tail each time the front door opened.

"Jimmy probably didn't give Max your number. Maybe you should say something to Justine before you leave," Carly said as she slid Elise's wall hangings into her trunk. "Have her remind Jimmy. Or just stop by his shop. You know he wants to talk to you."

"I feel weird doing that. I don't know why. I just do. If it's meant to be, it will work out. Somehow."

"That's a bad attitude. You have to take charge of your life."

"So, what did you do last night?" Elise asked.

"Oh, just went out to happy hour with some work friends, and it turned into an all-night thing."

Elise couldn't help but feel a pang of jealousy. In the past two months she had asked Carly to go to happy hour at least a dozen times, and she always said she had to work on her ad campaign or meet with a client. Yet she seemed to have plenty of time to go out with her work friends. Why couldn't she invite Elise? She wasn't jealous. She felt left out.

As she headed inside she wondered why Carly wouldn't invite her. Perhaps she was jumping to conclusions, and it was just a last-minute rendezvous. Pure spontaneity. She couldn't expect Carly to invite her to every little event. Furthermore, she couldn't rely on Carly so much. She needed to make new friends.

She was just slightly disappointed because she thought they

would spend more time together after she moved back to San Diego. They used to speak to each other at least three times a day, and if they weren't on the phone with one another they would e-mail back and forth. Now it seemed like a challenge to even get a hold of her. Oddly, it seemed like they were better friends when Elise was in Arizona.

The idea that they were drifting apart was almost unfathomable. Carly was her best friend in the world. Elise just needed to be patient, more understanding, and in the meantime she needed to make more friends. She was tempted to ask Carly about her project at work but knew better. She held back for the same reason it bugged her when people asked her about the movie rights. These things took time.

"So how are we going to move your bed and strap it to the car without Stan?" Carly asked.

"Glorious D said he would help. Since we're only driving fifteen minutes, I figured we could just tie the bed to the roof of your car. Justine should be coming home from work any minute to say good-bye and help, too."

Elise was emptying her sock drawer into a box when she heard Glorious D rapping to someone outside. She automatically assumed it was Justine until she heard him say, "You no hike. You got the bike." Unless Justine had pedaled her way to work that morning, he was rapping to someone else.

She shot a surprised glance to Carly when the doorbell rang. Perhaps it was Walt issuing a complaint because she was taking up two parking spaces in front of the complex while she moved her stuff. Or maybe it was the armed fugitive the helicopters had been hunting the previous day. She tiptoed to her window and peeked from a tiny slit in the blinds. "Oh my . . . It's Max," she whispered.

"No way!" Carly said gleefully.

"Shhhh."

"What do you mean *shhhh*? Go answer the door."

"How do I look?"

"Gorgeous."

She caught a glimpse of herself on the way to the door and noticed that she looked a little pale. She wished she had time to run back to her bedroom for some blush. But when she heard Max's second knock, she knew she couldn't waste any more time. He'd leave if she didn't answer soon. She remembered a brief scene in *Gone With the Wind* when Scarlett O'Hara had pinched her cheeks before meeting a suitor. Elise grabbed her cheeks and smashed them between her fingers.

"Hey stranger." She cringed at how corny and trite she sounded.

"Hope you're not too busy," he said.

"No. Just packing."

He looked at her strangely, and she wondered if she had broken blood vessels when she'd tried to add color to her cheeks. Then she realized he was probably waiting for her to ask him in.

"Oh, c'mon in. Sorry, I've just been kind of overwhelmed with the move and everything."

"Yeah, I heard about the eviction. Where are you headed to?"

"Mission Beach."

"I was wondering when you guys were taking off. I was just coming back from my buddy's shop down the street and I thought I'd drop in and say hello . . . or good-bye, I guess." He shrugged before setting his helmet on her coffee table.

Her hopes sank with the mention of good-bye. Apparently he planned on never seeing her again.

"So how is the book coming along?" he asked as he rubbed the side of his nose. Strangely, this turned her on, and she imagined his hands rubbing her skin.

"The book is coming along well. I got signed with a film agent, actually. One of the best in Hollywood." It was hard to believe she had let the words leave her lips. If she was jinxing her chances of walking the red carpet with Sandra Bullock, that was just fine. Watching his eyes widen and the dimples that came over his face were worth it.

"Really? Congratulations. Is this the new book that you just finished?"

She nodded. "Yes. With the same detective, Ashley Trent."

"That's great. I will definitely keep my fingers crossed for you."

"Well, you know just because I got signed doesn't mean that anything will happen. The film industry is even worse than the publishing world, and the odds are slim." Downplaying everything again, just in case of being jinxed.

"Well, never give up. I have confidence in you. I'm sure you'll make it."

"Thanks."

She felt her hopes drop like the *Titanic* when he reached for his helmet. *Don't go,* she wanted to shout.

"You ever been to the races?" he asked.

"The races?"

"Yeah, the horse races. Del Mar."

"Born and raised in San Diego, and I've never made it to the track."

"They start next week. I was thinking about heading over there on a slow day at the shop. You wanna come with?"

"Yes. Sure." Hee! Hee! He'd asked her out.

"Cool." He rolled his helmet between his hands. "All right, then. Why don't I grab your cell phone number, and I'll call you?"

She wrote down her number on a scrap piece of paper and wondered how men managed to be so cool and collected. So patient. *I'll call you?* When? She was dying to know.

As soon as she closed the door behind her, she ran to her bedroom.

"You are going to have so much fun," Carly said. "That is going to be the best date, so much better than getting dressed up and dealing with dinner and worrying about conversation. You guys will have something to focus on. It will relieve some of the first-date tension."

They packed up all her boxes, and Glorious D even pitched in to help them carry the mattress.

"I'm gonna miss you, man," he said as they slid the last box into her trunk. "You been a real cool neighbor."

"Well, I'll miss you, too." She leaned in to hug him and realized how thin he was when she felt his bony shoulders and back.

"What does the D stand for?" she asked. "If you don't tell me now, I'll wonder for the rest of my life."

He smiled. "That's a secret. But I'll tell you. Cuz I like you. It's Dwayne."

They were just about to leave when Justine showed up. "Oh. Are you leaving already?" Elise had told her she was leaving around eleven, and it was now noon. How convenient for her to show up late. "Come give me a hug," she said, arms outstretched. "Jimmy sends his best, too."

Elise hugged her. "Take care," she said.

"You, too, and keep in touch." She had a feeling they weren't going to call each other up for girl talk, and it really didn't bother her that much. However, a tiny, teeny, minute part of her actually thought she might miss Jimmy a little. He did make her laugh.

"You have someone coming to fix that hole?" They had discussed the hole in the wall several times in the past two weeks, and Justine had always promised that she would take care of it. However, Elise hadn't seen her make any effort yet.

"Yes," Justine said firmly. "Consider it done."

Elise and Carly arrived at her new apartment around noon. She knocked on the front door and waited for her new roommates to greet her. However, no one came. She knocked again and waited. They hadn't given her a key yet, so she had no way of letting herself in. She was positive she had told them that she would be arriving around eleven thirty. A pang of guilt hit when she realized she was almost an hour late. Maybe they had gotten hungry and left. She hoped they hadn't left. There was no way of getting in, and they had double-parked so they could unload all her stuff. She pictured Iris and Megan hungry and unable to wait any longer, and she suddenly felt bad for not calling to tell them she was running late.

She pounded again with her fist and was holding her hand midair when a guy opened the door. He wore khaki pants and a baseball tee and squinted from the sunlight before rubbing the sleep from his eyes.

She looked over her shoulder, wondering if she'd perhaps gone to the wrong apartment. Carly waited behind her with a box.

Elise looked at the liquor store across the street, then back at the wrought-iron numbers next to the front door. She was definitely in the right place. "Hi," she said. "Are Iris and Megan here?"

"They're sleeping."

She had spoken with them twice the day before and had told them during both conversations that she would be moving in around twelve. She hadn't expected them to be waiting with moving gloves and a hand truck, but she had thought they would at least be awake at the crack of noon to say hello. "Well, I'm moving in today," Elise said.

"Uh . . . Really? Hmm."

"Yes." She waited for him to move aside, but he gave the girls a once-over. "All right," he mumbled before stepping away from the door.

Her first thought when she reached the top of the staircase was that Megan and Iris had gotten rid of the coffee table since the last time she was there. Then she realized it was still there. It was just buried beneath fifty million cans of Natural Light and a magic eight ball. Another young man snored in the recliner.

Elise wondered if he had a form of tribal art tattooed on his face. Perhaps he was Maori? Then she realized it wasn't actually the unique designs sported by native New Zealanders, but rather the work of his intoxicated friends. Apparently the poor soul had passed out and unknowingly been victim of a Magic Marker. Printed in jagged handwriting across his forehead was "I love wacking off!"

She turned to a noise in the kitchen and watched as Scrubbles ate from one of several pots that had been left on the stove. He glanced at Elise and Carly as if they had been there all day before he stuck his head back into his meal.

The guy who had let them in flopped back onto the couch, closed his eyes, and pulled a throw pillow over his head, attempting to block out the light. Elise glanced over her shoulder at Carly. Eyes wide, she looked equally as surprised.

"Let's go to my room," she whispered. They headed down the hall, past Iris and Megan's closed bedroom doors.

"Looks like we missed the party," Carly said as she set her box on the floor.

They set their boxes down and continued to unload while her new roommates' friends dozed in the living room. They were hauling Elise's dresser through the room when one of the boys sighed loudly and rolled over, as if he was being rudely awakened. All the while Iris and Megan had yet to make an appearance.

She noticed Scrubbles stretching one long front leg across the floor outside Iris's room. He was scratching at something, and Elise wondered what he was after until she realized he wasn't actually scratching. He was digging. Or at least attempting to dig a hole to cover up the mound of poop he'd just left outside the door. Judging from the faint animal odor that came from Iris's room, Elise assumed his litter box lay inside.

She debated waking Iris. Which was worse? Picking up cat poop or interrupting her roommates' sleep on the first day? She didn't want to get started on the wrong foot and decided she had cleaned up enough little doggie dumps on her walks with Bella that she could handle picking up a little cat doodle. She was about to head for some paper towels when Megan's bedroom door opened.

"Oh!" she gasped. "Elise! You're here."

"Yes. Today is *the* day."

She wore a pair of underpants and a tank top. Elise avoided looking at her nipples, which were glowing through her sheer white camisole like headlights. She waited for Megan to run to her room for a bathrobe, but instead she threw her arms around her. "I'm so glad you made it! Let me just wash my face, and I'll help you get unpacked."

Elise watched as Megan missed Scrubbles's little present by a millimeter. "Scrubbles!" she said. "I don't know why Iris even has that cat. She's always locking the poor thing out, and he's always crapping where he shouldn't be. "Iris!" She beat on the door. "Iris. Elise is here, and your cat shit in the hallway again!"

Iris emerged, also in her underwear, her legs sticking from the granny-style panties like bratwurst. "Whatever, Megan. The house is in shambles and it's totally your fault." She looked at Elise. "It was not my idea to have people over last night, but Miss Party Girl over here just *had* to invite people over."

"You didn't seem to mind so much when you were on your fifth shot of tequila."

Bella came out of the bedroom to see what the commotion was about, and Elise realized this was the first time the cat and dog had come face-to-face. A blunt vision of the two animals going for each other's throats popped into her thoughts. This was all she needed at this point. However, Bella wagged her little tail and trotted over to the cat. Scrubbles was more reluctant but politely stood while the dog sniffed every inch of his body.

Iris looked down at the box Elise held. Her Potter CD rested on top, and Iris immediately pointed to it.

"I love them!" she said. "They're my favorite band."

"Really? Interesting. I just lived with the bass player and his girlfriend."

"Jimmy Frankel was your roommate before here?"

"You could call him that."

"Iris is in love with the lead singer," Megan said.

"No I'm not." Her cheeks turned red.

"Uh. Yes. You. Are."

Who knew Potter had so many fans? She felt like she knew a celebrity.

Megan and Iris did little to help. Rather, they said good-bye to leftover partygoers, then argued over who was going to use their previous roommate's Saturn for the afternoon.

Iris wanted it so she could go volunteer at a homeless shelter for a summer class project she was working on. Megan wanted it so she could go to the library for her summer school English class.

"I can give one of you a ride," Elise said, trying to be helpful.

"Well, we have another car," Iris said. "It's just that the Saturn is so much cooler." Elise wondered what the other car looked like. How cool could a Saturn be?

She was putting her clothes away when her cell phone rang. It was a number she didn't recognize. Max? Should she answer? What if it wasn't him? She did have a strict policy of not answering the phone for unknown callers, and for a moment she remembered what had happened the last time she'd answered. She ended up at a baby shower with Jimmy. However, she couldn't take the suspense.

She let it ring three times before picking up. She didn't want it to look like she was carrying the cell phone in her pocket, even when she slept, which she was. She needed to seem busy.

"Hello?"

"Yes, hi, Elise. Thomas Yackrell here."

His glasses and loafers were practically a faded memory.

"I just wanted to see if you were still interested in going to my public speaking group. It's called the Podiummasters—all one word—and I thought you might want to come. It's a wonderful group of professionals. I think I mentioned it last time I saw you."

"Well, um, actually I'm going to be very busy these next few weeks. With the move and everything. And I'm starting a new book, so maybe down the road?"

"Well, they'll have a meeting at the end of the month. Lemme tell you what. I'll check the schedule and get back to you and we can set a date. How does that sound?"

She thought for a moment. Her instinct told her to just say no. But her heart told her not to be mean. "Uh, yeah. I can't promise anything, but that sounds fine."

"Who was that?" Carly asked as soon as Elise hung up.

"This guy my parents are trying to set me up with."

"Is he cute?"

"The lenses of his glasses are bulletproof."

Carly laughed.

"I shouldn't make fun of him," Elise said. "He's nice, but he's just so not my type. He wants to go to his Podiummasters Club, which I could probably use. But I don't want to lead him on."

"Just avoid him."

Elise was starting to wonder if that was Carly's attitude toward everyone.

16. Youthful Guidance

The day after Elise moved in with the Branston sisters she ate her Special K with a wooden spoon. She hadn't unpacked the ample silverware she owned yet, and there were no clean spoons in the kitchen. She tried to be brave and search the pile in the sink, but when she saw mold growing she decided to settle for the lone wooden mixer which rested in a drawer full of crumbs.

After living with Justine's anal retentiveness she had hoped for roomies whose mere presence didn't make her feel like she needed to make her bed. Living in squalor was what she had gotten.

"Good morning," Megan said when she entered the kitchen. She didn't seem to find her choice in utensils odd. She poured herself cereal in a glass. "So I was wondering," Megan said. "And you can totally say no." Elise watched as she searched for a utensil. "But I have this paper due, and I really don't have time to write it," she said as she pulled a dirty spoon from an empty bag of chips on the countertop. "So I was wondering if maybe I could pay you to write my paper. Being that you are a writer, I figured you might be interested." She ran the spoon under the faucet.

She could think of a dozen things she'd rather do. "What's it on?"

"Emily Dickinson."

"Well, I really don't know that much about her, and besides, to be perfectly honest, I don't really like writing essays." She wondered two things: One, how Megan didn't have time to write a paper. She didn't even have a job, and she was taking one summer school class. Two, how did she have the money? Their parents supported them, but wouldn't she rather spend it on other things? "I'll help you, though," Elise said. "I'll take a look at it, and we can work on it together. Okay?"

She shrugged. "All right."

After they ate their breakfast, she led Elise to her room. Elise felt bad about stepping all over Megan's clothes, CDs, books, and other belongings until she watched as Megan trounced over all her stuff as if it were carpeting. She sat down on her bed and handed Elise one paragraph. "This is all you have?"

"Uh-huh."

"When is this due?"

"Today." She didn't seem too worried. "And it's supposed to be five pages."

"What was the exact assignment?"

"I have to pick a poem from this book." She held up a completely thrashed hardcover book with remnants of Dickinson's portrait on the cover. "Then I have to analyze it."

"Let me see the poem." They spent two hours working on Megan's paper, and though she hadn't actually sat down and written it for her, she felt as if she should probably still be paid. She had stood over Megan's shoulders, practically telling her what to write verbatim.

The thought of money reminded her that she needed to go to the bank to deposit a check that Justine had given her for some of the bills before she'd moved out. Even though all the utilities had been in Justine's name, and Elise had typically written her checks, she had covered the bills for the last couple of months, and Justine paid her back. She wanted to deposit it right away while she was fairly certain that her former roommate had money in her account.

"Do you have any idea where there is a Mission Federal Credit Union around here?" she asked Iris.

"Oh yeah. There is one right by campus. I need to go there, too. Do you want to go together?"

"Okay. I'm going right now though," she said as she reached for her car keys.

"That's fine. But I'll drive."

They walked to a basic four-door sedan. The only thing unique about the Saturn was its light lavender paint. It wouldn't have been Elise's first color choice, but maybe it appealed to a younger crowd. Surprisingly, the car was immaculately clean and smelled like fresh lemons. A tree-shaped car air freshener dangled from the rearview mirror.

"That was nice of Nicole to let you use the car while she's away," Elise said.

"Yeah, she said we could drive it around because it's not good to leave a car sitting for that long." She opened the sunroof.

Elise sensed that Nicole had probably assumed they would take it to the grocery store every once in while. While eating brats and drinking Heineken, she probably had no idea that her roommates were using her Saturn as their primary source of transportation.

They waited in line at the bank. Elise looked at the tellers, girls her age, working behind the counter. She was just starting to think that it was rare to meet a male bank teller when her eyes landed on one. He was unique for a couple of reasons. One, he appeared to be the only guy who worked at the bank. Two, he was drop-dead hot. She guessed that he was no older than twenty-one, and way too young for her. But perhaps he could date Iris or Megan.

He looked like the type of guy who would be in a soap opera. All

those daytime actors looked as if they hit the gym six days a week
and had spent the last two weeks tanning in the Bahamas. Even from
where she stood she could see how bright his sea green eyes were.
They looked like crystals, and he had the kind of long, dark eyelashes
every girl dreamed of growing. The only thing that needed some work
were his clothes. He wore a white short-sleeved button-down shirt
and a very bland tie that looked as if he had borrowed it from his father's closet. She couldn't help but wonder what he was doing in
those clothes, or any clothes for that matter. Why didn't he run off to
Vegas and join Chippendales? He could probably make three times
the amount he made at the bank, just in tips.

She was thinking of ways to subtly point him out to Iris when she
realized he was staring at her. She smiled at him, and though he was
too young, she couldn't help but feel flattered that he'd noticed her.
He lifted his hand to wave, and that's when she realized that he
wasn't checking her out. He was waiting for her to come to the
counter. It was her turn.

She handed him the check from Justine and a very small check
she'd been meaning to deposit for some time. When she was in ele-
mentary school her father had bought her stock in Nordstrom, and
she still received very small checks from the department store a few
times a year. She handed the hot bank teller the money and glanced at
his name tag while he typed her checking account number into the
computer. Billy.

He looked at her Nordstrom check, flipped it over, then looked at
it again. She suddenly felt really absurd for depositing a four dollar
check. He looked puzzled. He flipped the check over and examined
the front of it. "This check isn't made out to you," he said.

She'd been depositing these checks for over ten years, and no one
had ever said anything to her. "Well, yes it is. My name is right beneath my father's on the check. See." She pointed.

"Yeah, but the way it's written it means that you're a minor and
that your father is the payee."

Maybe she should just roll with this and pretend she was a minor. It would work to her benefit if she was ever feeling lonely. "Well, I have to be honest. This is the first time anyone has ever said anything to me about this, and I've been over eighteen for some time now."

"That's really strange. I can't figure out why anyone hasn't said anything to you."

"Well, we're talking about checks that are under four dollars here." She found herself approaching The Cliff of Babble. "I mean, I just never really thought they were that big of a deal. I always just saw them as meaningless little checks. Little ones here and there to cover the fees when I was overdrawn from my checking account." This was only getting worse. Not only did she appear totally over the hill, but also poor and irresponsible in front of the Chippendales bank teller.

"Meaningless money?" he said. "I've never heard anyone call money meaningless before. If you saved five of them, it would be a tank of gas."

She felt her cheeks going red and was tempted to explain that he was completely right, and she didn't believe money was meaningless at all, but people were starting to stare, and Iris had finished taking care of her accounting and was now waiting in the back of the bank with her arms folded over her chest.

He lowered his voice. "But listen. I'll deposit this check for you today. You have to call Nordstrom though and have them change the account to just your name." He winked at her. "I'll hook you up just this once."

Was he flirting with her? She hadn't been winked at in ages. She deposited her checks, and as she said good-bye, she thought maybe she would need to return to take out a loan or open a new savings account. She loved feeling like Demi Moore.

They stopped at Rubio's in Pacific Beach for fish tacos on the way home. She was fishing in her purse for money when she noticed the light on her cell phone blinking. She had messages. The first one was from Carly.

"You still have stock in Nordstrom? I can't believe you haven't sold that thing by now. The market is good—you should cash in. But first you need to learn how to lock the keys on your cell phone. You dialed me again, and I just heard your whole conversation at the bank. You better be careful. Anyway, call me!"

Oops. Thank God it had only been her weird encounter with the bank teller. One of these days someone was going to overhear her gossiping.

Next message. "Hey Elise. It's Max. I was thinking about heading to the track on Thursday and wanted to see of you wanted to come with me. Give me a call when you get a chance."

She was going out with him.

17. And They're Off

The morning of Elise's date with Max she woke filled with nervous energy. Bella slept next to her, and Scrubbles slept at the foot of her bed. Lying next to the two pets made her relax a little more.

If it were up to Bella, the two pets would be best friends. She wagged her tail furiously and even jumped in circles sometimes when Scrubbles entered the room. However, the cat had kept his cool. He wasn't entirely sure about the dog yet and often eyed her suspiciously if she came too close. Despite his trepidation, Scrubbles had seemed to find comfort in Elise's room. Who could really blame him? The apartment was too gross, even for an animal.

She pictured Max in his shop, his toned arms peeking from a T-shirt while he tuned a Gibson. He was probably as calm as could be. She felt hungry, but when she thought of food, nothing sounded good to her. She opened the fridge and scanned the contents. Leftover pizza. Yogurt. Beer. A bottle of vodka. The only thing that sounded good to her was toast, and she headed for the pantry, nearly tripping over Iris's Ugg boots en route.

While she waited for her toast to cook, she thought about what she should wear. Her only experience with the track had been seeing *Seabiscuit* on the big screen. Since watching the movie she'd been under the impression that horse races were a dressy affair. Women wore sundresses with matching gloves and glamorous hats. What would Max think if she greeted him at the front door, wearing a flowered sundress with gloves to her elbows and a hat that Princess Diana would've sported? She envisioned a look of panic washing over his face, the color draining from his cheeks. She'd stick with jeans and a blouse.

The toaster let out a loud ding, and she pulled out the bread with the tips of her fingers. When she opened the silverware drawer it was almost empty. Except for the dull butcher knife Elise had taken from her parents' Salvation Army pile eight years ago and a cheese grater, there was nothing else. She looked at the mound of dishes in the sink and decided she would rather not pick through lasagna explosions and bowls with cereal mush to find a butter knife. She'd unloaded her silverware, but Megan and Iris had already used every single piece, discarding them all in the wasteland known as their sink when they were finished.

While buttering her toast with a butcher knife she debated waiting for Max on the street corner a block from their apartment. This way he wouldn't have to see the dish heap in their sink or the three-day-old cranberry vodka cocktails on the coffee table, a roach clip floating in one.

Though she didn't want to get off on the wrong foot, she decided to ask them to help her tidy up a bit before Max arrived. It was only fair, considering she hadn't mixed one cocktail yet. However, it was ten o'clock, and Max was picking her up at two. The girls were still asleep. So far they hadn't gotten out of bed before eleven. And the odor of cat urine that wafted from Iris's room was enough to keep her away for the moment.

She took a trip to the Dumpster and when she returned, she heard music coming from Megan's room. She knocked on the door and waited. "Coming!"

When her roommate opened the door, she wore a G-string and

pink tank top, which didn't leave much to the imagination. Elise waited for her to explain that she hadn't done laundry in six months and thus had run out of clean pants and a bra. Instead she waited for Elise to explain what she was doing in her doorway with the vacuum and a bottle of 409.

"Hi," Elise said. "I don't mean to bug you, but I have a date today, and he's picking me up here . . ." She hated being the anal one and could feel an uncontrollable babble attack coming on. The moment she stumbled off, she'd uncontrollably spew out sentences like a broken sprinkler head. She tried to remain placid and continued, "And anyway, I was wondering if you guys could help me clean up because well, he's going to be here in about two hours, and he hasn't seen my place yet, and um—"

"You have a date? Yeah, I'll help you clean. But you know most of the mess is Iris's. And if she didn't sleep all day, our apartment wouldn't look this way." She immediately headed to her sister's door and let herself in.

"Iris! Elise has a date, and we need to clean the apartment."

"What?"

"Get up. We need to clean the apartment. Elise has a date, and he's gonna be here soon!"

"Get out." Hangovers had a way of making people sound like they were dying.

"Get up and help. You can start by cleaning out that cat box. It's disgusting."

"What's disgusting is the sound of you having sex every night. Maybe I wouldn't sleep so late if there was any peace and quiet around here."

"Shut up, Iris," she hissed. "He's still here."

Iris looked at Elise. "Did you hear her last night, Elise?"

She had heard something but was so tired she never quite figured out what the noise was. "Um. I fell asleep early," she said not wanting to get involved. She was thinking of ways to prevent them from fighting when out of Megan's room sauntered a guy with a severe case of bed head and extremely wrinkled clothes. Elise thought that perhaps she would be introduced to this gentleman, but instead he walked past them and mumbled, "Later."

Who was this? Obviously he was responsible for keeping Iris up all night, but Megan was clearly not going to provide many details about his identity as she sat there bantering with Iris in her underwear. Elise really hoped she got dressed before Max arrived.

Iris hopped out of bed, also wearing only her underpants and a tank top. "That guy is such a loser," she said. Elise wondered if he could hear them. "Such a player."

It was awkward standing there while the two of them fought in their underwear. However, listening to them argue was way too good to pass up. She had no idea Megan was romantically involved with anyone, let alone some cad who apparently enjoyed loud sex.

She avoided looking at them and let her eyes wander over Iris's room. The carpet was covered in dirty laundry, crusty underwear, and jeans with grass stains around the lower hems. If Elise were asked what color Iris's carpet was, she would honestly have no clue. There was not one square inch of unoccupied floor space.

A congealed Salisbury steak dinner rested on her nightstand next to several half-full glasses of wine. Cigarette butts floated like dead logs in her Chardonnay, making the liquid appear piss-colored. There was dry cat food sprinkled over her dirty clothes, and Elise noticed a small stain of blood on her sheets.

"Whatever, Iris. At least I get some. When was the last time a guy even called you?"

Elise cleared her throat. "Listen guys, I didn't mean to start a huge argument. But um . . ."

"I'm not the one who had people over to watch *The Real World* last night," Megan said to Iris. "The living room is your mess."

"Why don't we all just pitch in and take different tasks?" she asked. "It will make things go faster."

"I'm not doing the living room." Iris was clear.

"Well, I'm not—"

"Okay, I'll do the living room," Elise said. "Iris, why don't you do the bathroom? Megan, you do the kitchen."

They spent all morning cleaning. Elise suspected they were doing a half-assed job, shoving everything in closets and cupboards just to make things look tidy. But there was no time to complain. After showering she spent several minutes picking out an outfit and settled on her favorite jeans and a white Spanish-looking top with red flowers that fell off her shoulders.

While she waited for Max she watched a rerun of *The Real World* with Iris and Megan. She'd never been a huge fan of the show, but since she had moved to Mission Beach she had really begun to conclude that you had to be a total nut to qualify for the show.

The doorbell rang, and Iris and Megan didn't even bother to take their eyes from the television. This was fine with her, because she didn't really want a huge audience while she greeted Max.

There was something about a guy with wet hair that turned her on, and seeing Max with his damp hair slicked away from his face made a flock of butterflies explode in her stomach. He smelled delicious, too, and except for his little soul patch beneath his lip, his face looked smooth and clean from a fresh shave.

Thank God she hadn't run out and bought a Princess Diana hat and dress. He was dressed in jeans and a green T-shirt.

"Come on in," she said. She wondered what he would think of her after meeting her college-aged roommates and seeing her rundown apartment. He owned his shop and the loft that he lived in above it, and she suddenly felt slightly insecure about her living situation.

"I gotta admit," he said. "I was a little jealous when I drove in here."

"You were?"

"Yeah, I mean, you must get the best sunsets every night living down by the water. I grew up at the beach, and that is one thing I really miss living out in North Park."

"Well, you're welcome to come over anytime. We can actually see them from our balcony."

"I might have to take you up on that."

"Max, this is Iris and Megan."

Her roommates sat with their feet on the coffee table and each waved a hand at her date. "Great to meet you guys," he said.

She felt a need to get him out of there before he noticed the stains on the carpet or Megan's butt peeking from the bottom of her shorts. "Well, all right. We should be on our way." She reached for her purse.

"You mind riding on my bike?" Max said. "I have an extra helmet."

She had forgotten about his motorcycle and wondered how she could miss such a huge detail. She'd be touching him. "No. Not at all." However, this suddenly changed everything. If she had dragon breath she could forget making it to date two with him.

He looked at her flip-flops. A small smile lifted the corners of his mouth. "You can't wear those on the bike though. You gotta wear something that covers your feet."

She quickly headed back to her room and changed into her Pumas with the silver stripes up the sides. After sliding into her sneakers she tore through her desk drawer like an animal. Of course she was out of breath freshener when she needed it most. For a moment she debated brushing her teeth again. However, he was waiting around the corner, and would probably hear the frantic sound of her grating toothbrush. Instead, she slipped into the bathroom on her way back to the living room, squeezed a dollop of toothpaste onto her finger, shoved it in her mouth, swished it around, and swallowed before joining them.

The air outside was unusually warm and dry for the beach. She was glad they were experiencing a dry, hot summer, because this meant the ocean's humidity wouldn't make her face look like wet spaghetti.

When they reached his motorcycle he handed her a helmet. "Here's the spare." It looked like a giant beige pumpkin. "I know it's ugly," he said. "I'm sorry. I'd trade with you, but mine will be way too big for you."

When she slid it over her head she knew she looked like a fool. She could feel her cheeks squeezing together as if her grandmother were sandwiching them between her hands, telling her how much she'd grown. And her head suddenly felt as if it weighed more than her body. Furthermore, she wished she'd worn her hair up. It was sticking out of the bottom like a shag rug caught in a doorframe.

"Let me help you with the chin strap. It'll loosen it up a little." His big hands moved beneath her chin, and she could see the callused edges of his fingers while he loosened the strap.

He slid on his black, edgy, *I own a guitar shop and hang out in North Park* helmet, and she wondered what he must think of this little peon riding on the back of his bike.

The only time she had ever climbed onto the back of a moving object was when she had been horseback riding in college. She knew it was going to be a little awkward climbing onto the back of his Harley-Davidson. Even worse, in fact. When she'd been horseback riding, she'd had the horse to herself. Was she supposed to hang on to Max? Did she slide her arms around his waist? Prop her hands on his shoulders? Hang on to the seat for dear life? Maybe she should ask. He motioned with his thumb for her to hop on the back.

"You can just hang on to my waist," he yelled over the noise. Thank goodness he had told her.

She slid her arms around his waist and put her feet on the tiny little kickstand that they shared. Even though he wasn't wearing a jacket, he smelled like leather and mint gum.

Riding on the back of his motorcycle was like hanging out on one long, fun ride at Disneyland. The fresh air on her face and the way her heart raced when he sped up made her wish they were driving to Cabo San Lucas rather than just twenty minutes to Del Mar. His waist felt firm and strong, and his T-shirt soft and clean against the side of her face.

Dust swept up around them in the parking lot at the track. "You all right back there?" he called over his shoulder.

"Yeah! Great!" Then she realized that she didn't have to yell. He was sitting right in front of her.

The scent of clean Del Mar salt water and the soft breezes that filtered beneath her thin cotton shirt were enough to make her already love the races.

They walked to the open-air Spanish-style stadium. She was surprised at how clean the grounds were, not a piece of trash to be found. When she went to Padres games there were peanut shells and empty beer cans even at the entrance. It was the first time she had ever been to a sporting event and seen valet parking in the front. Every kind of luxury imaginable lined the driveway of the track, and she wondered if she should've worn the hat and gloves after all.

Max bought their tickets and gave Elise a small guide that showed which horses were racing, which jockeys were riding them, and a million other abbreviated things she decided to try to figure out later. He showed her in detail how to bet, and she asked if they could just watch the first race just as a practice round so she could get the hang of it before blowing any money.

He smiled. "Of course. Let's grab drinks while we're waiting." He bought them each a beer. As she took the first crisp sip she couldn't imagine doing anything better than playing hookey and sipping a cold beer on a sunny day with him. If the date ended now, she would've had a blast.

"C'mon. I want to show you something," he said as he pulled her hand. As he led her around the grounds, she looked around. She had never seen such a variety of people in her entire life. There were old men in polyester and orthopedic shoes studying the odds from newspaper clippings. She suspected they probably knew a lot more about betting than the surfers who had taken a break from the swell and were still wearing their swim trunks, or the tourists who appeared to be just as confused as Elise was about betting. There were people still wearing their suits from work and parents who had brought their little kids.

She scanned the stands for Lady Di hats and spotted a handful of women who looked as if they were attending a presidential inauguration. But for the most part people were dressed like Max and Elise.

They walked down to a small track where several horses slowly pranced around a fence, their jockeys riding atop them like little mice dressed in colorful caps and black boots. A number of gamblers and photographers hung around the rail of the Paddock and watched the horses as if they were studying for an exam.

"This is where all the horses come before they race." Max said. "You can check them out, see if you want to bet on them."

She remembered the time she had gone horseback riding at a dusty dude ranch near Tucson with several of her girlfriends. She had blown her nose later that day, and her boogers had dirt in them. Their guide, a skinny cowboy with the worst teeth Elise had ever seen in her life, handed her the reins of a brown horse with a rough coat the color of a seventy-year-old copper penny. The horse's name was Pappy and had absolutely no spark in its eyes.

The stallions that Elise admired today clearly bore no relation to Pappy. Dark chocolate in color and as sleek as brand-new Ferraris, these horses lifted their necks and knees like dazzling showgirls as they looped around the paddock. Instead of kicking up manure-laced dirt, their polished hooves tossed up dark earth similar in texture to the expensive potting soil her mother used in her rose garden. They carried themselves in such a way that made arrogance look absolutely beautiful. Just watching them made her heart beat faster.

"They're gorgeous," she said.

He nodded. "A lot of people like to see them before they bet. Sometimes if a horse is acting temperamental it might mean they're distracted. They may not race as well."

She was admiring a horse the color of fresh coffee beans when she heard a vaguely familiar voice behind her. "Elise? Elise Sawyer? Is that you?"

Her gaze moved from a polished set of hooves to Thomas Yackrell. Dressed in slacks that made his kneecaps look knobby, he wore the same tasseled loafers he'd sported at her parents' house. His legs looked like chopsticks, and he seemed much taller and paler than she remembered.

"Thomas! Good grief. This is more than I had even imagined. What a surprise."

He didn't even glance at Max. "I know. I buy a booth here every season for my company. We're up there." He pointed to the section where she'd seen the Lady Di hats. "You're more than welcome to join us." When he turned his head toward Max, she noticed how severe the part in his hair was. "And, um, you can bring . . ."

"Max, this is Thomas Yackrell."

Max's hand was curled around his beer, his star tattoo as bold and bright as any jockey uniform. When he moved his beer to the other hand to shake with Thomas, she noticed veins twitch in his forearms. His skin looked tanned next to Thomas's pink hands. "Nice to meet you," Max said.

"And you." His eyes quickly darted to Elise. "I found out the date for the next Podiummasters meeting. You still interested?"

She sort of wished that he would be silenced by a freak stampede. "Well actually . . ."

"Great. I'll call you. Let's try to get together for dinner, too. Enjoy the races." He spun on his loafers and almost left. Almost. However, he paused to look over his shoulder. "Oh and it was a pleasure meeting you, Mike."

"What a moron," Elise said as soon as he was gone.

Max shrugged. "He seemed all right."

"He's a friend of my parents. I hardly know him."

"You ready to bet? Or you still want to wait?" he said.

"I think I'm ready to bet."

"I'm betting on the female jockey," Elise said as she flipped through her little guide. "Julie Krone is her name. And I like the name of her horse. Tigermite. Screw checking the odds and all that other nonsense. I like that name, and I've gotta support the chick rider."

Max looked at her choice, then raised an eyebrow. "That horse is the long shot. But you should go with your first instinct. Sometimes it's lucky just to pick the names you like. And if the long shot wins, you'll really cash in."

Elise looked at her race program while they waited in line. There were trifectas and all kinds of things Elise had yet to understand. She sort of felt nervous. Everyone seemed to know what they were doing. What if she screwed up and held up the whole line? What if the bet-taker guy got mad at her for being a novice gambler?

When she walked up to the counter she handed the attendant two dollars and remembered everything Max had told her. Apparently, there was a sequence in betting. "I'd like to put two dollars on number seven to show." It was a very safe bet.

The man took her money and handed her a ticket. Max was next, and his betting was much more calculated and complex. She still wasn't certain what he had done after they left the counter. She just knew he'd bet on Ice Princess and Happy Dayz.

Even though they had paid for seats in the grandstand, they watched the first race from the lower level of the track. "This is where all the real action is," Max said as he leaned against the railing.

She could practically reach out and touch the Spanish bugler that came out and played a little tune before the horses headed to the gate.

"Tha hawses are approaching the starting gate," a male British accent announced. She had expected the same British man to stroll onto the green wearing plaid plants and carrying a pistol that he would shoot off before sending the horses bolting in terror. However, the British voice returned and simply said, "And away they go," just as casually as if he were saying "Cheerio, love."

At first she couldn't keep track of what the Brit was saying because he was talking so fast. The starting gate was clear on the other side of the track, so she couldn't really see. But when the horses came around the corner she could see that Tigermite was somewhere in the front. She clung to the fence.

"Tigermite taking gain over You Betcha Luck," she heard him say in his speedy announcement. "First place Tigermite! Second place Bridesmaid. And third place Neverending Story."

For a moment she didn't realize she was jumping up and down and screaming like a maniac. She couldn't help it.

"Mine won! It won!"

He smiled and rubbed her back. "I know. Lemme see your ticket." He looked at the little square of paper. "You probably won about eighty bucks. We'll see when we cash it in."

"Oh my God! I love the races." She grabbed his arm. "The next round of beer is on me."

She made eighty-five dollars and bet four on the next race. When the races started, she watched as an ambulance circled the track. She'd been so excited during the last race that she hadn't noticed it. "What's the ambulance for?" she asked.

"It's so dangerous they have to follow them."

She had never been to something more exciting. She didn't win every race, but found that the thrill and anticipation of watching her horse outweighed any losses. At the end of the day she and Max both walked away with a little extra cash in their wallets.

"Thank you so much," she said as they walked back to his motorcycle. "I had so much fun."

"Good. I'm glad. We'll have to do it again soon. You hungry?"

She wasn't. Butterflies had moved into her stomach and taken control since he'd picked her up, but she didn't want the date to end. "Yes. I am."

* * *

The Red Fox was located on the lower level of an old hotel in North Park. Like the hotel, the décor looked as if it hadn't been updated in years. Part restaurant, part bar, it was dimly lit. It was crowded with young North Park barhoppers. But the most interesting part of the Red Fox was the entertainment. An elderly woman with a cap of snow white hair sat in the corner of the bar playing a large keyboard. In front of her, a row of retired people waited to karaoke to their favorite old hits. A man who appeared to be pushing eighty was singing "It Had to Be You" when Elise and Max slid into a booth.

The man sang with the same enthusiasm any twenty-year-old would've given the song, and his smile seemed to send rays of light over the bar. Elise could've sat in the Red Fox for hours, watching the geriatric karaoke.

She decided to splurge and order a steak dinner. Max did the same.

"So, what did you do before you opened the guitar shop?" she asked.

"Well, I went to college in San Francisco. But I quit after a couple years. My band was touring all the time, and school wasn't working out with touring and everything."

"And?"

"Well, I played music for about ten years. Finally realized I couldn't take it anymore, and opened up my shop."

"What couldn't you take?" she before dipping a steak fry in ketchup.

"I'm sure you understand what it's like. It's like any other industry where you're creating your own product. You never know where you're going to be. I wanted more stability."

"I know exactly what you mean."

"We were signed by a big label when I was playing music, but our album never took off. I had a lot of money from my advance though, so I quit the band and cashed in."

"Good for you. If I had money to buy a place, I would in a heart-beat. Sometimes I feel like it's pointless to even save. By the time I do have enough money, condos will be a million dollars."

"You'll get in there."

She could've sat there talking to him all night about life. They ate steaks and drank red wine, and Elise watched women who probably belonged to her grandmother's gin club belt out songs like "Some-where Over the Rainbow."

He drove her home, and she could feel that awkward part of the evening approaching. The part where she didn't know if he would kiss her, or maybe even ask to come in. What she really hoped is that he'd make plans to see her again soon. Or would he politely say he had a good time and disappear into the starry night, never to be heard from again, which had happened to Elise a couple times.

He put his hand on the small of her back as they walked to the front door. "I had a great time with you today," he said.

"I did, too. Thanks for everything."

"We'll have to do it again." She sensed he meant it and wondered if he would kiss her on the cheek, the lips, or would he just go for a nice hug? These all meant different things. She hoped her breath smelled okay and tried to catch a whiff of it while she searched for her keys.

"I had so much fun," she said.

"I did, too. Let's—"

The staccato sound of rapid heels came running up behind them.

"Open the door!" a voice screeched.

Elise whipped around to face Iris, Megan, and a fellow she'd never met before holding a gigantic, life-sized poster. Elise wasn't sure what was more interesting, the fact that they were sprinting full speed down Mission Boulevard dressed as hookers and a pimp or the half-naked men featured on the poster that flapped in front of them as they sped toward the apartment.

"Elise! Open the fucking door! Quick!" Megan shouted, her eyes wide from terror. "We'll be arrested!"

Elise fumbled with her keys, while their feather boas flapped up around their necks. As soon as she pushed their door open, they ran through like fugitives. "Close the door! Close the damn door!" their friend shouted as he dove onto their staircase.

"Holy shit! That was close!" Iris yelled.

"Oh my God!" Megan said.

Elise looked at Megan's fishnet tights and leather skirt. "What happened?"

They burst into laughter and didn't stop for a good minute.

"You'll never believe!" Megan finally managed to say.

"We were coming back from a pimp and ho party," Iris explained, "when Megan here noticed this poster at a bus stop bench." Their friend held up a poster of several men with huge muscles and the same hairstyles as Fabio. Their weenies bulged from black Speedos like sacks of potatoes, and bow ties clung to their necks. *Thunder Down Under at the Pala Indian Reservation* was boldly advertised on top. "It's a poster for a strip club!" Megan exclaimed. "I told Iris and Joe that I wanted it, and the next thing I knew, Joe had broken into the poster's holder and ripped it out. We were all looking at it when a flashlight came toward us, and it was this stupid security guard on a bike. We just fled."

"With the poster!" Iris yelled.

"I can't believe we made it," Joe sighed. "That was *such* a close call."

"That poster is going to look fantastic in our living room! Aren't you excited, Elise?"

Thrilled. Just what they needed: a six-foot poster of gay male dancers whose privates were as big as her face.

Max chuckled. "I ripped off a poster for that movie *Natural Born Killers* when I was in college. We had Woody Harelson's gigantic head in our apartment forever."

"It's the coolest ever!" Megan yelled as a run spread down her tights.

"We're keeping it for the rest of our lives," Iris said.

"Well, hey," Max said. "I gotta open up early tomorrow, so I should get going."

"I'll walk you out," Elise said.

"No!" Megan shouted. "Don't draw any attention to our apartment."

He patted her shoulder. "I'll call you. Let's hang out this week."

She knew she wasn't going to get a kiss with an audience there and sort of felt like kicking a hole through their Chippendales poster. For tonight, she'd just have to settle for a pat on the shoulder.

18. Thieves

The next morning she woke up bright and early at eight a.m. She'd usually sleep a good hour longer, but she was too excited. Going to the horse races was enough to put her in a good mood for a decade. She could not only see herself becoming a chronic gambler but also falling head over heels in love with Max.

As she opened her bedroom window, she decided that the ocean air smelled a little bit better, the sun shined a little bit brighter. Bella propped her paws on the ledge, and Elise decided that they were going for a walk. It was rare that she was up at this time, and she decided to take advantage of the morning hours. Bella began to run in circles when she noticed Elise pull the leash from her desk drawer. She jumped on the bed, skidded across, and then looped around the bedroom twice, knocking over the wastebasket. Walking Bella in City Heights had been out of the question. It had been a long time since she had seen her leash.

Throughout life most of her visits to the boardwalk had been on the weekends. Being on the boardwalk on a weekday drew in a different crowd and was not as busy as the weekend. The skateboarders and singles crew looking for a potential date while meandering on Rollerblades seemed to have rolled off to class or work.

Rather, she noticed a lot of strollers, young mothers wearing visors and pushing their babies all the way from North Pacific Beach while they tried to burn off their pregnancy weight. The area was much more peaceful. Without the usual buzz of voices and wheels, the sound of crashing waves seemed louder. Bella was so excited that it was hard for Elise to walk fast enough to keep up with her. Her little nose drew its own trail over the cement.

When she walked a half mile and realized that she had not spotted one person without a child or a wedding ring, she realized that she lived her life like a housewife. She had the freedom to walk at will, run errands when most were sitting in a cubicle. She could go to the mall when there was no traffic, do laundry in the middle of the day, and clean her house at lunchtime. The only thing was, she didn't have a house. Or a husband. Or a child.

She was working hard to get the house, and she'd never planned on relying on a man for anything. She wanted to earn her own things and to feel the success that came along with making her own money. If she sold her movie rights, she might be able to have her own place. But then what? Ever since she'd moved from Arizona her roommates had driven her to work even harder. But what would it be like when she lived alone? It would just be Bella and her. She'd be hanging out with all the housewives during the week and hitting the singles scenes on the weekend.

It was way too early to speculate what would happen with Max, and she didn't want to pursue him just because she wanted a boyfriend. She liked him, really liked him, and if things worked out with him, she'd be happier than if she had any condo or movie deal. She wanted him in her life.

When they returned she noticed the previous day's mail on the counter. Atop the pile was a letter from her landlord in City Heights. Her deposit. The stars were aligned for her. First her fantastic date with Max, and now she was getting her eight hundred dollar deposit back from the place she had shared with Justine. She tore open the envelope and pulled a check and letter from the inside.

A surge of irritation bolted through her when she looked at the check. Six hundred dollars? It was supposed to be for eight hundred dollars. Clearly there had been a mistake. She quickly read the letter, which outlined how much money had been deducted. Two hundred dollars for a hole in the living room wall.

She didn't know who to be more angry with—Justine, or the landlord. The hole wasn't her fault, and Justine had promised to take care of it before they moved out. It was definitely Justine's fault, but she figured she had a better shot at getting money from her landlord.

She dialed him first. "This is Rich," he said when he answered the phone.

"Yes, hi. I recently moved from one of your units in City Heights, and I just got my deposit back, and two hundred dollars was deducted for a hole in the wall that I didn't create. That was my roommate's fault, and she was supposed to cover that."

"I understand." She was right about her instinct that he was a reasonable person, much more responsible than the fool she'd been living with. "However," he continued. "I don't know who is responsible for what when I look at the damage. All I know is there was a hole in the wall when I did my walk-through. I will have to hire someone to come in and drywall and paint, and it's money out of my pocket. It says on the lease that damage will be divided among the tenants. I apologize, but this is something you'll have to sort out with your roommate."

He had a point. It really wasn't his problem. She knew it would be pointless to argue with him, so she thanked him, then said goodbye. She wasted no time calling Justine. Elise didn't expect her to answer and wasn't surprised in the least when she was greeted with her voice mail. While she listened to the same voice she'd heard squealing

"Cheecher Meecher" for four months, she knew Justine was probably sitting right there next to the phone waiting for Jimmy to call. She was just avoiding Elise. "Hi, Justine. It's Elise." She debated explaining that she owed her two hundred dollars but figured she would never hear from the girl again if she let on that she was after money. "Please call me back when you get a chance. I miss you and just wanted to see how everything was going for you. Thanks!" *Asshole.*

She decided to head to the bank and deposit the six hundred dollars she did have into to her savings account. She tried not to think about everything she could spend two hundred dollars on. Gas for two months. New clothes to wear on her date with Max. Cleaning supplies for Iris and Megan. It was a lot of money in her world, and she tried not to burn with annoyance when she thought about her inconsiderate, boyfriend-obsessed ex-roommate.

She took a shower and ten minutes into it realized she was singing "Somewhere Over the Rainbow" loud and in a terrible Judy Garland voice.

Just as she tried not to think about her two hundred dollars she also tried not to think about when Max would call. Or if he would call. She opened her closet door and looked for something cute to wear. Call it ego, but she needed to look good for the hot bank teller. She searched for her halter top with the large floral print on it. It had an apron back and revealed just enough of her back to make her appear sexy without looking slutty.

She pulled the top out and began to put it on. While tying it around her neck she caught a faint odor of cigarettes and a perfume she didn't recognize. Odd. She couldn't recall wearing it. As far as she knew it was clean. When she put the top on she noticed that it looked a tad wrinkled. There was only one conclusion. Someone had been wearing her clothes.

This was completely fine with her. However, the idea of Iris and Megan looking through her closet when she wasn't home kind of gave her the creeps. Snooping was fine if the person under invasion had left their stuff in plain view. For example, if a roommate left prescription drugs sitting on a countertop, well then it was fine to peek and see if it was Prozac or Viagra. Obviously, it was no big secret if the roommate forgot to put their medicine away. However, going into people's closets and wearing their clothes without asking was not cool. She searched for a different shirt and threw the dirty one into her laundry basket.

She didn't like the idea of her roommates going through her closet and wearing her clothes, and as she headed to the bank she wondered how she was going to tell them. She really had no proof that they were going through her stuff. She was pretty sure, but what if she confronted them and they hadn't even set foot inside her room? Then they would think she was uptight and selfish. Maybe she should just wait and see if it happened again.

Billy the bank teller was hotter than hell, but she wasn't as excited to see him now that she had Max to daydream about. She ended up being helped by a different teller anyway. But when she was leaving she caught him watching her over the ledge at his station. Instead of quickly shifting his eyes back to the customer he was waiting on, he just watched her. She smiled, and he lifted his head in acknowledgment before turning back to his work.

Even though she couldn't stop thinking about her day at the races, she knew she had to get some work done, so when she got home she immediately went to her computer.

Bella curled up at her feet, and Scrubbles hopped onto her chair and cuddled his warm body against her back. When she turned her computer on and went to the file section, she was alarmed to see that there was a file she didn't recognize. "The Work of Mark Twain" was the last thing that had been on her screen. From what she remembered it had been seven or eight years since she had written a paper on Mark Twain. It had to belong to Megan, who was currently enrolled in a summer school course about American writers.

This was where she drew the line. She didn't mind if they borrowed her clothes, so long as they didn't ruin them and they asked first, but she did mind if they used her computer without asking. She had a lot of important work stored in her computer. If anything was lost or ruined or destroyed from some kind of cyber virus, she could never replace it.

She worked on her novel the rest of the day and tried to ignore the fact that Max hadn't called. Around four o'clock she went to the kitchen for a snack.

Her roommates were both dressed in hula skirts. She watched as Iris pulled a lei over Megan's head. "Aloha," Megan said when she noticed Elise.

"Hey. What are you guys doing?"

"We're going to a luau down the street," Iris answered.

"Cool. Um, listen, I hate to be a stickler, but if you guys use my computer, could you just ask first? I have a lot of really important stuff on there, and if it gets lost or destroyed, it would be a real problem, so could you just ask in the future?"

"Yeah. Sorry," Megan said. "I just had to hand in that paper today, and I didn't have time to go to the library."

"No biggie. Just let me know first from now on when you want to use it."

"Oh, I almost forgot," Iris said. "Max called you."

"He did?"

"Yeah. I don't know where you were, and I forgot to write it down."

"Thanks."

She went back to her bedroom and called him on her cell.

"Hey," he said. "I only have minute, but what are you doing Sunday night?"

She thought for a moment, even though she already knew the answer. She had to look a little bit busy. "Nothing. I'm free."

"Great. Why don't you come by? I'll cook dinner for us."

"Okay. Can I bring anything?"

"Just yourself."

She hung up the phone. "Yes!" she whispered. Sunday was four days away. It seemed so far.

19. A Wild Ride

A few days later Melissa called in deep and dire need of a babysitter. "Brice was supposed to take the afternoon off, and he had an emergency, and I have a doctor's appointment. I really don't want to take Jeffrey with me," she said. "I'll only be gone a couple of hours. Please. I'll pay you well, and if you want to lie out at the pool while he's sleeping, you can."

"All right. I'll be over in an hour."

"Thank you!" She heard Jeffrey squeal loudly in the background, and she wondered what in the hell she had just gotten herself into. However, now that she had a date lined up with Max, she could use the money for new clothes. She thought about how much more she could buy if she had the two hundred dollars that Justine owed her in her pocket. At times the irritation was so overwhelming that she couldn't even think about it.

Melissa was holding Jeffrey when Elise arrived, and he looked huge in her arms. "Isn't that bad for your back?" she asked. "I mean with the baby and everything."

"Yes, but he begs to be held all day, and I'm afraid he'll think I don't love him if I don't hold him."

Jeffrey was sucking on a cherry popsicle, and he stuck his bright red tongue out at Elise when she looked at him. "Hi, Jeffrey."

"Let's show Aunt Lise your new toy. She followed them to the backyard. Jeffrey immediately squirmed free of his mother's arms and ran toward a small child-sized Jeep. It was camouflage and had thick black tires and a fake walkie-talkie next to the steering wheel. "Show Aunt Lise how you drive it," Melissa called.

He jumped into the little vehicle, and Elise imagined that pedals rested somewhere beneath the steering wheel. This would be great exercise for him, she thought. He could really use the cardio. She waited for him to pedal with all his all his strength back toward them, but instead his chubby fingers turned the ignition, and his little off-road vehicle came buzzing to life.

"It actually drives?"

"Oh yeah. It's so neat." Her sister smiled from ear to ear, and Elise wondered what kind of drugs she and Brice were on. They gave him control of a car? No matter how small it was, the child was insane. She watched as Jeffrey steered the Jeep in circles around their hedges. Melissa didn't seem to notice when he took out two branches on their Double Delight rose plant. Instead she waved to him, then turned to Elise. "Isn't it fun?"

It was cute watching him drive the Jeep around the yard, and he seemed to be careful, so maybe there wasn't any harm.

"Anyway, I should get to my appointment. Make yourself at home."

She watched Jeffrey ride over safe terrain, keeping within his concrete path for several minutes. He occasionally sliced the side of a hedge and sent leaves scattering like confetti over the ground, but for the most part he was a decent driver.

Shortly after Melissa left, Goldie, their golden retriever, came bounding out from her dog door and ran to the lawn. Elise watched as the dog sniffed the ground for a moment, then squatted her hind legs to pee.

Jeffrey was heading in the dog's direction, and she thought for sure he would slow down when he noticed Goldie. However, she became a little alarmed when he didn't. Rather he pursed his lips together and continued on the same route.

The dog was taking care of business and didn't seem to notice the little army vehicle heading toward her until the last minute. Elise screamed for him to slow down, but he didn't stop. Goldie bolted just in time, barely missing the Jeep's front bumper. Ears back, she ran back to the house with her tail between her legs.

Elise was wondering how much longer he was going to ride the Jeep when she realized he was headed her way. She held up a hand and chuckled. "Uh, real cute, Jeffrey. Now slow down," she said as calmly as possible while backing away from him. "You're not going to run me over. Are—" She crashed into the a patio chair and fought to stay balanced. When she regained her composure she quickly headed for the grass.

As he sped up, a look of sheer delight crossed his face. At the last minute she jumped onto the lawn, coming within a millimeter of landing in the fattest pile of dog poop she'd ever seen. She was trying to maneuver her feet so she could flee without stepping in crap when she noticed that he was reversing right toward her. "Jeffrey!" she screeched as her eyes darted for a way out. She had no choice but to jump onto the Jacuzzi cover. He slammed on the brakes before crashing into the hot tub. She thought this might deter him, but he backed up and peeled out.

She stood atop the spa like a hostage, watching helplessly as he took out everything in his path.

How was she going to stop him? And even more important, how did her sister deal with him every single day? Maybe he was different around Melissa. She watched as he tore around the yard, leaving skid marks on the lawn and shouting with glee every time a bird fled his path.

He was taking corners quickly, occasionally riding on two wheels. How would she stop him? Was she going to have to yell for a neighbor? Would the police come with a stun gun?

His arms were as stiff as missiles and his brows furrowed as he headed back toward her. He rounded the corner next to the spa, and his hair flopped over his head when the Jeep turned on two wheels. She watched in horror as the tiny auto flipped onto its side and sent Jeffrey flying from the driver's seat like a small rocket.

She covered her mouth when he landed on his side, his shoulder hitting the pile of dog shit like a target.

"Oh my God," she breathed as she jumped from the spa. She didn't hear tears, only the buzz of the Jeep's engine, its wheels still spinning even after the collision.

He sat up just as she reached him. He looked dazed, and a long piece of dead grass dangled from his hair. "I crashed, Aunt Lise," he said quietly.

"I know." She picked him up. "Are you okay?"

He nodded, looking more embarrassed than hurt. She caught a pungent whiff of poo and remembered where he had landed. "Let's put you in the shower," she said. "You landed in Goldie's poop."

"Okay," he said quietly.

He seemed to enjoy showering, as he refused to get out once he was in there. She thought for sure he would get sick of sliding around on the shower floor, but he sat behind the glass in their guest bathroom, his hair matted to his face like palm fronds, while his bare butt slid across the tile. Every time she went to turn off the water, he screamed so loud she was afraid the neighbors would call the police. So she waited, figuring he'd get bored sooner or later. It wasn't until they ran out of hot water that he decided he'd had enough. After that, he fell asleep in front of *Bob the Builder*.

She was starving and was delighted to find their cupboards and refrigerator stocked full of good food. And it wasn't even the generic stuff that Elise was forced to buy due to financial constraints.

How nice it must be to buy in bulk, she thought, as she pulled a chocolate-chip granola bar from a Costco-sized box. She could only hope for the day when buying things like granola bars didn't seem like a luxury. She also helped herself to a soda before making herself a bagel with garlic cream cheese.

She was cleaning up her crumbs when Melissa returned. "If I'm not in labor by the thirtieth they're inducing me," she said. "I'm so ready to have this baby. I can't sleep anymore because it's hard to breathe when I lie down. Anyway, how was everything?"

"Fine, except he crashed his Jeep."

"What?"

Elise explained his little accident. "I'll have Brice throw it out," Melissa said. "Anyway, how is everything going with you? Your new place? Your love life? Any developments with the movie rights?"

"Well, everything is so slow in the book world. I've learned not to think about it that much. It could be a while before I hear anything about the movie rights." She debated telling her about Max but then remembered how bored Melissa was and how she would undoubtedly tell her parents. Elise's love life would be the most exciting thing that had happened in their country-clubbing world. She told her about Justine ripping her off instead.

"The girl has no class!" Melissa yelled. "And why can't she pull her head out of her ass and quit thinking about her dumb boyfriend for one minute? If you don't get that money back, sue her ass!" Elise hadn't heard her sister cuss like this since she had become a mother. Clearly, her hormones were raging in the last part of her pregnancy. Talking about Justine with someone else made her even more angry and for some reason seeing her sister's anger just fueled her irritation.

She decided to change the subject. "Well, I should be on my way."

On the way home Max called her. "What are you up to tonight?" he said. "I have to go to The Casbah to do sound for The Dragons. But why don't you stop by?"

She was not only happy that she would get to see him before their

dinner date on Sunday but ecstatic that he, too, wanted to see her before Sunday. She was so glad he wasn't the type of guy that played
games, or that she wouldn't end up borrowing Carly's copy of *He's
Just Not That Into You.* He *was* into her, and after her day with Jeffrey she couldn't think of a better way to spend the evening.

He'd told her to call him when she was parking, so he could come
outside and meet her. She was sort of glad he'd made the suggestion
because The Casbah wasn't located in the friendliest part of town. It
was situated just minutes from the airport and located in a neighborhood similar to her old one. She called him on his cell phone, and he
waited on the corner for her while she parked.

He kissed her on the cheek when they found each other. She
caught the same whiff of mint and leather. "Nice jacket," he said.

She had stopped at the mall on the way home from babysitting
and splurged on a velvet jacket with gathered sleeves. She'd also
found a pair of delicious Marc Jacobs heels on sale at Nordstrom.
The pink peep-toe heels were a little steep, but it was Max, she'd told
herself.

"You look cute."

"Thank you." *But drinks won't be on me tonight,* she wanted to
add. If he only knew.

The bar was dim but had a red glow cast over it, and she noticed
some goats' heads painted on the wall. So it wouldn't be up Marge's
alley, but it was a mecca for local rock bands.

They chatted on stools in the back. Then he taught her how to
play pool while the opening band played. She decided there might not
be anything sexier than a man with a pool stick. Watching him lean
over the table to concentrate on his shot stirred visions of him hovering over her, and she wondered what he would look like with no
clothes on.

"Here," he said, coming up behind her. "Aim to the left, and you'll get that shot." His hands brushed over her arms as he helped her reposition her pool stick. She knew she didn't look nearly as skilled or sexy with a cue, but she didn't mind him touching her.

He seemed to know everyone, and he introduced Elise to all his friends.

She would've stayed all night, but he was going to be doing the sound for for the headlining band and she didn't want him to feel like he had to entertain her. When she left, he walked her to her car. She felt her stomach turn with butterflies at the thought of him kissing her good-bye.

She pulled her keys out and stood beneath the streetlight. "Well, are we still on for Sunday?" she asked.

"Of course." Then he lowered his head slowly, and without giving it much thought, she moved toward him. He was a fantastic kisser, very little tongue and mostly soft lips. She loved feeling the roughness of his soul patch on her chin.

He pulled her into his arms, and she felt him get hard right there in the alley near The Casbah. If she wasn't concerned about the drug addict going through the trash ten feet away from them, she probably would've pulled him into the backseat of her bug and taken his clothes off right there beneath the glow of a streetlight. "You should probably get back to work," she said as he kissed her forehead.

He looked down at the bulge in his pants, and they both started laughing. He waited until her car was started and she had pulled out of her space before heading back to The Casbah.

She smelled beer as she walked up the staircase. She expected to see a dozen random people passed out on their couches, but to her relief the party had apparently dissipated. However, a load of evidence remained. Dozens of beer cans littered the coffee table. A bag of potato chips lay on the floor, its contents scattered like shards of glass all over the carpet. She stepped over a spilled beer and headed to the kitchen.

She wanted tuna. Ever since she went to the horse races her appetite had gone on vacation, and she had started craving the strangest things at the oddest times. She'd lost weight, too. Just this morning she'd caught a glimpse of herself laughing in the mirror and was thrilled to see that the little ridges in her neck were showing, rather than the double chin she'd caught sight of only a month ago.

She opened a can of tuna, and since there were no clean bowls, she decided to eat straight from the can. She washed a fork, then took her low-carb meal to the couch. *Fargo* was on, and she watched the tail end of the movie while eating. *Fargo* was one of those movies she could never get sick of watching. She'd probably seen it thirty times and still got excited when it was on television.

When she got up from the couch she felt as if her hair had gotten wedged between a couple of couch cushions. She reached her hands back to feel what it was and release her hair and quickly withdrew when her fingertips touched something sticky. It felt like gum. Her suspicions were confirmed when she smelled her fingertips and got a blast of icy mint.

The last time she had gum in her hair had been in preschool. She couldn't remember the specific incident, just that her mother had tried for several minutes to slip the strawberry pink gum from Elise's hair with peanut butter. She'd gotten most of it out but eventually had to pull out the scissors and snip a small lock from Elise's head. The damage had lasted a lifetime, because their family portraits were taken the following week, and Elise looked as if she had cut her own hair.

What would Max think the next time he saw her and one lock of hair was several inches shorter than the rest? She would have to cut her hair short and would look like a boy. She immediately went for the peanut butter. It wasn't hers, but she didn't care. She unscrewed the lid and noticed several blobs of various jelly flavors and streaks of greasy butter around the top of their Skippy. Wiping the knife clean before dipping into the peanut butter was just too much work for them. She used a wooden spoon to dish out some peanut butter and then rubbed it generously between her fingers.

She worked hard, rubbing it like grease into her hair where the gum was stuck. It took several minutes, but she actually felt like she was making some progress. She headed to her bedroom for a comb. She'd started stashing most of her toiletries in there after she'd noticed blonde silky hairs in the teeth of her hairbrush a few days earlier.

She passed a small pile of cat shit outside Iris's door and avoided stepping in it. Elise's bedroom door was closed, as she had left it. When she opened it, she was confused. There was a giant mound beneath her covers. Then she saw a dark mound of hair—no, two mounds of hair. There were people in her bed.

"Ah-hem." She cleared her throat, and Scrubbles and Bella both looked up at Elise from the floor. Bella ran to Elise and jumped all over her calves. She even released a few yips. However, the dog barking did nothing to wake the two intruders. She looked at their shoes lying next to her bed. His and hers. If they had sex in her bed, she was buying a new mattress.

She cleared her throat again, but they didn't even stir.

She didn't know which roommate to blame for this, but due to the cat crap outside Iris's door, she decided to try Megan first. She carried Bella with her to Megan's room and held her with one arm while knocking with the other.

She waited, then knocked again. Nothing. Maybe she wasn't knocking loud enough. She began to bang, and the dog squirmed.

"Geez." She heard a male voice, groggy and irritated from the bedroom. "Tell her to go away."

Oh no. Elise wasn't going anywhere.

She knocked again.

"What?" Megan finally shouted. "What, Iris?"

"It's not Iris. It's Elise," she said as kindly as possible.

Her tone immediately softened. "Oh. Elise, sorry. I thought you were Iris." She heard footsteps. Then Megan opened the door with a towel around her chest. "What's up?"

"Well, after getting gum in my hair, I went to my bedroom for a comb and found two people in my bed. Are those your friends in my bed?"

She thought for a moment. "Oh yeah. Uh-huh. They are. Brittany and Hunter slept in your bed. I thought you were staying with Max." She walked out of her room, holding a towel around her thin body. "I'll tell them to get out."

Megan opened Elise's door. "Hey you guys. Wake up. My room-mate is home, and she wants her bed back. You guys have to get out."

"Okay," the girl said, squinting from the brightness.

"What time is it?" the guy asked.

"Two o'clock."

There were no apologies, and they didn't even really seem to be embarrassed for that matter. Elise was just thankful they were wearing clothes.

After they left she spent an hour removing the gum from her hair. She was tired but relieved that she wouldn't end up looking like Chynna Phillips in the early days of Wilson Phillips. It was too late to do laundry, so she ended up sleeping on the top of her covers. Bella slept curled against her side, and Scrubbles slept at her feet.

20. Dinner at His Place

Sunday came quickly. She called Carly while she was getting ready. Luckily, she answered the phone. Elise needed some good girl talk before her date with Max.

"He's having you over for dinner?" Carly asked.

"Yes. He's cooking."

"I don't think I've ever even had a guy cook for me before. In fact, half the time they don't even pay when we go out to eat." Carly said. "But do you know what this means?"

"He's comfortable in the kitchen?"

"No. It means he really likes you. Most guys don't even want the girl to know where they live until at least the tenth date. How many dates have you gone on now?"

"Two, I guess, if you count The Casbah."

"This is your third date, and he's having you over to his place. He's investing time and effort into making you something with his own little hands. It's so sweet."

"Or maybe he just wants to get laid, and this is an easy way to get me over to his house."

"Please. You are so cynical sometimes. He likes you. I can tell. I could tell the night at Winston's in Ocean Beach."

"Really?" She didn't know why she was surprised. She knew he liked her.

"Yes. I even caught him watching you a couple of times."

"Why didn't you tell me this?"

"I'm sorry. I just forgot. I've had a lot on my mind since then."

"With the project?" She didn't want to come right out and ask how the project was coming along, but she figured this was a subtle way of getting Carly to tell her.

She was quiet for a moment. "Yeah. With the project. But there—"

"Can you buy us a keg?" Megan asked as she entered Elise's room. "Oh, and do you mind if we have a party here tonight? *Survivor* is on."

"Um. Hold on, Carly."

"Well, you know what?" Carly said. "Let me just call you back later. My other line is beeping."

"Well, really. It'll just take a sec." She sensed Carly was about to tell her something, as if she had something on her mind.

"I really gotta take the call. So I'll just talk to you soon. Love ya, hon. Bye."

Elise was left with a dial tone.

On the way to Max's loft she stopped for flowers and a bottle of Chianti. She didn't want to arrive empty-handed. She found a flower stand in North Park next to Ray's Liquor and chose a bunch of firey orange sunflowers. They were large and thriving and bright with color, and she'd never seem anything like them.

When she arrived at his loft she followed his directions and walked up the steps on the side of the shop. The front door was open, but he had a screen protecting the entrance, and she could smell something delicious cooking. She pressed the doorbell and instead of releasing a melodic ding-dong, it released a loud buzz.

He wore a vintage-looking western shirt, jeans, and he was barefoot. "Hey thanks," he said taking the flowers. "These are awesome. I've never seen sunflowers this color. And I don't think I've ever received flowers from anyone before."

His home was tiny but not as bad as Elise had imagined. She pictured him in a studio with a lone mattress in middle and a lightbulb dangling from the ceiling. She'd actually imagined them sitting on the edge of his mattress with plates in their laps and wineglasses resting at their feet. However, the place was completely furnished, with an Art Deco twist. Her heels clicked on his hardwood as she followed him into his tiny kitchen. Maggie nudged Elise's hand with her nose.

"Someone wants to be petted," Elise said as she scratched the dog behind the ears.

"You would think that dog was starved for attention the way she goes around nudging people like that. But trust me, she gets plenty of love all day. Have a seat. We can chat while I cook," he said as he took the wine from her hands.

"Let me help with something. Why don't I put the flowers in the vase?"

He raised his eyebrows.

"You don't have a vase. Shoulda known." She smiled. "Actually, now that I think of it, I don't even have a vase."

"Here. We can use this." He pulled a cardboard milk carton off the top of the counter. "I just emptied it. It was headed to the recycle pile."

He gave her a pair of scissors, and she cut the top of the carton off. "Very shabby chic," she said as she set the flowers on the table. "So what are we having?"

"Chicken curry." He stirred something luscious and creamy looking in a saucepan, and she felt an urge to throw her legs around his waist and make out with him right there over his dish.

"So tell me about your new roommates," he said as he put the wooden spoon down. He reached for the bottle of Chianti she brought over.

"Well, they're in college, so I think they're still in that phase when getting wasted and puking in someone's car is okay. But they seem nice enough."

He handed her a glass of wine. "I hope you're hungry," he said as he carried two heaping plates of food to the table.

They ate at his tiny table, and by the time they were finished, Elise realized they had gone through two bottles of wine. She could not remember the last time she had felt so happy. Maybe she had forgotten what it was like in the early days with her ex-boyfriend, Tim, but she didn't think she'd ever felt this way before. It seemed like there weren't enough hours in the night, and she truly did not want it to end.

They tried to watch a movie but ended up talking throughout most of it. By the end, Elise wasn't even really sure what the plot had been about. They talked about their families and places they'd traveled, too. Except for Alaska and both Dakotas, Max had been to almost every single state. Touring with this band had led him all over the country.

"That must have been so much fun. I always wanted to go on one huge road trip all over the country. See Graceland and The Alamo. I've even kind of wanted to see Mount Rushmore."

"That is the one place I've never seen. Mount Rushmore. Graceland was cool. They won't let you see any of the bathrooms. And they won't let you see Elvis's bedroom."

"Really?" She imagined Max, looking hotter than ever, following a tour guide through Elvis's house, looking for some kind of sign of a toilet.

"Rumor has it Elvis died in the bathroom in the master bedroom, and I think he may have died right there on the toilet. That's why they won't let you see the bathrooms. It's actually a really small house."

"I never knew he died on the toilet."

"Well, nobody ever says that. They only say he died in the bathroom. I also saw Loretta Lynn's house. It's supposed to be really haunted there. Ghosts from the Civil War. You can swim in her creek, too."

"So, why'd you leave the band? It seems like it would've been so much fun, touring the country with all your friends."

"There were a lot of reasons." He reached for the wine and filled both their glasses.

They were on the second bottle, and she hoped her mouth didn't look like a plum with teeth. Red wine did this to her, and she had several photos where her teeth were stained a deep purple and her lips outlined in wine lip liner.

"It was fun. But I think I really lost myself. The partying, everything. Half my tattoos were done in drunken stupors."

"Do you regret them?"

"No. What I regret is the way I treated people. I never called my family. And I was engaged."

Elise swallowed. "You were?"

He nodded. "Yes, I was. And I really messed it up."

"Did you cheat on her?"

He shook his head. "What really ruined it was just my own stupid selfishness. I just took her for granted while I was away, which was a lot. But let's not talk about any of this. It's in the past."

She felt her stomach turning with nausea. She didn't want to imagine him engaged. But the other part of her wanted to know more. Was he still in love with this woman? Had he gotten over it?

"So, she was the reason you quit?"

"Not really. I think breaking up with her made me realize a lot. I was gone for eight weeks right before we broke up. I was going on two hours of sleep every night, partying in different towns. She and I were fighting a lot, and when I came back, she told me she had been seeing a guy she worked with. Gave me the ring back, and it was over. I don't blame her, though. I was a real asshole. She deserved more. And she got it. She married someone else a year later. And I'm happy for her."

"You are?"

"Of course. We're friends. I'm glad she's happy. But enough about this. I'm sure you don't want to hear about it." He smiled. "Please don't tell me about your exes. I think I'd be jealous."

Maybe it was the wine that made her bold, but she leaned in closer to him, and he took her face into her hands. Their kiss was slow and soft, and his lips had a distinct taste of something she couldn't define. She felt herself wanting to be closer to him, to feel his warm skin on hers. She wanted to wake up next to him in the morning, but this was only their third date. A very faint part of her conscience reminded her what had happened last time she rushed into something like this.

Shortly after Tim she went out on a few dates with another student from the criminal psychology program, Aaron Terry. On the third date she and Aaron had ended up back at her apartment. Buzzed and completely aroused, she couldn't help herself. The sex had lasted a whopping two minutes, and he waited two weeks before calling again. When he did finally call, he seemed more interested in meeting up for a late-night booty call than going to dinner.

But Max is different, she told herself as her hand brushed over the hard bulge in his pants. She and Max had a connection. She could talk to him all night about landmarks in the United States, and it would be terrifically interesting. He had cooked for her, and he had opened up to her about his past. His mouth traced its way down her neck, and she found herself pulling her V-neck shirt aside. He moved the edge of her bra away and gently latched his lips over a nipple. She suddenly wanted every inch of him on her body. She wanted to be filled with him.

Aaron Terry. Aaron Terry, her conscience shouted. Max must've sensed some hesitation in her, because he took his mouth away from her breast and sat up.

"We should stop," she said as she twisted her bra and shirt back into place.

"Okay. That's fine." He rubbed her arm. "I don't want you to feel uncomfortable."

Actually she felt totally horny, but kept that to herself. "I just don't want to rush."

"I completely understand."

They stayed on the couch, drinking wine and laughing at his stories about the wild days in the band. "Show me your tattoos," she said, lifting his sleeve. The naked lady on his arm was not the same type of naked lady say, Axl Rose would have. She wasn't *Penthouse* but had the same classic style of Ann Margret or Marilyn Monroe; big, soft curls weighed down her hair, and long lashes that looked like dark, dainty fans rested over her eyes. "Is the woman someone famous from the forties or fifties?" she asked.

"I don't think so. She's a Vargas Girl. Maybe at that time she was a famous pinup."

The model peered with catlike eyes over her left shoulder while unlatching the straps of her bra with long, feminine fingers. The curves of her left breast and nipple were exposed suggestively, and her waist seemed to join her butt like the tip of a heart. She had long and curvy legs and wore sexy, timeless heels similar to ones that Elise had imagined herself in if she ever had money.

She'd always secretly wanted to wear a pair of heels like these. Her fantasy had included a white-fur-trimmed silk robe and matching heeled slippers. She'd strut to a chaise longue near a sprawling swimming pool. Of course, only her maid would know that she was prancing around like Ava Gardner. Naturally, she'd never show up at her parents' country club dressed this way, but in the privacy of her mansion she could dress like this, sipping martinis and smoking skinny cigarettes. In the fantasy, she smoked.

He lifted the back of his shirt, and her eyes were immediately drawn to his lower back. Michelangelo's *Creation of Adam* covered the area above his tush. Not the entire painting from the ceiling of the Sistine Chapel, but only the most well-known aspect of it—the two hands, the index fingers of God and man delicately touching for the first time.

"I've been to the Sistine Chapel," she said.

"Me, too. It's awesome."

When she noticed the lightning bolt with the initials TCB printed next to it on his left shoulder blade, her heart instantly sank. What if those were the initials of his ex-fiancée? She wanted to ask but also kind of didn't want to know the answer. How could she be in a relationship with someone who had another woman's initials permanently written on his body? And what kind of girl asked for a lightning bolt to accompany her initials? Even a cheesy rose would've been classier.

What was her name? Tracey? Theresa? Tamara? Tammy Christine Brown.

"Who is TCB?" she asked, unable to control her tormented curiosity.

"TCB is Elvis's trademark. It stands for Takin' Care of Business. He always had the lightning symbol with TCB on everything."

"Oh," she said, trying not to sound too relieved.

He showed her all kinds of pictures from his rocker days. He reminded her a little of a young Jim Morrisson back then with his shaggy hair and suede pants. They looked at all his photos on his bed, where they ended up making out again. She wished she could hit a Fast Forward button to a few more dates from now when she felt more secure about their situation, but she couldn't.

"You're sleeping here tonight," he said. "Not that anything will happen. I just think you should stay with me."

They ended up falling asleep entwined in one another's arms. It had been ages since she'd spooned, or felt someone's breath on the nape of her neck. It was the most deep and satisfying sleep she'd had in some time.

21. The Ultimate Invasion

She left his apartment early the next morning while he was still groggy with sleep. It was hard to leave the warm blanket his body had created against hers, but she didn't know how she looked. The possibilities were endless. She could look as fresh as the moment she'd walked in, or she could have mascara running down her cheeks and two new zits from sleeping with foundation on.

He called her that afternoon but unfortunately had to help a local band install some equipment in their studio. He wanted to see her the following night, but it was Brice's birthday, and she had to drive to Poway for dinner at her parents' house. After that it seemed like an eternity until she would see him because his sister and two nieces flew in from San Francisco for the week, and he'd be tied up with family events. It seemed like she would never see him again.

She spent her days working on the next Ashley Trent novel in the morning and spending a couple of hours at the beach in the afternoon. She checked her e-mail obsessively for any news of the movie rights. Near the end of the week her curiosity got the best of her, and she decided to e-mail her agent to see if there had been any word on the film rights.

> *Hi Cheryl,*
>
> *Just wondering if we've heard anything. Thanks!*
>
> *Elise*

As soon as she sent the e-mail, she knew the only news she'd be getting would be probably be bad. If there had been good news, she would've heard. After sitting in front of her computer screen for nearly an hour and clicking Refresh on her e-mail nearly five hundred times, she decided it was time to clear her head a little.

She decided to go to the mall. She needed some cute clothes now that she was dating someone. She had no money but reasoned that credit cards were for emergencies, and having a new beau and no cute clothes was an emergency.

When she returned home her roommates were gone and her computer was on. She could've sworn that she had turned it off, because she was paranoid about losing stuff ever since Megan had used it without asking.

When she looked at the screen there was a gigantic image of Iris's face wearing a blonde wig that looked as if it had been pasted on her from a different computer file. The style of the wig was much different than her frizzy, shoulder-length hair. The new Iris had a trendy little shag. She clicked on the box, and when she did so, Megan's face popped up sporting a black, short, Joan Jett–like hairdo. She clicked again, seeing them each with red hair, long hair, curly hair. Then an icon came up that said, "Welcome to the Makeover Program. Would you like to pick out makeup?" She clicked Yes and watched as several different shades of eyeliner popped on the screen. She clicked on turquoise blue and then requested fuchsia lipstick. She tried to close the screen, but it wouldn't, and the little hourglass came on. She waited and waited and it didn't close. They had frozen her computer with their makeover stuff, and now she wouldn't be able to find out if her agent had e-mailed her back.

She hit Control-Alt-Delete, but nothing happened. She pressed the Power button, and the computer did nothing. She was stuck gazing at Iris with short, black curly hair and cat's-eye reading glasses.

Her phone rang, and her irritation quickly dissolved when she realized it was Max. "Hey. You busy?"

"No. I'm just trying to fix my computer."

"I'm meeting my sister and her kids at the coaster in a half hour, and I thought I'd stop by if you aren't doing anything."

"Okay," she said, trying to stifle her glee. "Come on by."

Luckily, their apartment was in fair shape. Her roommates' parents had stopped by the previous day for lunch, and Megan and Iris had been forced to clean. After she hung up the phone with him, she did a quick sweep through their living room and kitchen and shoved a few things in a cabinet. While she waited for Max to arrive, she called her brother. Surprisingly, Stan actually knew a lot about computers, and she needed his help.

She explained what happened. "Well, what are you doing right now? I can come by to help you fix it, or you'll have to wait till this weekend."

She couldn't go that long without e-mail. It would drive her nuts. However, Max was on his way, and she hadn't told Stan they were dating yet. Not that it was some big secret. She just hadn't had a chance to tell him. On the other hand, now was as good a time as any. "All right. That's fine. Max will be here, too."

"Really? That's cool. Are you guys dating now?"

"We've hung out a couple of times, but please don't tell Mom and Dad."

"Why not?" This coming from someone who never revealed anything about his love life to anyone.

"Because I'm just not ready. Do I have to explain? They were trying to set me up with Thomas Yackrell. You think they're going to welcome Max and all his tattoos with open arms?"

"Who cares what they think?"

"I'm just not ready, okay? We've only been on three dates. It's the same reason why he's not taking me to meet his sister and nieces tonight. It's too soon."

"All right."

Max arrived first. He handed her a single yellow rose. "I didn't know you had roses in North Park," she said.

"I don't. I snagged it out of someone's yard on the way over here."

He was cute even when he was a thief. She stood on her tiptoes and kissed him.

Stan arrived a few moments later, and while he fooled with her computer, she put the rose in a glass.

She put her rose on the nightstand. Max and her brother chatted and joked with one another, and she was really glad that they got along so well. Next to Carly, he was her closest friend, and she always did secretly hope he approved of all her boyfriends.

"I put a password on here, too," Stan said as he finished working on her computer. "So now your roommates can't get in here anymore."

This was good, because now she wouldn't even have to confront them. They would just learn on their own that they would never be able to figure out what her password was.

"What is my password?" She waited for him to say something perverse or disgusting, and she'd never be able to figure out how to change it.

"Bella," he said.

After her computer was fixed, she figured Stan would leave, but he just sat there chatting with them. His cell phone rang, and he didn't leave the room to answer it. "Hi, Mom and Dad."

What was wrong with him? Hadn't she just finished telling him that she didn't want her parents finding out about Max just yet, and here he answers his phone while they're all hanging out.

"I'm at Elise's," she heard him say. "You are? Well, I don't know if Elise can, but I'll go. Okay, see you in five minutes." He snapped his flip phone shut. "I'm going to World Famous with Mom and Dad. You guys want to come?"

"I actually have to meet my sister and her kids at the roller coaster in a little bit. So I can't."

"No. I'll pass," Elise said. She expected Stan to get up and leave to meet her parents, but instead he just sat there.

"Don't you have to meet Mom and Dad in five minutes?"

"No. They're coming here. They want to see your new place."

"They are?" she said, trying to keep herself from jumping across the bed and beating Stan senseless with his cell phone.

The only thing she could figure was that he had been dropped on his head at birth. Had he not heard anything she'd said to him before he came over? She wasn't ready to introduce them to Max. He was someone she was going to have to slowly expose to her parents to, like maybe next year. In fact, she had it all planned out. She was going to subtly start mentioning him, little by little, eventually slipping in that he hadn't finished college and had a number of tattoos, specifically one of a seminude woman. Then gradually she planned to slip in that they were dating. If things went well with Max, maybe by the following year she'd mention that they were serious. But they couldn't meet *now*. It would be too much of a shock. And it was too early for Max, too. Meeting her parents could have an equally traumatizing effect on him. They could permanently scare him away.

For payback, she would run classifieds in every publication in town with Stan's number: *Free AKC golden retriever pups. Parents are both champions. Must find good homes soon! Call Stan.*

Shit, how was she going to get out of this? Even if she did say she wasn't hungry, they were still coming over. It was inevitable, unavoidable for them to meet Max. Maybe she could intercept them in the driveway and tell them Max was one of Stan's friends. She'd never be able to say this in front of Max, but for now it would probably just be best for everyone if she fibbed a little. That's what she'd do. Then down the road when she started mentioning that they were dating, she could just say, "Remember that nice friend of Stan's you met? Well, we're dating! Imagine that."

She had no doubt Max would be polite and likable around her parents. So maybe this would just work out for the best. He could lay the foundation for being liked before they even knew he was dating their daughter.

She'd quickly give them a run-through of the apartment and politely send them on their way.

Max excused himself to use the restroom, and Elise immediately turned to her brother. "What the hell is wrong with you?" she hissed.

"What?" He threw his arms to either side of his body.

"I told you I didn't want them to know anything."

"What could I do? They offered to pick me up, and I want to have a couple of cocktails at dinner, so I wasn't about to drive there."

"You are unbelievable."

"Just say he's friends with your roommates."

"What? In front of him? When I introduce them?"

Stan was about to suggest something when Max returned, and they both maintained their composure.

"I'm going to take a bag of trash out before my parents get here," she said, even though she had already thrown everything out before Max arrived.

"I can help," Max offered. "I'll go with you."

"Um no. That's okay. While you're both here I actually need you and Stan to move my dresser. I don't like it there."

"Why?" Stan asked, puzzled.

"Where else would you put it?"

"I just think maybe it should be moved another five or six inches to the left. Thanks. I'm sure you guys can handle it."

She waited on the sidewalk until she saw Marge's pink outfit heading toward her like a firecracker. They were surveying the place as if they were the ones moving in. Her mother's lipstick and blush were both pale pink, and her hair looked as if it hadn't moved a millimeter since she'd styled it that morning.

"Well, this is much better than that *place* you were living in before," her mother said as soon as she noticed her.

"Much better. But what about the noise?" her father asked. "Aren't you going to get tired of hearing that roller coaster?"

"I'm only living here for three months. Their roommate is studying abroad in Germany, and she wants her room back."

"Stan has a friend here," Elise said as hey walked toward her front door. "He's not going to dinner with you guys though."

"Oh? Have we met this friend?"

"No. I don't think you've met this one," Elise said. She waited a moment before opening the door.

"Speaking of meeting people," her father said as they stepped inside. "What did you think of Thomas Yackrell? Isn't he something?"

Max was sitting just a small flight of stairs away, and didn't sound travel up?

"Oh yes," her mother added as they ascended the staircase. "His mother called me and told me he was just taken with you."

She searched for something to distract them. "Have you lost weight, Mom?"

"Uh . . . well. Gee, no one has noticed. But yes, I have!"

Thank God she had thought of something to get them off Thomas Yackrell. "I've been doing Pilates and trying to get your father involved, too."

Hal rolled his eyes.

When they reached the living room Max and Stan were engaged in conversation, and Elise hoped that he hadn't heard a word of

Thomas Yackrell. He stood up when her parents entered. Hal and
Max went to shake hands, and Elise couldn't help but notice her father's eyes wandering to Max's hand. They lingered there for a moment. The star tattoo.

"I'm Max."

"Pleasure to meet you, Max."

"Yes," Marge said. "Will you be joining us for dinner?"

"Um, actually I'm meeting my sister and my two nieces in a little
while to take them to the roller coaster."

"Oh, that's nice." Marge said. "So what do you do?"

"I own a guitar sales and repair shop."

"Lovely."

"Let me show you around!" Elise interjected for Max's sake. She
didn't want him to endure a Hal and Marge inquisition.

The entire group followed her throughout the apartment, and she
silently prayed they would leave soon. Her parents asked all kinds of
questions about Iris and Megan. What they were like. Where they
were from. Their bedroom doors were open, and naturally her
mother had to look inside. Miraculously, their rooms were cluttered
but cleaner than usual.

"Megan is a lovely girl," her mother said as she glimpsed a picture near her bedroom door. It was of Megan standing with about five
girls who looked as if they had been drinking for hours on end. They
all held red plastic cups and wore celebration on their faces.

"Ha! Look at that," her mother said, pointing to a poster of
Lenny Kravitz. "I remember when you had posters of him on your
wall."

"And before that she had posters all over her walls of those, what
were they . . . ?" Her father thought for a moment. "New Kids on the
Block!"

Stan threw his head back, laughing wildly. "You were obsessed
with them. And Milli Vanilli."

Her mother laughed, too, and Elise wondered if it was possible for people to choke on their own laughter. "I remember," her mother said in between peals of laughter. "When you wrote Jordan What's His Name from New Kids on the Block and asked him if he would attend the sixth grade dance with you."

"I remember that!" Stan said, fighting for air as well. "You even included a picture of yourself. Or how about the time Elise started a Kirk Cameron fan club on our street and turned the garage into the club's headquarters."

Now everyone was laughing. Except Elise. Her parents may as well have busted out all the pictures of her from the eighth grade air band when she wore fluorescent spandex and lip synced "I Think We're Alone Now" by Tiffany, her braces flashing beneath the spotlight. Could she look any less cool in front of Max?

"Ha-ha," she said flatly. "Laugh all you want. I can think of a million embarrassing things you've done." But funny, she couldn't think of one.

When she looked at Max, his lips were pursed, dimples puckered in amusement. She couldn't tell if he was smitten or laughing at her. She was certain he had been cool for his whole life. She just knew it.

"Let me show you Iris's room," she said in an attempt to distract them from remembering anything else from her cornball past.

When they moved to Iris's room, they all crowded into her doorway, and what Elise saw made her arm hair stand on end. Right there, in plain view atop Iris's dresser, was the tallest bong that she'd ever seen. She didn't care if her roommates smoked pot, but her mother might have a stroke right there in the hallway. Her parents had grown up in the sixties and were probably the only two people who had never inhaled a smidgen of pot, not even secondhand. Granted, everyone's parents tell their kids they have never smoked pot to keep their teenagers from calling them hypocrites when lecturing about drugs. However, Elise was positive her parents had never smoked pot. It had been confirmed by her cool Uncle Joe on her father's side of the family who ordered all the cousins' cocktails at family weddings in the days when they were underage. Not only had her parents never smoked pot, but they thought it was on the same scale as smoking crack.

She tried to back out of Iris's room, and her mind went wild thinking of ways to distract them. She waited for them to flip out or call the police. However, their eyes wandered over the room, and they didn't say a word. Not a single word about the bong. There wasn't even a frown of disappointment. It was like the purloined letter. It was in plain view, and they didn't even notice. Or they didn't know what it was. At any rate, she didn't care. She just wanted them out.

She led them back to the living room. "Well, you guys better get to World Famous before it gets too crowded in there. You know how hard it can be to a get a table."

"Are you sure you don't want to join us?" her father asked.

"Yes, why don't you come?" her mother said.

"No. I have a lot to do." She still hadn't even checked her e-mail.

"Very well." Her mother shrugged.

Her father extended his hand to Max. "It was nice meeting you, Mark."

"It's Max," Elise corrected.

"Oh. Oops. I mean Max."

She was just getting ready to close the door behind them when her mother leaned in and whispered, only she wasn't whispering as low as Elise would've liked, "I have something I need to drop by for you. All my feminine stuff for a certain time of the month. I won't be needing any of that anymore, if you know what I mean."

Get out! she wanted to shout. "All right. We'll discuss this another time. Thank you. And good-bye." She bolted the door behind them.

She looked at Max, hoping he hadn't heard a single word about menopause. "They seemed nice," he said.

"Oh. Good. I'm sorry you had to get sucked into all that."

He shrugged. "Don't be sorry. It was fine."

They chatted for a little while before Max stood and said he needed to get back to the roller coaster.

After he left she went to her computer. There was a reply from her agent in her in-box.

Hi Elise,

I spoke to the film agency today, and they've heard back from mostly everyone, and at this point they have all passed on the project. However, there will be other options to explore. I'll keep you posted.

Cheryl

Any immediate fantasies of buying her own condo in the near future suddenly went out the window. She may as well start looking for a new place. She only had two and a half months left with Iris and Megan.

22. The Best Steak of Her Life

"Have you ever been to the Turf Club?" he asked.

"No." She had met him at his house. They had never discussed what they were doing. They'd just decided that they were going to hang out.

"Good. It will be fun then."

The Turf Club was split in two sections. One was a crowded, dark bar people waited for hours to eat in the other half. The second part was a restaurant filled with smoke from the gigantic grill in the middle of it. The place was a novelty in San Diego, and Elise found that she didn't mind waiting for an hour and a half for a table.

There was A.1. steak sauce galore, and one big party. She and Max each ordered from a selection of raw meats and then headed over to the big bonfire. Standing around the flames was like mingling at a cocktail party, and Elise immediately started to make friends. Waiting in the bar had seemed to make everyone buzzed and chatty, and Elise found herself discussing s'mores with a girl who had a hoop through her left nostril and enough mascara to raise the stock in Revlon.

"They should really have a dessert menu here," she said.

"Imagine what a hit that would be."

She watched as Max doused their steaks in A.1. and flipped them. Then he touched her arm. "Let's go sit down while they cook." They headed back to their booth. After Elise sat down, Max motioned for her to come closer. She leaned over the table, expecting him to tell her something that couldn't be said too loud—like maybe there was a weirdo he wanted to point out.

"No," he said, grinning that boyish grin that made her absolutely wild with lust. "C'mere. I mean slide over here."

"Oh." She moved to the other side of the booth, and he put his arm over her shoulders.

They watched as someone's T-bone went up in flames. The poor soul put the little inferno out with steak sauce and then picked up a totally charred piece of meat with tongs. After several minutes of waiting they went back to the grill. Elise picked up their garlic bread with tongs and watched as Max first picked up his steak, juicy and dripping with marinade, and slid it onto a plate. He was moving the tongs in the direction of Elise's steak when a skinny redheaded guy in a leather jacket swerved in and snatched it with the tip of his steak knife. She watched in horror as he plopped it on his plate and quickly scurried off.

"Excuse me," she shouted. "That's my steak!" But he didn't hear.

Max hustled past her and Elise trailed behind, holding the plate of garlic bread. He followed the meat stealer back to his table. The thief had slid into his booth. He had several friends, and they all looked up at Max and Elise, waiting for them to explain why they were hovering over their table.

"Sorry to interrupt, man," Max said, armed with a pair of tongs, "but you took my girl's steak."

"Huh?" he said over the music.

Max had called her his "girl." Did that mean girlfriend or fling? It could mean either.

Clearly oblivious to his mistake, the redhead gazed up at Max through eyes that suggested hours of solid drinking.

"I said. You took my girlfriend's steak."

Elise never imagined that a stolen piece of meat at the Turf Club would not only make her heart soar with euphoria but also move her relationship with Max to another level. One piece of steak changed everything. He'd called her his girlfriend. She had . . . a boyfriend. Stunned, she stood over their table, paying little attention as Max held out his plate and accepted the redhead's apologies as he returned the meat. He had called her his girlfriend.

It took her a moment to realize that Max was walking away with her meat. She needed to follow . . . her boyfriend.

"Drunk idiot," Max muttered as they walked back.

She felt a need to say something, just to clarify that he wasn't calling her his girlfriend for dramatic effect to get the meat back. This was how people became confused in relationships during the early phases. One person says something in passing, and the other person takes it literally and ends up with a totally different perspective on the relationship. Then when the confused individual ends up dumped, they can't understand why. She'd seen this happen many times with Carly. Poor communication led to misunderstandings.

"You called me your girlfriend," she said as they approached their booth. Still holding a pair of tongs and a plate with both their steaks, he kissed her on the forehead.

"Well?" he said.

"Well what?"

"Does that bother you?"

"No. I just wasn't sure what . . ."

He kissed her again, on the mouth this time. "Good," he said. "I'm glad it doesn't bother you. Because it's perfectly fine with me."

*   *   *

After polishing off what seemed like the best steak in her life, they rode on the motorcycle back to his studio. She held on to his waist and breathed in the scent of leather and mints. She pressed the left side of her cheek into his back and closed her eyes.

When they returned, Maggie was asleep on the couch and only lifted her head to look at them while they shuffled past, pulling each other's shirts off and kissing various parts of exposed flesh. They tumbled onto the bed, and for once she felt perfectly safe letting him remove every article of her clothing. She was dying to feel every part of him covering her. But he was slower, soft, and eventually she met his pace. They felt perfect together.

The following morning they ate breakfast together. She set his kitchen table wearing one of his T-shirts and her underwear while he stood over the stove, frying bacon and scrambling eggs.

She had a boyfriend. She was going to have to tell her parents sooner or later, because she even thought she could be falling in love with him. Real love, like he could be the father of her children love. It was going to be hard to tell her mother she was dating a man Marge couldn't flaunt at one of her women's league meetings, but she'd have to do it, because he wasn't going anywhere as far as Elise was concerned.

She'd tell Stan first. He'd have some advice on the situation, because he was always the one who had stirred up Marge and Hal's hot spots when they were growing up. To this day both her parents blamed him for every gray hair on their heads.

Max kissed her on the forehead before pouring them both glasses of orange juice.

"I had fun last night," he said.

"I did, too." She ran her fingertips over his chest before he pulled her close.

"I wish I didn't have to work today. You know you can hang out in the shop with me if you ever feel like ditching your book for a few hours."

"All right. I'll come back later this afternoon. With a white pizza."

"Now you're talking."

They sat down for breakfast, and Elise wasn't even hungry. Every nerve in her body was consumed with the best kind of happiness, the bliss of newfound love. She had not been caught in bliss like this in seven . . . maybe eight years. The last time she had felt this way was with Tim. They'd go to dinner and all she would eat was a tiny Caesar salad, and she could hardly even finish that. She was too consumed with happiness. She'd wake up feeling content, knowing that even if she had a horrific day it wouldn't matter because she was in love.

Maggie sat beneath Max, begging for scraps of their breakfast, her golden eyes staring up at him with longing. "Quit begging, Maggie," he said. But she whined and moved closer. "Maggie. Go away." He pointed to the living room. "Go!"

Instead of moving to the living room, she inched over to Elise and rested her head in her lap.

"Nooo," Max said. "Don't go to her." They both laughed. "She likes you," he said.

Elise rubbed Maggie's ears. "My poor dog's at home. Her bladder is probably ready to explode."

"You can always bring her here if you want. Maggie's good with other dogs. She'd be sweet to Bella."

After eating they cleared the dishes. Elise began to wash them, but Max moved up behind her. She could feel the rough edges of his face against her neck as he kissed her throat. "Come take a shower with me."

"Okay." She dropped the fork she was holding in the sink.

They tried to make love standing up, and at one point he even had her straddled around his waist, pinned to the shower wall. But whoever wrote those love scenes for the movies where people had sex in the shower, had clearly never had sex standing up in the shower. They ended up on the bathroom floor, Elise on top while Max's wet hair created a puddle on the tile beneath them. They didn't bother to turn off the water.

Her hair was still wet when she returned to Mission Beach. She could've walked into her apartment and found all of her possessions in the midst of Iris and Megan's clutches and she wouldn't care. This was he kind of effect love had on her. This was why it happened very rarely.

She wondered how on earth she was going to write with her head continuously floating back to the moment he'd called her his girl-friend, or the way he had hovered over her the night before. She decided to head to Starbucks in Pacific Beach for a coffee before she got to work.

Scrubbles was crying incessantly on the front door step when Elise returned to her apartment. Obviously hungry, Elise wondered how long he had been locked outside. Her roommates were both sprawled across the couch wearing last night's makeup and watching a *Real World: Mexico* marathon on MTV. A graveyard of empty vodka bottles and beer cans covered their coffee table, their glass necks sticking up like tombstones. The remnants of a DiGiorno pizza lay on the floor beneath their feet, and if Elise wasn't mistaken, she thought she had actually seen the pizza there three days ago. They hardly even looked up when she passed them. She wondered how they couldn't have noticed the cat.

Before changing out of her clothes from the previous evening she called Carly. She was dying to talk to someone, especially her best friend. She was greeted with her voice mail and wasn't surprised. "Call me as soon as you get this. I have to tell you about last night," she said before hanging up.

When she returned to the living room, it was a commercial break. "What are you up to?" they asked.

"I was just gonna head out for a coffee. You guys wanna come?"

"Yeah. Let's take the Saturn," Iris said. "You coming, Megan?"

"Sure. I'll drive."

"You drove the Saturn yesterday. I'll drive it."

One would've thought they were arguing over a convertible Porsche, but it was actually the lavender four-door sedan in their parking garage with cloth seats.

"I got it washed, though, so I should get to drive it."

"I'll drive there, and you can drive home."

"Fine."

They both wore pajama bottoms and T-shirts and Elise sort of wished she hadn't asked them to go. She would have to wait for them to get dressed, and she really just wanted to get her coffee and return. However, the girls slipped on sandals, grabbed their wallets, and headed to the front door in their pajamas.

They passed the fifteen-year-old minivan that Iris and Megan shared on the way to the Saturn, and Elise now understood why they argued so much over who got to drive their roommate's car. The gray van had a cracked windshield and was missing every single hubcap.

Elise climbed into the backseat. As soon as Iris turned the ignition, Megan rolled down all the windows and the sun roof and quickly cranked up the Potter CD in the stereo. She swerved out of the space and backed directly into a metal trash can behind her. "What the hell, Iris!" Megan screeched. "I knew I should've driven."

"How the hell was I supposed to see that? And you're the swift one who parked right next to the trash can."

"Oh, so it's my fault?"

Elise put her seat belt on.

Iris turned up the stereo to deafening volumes as she peeled out of the alley. As they headed down Mission Boulevard, Elise noticed Megan checking herself out in the rearview mirror as she propped an elbow on the window's edge.

"So, how was Max's last night?" Iris yelled over the music.

"Great! Things are going awesome with him."

"Really? Did you guys have sex?" Megan asked as she spun around.

Elise smiled.

"You did!"

"Hey," Elise said. "Carly's here." She was so happy to recognize the black Jetta that she was tempted to ask them to drop her in front of Starbuck's while they circled the parking spot for a space. She could not wait to share what had happened the night before.

As soon as they entered the coffee shop, Elise's eyes scanned the place for Carly. She spotted her blonde bob in the corner. She didn't see Elise, and Elise couldn't tell over the crowd who Carly was sitting with. "Will you guys order me a café mocha?" she said as she handed them a five. "I want to go say hi to Carly real quick."

As she headed closer it became evident that she was with a guy. She could see the back of a San Diego Padres baseball cap. Perhaps it was her gay neighbor that she sometimes went out with. She felt a surge of envy and confusion again as to why she wouldn't include her. It was like she didn't even care that she had moved back to San Diego. But maybe it was someone from work. They were going over stuff for her project. She quickly stopped when she noticed the way Carly was laughing, no, actually glowing when she giggled at something the guy had said. This was no gay guy, and if it was a colleague she apparently had the hots for him because she leaned across the table and kissed him quickly on the lips. Now she was really hurt. Why didn't she know about this? She was the first person Elise had called this morning after her evening with Max. Was this guy married?

Her eyes left her lover's face and the bright look of love quickly vanished when she saw Elise. Not only did it vanish, but sheer terror flashed across her eyes. Elise waved, and as she did so, Carly's companion looked over his shoulder.

"Stan?" she said it so loud that the entire coffee shop shot her a look. "And Carly?" This was even louder. "What? How . . . Why?

Oh my God!" It all made sense now. Everything. Her best friend had been shagging her brother. They had both been lying to her. There was no project. There was a secret love affair going on between two people that she considered family. She could feel the entire establishment watching them but hardly noticed when Megan came up behind her, holding her mocha. "Here is your coffee, Elise," she said quietly before turning her gaze to Stan and Carly, who were just as speechless as Elise.

"Thank you," she said without taking her gaze away from them. "This is . . . I can't . . . I've gotta get out of here. Now!"

"Elise, wait," her brother said. But she was already racing from the café. Megan and Iris trailed behind her. She quickly hopped in the backseat of the Saturn. "Wow," Megan said as she slid behind the wheel. "Your brother is screwing Carly!"

Elise wanted to tell her to pay attention the road.

"Look!" she shouted as the car reversed from its space. "There they are. They're looking for you."

Elise watched as Stan and Carly searched the lot for them. From the corner of her eyes, she noticed a black pickup truck rounding the corner right next to them. "Megan, watch where you're—"

The Saturn nailed the truck so quickly that it felt like a rubber band snapping. "Good going," Iris said to her sister. "You've crashed the Saturn."

23. Reckless Dialing

Lucky for Iris and Megan, there was little damage to the pickup truck. However, the Saturn was another story. The back bumper was crunched beyond recognition, and the trunk wouldn't open. The accident was bad news for Elise, too, because when they slid back into the car after surveying the damage Iris moaned, "What are we going to do? Nicole is coming back in a month."

That meant Elise had to move again soon, and she still didn't have a roommate lined up. But she couldn't even think about that. All she could think about was Stan and Carly—the liars.

Stan was waiting outside her front door for her when she returned to her apartment. "Can I please come in and talk to you?" he asked.

Iris and Megan watched the two of them with a flicker of glee in their eyes. She couldn't blame them. This was far more interesting than any of their fights over the car. She wondered if she had watched the two of them with the same look in her eyes. For once, she was the one fighting with a sibling.

"Come in," she said to Stan.

He followed her up the stairs, and when they reached the top they both stood staring at one another. It was the first time she had ever seen her brother look frightened. "Look," he said, then stopped. "I . . ." He stopped again.

"Where is Carly?"

"I told her not to come with me."

Elise folded her arms over her chest. "Why?"

"Because I just wanted to talk to you myself first."

She sat on her bed and pulled Bella into her lap. Scrubbles hopped on the mattress and began to purr. He stepped on her purse as he climbed closer to Elise. She didn't mind that his little feet were walking over her bag. She was too pissed to care. It was strange, listening to a purring cat when she felt like she could explode at any given moment.

"Why didn't you guys tell me? I have felt like neither one of you have wanted to be around me all summer. I've felt like I've had no friends."

"I am so sorry. Really, I am. I just . . . we just didn't know what was going to happen with us. It started out as a drunken fling that night at Winston's. And we figured, what was the point in telling you when it was just one of those things that would never happen again? But then it turned into something more, and by that time it had all snowballed. Every time I saw you I wanted to tell you, but it just became harder and harder."

"Look, I'm really pissed. And I have to be honest with you. I don't think I'll get over it any time soon. So you guys are just going to have to leave me alone for a while."

"You're so ridiculous." He became angry. "How is this any different from you hiding Max from our family?"

"It's very different."

"No. It's worse, actually. Because you're ashamed."

"And what? You weren't ashamed to tell me about Carly?"

"No. I wasn't. I didn't want to tell you because if things didn't work out with us, I didn't want it to put a strain on your friendship with her. But you . . . you won't introduce Max to our parents because you're ashamed that he isn't some freaking CEO of some Fortune 500 company. You lied and said he was my friend the day they came over. You are afraid of what they'll say about his tattoos."

She didn't know what bugged her more. The fact that he had a point—She had lied, and for the past two and half months she had been having the time of her life with Max and hadn't once mentioned that she was dating him to her parents or sister. However, he was twisting this all around on her. This wasn't about Max and her. This was about the fact that her brother had been sleeping with her best friend behind her back. It was weird, and she felt deceived. "You know what? Just go home. I don't want you here anymore."

"All right. Fine," he said as he headed for the front door.

As soon as he was gone, she went to her cell phone. She wanted to call her sister to see if she had known anything about this. When she fished her phone from her bag, she felt the color drain from her face. When Scrubbles had stepped all over purse he had stepped on her cell phone and dialed someone. She picked up the receiver, praying her mother wasn't waiting on the other end.

"Hello?" she said with a twinge of fear and emergency in her voice.

Dead air answered her, and she wondered if she was speaking into someone's voice mail. How much of their conversation had this person heard? Would her parents come home from the country club and find out everything about their kids' love lives? Frankly, she didn't care at this point. It's not as if they were porn stars. She had found someone she liked, and it was about time they found out.

She scrolled to her dialed calls box, praying the whole time it was one of her friends from Arizona that she'd called, or perhaps even Justine. She felt a surge of something worse than adrenaline when she looked at whom she had dialed. Her worst fear was confirmed when she realized who it was. It was not her mother. It was Max.

* * *

How her life had gone from pure bliss to utter hell in one morning was a total myth to her. Just a few hours earlier she had been sitting in her underwear eating eggs and bacon with the love of her life, and now she was trying to figure out if he would ever speak to her again. She prayed that by some miracle their voices had been muffled and he hadn't heard, but she had a bad feeling. If his voice mail picked up, there was the slight possibility she could intercept him before he heard anything.

She could always call him and tell him to just disregard her previous message. But then what if that piqued his curiosity and drove him to listen to every single word they had spoken. She needed to see him remove the message in her presence. She grabbed her purse and headed for Maxes Axes.

She'd never felt more anguish in her life as she sped into North Park. She parked directly in front of his shop and could see him behind the counter inside. Maggie lay in a beam of sunlight in front of the door when she entered. "Hi," she said. He took his eyes away from a mustard-colored Les Paul and looked up at her. It was hard to read him.

"I, uh. You said to just come on by, and so here I am. Um, I think I may have left you a message earlier that you can just disregard."

"I got your message." He stared at her. She felt her stomach turn, and she thought she might actually barf on his carpet.

"The one with Stan and I sorting out some—"

"The one about your parents and all that."

"Look. I really wish you hadn't heard any of that. Stan was angry, and he said a bunch of things that just aren't—"

"You know, I'm probably not the right guy for you. Not that I could see you with that Yackrell dipshit, but I just want a girl who wants me back. Not someone who has a bunch of issues about my tattoos." His voice was growing colder. "I have never in all my life had anyone be ashamed of me because of that, and I'm not going to start now."

"You shouldn't start now. I'm not ashamed of you. I swear. I'm in lo—"

The front door swung open, and a bald guy wearing makeup and a fedora came in holding a guitar case. Max acknowledged the rocker, then turned to Elise. "Look, I can't talk right now. I've got work to do. These guys have a show tonight."

She wanted to tell him to say they'd clear everything up later, that he'd call her. Instead he shook his friend's hand. She turned and left, crying the whole way home.

24. Monster Situation

A week went by, and he didn't call. She called him endlessly, apologizing, but he didn't pick up or return her phone calls. She grew more miserable with each passing day and eventually quit hounding him. Stan and Carly had both called her relentlessly. They'd even tried to stop by a couple times, but she had made Megan and Iris lie and say she was walking Bella.

She had no desire to speak with Carly or Stan or even her agent, for that matter. Even if her agent called with a million-dollar film deal, her heart would still be broken. Iris and Megan played the Ryan Adams *Heartbreaker* CD when they had friends over one night, and she had to leave to take Bella for a walk. She ended up sitting on the boardwalk with her dog, watching the sunset and thinking of the last time she had woken up next to Max, the way his chin was dark with whiskers from not shaving. She didn't think she'd ever be able to look at another guitar or even listen to the mention of horse races without feeling pain in her chest.

It was clear—he was over her. Who could blame him? She tried to put herself in his shoes and had realized that she would probably be just as hurt and angry. He'd been around the world and back, and he didn't need this kind of crap in his life. At times she wanted to excommunicate her brother for the rest of her life for dragging Max into their argument. But it was her own stupid fault. If she hadn't cared so much about what her parents thought, she wouldn't be in this situation.

She only had a few weeks with Iris and Megan, and then she had to start looking for a roommate, depressed or not. She scoured the ads, called people, and typically reached the same frustrating conclusion she had come to every time she had searched for a roommate. She finally saw one ad that surprisingly took pets and had affordable rent in a desirable location.

> Beachfront Property in upper Pacific Beach. Looking for a
> female roommate. 2 huge rooms, each with own bath. Two
> parking spaces and plenty of storage space. Pets ok.

When she'd talked to Delores on the phone she seemed to have a good sense of humor, which was good, because Elise hadn't seen humor in anything ever since Max had written her out of his life. They scheduled a meeting for the following day.

She followed Delores's directions the next day, and was torn between sadness and joy to see that Carly just lived a few blocks over. Seeing Carly's neighborhood made her miss her best friend.

She pulled up to a little house with white stucco walls and a red roof. The lawn was overgrown by several inches, and a small pile of cat litter stood in the middle of the driveway. So it needed a little TLC, but it was better than any other living situation she'd had since she'd returned to San Diego.

She kept an open mind as she walked up the driveway. A few weeds brushed over her calves as she continued down a path to the front door.

She searched for a doorbell and found an older model one. The tip of it was stuck at an awkward angle inside a little hole, as if the last person to ring it had pressed too hard. She tried dislodging it with her finger but frustratingly came within a hair of touching it. She knocked. No response. She banged and felt the side of her hand sting the harder she pounded. Still, no response.

She rummaged through her purse for something small to stick in the hole—the tip of a pen, perhaps tweezers. Just a week ago she'd seen both of these items in her bag, but now they were gone. She decided to try to squeeze her car key into the doorbell hole. But instead of producing a ring, small shards of glass shattered from the cavity. She hadn't realized the doorbell was made of *glass*. She stared at the opening of the hole, trying to figure out ways she could fix it so Delores wouldn't notice. How was she going to explain this? She hadn't even met Delores Ditson and had already broken something.

It occurred to her that doorbells had live electricity running through them. If she stuck her pinky too far in there, she could shock the hell out of herself and die on the doorstep before she even saw the inside of the house. Then she'd never be able to live in Pacific Beach.

She debated turning around, running to her car, and forgetting that she'd ever come across Delores's listing. But then she remembered her only other option at the moment was staying with her parents, which could land her a permanent residence at a mental institution. She felt the cool caress of an ocean breeze and the sound of seagulls cawing overhead, and she decided explaining the doorbell would be worth it. She could always just say it was already broken when she got here, act as if she were doing Delores a favor by informing her.

She was about to yell for Delores when what sounded like a tank approached the driveway. Covering her ears, she spun around. Over the weeds she saw a black truck that looked as if it had driven directly from a monster truck rally. Each wheel alone was bigger than Elise's Volkswagen. The frame of the truck rested atop the massive tires like a little matchbox car. She imagined it in a monster truck rally commercial, tossing up mud and squashing Cadillacs like they were ants.

She waited for a guy with a mullet and a muscle shirt to pop out. Instead, a petite, muscular brunette with hair curlier than Little Orphan Annie jumped from the driver's seat. She wore a miniskirt with a button-down pinstriped top and platform shoes with the thickest square heels Elise had ever seen. Even in her five-inch block shoes Elise was still taller.

"Are you Elise?" she said as she walked up the path.

"Yes. I am."

"Right on. I'm Delores. Sorry I'm late. I'm selling Kirby vacuum cleaners, door to door. I just got the job, and man, does it suck! But you'll never believe what just happened to me. Come check this out."

Elise followed her back to the truck.

"Just now when I was on the freeway, this dry cleaning delivery van was passing me, and somethin' must've been loose on his trailer because a small part of his bumper flew off and hit my truck." Strangely, she sounded very excited when she explained this to Elise. "Look. Right here." She was smiling as she pointed out the tiniest, faintest dent in the history of automobile collisions. It was smaller than a door ding, and Elise had to squint to see it.

"I can hardly see it," Elise said.

"Uh, are you kidding me? I can!"

Elise shook her head. She wasn't kidding. However, she was visibly aware of the gigantic lettering on the back window on the extra cab on her truck. "Move Over, Princess. The Queen Has Arrived." was airbrushed on the glass. Not even a bumper sticker. Airbrushed. Each letter was painted in a sunset of pink, beginning from the top in hot pink and fading to light pink toward the bottom.

"Anyway," Delores said. "I wrote down the number of the dry cleaners, called them right away on my cell phone, and told them I'd been hit by something off their tailgate. They told me to get an estimate and they'd cover it." She grinned again. "And guess what?"

"What?"

"My boyfriend happens to work at an auto body repair shop, so

we're going to estimate the damage to be worth about three grand."
She shrugged. "Value Dry Cleaners will never check."

Three thousand dollars? The mark was smaller than a door ding.
"Well, lemme show you the place."

As they entered the house, Elise wondered if Delores would try to
rip her off in some way.

Once inside, Delores kicked off her platforms. "These damn
shoes are so hard to walk around in."

"Have you considered wearing flats?"

"Duh? I wanna look *professional*."

She looked at Elise's clothing. "But I guess you wouldn't know
what that means." Elise ignored her remark and reasoned that the
poor girl's mother had never taught her any manners.

Up until this moment, Elise had always thought her home décor
looked as if it was the epitome of hand-me-downs. However, looking
at Delores's living room made her feel as if her stuff was actually kind
of nice. Delores's furnishings looked like an organized garage sale.
Beat-up corduroy couches with thick, seventies-style oak frames. A
fake wood entertainment center that would've been fantastic in 1981,
and a papasan chair that appeared dangerous sat on a stretch of dirty
cream-colored shag carpet.

"You gotta rug?" Delores asked.

"No. Actually, I don't."

"Damn. I need a roommate who has a rug. When my old dog lost
control of his bladder he pissed all over the place. We need a rug to
cover that shit up." She pointed to a stain the size of a twin mattress.

"How big was your dog?"

She shrugged. "He was a Rottweiler. Maybe eighty, ninety
pounds."

It wasn't the furniture that bothered Elise. Over time, she knew
they could buy better stuff. And things could always be spruced up
with cute throw pillows and some sheets. It was more the choice of
décor that Delores had hung on the walls that made her have doubts.

A mirror with a Bud Light logo hung over an old Pac Man machine. A massive photo of dirt bikes flying over sand dunes occupied one wall, and an orangey-brown wall hanging made of carpet and featuring a shit-colored sunset over a barfy orange–looking beach was displayed near the entertainment center. What could she say? Get rid of all your art. I wanna hang something better up?

And something smelled. Ripe. A pungent, sour odor. She looked around for trash, but despite Delores's hideous style, the house was actually clean. Tidy, but outdated.

"So how the hell did you get a last name like Sawyer?" Delores asked.

"Uh . . . what do you mean?"

"Well, it's just like that book. Tom Sawyer. Don't you get that a lot? Tom Sawyer. Elise Sawyer."

"Not really." *And what? 'Ditson' is a charming last name?*

Delores giggled. "I just think it's kind of funny. Like your best friend could be Huck Finn."

Elise realized she wasn't trying to be rude. She was just a complete idiot. In a strange way, Elise was really enjoying the whole encounter. Talking to this scam-pulling little case study was the most interesting thing she had seen in days, and it was taking her mind off all her problems.

The kitchen was just as retro, with linoleum floors and Formica countertops. There was another wall hanging made of carpet and featuring a fruit basket with purple bananas and a variety of other things that resembled fruit but looked more like a science project gone bad. "Do you want an RC cola?" she asked, as she pulled one from the fridge.

"No, thanks."

Elise realized that the odor was in the kitchen as well and wondered if some kind of sour mold grew in the walls.

Upon entering the bathroom Elise reached for her cell phone. They needed to call the police. The place had been ransacked, literally turned upside down while Delores had been out selling vacuums. The medicine cabinet was open, and all its contents were scattered around the floor and over the countertop. A bottle of Tylenol floated in the toilet. Towels were ripped from the racks and strewn around the room like lifeless rags.

The toilet paper had been unrolled and shredded into a million cushiony pieces.

"Shit," Delores mumbled. "Not again."

"Uh . . . what hap—" Elise was in midsentence when she felt the tickling sensation of something brushing against the back of her calves. "What the . . ." she turned around and looked into the eyes of something wild. The creature, resembling a raccoon, gazed up at her as if it were checking her out—as if Elise was the foreigner. It had long, menacing teeth and a snout that looked as if it could pick ants out of a crack in the tile.

"Oh Ariel! You've scared Elise. And you've made a mess again." The animal jumped on Delores's shoulder. It was twice the size of Bella, and she wondered how on earth it managed to balance itself on Delores's small frame.

"What is it?" she asked.

"She's my coatimundi. She usually doesn't make messes like this, but sometimes she manages to escape her cage. Don't you?" she said rubbing Ariel's ears. "She can be a little monster sometimes."

"Does it live in the house?"

"Well, yeah . . . Where else would it live? Do you like camping?"

"Uh . . . I guess."

"Cool. I love camping."

The stench had followed them to the bathroom, and Elise suddenly felt a need to get the hell out of there. However, she had dropped her purse when Ariel had snuck up on her, and some of her stuff had fallen out. She reached down to grab her stuff, and the odor became stronger. It suddenly occurred to her: It was Delores's feet.

Within five minutes she had politely said good-bye and explained that she had several other roommates to interview before she could commit to anything, and not to count on her. As she drove home she wished more than ever that she *did* have other roommates lined up for interviews.

25. Slow Down the Hoedown

Upon her return from Delores's, Megan thrust a plastic cup filled with something fruity into Elise's hand. "We're having a party for you!" she raised her voice over the music.

"For me?" she said, looking at the crowd in her apartment. They all looked like they were going to a rodeo.

"Yeah. Since you're leaving and since you've been so sad lately we decided to have a hoedown."

She sensed they would've had the party regardless of her circumstances, but in a weird way she felt honored. She looked at the crowd in her house, all under twenty-three and no one she knew. But hey, at least she could get drunk. She was about to ask what she was drinking when her eyes caught on someone sitting on her couch. Sitting in the midst of several people Elise didn't recognize was Billy the bank teller.

"Elise!" Iris called. "Come play Asshole with us. I'm president." Then she pointed to three people who sat next to her at the kitchen table. "You will all only refer to my roommate, Elise, as Princess Elise." So far the party was off to a great start. She took her eyes away from Billy and headed to the table. A girl wearing a

G-string strapped around her forehead dealt her a hand. "I'm the ass-hole," she said as she looked at Elise with misery in her eyes.

"Yes!" Iris's voice boomed power over the table. "The asshole must deal cards and wear a lei made of Megan's socks."

She hadn't played Asshole in ages. From what she recalled it was a drinking game that was designed to create a democracy but really ended up creating a dictatorship. She knew she'd probably end up being the asshole the first round. She was tempted to skip the game and the whole party for that matter. She was seven or eight years older than most of the people at the table and had outgrown the humor in wearing leis made of dirty socks.

It was supposedly her party, but Elise sensed no one else in the room was aware of this. If she went back to her room she would end up thinking about Max and Carly and Stan for the rest of the evening. She'd just sit by the phone waiting for Max to call and wondering how her best friend and brother had managed to lie and elude her for months on end. Getting drunk and being called Princess all night was a much better option. The first round of Asshole worked to her advantage. Everyone else had been drinking for at least two hours, and she had outwitted almost all of them, except Iris, who was still president but going by "Queen Iris." Elise was vice president. "I got accepted into a study abroad program for next spring," Iris said. "I'm going to London."

"That's exciting news," Elise said.

"Yeah, so you could stay here until February and sleep on the couch and then sublet my room when I'm gone," she suggested.

She couldn't think of a worse plan. "Oh, that's okay. Thanks, though. What are you going to do with Scrubbles while you're away?"

She looked at Elise blankly for a moment. "Oh yeah. Scrubbles. I don't know. Either Megan will watch him or maybe he'll go to the pound. I'm sure someone will adopt him."

"I need another drink," Elise said as she excused herself from the table.

"All right. But come back," Iris called.

She was pouring vodka into a glass when a cup slid in right next to hers.

"What are you having?" he asked.

"A vodka cranberry." She looked at the sea green eyes that had motivated her to create a savings account and deposit spare change into her checking on a regular basis. His only participation in the hoedown was the cowboy hat he wore on his head, and quickly removed.

"Great. Can you make me one, Elise?"

He knew her name. She was always Ms. Sawyer at the bank, and now they were on a first-name basis. "Of course."

"You come into the bank quite a bit."

"Yes. That's right. You're Billy. Right?"

"Yes. Did you ever straighten out that thing with your Nordstrom stock?"

She lied. "Yeah. So how do you know Iris and Megan?"

"I have summer school with Megan."

"Small world." She wanted to suggest that he quit school and pursue something with entertainment. His looks were amazing, but she held her tongue.

"Do you go to USD, too?"

"Oh, no. I'm out of college. Have been for a while." She felt herself falling off The Cliff of Babble again. "I'm actually just living here for three months. It's temporary. I am a lot older and needed a place, and I mean, San Diego real estate is so out of control."

"Yeah. I know. I just bought an apartment."

It didn't make her feel any better knowing that a college-aged bank teller was a step further in real estate than she was. She downed her vodka cranberry and began mixing another. "How old are you?" she asked.

"Twenty-one. And you?" She remembered the scene in *Vacation* when Chevy Chase had reached the end of his rope with their whole trek to Wally World and had gone down to a seedy cocktail lounge where he met a much younger Christy Brinkley and ended up telling her all kinds of lies to impress her. She felt like she could easily model his character at the moment. But then she asked herself why she would lie. To impress this guy? He was just a hot bank teller. "I'm twenty-three."

She was on her third cocktail in twenty minutes and feeling fantastic when someone offered her a shot of Jägermeister. *Why the hell not?* she thought as she pounded the shot. Unless he got a hold of her driver's license, she was on the right track.

She ended up chatting with Billy for two hours, getting drunker as each minute passed. He seemed to be stone sober to her, but then everyone seemed sober to her when she was drinking.

"So, can I see your book?" he asked.

"Sure, why not?"

He followed her to her room, and she showed him the book. "I don't think I've ever read a whole novel unless I've had to for school," he said as he quickly looked at the cover and set the book back on her desk.

This should've been a total turnoff to her, but she was buzzed and kind of liked being Demi Moore. After all that she'd been through in the past week she was entitled to rob the cradle. She looked at her dog, who eyed her with scolding eyes, as if to say, "What the hell are you doing? This guy hasn't even acknowledged me."

When she took her eyes away from Bella, Billy leaned toward her. He started to kiss her slowly. Maybe it was her feeling bold, but the kisses soon became strong and heated. She rubbed her hands over his shoulders while she kissed him back. She'd never felt such strong arms and shoulders, and expected them to feel as hard as they did— like a mannequin. Then, to her amazement, he just stripped down right there in front of her. No foreplay. No sensual unbuttoning. He just took all his clothes off. Not that he was a sight for sore eyes or anything. She just wasn't expecting it. His penis was massive, and he had a six-pack. However, something about the whole situation made her want to leave her clothes on. Even in her drunken haze she felt as if he was too bold, as if he was used to just getting nude and getting action. As if seeing him nude were supposed to make her follow his lead and strip down, too.

Bella's head rested on her paws, and her face looked sad when Elise glanced at her. She suddenly wanted him to put his clothes back on. She thought of tactful ways to get rid of him, but nothing really came to mind, so she just came right out with it. "You know what? I don't want to do this."

"Do what?" He sprawled out on her bed, and she wondered how he could feel so comfortable in the nude. He was better suited for one of her roommates.

"I just don't feel like hooking up with you. I'm sorry." A small part of her didn't want to make out with him because of Max. She missed him, and the thought of touching someone else, no matter how hot he was, just made her miss Max even more. But most of all, she just wasn't into him. He'd never read a book. He'd stripped down totally nude as if Elise were supposed to go wild, and she didn't want to be Demi. She wanted to be Elise.

He shrugged as if he'd just been told she'd prefer pineapple juice over cranberry with her vodka. "Whatever. Do you mind if I crash in your bed though? Because my ride is drunk and I can't drive and I just want to sleep somewhere."

"Sure. Whatever." How was she ever going to be able to deposit checks again, knowing that she had seen him totally in the buck? She thought he'd put his clothes back on, but he slid under her covers, rolled over onto his left side, and said, "Good night."

She was feeling rather tired herself and really just wanted the whole night to be over with. She ended up asleep on top of the covers, fully clothed, even wearing shoes. Bella climbed in between them. She licked Elise's face, then walked in a small circle before lying down right next to her. Her back felt warm against Elise's, and she could hear her tiny doggy breaths. She wondered what Max was doing, if he was lying next to someone. If he'd even thought about her since their last conversation. Though her bed was full, she'd never felt more alone.

26. Labor Day

For the first time in Elise's life she loved being awakened at the crack of dawn by a ringing phone. Every time she heard the sound of her cell phone she plunged down a pathway of hope that it was Max on the other end. He'd apologize for waking her before explaining that he hadn't slept in days and he couldn't wait another minute to talk to her. He'd then invite her over, they'd make up over passionate kissing and embracing, and have splendid sex in his bed where they would remain entwined with one another for the rest of the day. She experienced fleeting fantasies such as these every time her phone rang.

The dream ended as soon as she heard her mother's voice. "I have wonderful news."

"What is it?" Elise said, unable to conceal the disappointment in her voice. It was seven a.m. Max was probably sound asleep and moving on with his life, and all she wanted to do was return to the deep and satisfying slumber she'd been in two minutes earlier.

"Your sister is in labor."

She sat up and screeched. Lying next to her in bed was the bank teller. "Shit!"

He rubbed the side of his head. "What time is it?"

She remembered her mother. "I mean, really? Oh my God. That's so exciting."

"Yes, I know. Her water broke at five o'clock this morning."

She flashed Billy a look before holding a finger to her lips.

"Your father and I are here at the hospital with Brice and Melissa, and we were wondering if you could come take Jeffrey."

Of course they were wondering if she would come take Jeffrey. By now the entire labor and delivery unit was probably wondering if someone could take him.

"Yeah. Of course," she said. This would give her an excuse to get Billy out of her bed. "I'll be right over."

After she hung up, Billy slid from her bed. He was completely nude and had no shame about walking across her bedroom in broad daylight with his privates showing. She wondered why he was naked when she was fully clothed but then remembered everything that had occurred.

When she arrived at the hospital, her parents were in the waiting room with Jeffrey. He wore purple knee-high socks with cartoon wolves on them, his cowboy boots, and a pair of swim trunks. He was entertaining the entire waiting room with a yo-yo. Her mother stopped smiling when she noticed Elise. "Humph. Here she is."

"Take me to the beach," Jeffrey said as soon as he noticed Elise.

"Oh. Sure. Maybe we can go later."

"No. Beach now."

Her mother laughed. "I told him Auntie Lise lives by the beach, and that's all he's been talking about."

Elise had visions of Jeffrey running ten yards ahead of her across the sand in his boots, heading into the Pacific Ocean during riptide, while she fought to catch up to him. She didn't know how to break it to him, but the beach isn't exactly how she imagined spending the day with him. Perhaps they'd rent some Disney movies or finger paint. "Do you like popcorn?" Elise said. "I was thinking we could make some microwave popcorn and watch *One Hundred and One Dalmatians*." She thought the dog thing would appeal to him with his socks and all.

However, rather than running to the hospital exit so they could get home to watch the movie, he suddenly turned British. "Condy. Condy at the beach."

"How 'bout we go see Mommy before you leave?" Grandma suggested before flashing another cold look Elise's way.

"That's a fantastic idea," Elise chimed in, wondering what she had done to piss her mother off. She thought she was doing everyone a favor by picking up Jeffrey.

Jeffrey ran ahead of them, and her father trailed behind with the yo-yo. "Just so you know," her mother said under her breath. "I heard that young man this morning. And don't think for a minute I'm going to believe you had a friend over for breakfast at seven a.m. I hope you're not acting like a harlot, Elise. Girls who act like harlots never get married." And with that she sped up behind Jeffrey and her father.

"But—" She wanted to explain that nothing happened. They'd just kissed. She didn't even like him. But there was no use. Her mother would never understand. The only thing that could be worse at this point was Max finding out that Billy had slept in her bed.

Elise had imagined her sister to be like Melanie Wilkes during the birthing scene in *Gone with the Wind*, pale, drained of every last ounce of energy, the dark circles under her eyes indicating hours of excruciating pain. She was very relieved when she found Melissa lying in a hospital bed wearing her pink terry cloth robe, sucking on a Popsicle, and watching the *Today* show. Her feet were propped on two pillows, and every strand of hair was coiffed and fashioned like the fabulous mother she was. "They just gave me an epidural," she said as Jeffrey ran toward her bedside.

"You look great," Elise said. She was really glad to see that her sister wasn't suffering.

"Thanks so much for taking Jeffrey. It would just be such a long day for him here."

"Uppy," Jeffrey begged from her bedside as he offered his arms to her. "Uppy! Uppyyyyy! *Upppppyyyyy!*"

"I'm sorry, sweetie," Melissa said. "You can't come up here. Mommy is going to have your little sister and has to stay in bed, and there just isn't room for you right now."

He looked at her as if she were speaking Latin. "Uppy."

"Maybe we should be on our way," Elise said.

"Great," Brice quickly led them to the door. "Let me get my car seat out of the minivan for you. You know, even better yet, why don't you just take the minivan. I'm not leaving anytime soon, and you can just bring him back this evening. Grandma and Grandpa said they would take him home tonight."

"Why don't you bring him back around five?" Marge chimed in. "We'll take him to dinner and then home for a bath."

"Okay."

Brice gave her the keys to the minivan and a gigantic diaper bag. "There's also sunscreen in there," he said.

"Oh, yes," Melissa called. "Make sure he wears sunscreen. Call us on Brice's cell phone if you need anything!"

The first five minutes of the drive consisted mostly of Jeffrey kicking the back of her seat and asking to listen to music. She flipped on the radio, falsely believing this would satisfy him.

"Noooo," he whined. "Music."

"What kind of music?"

"Music."

"Rock music? Folk music? Country?"

"Music."

She had no idea what he was talking about and nearly smashed the van into the guardrail on Interstate 5 trying to figure it out. "Is it on a CD?" she asked, fumbling with the glove box while avoiding swerving into the lane next to her.

"I WANT TO HEAR MUSIC, AUNT *E*-LISE." It was the first time he had ever pronounced her name correctly, and he said it with such conviction that he sounded as if he were telling her off. Then he kicked the back of her seat.

"All right. All right. Please just stop kicking," she pleaded. She pulled off the freeway two stops before her exit and dialed Brice's number.

While waiting for him to answer she could feel her back vibrating with each thrust of his foot. She imagined Brice applying cold compresses to her sister's sweaty forehead while a nurse encouraged her to push.

"Brice!" she exclaimed with a load of relief in her voice.

"How's everything going, Elise?"

What was she supposed to say? *Terrible. Your child may be the next member of the Trench Coat Mafia. Could I actually bring Jeffrey back at nine? This morning?* She didn't want to hurt their feelings or be a bad aunt. She really wanted to like the kid. She did. And certainly there had to be redeeming qualities about him. Otherwise they wouldn't be bringing another one into the world. "Oh, things are going just fine. I had one quick question though. I know it seems trivial, but he keeps asking to hear music, and I'm very sorry to bother you about this but—"

"MUSIC NOW!"

"Ah yes," Brice said calmly. "It's that song by Madonna."

" 'Music,' " Melissa called from the background. "Tell her it's in the CD case in my glove box."

"MUSIC! MUSIC! MUUUUUSIC!"

"The song is called 'Music,' and it's—"

"In the glove box." Elise finished for him.

She opened the glove box, praying the whole time this Madonna CD was in there. She found the CD. Upon putting it in the stereo Jeffrey immediately began to bounce up and down in his car seat. "Music makes the people come together," he sang.

Never in a million years had she thought she'd be driving a minivan into Mission Beach with a two-year-old Madonna fan in the backseat, singing at the top of his lungs to one of the biggest clubbing songs in history.

"Again!" he demanded as he threw his fist in the air. She had no qualms about playing the song again. She could've driven around all day watching him from the rearview mirror.

He reminded her of a South American dictator, only he was two and riding in a car seat. "Hey Jeffrey. What'd ya say we go shopping on Melrose today?" she asked. "It's about two and half hours away, and I could really use some time away."

"Hey Mr. DJ," he sang, throwing his neck back.

"Perfect!" She didn't have to worry about him drowning, and she'd escape watching *Barney* or those queers from The Wiggles. "But first, let's head to McDonald's. I'm starving."

By the time they had reached McDonald's they had listened to "Music" five times, and she really started to think that if she heard that opening riff again she might have to throw the CD out the window. She tried playing some other hits from the CD, but they were received with a jarring kick in the ribs and a demand to hear "Music." It was amusing until tears began to spring from his eyes and his voice became staggered.

"All right. Okay. We'll just keep it on your song," she said, calling off any plans for a long drive. "Guess what? I bought you a Happy Meal."

He bounced up and down. "Want Happy Meal now?"

"Let's wait till we get home."

"No. Now."

She started "Music" over again, and they headed back to her apartment.

* * *

Thankfully, no partygoers had passed out on their couches, but the place was in shambles. Beer cans and cocktail glasses littered every corner of their living room. The limp lei of socks was draped over the television set, and she found herself asking what kind of babysitter she was.

After eating their McDonald's Jeffrey threw on a cowboy hat from the night before and began to jump from foot to foot asking loudly to head to the beach. Iris and Megan were still sleeping, and she thought this might be a good idea. She didn't want to wake them up. It was still early and the air was crisp outside, so maybe she could even talk him out of going into the water. They could build sand castles and dig for shells along the shore.

"All right. We can go to the beach, but first we have to put sunscreen on," she said, dreading his response. She expected him to react the same way he had the last time she had changed his diaper. Kicking, screaming, and basically resisting the whole effort.

However, he hopped from the couch and said in a singsong tone, "Okay, Aunt Lise. Put sunscreen on." She resisted an urge to jump up and applaud. Rather, she quickly reached in the bag Brice had given her and pulled the tube out before Stalin-like Jeffrey returned and refused to protect his skin. She took off his little T-shirt and helped him slide into his swim trunks. His pudgy tummy was as pale as a jellyfish and protruded from the edge of his swim trunks, but he looked absolutely adorable. He really was a cute kid.

She squeezed some sunblock on her finger, and he held out his hand. "Let me put on, too, Aunt Lise!"

"Okay, great. Thanks so much for helping," she said as she squeezed a generous dollop of lotion onto his tiny little fingers.

They were finally connecting. She was so glad and excited, mostly to know that the bloodline of Satan didn't run in her family, but also to know that it was possible for them to get along. She moved quickly, afraid that this opportunity to click might suddenly turn volatile.

He didn't even protest when she rubbed lotion all over his face. In fact, he told her not to miss any spots as he eagerly spread SPF all over his chin, neck, and shoulders. She helped him rub it on his arms and tummy, and he smiled at her. She reached for the tube to apply more to his back. She was squeezing lotion onto Jeffrey's palm when she noticed something so alarming that she witnessed the hair rise on her arm. The tube she held in her hand was not the pink and blue Johnson & Johnson SPF for kids she'd seen in the bag earlier. Rather, it was a pink and blue look-alike tube of Johnson & Johnson diaper rash ointment. Dear God, she'd rubbed butt cream all over him.

"More, Aunt Lise, Jeffrey want more sunscreen." He thrust a wiggling set of fingers toward the bottle and began to squeal.

"Actually, Jeffrey. There has been a slight change of plans. Guess what we're going to do?"

He looked at her suspiciously. "Have condy?"

"We're going to apply sunscreen twice!"

"No," he whined. "Go to beach."

"We are going to the beach!" she said enthusiastically. "But in or-der to get there, you have to first take a shower. Then we'll apply sun-screen again! And *you* can rub most of it on!"

"Nooooo! Jeffrey no take shower!" His voice was so piercing she thought the television might crack.

"We're going to take a special kind of shower. We're just going to wash your face and chest and arms. You don't even have to take your swimsuit off. It will be just like going to the beach, only there will be no sand."

"No."

She tried to pick him up, and he pushed his hands toward her. "Nooooooo." His voice became staggered, and she sensed tears ap-proaching the same way animals can detect natural disasters before they strike. She frantically began searching the kitchen cupboards for a bribe. Microwaved popcorn? Could she bribe him with that? "Hey Jeffrey. Look what I have." She held up a box of Smart Pop as if it were a gigantic box of grape-flavored Nerds.

"No." He held a hand toward her.

Finally she found one mint wrapped in cellophane. It was the kind of treat that was offered in bowls on hostess stands at restaurants. For all she knew that mint could've been sitting in there since two summers ago. But she tried not to think about that.

"Look what I found." She waved the candy in front of Jeffrey, and he became calm and quiet, the same way Bella did when presented with the opportunity for a treat. She had an urge to tell him to sit—lie down. However, his hand lunged toward her, and she snapped the treat back. "You can have this if you let Aunt Lise wash the diap— I mean sunblock—off you."

"Okay!"

They ended up at the kitchen sink, Jeffrey squirming in her arms as she tried to splash water onto his torso. She was rubbing his face with a damp paper towel when he screamed, "My mouth is on fire!" He spat the candy from his mouth and it whizzed across the room like a meteor before hitting the cabinet and remaining stuck to a white cupboard door.

"Hu, hu, hu," he panted. "Mouth on fire. Condy hot."

She quickly got him a glass of water and prayed he had a horrible long-term memory. Hopefully, he wouldn't tell his parents about any of this. She figured it was fine to give the boy peppermint. When she offered him the treat he seemed to be a candy connoisseur and very acquainted with mints.

Before they left she searched for things they could use to dig in the sand with. She found a bucket with an unused mop and a layer of thick dust on it in the hall closet. She wasn't surprised in the least that it looked as if it had never once been used. Then she took a stack of leftover plastic cups from Iris and Megan's last keg party.

They left the apartment and headed down Mission Boulevard. "Jeffrey, let's hold hands," she said as several cars whizzed past them.

"No!" He folded his pudgy arms over his chest.

"Listen, I'll show you something really neat at the beach if you hold my hand."

He moved a few steps away from her.

"Jeffrey, give me your hand." She was getting impatient, and she didn't trust him. She sensed if she didn't hold on to him, he might run into the street or play chicken on the roller coaster tracks.

She pried his arms from his chest and held on to his wrist the rest of the way to the beach.

They finally arrived at the beach and, naturally, he wanted to go in the water. *Distractions,* she thought. *It's all about distracting him— diverting his attention to something else.* "Let's build a sand castle!"

"Okay, Aunt Lise. Let's build castle."

She pulled plastic cups from the bucket, and they began to dig. Perhaps she would become closer to him by the end of the day. They seemed to be hitting it off with the sand castle plans, and she had visions of them building a four-story mansion with pillars and French windows. They'd be the envy of every little castle-builder up the south Mission coast. As she dug and began to shape her sand into the frame of the castle, she imagined passersby stopping to admire their creation, tourists even asking for a photo with the grainy palace. Jeffrey would love this day and always want to come to the beach with Aunt Lise. He'd now prefer her over Stan, and she'd be his favorite relative.

She was making a pile for one of the pillars when Jeffrey dropped his cup and swung his head toward her. "You! Dig over there." He pointed the smallest index finger she had ever seen to a pile of stinky seaweed with fifty million sea flies hovering over its slimy strands.

"How 'bout I just move a little bit to the side," she suggested, trying to save herself from becoming an outcast in the kingdom of Jeffrey the First.

"Nooooo. Don't dig near me. Go way Aunt *E*-lise."

"But Jeffr—"

"Goooooo!"

"We're going to build the biggest castle on the beach, and it will be the best, and I'm going—"

"You no dig with me. This is my sand castle. My sand castle!" He could've been the mayor of a Columbian town, the way he threw his fist in the air.

"All right. Fine." She put down her cup and retired from building. As she sat in the sand she tried not to think about Max. Jeffrey stopped digging, flashed her a look of death, and firmly said, "Stop singing."

She couldn't sing. She couldn't dig. All she could do was sit and rot in the sand. She began to run her fingers through the wet sand near her toes, and she found a sand crab. She instantly grabbed a cup and captured the little critter. This had to win her nephew over. Kids loved animals. "Hey, look at this, Jeffrey. Look what I have in my cup."

He peered over the edge of her cup, and she showed him the little beige-colored sand crab she'd found. It moved around like a spider inside the cup, and Jeffrey was absolutely fascinated. "Find more," he said as he began digging in the sand.

After they had collected a dozen crabs they put them into their bucket with a load of sand and some water. "Me take home," he said.

"Actually, we should let them go so they can be with their mommies."

"Me take home! Mine."

Elise could see her returning Jeffrey to the hospital. "Oh. Before I forget. Here is his diaper bag and a bucket full of sand crabs."

"But this is their home. They need the salt and the sand and . . . and their food. Just like you need Happy Meals and all your toys."

"But I waaaant theeeem."

"They'll be much happier here. Think if someone took you from your bed and away from your mommy and all your toys and your favorite things to eat."

He looked at her as if she were speaking a foreign language. "Me take crabs home."

Distractions. "Let's go put our feet in the water."

The only place he put his foot was down. "No. Jeffrey dig for more sancabs."

She tried every kind of bribe she could think of, renting movies, buying "condy." Everything. But he wouldn't have it, and when he started screaming and people stared as if she were hurting the child, she finally caved. "All right. All right. You can take the sand crabs back to my apartment, but you can't take them to your house."

He'd won.

When they returned to her apartment it was around lunchtime. Iris and Megan were sitting on the couch watching reruns of *Amish in the City*. It was an episode Elise had now seen three times with them, which meant they had probably seen it a dozen.

"Well, who is this?" Megan asked in a playful tone.

"This is my nephew, Jeffrey. My sister is in labor, and I'm watching him."

"Oh," Iris said, not very impressed by the child. "What's in the bucket?"

"Sand crabs. He insisted on bringing them back from the beach, so I'm going to put them on the balcony."

"Her is sad," Jeffrey said, pointing to the screen as an Amish girl cried.

Elise made him a snack of cheese, crackers, and an apple slice before they went into her bedroom to see what they could find on the Disney Channel.

Her mother called to tell her that Melissa had given birth to seven-pound Cassidy Renee, who looked just like Jeffrey. "You can bring him back to the hospital in an hour or so if you'd like. Brice and Melissa are tired, so we'll probably take Jeffrey and go home soon."

Since she was having a hard time keeping her eyes open in front of *Barney*, she decided that might be a good idea. She hung up with her mother and told Jeffrey the exciting news. He seemed oblivious as he chewed on a piece of cheddar cheese.

"Aunt Lise?" he said.

"Yes?"

"This makes my tummy feel happy." He smiled, and she wanted to hug him.

27. Motherly Advice

The following morning Elise went to the hospital to see her sister and meet her new niece. When she'd dropped Jeffrey off the previous day both mother and baby had been sleeping, and she didn't get a chance to see them. Brice was picking up Jeffrey from her parents' house when she arrived, so it was just the three of them. She was glad there wouldn't be a toddler to interrupt them or her parents there to listen to their conversation. She hadn't been able to have a decent minute of girl talk with her sister since she had returned to San Diego.

Melissa looked tired but content when Elise entered the room. The circles under her eyes were obvious, and all the color had left her lips. However, she was smiling. "You got here just in time," she said. "She is awake. Mom and Dad haven't seen her with her eyes open yet."

Elise had stopped at the gift shop on the way up and bought a pink balloon with a bear holding a sign that said, "It's a Girl!" She set it next to Melissa's bed before peering at the bundle Melissa held in her arms. The baby's face was as pink as a rug burn, her little hands were as wrinkled as an eighty-year-old's, but she could already see features forming. A tiny little square nose like Melissa's, and though her eyes looked vacant and small, she could see her sister in them.

"She's beautiful," Elise said.

"Do you want to hold her?" Melissa asked.

"I'd love to."

She passed the tiny bundle into Elise's arms. For some reason she expected the baby to immediately begin wailing as babies always seemed to do, but instead her eyes wandered over Elise's face, and her little fingers locked onto the edges of the blanket she was wrapped in.

Elise sat down in a chair near Melissa's bed. "She is precious, Melissa."

"Thanks," her sister said as she limped to the bathroom. She moved as if she had spent the previous day atop a bareback, galloping stallion.

"Are you okay?"

"Yes. Just extremely sore. Her head couldn't fit through, so the doctor cut me all the way back to well . . . you don't want to know. I have seven stitches."

"Holy shit."

"Yeah, Brice almost passed out when the Dr. Sims cut me. I've never seen his face turn so white. But honestly I have to say it didn't hurt that bad."

"Did they numb you before they did that?"

"No. There wasn't time. The baby was coming out."

"What did they cut you with? Scissors?"

She shrugged. "I couldn't really see. Some tool. But honestly, it didn't really hurt at the time. I'll tell you what hurt. What really hurt was after the baby came out everyone was standing around looking at her. The nurses. Brice was saying how beautiful she was and the doctor had to put his entire arm back inside me because the placenta was still in there. I can't even describe the pain I felt when he ripped that out."

Please don't, she wanted to say. Elise was starting to think she didn't want kids. Stitches? Cutting? Placentas being yanked from your body when the doctor is forearm-deep in your privates? It sounded awful. "Then he stitched me up." Elise looked down at the child whose tiny little mouth was agape. At first she thought she was yawning, but when her grapefruit sized head turned to the direction of Elise's breast like she was a magnet and she began sucking on her sweater, Elise knew the child had other intentions. "Uh . . . What's she doing?"

Melissa laughed. "Being a rude little thing," she said in baby voice. "Jeffrey used to do that, too. She's looking for a breast to nurse on and she just hasn't realized that milk only comes from Mommy. Have you, little sweetie?" Melissa cooed as she limped back to Elise.

"Here," Elise held her toward Melissa.

"Will it make you uncomfortable if I nurse in front of you?"

Elise thought for a moment. "No. It's fine." They were sisters. They had bathed together as children and changed clothes in front of each other enough in life that it really wasn't a big deal.

Elise made a conscious effort to focus on Melissa's face and not her bare chest.

"Now let me tell you how this feels. Take your nipple. Squeeze it as hard as you possibly can, then twist it over and over again while still pinching it together."

"Why does anyone have kids?"

"I don't know. You just get used to it."

"Is Stan coming by?"

"Not yet. I think he's coming by later."

Elise wondered if she should say something, or if she should let Stan do the honors of informing her about his relationship with Carly. "So, did Stan tell you about Carly?"

"No. What happened?"

"They're dating."

Her eyes grew wide as she took her gaze away from the baby. "What? Stan and Carly?"

"Yes. For quite some time now. They've been lying to all of us."

"I had no idea!" Her eyes were aglow with excitement and delight. "Is it serious? Did they do it?"

"I'm pretty sure. But who even wants to think about that?"

Melissa released a loud, snickering laugh. "What scandal. I never would've suspected Carly to be the type to create such drama." Ever since Melissa had married and had children, the most entertaining thing she was exposed to was a purple dinosaur. If there were ever any kind of gossip or excitement in anyone's life, she felt it was the equivalent to when J.R. was shot on *Dallas*. She clapped her hands together. "Mom and Dad will flip. They love Carly! And think. If they got married, Carly would be our sister-in-law. She'd be family."

"Well, she hasn't been acting like much of a friend these past few months, blowing me off. Sneaking around. Lying. She must've told me a dozen lies, and the whole time I just thought she didn't want to be as good of friends as we used to be. I thought she was getting sick of me."

"They were being sneaky?"

"Yes, I think I even almost walked in on them having sex."

"You did? What happened?"

It was an incident Elise would rather not spend a ton of time recapping, and she quickly filled her sister in.

"Oh my God. Think if you had seen them. Actually caught them in the act."

"It would've scarred me for life. Let's not even go there."

"Well, I know you're probably hurt because they left you out of the loop. But you have to think of why they did it. Everything probably just snowballed. They probably wanted to tell you, but the longer time went by the harder it became."

She nodded. "I know. You're right." She felt a lump in her throat. "But now everything is such a mess." Tears trickled down her cheeks. "Not just with them. I've screwed up my love life, too."

"You have a love life?"

"Yes, but please don't tell anyone."

"What? Are you gay?"

She stopped crying. "No! Please. Do I seem gay?"

"No. But you have gone quite some time without a boyfriend."

"Well, it was because I couldn't find anyone I liked. And I finally did. He's gorgeous and sweet and successful with his business, and I totally screwed everything up."

Anticipation was practically jumping from her sister's eyes. "Who is this person? And why didn't you tell me?"

"His name is Max, and I met him when I was living with Justine and Jimmy. He owns a guitar shop. I didn't want to tell anyone because I thought Mom and Dad would flip out when they found out he has tattoos and drives a motorcycle, and now he knows that I was afraid to introduce him to our parents, and he thinks I'm ashamed of him, and it's one huge mess. And now I'm the most miserable I've ever been."

"Okay. One thing at a time. Start from the beginning."

Elise told her all about him, and the past few months that they had spent together. She told her about walking in on Stan and Carly at Starbucks and how her cell phone had accidentally dialed Max.

"Look," Melissa said. "Mom and Dad love you. They want you to be happy. I know they're hard to deal with sometimes, but they would accept Max."

"I know. At this point I would tell them in a second. I don't even care what they have to say, but it doesn't matter anymore. He's gone."

"Give him some time to get over his hurt feelings, and he'll be back."

"He will?"

"Yes."

"But he won't even answer the phone. And why should he come back? Now that he thinks our parents are total assholes."

"If it's meant to be, it will work out. Now as for Stan and Carly, they're your best friends, and you have to get over it, too."

28. An Offer

When she returned home, Iris and Megan were gone, most likely getting an estimate for the Saturn. There was a strange envelope with no return address sitting on the counter. Her address and phone number had been typed on the envelope. She opened it, hoping by some off chance it was a check from Justine, but who was she kidding? After several phone calls, she was never going to see the money again. She tore open the envelope. The letter inside was also typed.

Dear Elise,

Please don't rip this up, or throw it away. Typing this was the only way I figured I could get your attention. I'm sure you've looked at the signature and realized by now that it's me, Carly. First, I want to say that I am so sorry for lying to you. I could explain to you why, and it might make sense to you, but the more I think about it the more I realize there is no excuse. You are my best friend, and I should've never misled you.

Over the past several months I have wanted more than

*ever to let you in on everything, mostly because I just wanted
to tell you that I have never been this happy. I know this
might be weird for you to hear, but I have never been in love,
and now I really think I am.*

*Honestly, I'm glad you found out. There were so many
times that I wanted to tell you, and I lost so much sleep thinking about when and how I should tell you. But now you know,
and I've missed you more than anything. I miss my best friend.
If you need time, I understand. But please try to forgive me.*

*Love,
Carly*

She didn't know how to respond. Thinking of Carly and her
brother in love was still so strange to her. But she missed her best
friend, too. The phone rang, and she set the letter aside.

When she looked at the number, her heart skipped a beat. Her
agent. The agency only called if there was good news or they needed
something from her. Bad news was usually delivered via e-mail, and
even minor good news usually took the e-mail route, too. A phone
call constituted something important.

"Hello," she said.

"Hi Elise. It's Carissa at the Adams Agency. Cheryl wanted me to
get a hold of you, so let me buzz her and put her on."

"Okay, great," she managed to calmly squeak out, even though
she felt like shouting, "What is going on? Just give me the news!"

There was a buzz, then the familiar voice of her agent, coming
from afar, as if she were on speakerphone. "Good news here, Elise. I
just got off the phone with Jennifer Bloom, and apparently we got an
offer we weren't expecting. It's not for the big screen, but Kelly
Goldberg, a television producer, is putting in an offer to buy the
rights for a television series. An hour-long program, like *Alias* or
Murder She Wrote. She's working out an offer today with Jennifer,

but it looks like your book will at least end up being a pilot. If it is picked up as a major show, you're looking at residuals for many years to come. I wasn't sure if television was okay with you, but I think in the long run this will work in your favor."

She felt tempted to fall to the ground and flail her arms and legs around with excitement, but she had to maintain her composure. "Television is fine. Perfectly fine."

"I figured that's what you'd say, but I just wanted to make sure. We should have more details about the offer later today, but I'm expecting it's going to be pretty decent."

"Ballpark figure?"

There was a certain caution in this industry. No one ever made predictions, because if they were wrong, they didn't want to assume blame. "I would say anywhere from ten thousand to half a million." That was the other thing. People never gave a close estimate. An estimate always covered all price ranges. "Either Carissa or I will let you know as soon as we have more details."

"Okay, great. Thank you so much."

She jumped up and down when she hung up the phone, and since there was no one there to share her excitement with, she planted a huge kiss across the Thunder Down Under poster. She decided to tell Carly first.

She wanted to talk to her in person, so she drove to Pacific Beach. Any nervousness she felt about talking to her for the first time since she'd caught them red-handed at Starbucks was squashed by her excitement over seeing her Ashley Trent novels as a television series. She noticed her brother's car in the parking lot and had second thoughts. Maybe this wasn't the best time. She was still pissed at him for saying all that he'd said about Max.

However, she was going to have to forgive him at some point, too, so she might as well start now.

29. Good-bye and Hello

Moving day was quite different from the past. This time she packed her boxes and hired movers. She sat back sipping a Sprite while two brawny young men hauled all of her belongings into a large truck. She put it on the credit card and vowed to pay the luxury off as soon as she got the money from her television deal, which had landed a decent six-figure advance.

She'd already been talking to real estate agents, and the day that check came in she'd be looking for a new home, her own home. For now her stuff was going in storage and she'd be staying with Carly for a couple of months. She spent every night with Stan and was never around anyway. Elise was happy for them but also couldn't help but feel a pang of envy that they had each other. They got to wake up to each other in the morning. She missed Max so much, and knew she would have to get over him sooner or later. There was nothing else she could do. He'd made up his mind and if it were meant to be, he would've forgiven her by now.

The only possessions the movers weren't taking in their truck were Bella and her suitcase that she'd be living out of for the time being. She went for Bella's leash and on the way passed Megan. She was throwing her purse over her shoulder.

"We're off to pick up Nicole from the airport. So this is probably good-bye. Thanks for being such a great roommate."

"Thank you for . . ." Elise hugged her thinking of something to say. "Being such a great friend. I'll miss you guys." It was true. They were good people, just slobs.

"Don't be a stranger. Come by and see us."

"I will. And you'll have to come see my place when I move in." The words were sincere, but Elise sensed neither one of them would ever actually visit. She was old enough to know that these invitations often went unfulfilled in life, as people grew up and moved on. Iris and Megan were too young to realize that you could be exposed to the most intimate moments of people's lives while you lived with them, and then once you moved out, you moved on.

Iris came around the corner, holding the keys to the Saturn. They still hadn't fixed the back bumper nor told their roommate about the damage. Roommates were such interesting creatures. Elise sort of wished she could be there to see Nicole's reaction when she saw her car. "Max is here," she said.

"Max? Are you kidding me?"

"No. I'm not," she whispered. "He's in the living room."

"What does he want?"

"I didn't ask him." Then she turned to Megan. "We have to go. Nicole's waiting for us." She opened her arms to Elise. "Hug me quickly, and then get your ass out there already."

Elise gave her a quick, sloppy hug before heading to the living room. Her heart pounded with every step. He was so cute it was almost painful to look at his dark eyes. "Hey," he said. "Looks like I always catch you at the last minute."

"Yes. That's right. The day you asked me to the races I was moving as well." She hoped this would trigger a fond memory and he'd suddenly be plunged into the depths of missing her.

He smiled, and for one hopeful moment she thought he might actually be here to mend the fences. But then she saw the bag in his hands.

"I ran into your brother yesterday at Winston's, and he mentioned you were moving. I thought you might want your stuff that you left at my place." She saw a sleeve from her hooded black sweater poking from the plastic shopping bag in his hands. She knew her hairbrush and her black bra lay inside the bag as well. Now she wished he would just drop the bag and go. This was it. There was nothing to tie them. And as stupid as it may seem, a sweater and some toiletries were her last hope of ever remaining in touch with Max. Having these back in her possession meant that she'd really never see him again.

"Thanks. I appreciate that. I uh . . . I really want to . . ." She wanted to apologize one more time to him, to let him know how truly sorry she was. But she wanted to find better words than the ones she had been using up until this point. Obviously, they hadn't been working.

Iris and Megan breezed past them and hollered a good-bye, and Elise hardly noticed.

"Look," Max said after the door closed behind them. "Do you mind if we sit down for a minute?"

"No. Not at all. I um . . . do you want something to drink?"

He shook his head as he sat on the couch. "I'm fine. I just . . . I wanna talk to you."

She sat down next to him and studied his face as his eyes wandered over the floor then back to her face. "When I met you I was so happy. I hadn't felt like that . . ." He thought for a moment. "Ever."

"Me, too," she said quietly.

"We really had the best time. And that day I heard you talking to Stan it just wrecked my whole image of you—"

"Max, I totally understand. I would feel the same way."

"I didn't think I could ever be with someone who wasn't proud of me. It just couldn't work. I mean, how could it work?"

"Max, I am proud of you. It's just that I was worried about—"

"Listen, I've tried my hardest to just wash my hands of the whole situation. Move on. I've worked my ass off at the shop. I've gone on a couple other dates."

She felt her heart plunge into her chest. The thought of him out with someone else made her feel ill.

"But I've been completely and totally miserable. I've never felt this way in my life. I've been through breakups with other girls. I left my band that I was with for ten years. But never have I ever felt this sad. Time passes, and eventually you feel better. Right?"

She shrugged.

"But I'm not better. I'm so down all the time. And I really think that if I could get over you, I would've by now. But I can't."

She wiped tears from beneath her cheeks. "I've been miserable, too."

He put his arms around her, and she finally felt like she was home.

"So I hear you're staying with Carly till you buy your condo?"

"That's the plan."

"So do you think she'll mind if you stay with me?"

She smiled. "I think it will be just fine."

He waited for her while she collected Bella and her suitcase. When she returned to the living room he took the suitcase from her hands. "I'll carry that." They headed down the staircase together, and when she reached the front door she took one last look up the winding stairs. Heading down the flight of steps was Scrubbles. His tail stood on end, and he let out a loud meow. She paused for a moment and felt her heart break as she thought of him stuck with Iris and Megan, underfed and deprived of his litter box. She envisioned Iris deciding he no longer fit in her life. He'd end up on the street or in the pound, lonely and hungry for the rest of his life. She looked up at Max. "Do you like cats?"

He chuckled as he shook his head. "Are you going to be sad without him?"

She nodded.

"Go ahead."

She reached down and picked up Scrubbles and then closed the door behind them.